DEATH
MESSAGE

ALSO BY DAMIEN BOYD

DEATH
MESSAGE

DAMIEN BOYD

Text copyright © 2023 by Damien Boyd
All rights reserved.

Published by Thomas & Mercer, Seattle

www.apub.com

Amazon, the Amazon logo, and Thomas & Mercer are trademarks of Amazon.com, Inc., or its affiliates.

ISBN-13: 9781662507359
eISBN: 9781662507342

Cover design by @blacksheep-uk.com
Cover image: ©Richard Nixon / ArcAngel; ©air_studio / Getty Images

Printed in the United States of America

For Tim, Phil and Matt

Prologue

IN THE CROWN COURT AT BRISTOL

THE QUEEN

– v –

CHRISTOPHER GREEN

SENTENCING REMARKS OF MR JUSTICE BARLOW

You have been found guilty of a single count of Causing Death by Dangerous Driving. You told a pack of lies in a feeble attempt to deflect blame for what happened on to others, but this jury saw through you very quickly.

The facts of this case are that in the early hours of the 28th of February this year an empty Iveco tipper lorry driven by the Defendant struck Mr Jackson Ogunwe. According to his tachograph, the Defendant had been travelling at speeds of 54–58 mph and was thereby exceeding the prevailing speed limit. Mr Ogunwe was struck by the nearside front of the Defendant's tipper lorry, before being crushed under the nearside rear wheels. It is perhaps some small crumb of comfort to Mr Ogunwe's family to know that he was killed instantly.

An eyewitness saw the Defendant's lorry veering towards the near-side crash barrier. He gave evidence that in his opinion the Defendant was exceeding the speed limit and appeared distracted. We shall never know what it was that distracted the Defendant, but the tachograph and evidence from the investigating officer confirm much of what the eyewitness saw.

Perhaps it was tiredness, which is nevertheless indicative of a reckless disregard for the safety of other road users. The tachograph confirmed the Defendant had been substantially exceeding his legal driving hours on the day of the collision, although in an appalling lie dismissed by this jury, the Defendant alleged that the tachograph before this court was not his, and had been switched by the police.

I have read the victim impact statements submitted by Mr Ogunwe's mother and father telling of their devastating loss. Both speak of their grief at the death of their son at such a young age. Jackson was a young man full of promise, with his whole life ahead of him; a dearly loved son and a talented artist. His parents have sat through the entirety of this trial, demonstrating the utmost dignity whilst being forced to listen to the Defendant's false and distressing allegation that their son was pushed in front of his lorry. Yet another allegation, I might add, that has been comprehensively dismissed by this jury.

I am obliged to consider the Sentencing Guidelines, and in my judgement the fact that the Defendant was exceeding the speed limit and driving in excess of the legal time limit adds to the Defendant's culpability. His conduct was reckless and I am satisfied that the eyewitness observations are accurate and that the Defendant's actions posed a substantial risk to other road users.

In my judgement this is a Level 2 case, and taking the above factors into account I take as my starting point 3 years' custody.

I am also obliged to consider whether there are any aggravating factors in this case and there are not. The Defendant has no previous convictions and remained at the scene until the emergency services arrived. It is right that claiming the victim was responsible for the collision is an aggravating factor, but the Defendant has not done that in this case, instead alleging that a person or persons unknown pushed the victim in front of his lorry. I have no doubt that this caused additional distress to Mr and Mrs Ogunwe, but it is not, in my judgement, an aggravating factor.

I have taken into account everything that has been said by Mr Bullock on the Defendant's behalf. The Defendant is 31 years of age and has been employed as a driver for the last 7 years with an otherwise unblemished record. He has a long term partner who is pregnant.

I am satisfied, therefore, that the balance of aggravating and mitigating factors does not warrant an increase in the starting point and, accordingly, the sentence that I pass is 3 years.

I am conscious that the Defendant makes his living as a driver, but I am obliged to impose a period of disqualification upon conviction for this offence and do so for a period of 6 years.

The Defendant will stand.

Christopher Green, I sentence you to 3 years' imprisonment. In addition, you will be disqualified from driving for 6 years. I further order that the disqualification shall continue until you pass an extended driving test, and the confiscation of your driving licence.

Take him down.

The Honourable Mr Justice Barlow

15th October 2002

Chapter One

'Let's go fishing, you said.' She glanced down at her trainers, saturated in the long wet grass, the damp creeping up the legs of her jeans. 'It'll be fun, you said.'

'It is fun.'

'I should've listened to my sister. She always said you were a dipstick.'

'Thanks!'

'I thought we'd be fishing for carp, not crap.' She chuckled at her own joke, watching the rain dripping off her golf umbrella on to a pile of rusted metal lying on the riverbank at her feet, like some sort of pagan offering. 'It's bloody freezing too.' A shudder. 'We're supposed to be curled up in a tent, with a stove and a few beers. Snuggled up all warm like, in a sleeping bag, y'know.'

'That's boring,' he replied, dragging the large magnet up the bank, a small coil of rusted barbed wire his 'catch' this time, trailing a clump of rotting weed behind it. 'You never know what you're going to get with this. I've had guns, knives, all sorts of stuff. When you're fishing you just catch fish. Big deal.'

He ripped the barbed wire free and dropped it on the pile, before swinging the magnet on the end of the blue nylon rope and lobbing it across the river. It landed with a 'splosh' just short of the far bank. Then he started pulling on the rope, dragging it slowly across the riverbed.

'You wouldn't get carp here anyway. Not in winter and not when the level's up like this,' he said, clearly hoping fishing rusting metal junk out of the river might be some sort of consolation.

It wasn't.

'A mate of mine found a hand grenade once.'

That wasn't either.

'Can we go now?' she demanded, with a stomp of her foot.

'We'll just go down to that bush. That's about as far as anyone could throw anything off the bridge.'

'Really?'

'Allowing for the current to carry it down a bit,' he replied, with a shrug to soften the blow, although he was still pulling the rope hand over hand so it was difficult to tell.

North Curry was less than a mile away across the Levels, but she couldn't make it out through the mist and rain. Even the green fields looked grey. Gave her the creeps at the best of times, the bloody Levels in winter. Miles and miles of farmland, spooky look-ing ditches and fast flowing rivers. Not to mention that serial killer on the loose.

'They did catch that bloke with the scythe, didn't they?'

'Yeah. Stop worrying.' He was swinging the magnet on the end of the rope. 'One more here and then we'll move down a bit. Can you carry that stuff?'

'No I bloody well can't.'

'Don't worry, I'll pick it up on the way back.'

She turned and started to scramble up the bank, her feet slid-ing on the wet mud. She put her hand down to steady herself and flinched. The stinging nettles were dying back in the winter frosts, but were clearly not dead yet. 'Shit!' she grumbled, rubbing the palm of her hand on her jeans.

'D'you want my gloves?'

'No.'

'Just wait there and I'll pull you up,' he said, scrambling past her, the magnet already lobbed up on to the top of the bank. 'Here.' He reached down. 'Give me the brolly.'

She resisted the temptation to throw it at him javelin-style, but soon wished she had when she lost her footing and ended up kneeling in the mud. 'Look at my effing trousers!'

'Sorry.'

'I can feel water trickling down the back of my neck as well now,' she said, snatching the umbrella back.

'I'm just going to try off the end of that slipway, then we'll call it a day. Ten minutes.'

A thick layer of grey slime coated the concrete slip that disappeared into the water at the bottom of the bank. It was a popular spot, judging by the footprints in the mud down to the water's edge.

'Looks like someone's beaten you to it,' she said. 'Can't we go?'

'That's just fishermen,' he replied. 'They'll be after the pike this time of year.'

She watched him picking his way down the slipway, his feet sliding on the mud. Then came the 'splosh' of the magnet landing in the water on the far side of the river. 'C'mon, it'll be dark soon.'

'Just a couple more throws.'

She sighed. 'I should've known from all that crap in the back of your pickup.'

'Will you stop going on about crap? It's scrap!' He was pulling the rope again, hand over hand. 'Worth a few quid too, if you get enough of it.'

'You'd be better off buying a lottery ticket.' She leaned on the fence near the top of the slipway, watching him trying to pull something off the magnet. Then a piece of shiny metal landed at her feet. 'What's that?'

'A hacksaw. New too,' he said. 'Blade's still sharp.'

'Why would somebody throw that in the river?'

'Maybe it was used to cut up a body?' He was grinning from ear to ear, waiting for her reaction.

'Don't be such a—' She turned away, stony-faced. 'What's that box up there?' she asked, looking up at the bridge above them.

'It's a webcam watching the water level on the gaugeboard over there. It's so the Environment Agency can control the sluice gate under the bridge. See it? It's supposed to stop a high tide going further upstream.'

'Oh, yeah,' she replied, although she couldn't really see it. There was some mechanism up on the bridge that looked familiar, but the sluice gate must've been underwater. 'Is magnet fishing legal?'

'Of course it is.' He was pulling hard on the rope, bracing himself with one foot against the edge of the slipway. 'It's just litter picking, really, innit.'

'Do you need permission?' One hand outstretched beyond the cover of the umbrella to check whether it was still raining.

'If anyone asks, I'll say I didn't know.' His feet were slipping now, the rope inching in even though he was pulling as hard as he could. It reminded her of the tug-of-war at the village fete. 'I don't suppose you could give me a hand?'

'No way am I going down there,' she replied, shaking the water off the umbrella.

Then his feet went from under him and he landed flat on his back in the mud, his stream of expletives lost in her loud cackle of laughter.

'Serves you right, you plonker.'

Up on his feet now, pulling on the rope again. 'It's come free,' he said.

'What is it?' Taking an interest, although she wasn't entirely sure why. She took a step towards the top of the slipway, using the umbrella as a walking stick to steady herself.

'Looks like a tin box.' He had manoeuvred it around to the bottom of the slipway and was dragging it up the slope, the box sliding out of the water below him on the thick layer of mud.

The magnet was stuck to the back, just above what looked like hinges, although that meant the box was upside down. Flakes of black paint were visible in amongst the rust as the water drained away.

He reached down and took hold of a small corroded handle on the side of the box, and picked it up, magnet and all, carrying it up the slipway dragging the blue rope behind him. 'It's not very big, but it ain't half heavy' – struggling to stay on his feet. Then he dropped the box in the long grass and turned it over. 'Who's J.M.C., I wonder?' He was reading what was left of initials painted on the lid. 'Or it could be J.N.C., I suppose.'

'Is it locked?'

'A keyhole, but no key,' he replied, rattling the lid with a hand each side. 'Yeah, it is.'

'What's in it?'

'How the bloody hell am I supposed to know that?'

'It could be gold,' she said, her eyes widening.

'C'mon, let's get it in the back of the van. We can worry about opening it later.'

◆　◆　◆

'Good luck with that.'

Detective Sergeant Jane Winter looked up from her computer just as Detective Constable Dave Harding turned away. He was loitering by the kettle in the CID Area on the first floor of the police centre at Express Park, clearly trying not to laugh. 'This is going to be good sport, mate,' he said when DC Mark Pearce appeared, carrying a bottle of milk. 'A lamb to the slaughter.'

They were watching a young police constable hovering nervously, her face reddened, trying to summon up the courage for something. Neatly pressed white shirt and black trousers; polished shoes. Keen as mustard, obviously. She looked younger than Jane's half-sister, Lucy, and she was only sixteen. A probationer, must be; carrying a file and looking for someone.

'You'll find DS Winter over there,' said Dave, loudly and with obvious glee. He turned round, leaned back against the worktop and folded his arms, settling in for the show.

Jane sighed. It had been a miserable morning spent in a Burnham-on-Sea supermarket, taking witness statements from a checkout supervisor and two security guards. Shoplifting; a bottle of gin and two packets of digestives. At least they'd been the chocolate ones.

Things hadn't been the same since Dixon left. Either that or someone was trying to wrap her in cotton wool. Or a bit of both, perhaps. Giving her all the boring jobs to keep her out of trouble. Jane had tried several protests, but they had fallen on deaf ears. 'I'm bloody well pregnant, not ill.'

'I am not sending a heavily pregnant officer into any situation that might turn nasty, and you can sue me for sex discrimination if you like,' Detective Chief Superintendent Deborah Potter had said, firmly.

A tick in the box, dated and initialled. Jane's pregnancy risk assessment review was over for another few weeks.

'I'm not heavily pregnant.'

'I can see your bump from here and you're not even sideways on.'

A few expletives had slipped out after that, but Potter had overlooked them, seemingly more interested in when Dixon was coming back. The truth of the matter was Jane didn't know *if* he was coming back, let alone when, but she'd kept that to herself, pleading ignorance on all counts.

'Sergeant Winter?' The young uniformed officer was peering over the partition, her short dark hair and pale complexion exaggerating a deep blush. 'Sorry.'

'What for?'

'I don't know really.'

'What's your name?' asked Jane.

'Sarah Loveday.' She was holding a file in front of her, using it as a shield possibly. 'They gave me this to review and said it might be worth running it past CID. I was told to ask for you.'

'Who told you?' Jane glanced over Sarah's shoulder at Dave and Mark, grinning like a pair of idiots. 'Don't answer that.' She leaned forwards, reaching out for the file. 'What is it?'

'A misper.'

'How long have you been a copper?'

'It's my first week,' replied Sarah. 'I was in the cadets for two years and now here I am.'

That explained the jargon. 'And how long has this person been missing?'

'Six months.'

'All right.' Jane reached down and picked up her handbag. 'Let's take this in the canteen. Away from prying eyes.' She glared at Dave and Mark as she brushed past them, deriving some satisfaction from their obvious disappointment. 'You look after this,' she said, handing the file back to Sarah. 'Grab that table in the corner. Tea or coffee?'

'Tea, thank you.'

Jane was watching Sarah from the queue, flicking through her notebook. Conscientious too, then. 'You've read the file?' she asked a few moments later, as she slid a mug of tea across the table, dropping two sachets of sugar next to it.

'Cover to cover,' replied Sarah.

'Well?'

'His name's Barry Mercer. He's one of those private detectives who does the surveillance – you know, personal injury claimants taking the mickey, benefit claimants, that sort of stuff.'

'Proof of life?'

'Nothing. No one's heard from him, bank account's not been touched, mobile phone's dead. Literally nothing.'

'What about his car?'

'He's got a van; no trace of that either. Tax and MOT expired a couple of months ago.'

'Well and truly missing then,' said Jane, taking a sip of tea. 'Where did he live?'

'He's got a flat in Bridgwater. His son's looking after that, but he lives upcountry. Solihull. That's near Birmingham, isn't it?'

Still using the present tense for a man who'd been missing six months; Sarah was an optimist – that would soon be knocked out of her. 'Family?' asked Jane.

'Just the son and an estranged wife. She's not heard from him for years, though.'

'Any work colleagues?'

'He's a one-man band, but he's got a secretary for the typing and stuff. She lives over Puriton. His office is all closed up.'

'Has anyone been over there?'

'Not as far as I can see. There's a short statement from the secretary, though. Last contact was June eighteenth. He sent her a text about some footage on a case that was listed for a pre-trial review the following week. The phone signal put him on the edge of Curry Rivel, which tallies with the case he was working on at the time: another personal injury claim.'

'You found her then?'

Jane recognised the voice straightaway. So did Sarah, who jumped up and stood sharply to attention, her heels snapping together.

'Yes, Sir,' she said.

Assistant Chief Constable David Charlesworth was liable to get himself reported for stalking, thought Jane. He'd been popping up at least daily for the last couple of weeks, always with the same question.

'How's Nick getting on, Jane?'

And there it was again.

'Sit yourself down, Sarah.' Charlesworth dropped his hat upside down on the table, a small puff of dandruff settling back on the black lining.

'Thank you, Sir.'

'Nick's fine, Sir,' said Jane.

'Out on the beach with his dog, I imagine?'

'He did say he might go fishing today.'

'What time's his interview?'

Jane hesitated. How the bloody hell could Charlesworth have found out about that? Could she risk lying to the ACC?

'Oh, come now.' Charlesworth was frowning at her over his horn-rimmed glasses. 'Isn't he meeting the head of corporate finance at Oxenden Hart this afternoon?' He pulled a chair out from under the table and sat down. 'It's all right,' he said. 'I know he is, and tell him I understand. He's got to explore his options. I get that. But he'll last five minutes in the legal profession. You and I both know that.'

'He's angry, I think, Sir,' said Jane.

'Of course he is. I would be if my own force charged me with murder. But he's a copper – not a word I use often – and a bloody good one at that. Do us all a favour and remind him why he left the legal profession behind the day he qualified as a solicitor.'

'I will, Sir.'

'It's been six weeks now and we need him back.' Charlesworth shook his head. 'In the meantime, you're going to be helping Sarah with a missing person case, I gather?'

'I was just briefing Sergeant Winter, Sir,' said Sarah.

'Good. We need to nurture young talent, Jane.' Charlesworth had stood up and was pushing his chair back under the table. 'Look after her and help her settle in.'

'Of course, Sir,' replied Jane.

'Anyway, I'll leave it with you, and be sure to give Nick a kick up the backside.'

Chapter Two

Jane's text arrived just as Detective Chief Inspector Nick Dixon turned into the visitors' car park at Oxenden Hart.

Charlesworth knows about your interview Jx

He switched off the engine and glanced into the back of the Land Rover at the large white Staffordshire terrier curled up asleep in his bed. Shame, it would be dark by the time he came out, but they'd spent the morning on the beach, so that would have to do for today. New suit and tie too. Maybe they'd just walk across to the pub when he got home?

He was twenty minutes early, so took out his phone and tapped out a reply to Jane.

Did you forget to wish me luck? Nx

He watched the speech bubble, Jane typing something. A digital slap in the face, as it turned out.

No, I didn't. Corporate finance lawyer my arse xx

The speech bubble was still there, so she was still typing.

She'd spent the last six weeks telling him he was making a huge mistake, so no doubt it would be something along those lines; with an expletive or two thrown in for good measure. Either she'd try the 'you'll last five minutes in the legal profession' line, or it would be the transfer idea again. She'd already suggested that umpteen times. 'Apply for a transfer if you don't want to stay with Avon and Somerset. Somewhere nice like Devon and Cornwall. Cumbria even, you love the Lake District.' He smiled to himself as he remembered her reply to the obvious question.

'You'd come with me?'

'I'd follow you to the ends of the earth. You know that.'

Not that you'd know it from her text messages, mind you.

You're being an idiot. I know you're angry but those gits from Professional Standards were only doing their jobs. You dealt with it. The charge has been dropped. Get over it.

Then, to sweeten the pill:

I love you :-)

He slid a letter out of his inside jacket pocket; a one-liner from his solicitor: '. . . pleased to enclose a copy of a letter received today from the Crown Prosecution Service.' That was a one-liner too: '. . . write to confirm that the Crown will offer no evidence in relation to the single charge of murder, which is formally withdrawn and all bail conditions revoked.'

No apology. Nothing.

Charlesworth had been decent enough to authorise paid leave, although probably hadn't been expecting it to go on this long. Dixon wondered how Charlesworth had found out about the job interview. The only other person who knew about it was Home Office pathologist Dr Roger Poland, and he wouldn't have said anything, despite agreeing with every word Jane had been saying.

Roger had tried a slightly different tack from Jane, though. 'You're the best I've ever known in twenty-five years as a pathologist. Do what you're good at. You'll hate doing anything else.'

Dixon closed his eyes and tried to remember how he'd felt the day he left the legal profession; the day his training contract finished. The firm had asked him to stay on, offered him a good job in the corporate team too.

Liberated, that was it. Two long years of drudgery. The six months spent in the corporate team had been bearable, just; the property department thoroughly miserable, his time spent fielding calls from pushy estate agents, and clients furious their purchase was taking so long. Divorce work had been an eye opener too; he winced at the memory of the client who'd broken into the former matrimonial home and cut everything in half, the child's mother spending the day racing around pet shops trying to find a rabbit the same colour before their boy came home from school. That was after she'd cleared up the pool of blood on the kitchen floor.

And the less said about his six months in the litigation department, the better.

He glanced in his rear view mirror at the grand entrance to the reception atrium at Oxenden Hart, and wondered what the hell he was doing about to walk into a law firm for a job interview.

Then he remembered how he'd felt when his own police force had charged him with murder and locked him in a cell; how he'd felt standing in the dock at the Magistrates Court.

Six weeks on and the anger was still raging as fresh as the day he had been handcuffed and led out to the prison van in full view of his colleagues. His subordinates.

'I've got a two o'clock appointment with Mr Page,' said Dixon, once through the automatic revolving doors.

'Mr Dixon, is it?'

'Yes.'

'Take a seat and I'll let him know you're here.'

Red leather sofas, a glass coffee table with a well-thumbed copy of *The Times*. A television had been mounted on the wall and was showing the BBC News channel, the volume turned down, subtitles appearing along the bottom of the screen. It reminded Dixon of the diabetic centre at Musgrove Park Hospital. It might have smelled different, but he had the same nervous sick feeling in the pit of his stomach.

One-fifty-seven, according to the clock on the wall above the reception desk.

The youngest detective chief inspector in the history of Avon and Somerset Police reduced to this? He'd even passed the selection board and was going for a superintendent's job at police headquarters just before his arrest. And now here he was applying for what was effectively a job as a newly qualified solicitor. After all, he'd had no legal experience in eight years, except crime perhaps.

A huge pay cut, as Jane had been at pains to point out. No taking your dog to work either.

Then there was the time recording, and the targets.

Best not to think about it too much. Dixon picked up the newspaper and flicked through the headlines. Someone had done the quick crossword on the back, which was a nuisance.

Ten past two.

Time had been dragging a lot lately; too much of it on his hands, possibly. It had started in police custody – a very long twenty-four hours that had felt like a lifetime.

Soon he'd be breaking it up into six-minute units, recording seven and a half hours a day chargeable time, watching his life pass before his eyes on a timesheet.

Twenty past two.

He glanced at the receptionist. 'I'll try him again,' she said, nervously. 'He does know you're here.'

Some bright spark at his old firm had thought it was a good idea for the trainees to get some experience of working on reception, although the reality was it was just a way of covering the receptionist's lunch break. Either way, it had been a pain in the arse.

Another flick through the newspaper headlines, the initials 'OH' scribbled in the top right corner of the front page by the newsagent. Dixon slid his pen out of his jacket pocket and completed the sentence for them.

'OH, NO.'

Then he walked out.

◆ ◆ ◆

A caricature of a detective, hunched over a magnifying glass and wearing a comedy deerstalker; it was hardly an imaginative logo. It had been stencilled on the inside of the toughened glass in the door, a flight of grubby stairs behind it leading up to an office above a chippy. 'Somerset Investigations', a member of the Association of Private Investigators, according to the only other window sticker.

'The phone number redirects to his mobile, which is dead,' said Sarah. 'Sheesh. You'd have to have a strong stomach to work here.' She turned away, the back of her hand over her nose.

'Or love fish and chips.'

'How's the morning sickness?' Sarah grinned.

'Only lasted a couple of days,' replied Jane. 'Touch wood.' Her hand on the door frame.

They were watching a woman picking up the junk mail that had been gathering dust on the floor inside the door; piles of it, freebie newspapers, charity collection bags and leaflets thrown in a box at the foot of the stairs, leaving a miserable three brown envelopes in her hand.

'What's her name again?' asked Jane.

'Carol Baynes. She said she'd meet us here, so I'm guessing it's her.'

Bolts top and bottom, then the door opened.

'Sorry about that. It's been a few weeks since I was last here and it soon piles up.' She waved her hand in front of her nose. 'Sorry about the smell; can't stand it now. I haven't touched fish and chips since I left.'

'Mrs Baynes?' asked Jane.

'Yes, yes, come in. Then I can shut the smell out.' She bolted the door behind them and squeezed past. 'This way, and watch the lino,' she said, setting off up the stairs. 'I gave a statement at the time, so I'm not sure how much help I can be, I'm afraid.'

'I'm assuming you haven't heard from him.'

'No, I haven't. I haven't been paid either.' Mrs Baynes threw the brown envelopes into a wire basket on the desk in front of her. 'More debts.' She picked up the basket, shaking it from side to side, as if panning for gold. 'The accountant's supposed to be dealing with them.'

'How long have you worked for Mr Mercer?'

'Eleven years.'

Sarah was sitting down at a desk, making notes; Jane was impressed.

'And what sort of work did he do?'

'He used to do the lot – tracing and process serving – till he got beaten up serving a bankruptcy petition on someone. Then he started specialising in the surveillance.'

'His website says he still does process serving, though, doesn't it?'

'He farms it out to someone else these days, lets them take the risk.' Mrs Baynes was leaning against a filing cabinet, a kettle sitting on a tray on top. 'I would offer you a tea or coffee but there's no milk, I'm afraid.'

'That's fine,' said Jane. 'You mentioned debts?'

'You'd need to speak to his accountant about that. All I know is I'm owed six months' wages.' Mrs Baynes ran her fingers along the top of the filing cabinet, before flicking the dust on to the floor. 'Look, they said you're a detective sergeant on the phone, so is there something you're not telling me? Have you found a body or something?'

'Nothing like that,' replied Jane. 'We're just reviewing the missing person case, checking for any suggestion he might have been a victim of crime.'

'There'd be plenty of people willing to do him a mischief, I expect. Goes with the territory.'

'What cases was he working on at the time of his disappearance?'

'He only had three on the go. He'd usually have four, or five at most, but one had just settled out of court.' Mrs Baynes shrugged. 'That's what usually happens when the defence disclose his surveillance footage, to be honest.'

'Personal injury claims?'

'Most of them are. Claimants pretending they'll never work again, can't walk more than fifty yards, that sort of thing. He did some work for the DWP – people claiming benefits and working at the same time. A couple of cases for employers too, keeping an eye on employees off long term sick.'

'What about the day he disappeared?'

'He was over at Curry Rivel. That was a new case that had not long come in; he'd only been on it a few days. Makes me wince just thinking about it,' replied Mrs Baynes, with a shudder.

Jane waited.

'It was a young lad – twenty or so – at a car breaker's yard. He was operating the crusher and they'd got it surrounded, for safety y'know, with a wall of crushed cars maybe fifteen feet high. They'd crane the car to be crushed over it and drop it in the crusher, and there was a gap in this wall a few feet wide for the workers to get in and out. Anyway, this lad was standing thirty yards away and, bang, a fire extinguisher blew and a piece of metal took his leg off just above the knee.' She was rubbing her thigh. 'Doesn't bear thinking about.'

'And why was he being watched by Barry?'

'He was claiming he couldn't walk without crutches and he'd never work again, usual sort of thing. Future loss of earnings – you can imagine it, can't you? It was a big claim. Only he'd got a prosthetic leg and Barry got footage of him playing golf at Brean.'

'Golf?' Sarah looked up.

'He was hopeless at it, according to Barry,' replied Mrs Baynes. 'It's not quite as simple as that, though. You need footage over several days, otherwise they just say they were having a good day. You need to catch them several times, doing different things.'

'What about the other cases he was working on? Let's start with the one that has just settled.'

'Stevens. That was a bloke claiming he'd never work again after a back injury installing an Aga. Turned out he was running a guest-house, so Barry checked in for the weekend and left a camera in his room.' Mrs Baynes smiled to herself. 'Stevens comes in, rummages through all Barry's things, then makes the bed and runs a hoover around. Back injury, my foot. He got him walking the length of Minehead High Street carrying two bags of shopping as well.'

'How much did the claim settle for?'

'We don't get to know that, I'm afraid. We just send the defence solicitors the footage with Barry's witness statement and a bill.'

'So, how d'you get to know the case has settled?' asked Sarah.

'There was a court date for that one, and he got a letter saying there was no need to attend anymore.'

'And the other live cases?' asked Jane. 'There were two more current at the time of his disappearance, you said.'

'One was benefits, claiming disability and doing cash in hand work. The other a nasty road traffic accident, I'll give him that, but he was claiming for whiplash while still working as a bricklayer. Barry got him up on scaffolding, carrying planks. When he disappeared I just let the solicitors have the footage we'd got and I've heard nothing since.'

'Presumably the footage is stored electronically?' asked Jane.

'It's all flash drives and USB sticks these days,' replied Mrs Baynes. 'Back when Barry first started it was video cassettes. He's got loads of them upstairs from the old days.'

'Upstairs?'

'That's where the old files are. Barry was too tight to pay for storage, let alone shredding.'

The staircase was narrow and dark, the only light coming from under a closed door at the top.

'Sorry, bulb's gone.' Mrs Baynes was fumbling for the key. 'He kept it locked; not sure why he bothered, really.'

Jane took out her phone and shone the light on the keys.

'Oh, thanks.'

The smell of damp mixed with the fish and chips when the door swung open, helped on the way by a sharp kick from Mrs Baynes. Light was streaming in through a dormer window, the paint all around it stained with water and mould.

'I never come up here, for obvious reasons.' Mrs Baynes stepped out of the way on the landing. 'Help yourselves. Everything up here is over a year old, I'd say. Anything more recent is still downstairs. The correspondence files are the thin ones in the boxes.'

The mantelpiece was piled high with video cassettes in their cardboard sleeves – names and dates scribbled on labels on the spines, the ink fading. Not that anyone could reach the fireplace for the boxes on the floor. A trestle table against the opposite wall was struggling to hold the weight of the boxes piled up on it, only managing to do so thanks to the boxes stuffed underneath it.

'Tell us about his van,' Jane said, raising her voice to Mrs Baynes, who had stayed out on the landing.

'Oh, that. It was an old heap, really. It had one-way glass in the back windows and there were small windows in the sides as well, so he could film people without being seen. He had it boarded up behind the seats, so it looked just like an empty van parked up. He even had an armchair in the back, and a commode, although he used to call it something else.'

'Did he have a car as well, for personal use?'

'No.'

'Was he in a relationship?'

A shriek from the landing. 'You've got to be kidding!'

'We have to ask.'

'Not since his wife divorced him. Let himself go after that, he did. And that's being polite. It was sad to watch.'

Jane gestured towards the door and followed Sarah out on to the landing, closing the door behind her.

'He was one of your lot,' continued Mrs Baynes. 'A copper. That was long before I knew him, mind.'

'Where?'

'Avon and Somerset. He was based in Bristol mainly, I think. It was a while ago, maybe twenty years or so.'

'What did he say about his time in the police?' asked Jane.

'Nothing. Except the contacts were useful – back in the day, when former colleagues would look things up for him on the computer. A hundred pounds plus VAT for a standard trace, and all it used to take was one phone call to an old colleague. You can't do that sort of thing now, can you?'

'We certainly can't,' replied Sarah, hardly able to contain her surprise at the very idea of it.

'Why did he leave?'

'He retired, he said.' Mrs Baynes looked puzzled. 'I don't remember him ever giving a specific reason. Was there one?'

'We don't know,' Jane replied. 'Yet.'

Sarah drew breath, waiting until the front door closed behind them. 'We didn't even know he was ex-police,' she said, her voice apologetic, as if it was somehow her fault. 'There's nothing on the file at all.'

'I was wondering why you hadn't mentioned it.'

Chapter Three

'Bit of a dive, isn't it?'

'I've seen worse.'

Another dark staircase, the same smell of damp, although without the fish and chips this time. Jane and Sarah were waiting on a landing again too, only now it was for a neighbour to ring Barry Mercer's son.

'He says it's fine to let you in,' said the man, appearing too close to them and wearing a shell suit that could've done with a wash weeks ago, Jane thanking her lucky stars she had a strong stomach. Deborah Potter may have been trying to keep her out of trouble, but she was sure as hell testing her nausea threshold.

'We'll push the key through your letterbox when we've finished,' she said, determined to get rid of the man.

'Oh, right, thanks.'

Sarah closed the door behind them and waited for the neighbour's to close opposite. 'Nosy bugger.'

'Has someone been here before us?' asked Jane, snapping on a pair of latex gloves.

'The investigating officer met the son and daughter-in-law here when Barry went missing. They must've had a bit of a tidy up, looking at the kitchen,' replied Sarah. 'It's very different to his office.'

'Who was the investigating officer?'

'Er, hang on.' Notebook again. 'PC 2575 Nigel Cole. Don't know him. Do you?'

'Yes, I know him.'

'What's he like?'

Jane was flicking through a pile of post on the sideboard. 'You wouldn't want him as a phone-a-friend if you get through to the final of *Millionaire*, but have him by your side if the shit hits the fan,' she said, idly.

'I'll try to remember that.'

'Bills,' said Jane, her lips still moving as she added up the figures on the credit card statements, dropping each in turn back on to the pile. 'Just under twenty one thousand on credit cards and there's an M&S store card too. He used that for food and drink, by the looks of things.'

Sarah had opened the fridge, the light coming on. 'Cleaned out.'

'Switch it off at the wall and leave it open, then.' Jane was opening the sideboard drawers one by one. 'Does he own this place or rent it?'

'Owns it with a mortgage, according to the file.'

'Where's his passport?'

'We've got it.'

Five large black bin bags of clothes lay on the bed, which had been stripped, the bedding in another bin bag. 'Somebody's taken this lot to the launderette,' said Jane.

'There's one a few doors up.' Sarah leaned on the door pillar, watching Jane opening the wardrobe doors. 'What exactly are we looking for?'

'You'll know it when you see it. Have we got a statement from that neighbour?'

'On the file. He saw him the evening before the day he disappeared. Just passed on the stairs, said hello, that was all there was to it.'

'And you've spoken to the son?'

'Briefly.'

'Not now, but ring him and get a detailed breakdown of exactly what cleaning him and his wife did in this flat, will you?'

'Yes, Sarge.'

'My name's Jane.'

'Oh, right, thanks.'

'Then we'll get Scientific in here with luminol; see if they can find any traces of blood.'

'You think he's dead then?'

'If he's done a runner, he's done it without any money or his passport.'

'Wow. My first case too.'

'It won't be your last.'

'Aren't you going to drop the keys back through—?'

'Scientific will need them tomorrow,' said Jane, closing the front door of Barry Mercer's flat behind them as silently as she could, not that there was any real risk of the neighbour hearing them leave over the thump of his music. 'Just tell the son you've kept them when you speak to him.'

'I think it's odd he hasn't been pestering us to find his dad, don't you? I mean, if my dad went missing I'd be climbing the walls.'

'We all have a different relationship with our parents.'

'I suppose we do.'

'Just keep it factual with him,' whispered Jane, tiptoeing down the stairs. 'This is what we're doing and we'll be in touch. What time are you on duty until?'

'Eight.'

'I'll drop you back to Express Park, then I'm off home. I'll take the file with me too, if you don't need it.'

'He's seen us,' said Sarah, when Jane started the engine of her car. 'He's in the upstairs window.'

'Too late now.'

'Someone said you're getting married on Christmas Eve?'

Idle conversation was fine with Jane, while she was deep in thought about what had become of Barry Mercer. 'Yeah,' she said, at the same time asking herself what Nick would do. And how he had got on at his job interview.

'To Nick Dixon?'

'Yeah.'

'We heard all about him at police college. Is he as good as they say he is?'

'Better.'

'How'd the interview go?' asked Jane, from the kitchen.

Dixon was stretched out on the sofa, a can of lager on the carpet next to him. He had paused *Hobson's Choice* when Monty heard Jane's car in the lane and the barking started. Now the dog was jumping up at her, Jane doing her best to fend him off.

'It didn't.'

'What d'you mean?' She was using a file as a shield, before casually dropping it on the sofa next to Dixon.

'A two o'clock interview and I was still sitting in the waiting area like a lemon at two-twenty-seven, so I walked out.'

'Charlesworth.'

'That's what I thought. The funny handshake brigade at work again; probably bumped into the bloke from Oxenden Hart at a

29

lodge meeting.' Dixon sat up, craning his neck to read the name on the file. 'I've got another one tomorrow in Weston, so we'll see if anything comes of that.' He knew her game; Burton had used it on Harris in *The Wild Geese*, and he could see her watching him out of the corner of her eye. It must be something interesting, mind you – code 400, so a missing person file.

'I can't believe they just left you sitting there all that time.'

'I can't believe I bloody well sat there all that time.'

'Gits.'

'I'd rather Charlesworth was behind it, because if that's the way they treat people then I had a lucky escape.'

'Maybe you should thank him?'

Dixon could hear Jane filling the kettle, so he turned the file on the sofa cushion to read the label.

'Tea?'

'I've got a beer, thanks.'

'Have you fed Monty?'

'Not yet.'

'I'll do it.'

That gave him enough time to pick up the file and take a peek at the fly sheet on the inside cover. Six months? Probably dead then. Nigel Cole the investigating officer, before he became the Rural Crimes Unit. Dixon hastily shut the file and turned it back around when he heard footsteps approaching.

'Has he been out?' Jane asked, sitting down on the sofa between Dixon and the file.

'On the beach this morning.'

'All morning, I expect.'

'Most of it.'

She kept glancing down at the file – trying to work out whether Dixon had looked at it, probably. 'It's a missing person file, in case you were wondering.'

'I wasn't.' Dixon took a swig of beer, as casually as he could manage.

'One of Nigel's.' Jane was holding her mug of tea in both hands. 'Would you like to hear about it?'

'Not really.'

'Barry Mercer. He's a private detective specialising in surveillance, personal injury claims, stuff like that. Just disappeared; no proof of life, nothing. I'm looking at it again with a young probationer, Sarah.' Jane smiled. 'Nice kid.'

Another swig; doing his best not to take the bait.

'He had three cases on when he went missing. An accident claim where a young lad had his leg blown off at a car breaker's yard, a benefits case for the Department of Work and Pensions, and a whiplash claim. Another had just settled out of court. They've all been spoken to, but only in the most general terms it seems, because Nigel didn't want to alert them to the fact they were under surveillance. After all, it's supposed to be covert, isn't it?'

'What d'you fancy for supper?'

'Look, I'm asking you for your help.' Never one to give up easily, Jane was trying a change of tack. She'd tried getting him interested in the file and that hadn't worked. Dixon suspected emotional blackmail would be her next tactic. 'It's what you do if you love someone – you help them.'

'Oh, I see. *Help*.'

'Will you help me, please?'

'When you put it like that, how can I refuse?'

'Thank you,' said Jane, placing the file in his lap. 'I'll nip over to the pub and fetch us a curry while you read that.'

'Not fish and chips?'

'Long story.'

'Well?'

'Very nice.'

'I wasn't talking about the curry!'

Dixon snapped open another can of lager. 'He might have had an accident and be lying somewhere, his body undiscovered. Or he might be holed up somewhere, not wanting to be found. He might even have gone abroad. Let's face it, a man like that will know how to go about getting a fake passport, won't he?'

'Don't be difficult.' Jane sighed. 'You know full well we're just trying to rule out foul play at this stage.'

'Get Scientific into his flat.'

'That's happening tomorrow.'

'Check his internet search history as well. That doesn't look like it's been done. And check the status of the cases he was working on when he disappeared. If they've settled out of court since then, interview them again; if his surveillance evidence was disclosed by the defence then go in hard. If the case is still going on and surveillance evidence hasn't been disclosed, move on.' Dixon stood up. 'They still won't know they were being watched.'

'They could've found out.'

'That's stage two, if you still can't find him. Ice cream?'

'No, thanks. And you shouldn't be having it anyway. You're diabetic, in case you'd forgotten.'

'If someone's killed him then it's most likely going to have been because he saw something he shouldn't, so you'll have to go back through his old cases as well.' Dixon was in the kitchen, stacking the dishwasher. 'Three years to begin with. Look for those where he cost the person a lot of money, or they went to prison and have since been released if it was a benefits cheat. Then rattle their cages.'

'We'll need to watch the surveillance footage, won't we?'

'All of it.'

'There's only me and Sarah.'

'You've got your work cut out then, haven't you?' Dixon appeared in the kitchen doorway, a piece of fruit in each hand. 'There's an apple or a banana.'

'What happened to the ice cream?'

'I'm diabetic,' replied Dixon, tipping his head. 'In case you'd forgotten.'

'I'll have the apple.'

'What about the footage he shot on the day he disappeared?'

'His cameras were in his van, so they've gone too,' replied Jane, then caught herself. 'I think. I'll need to check.'

'See if he had any cloud storage in that case. He may have had it set to back up automatically.' Dixon sat down on the arm of the sofa next to Jane. 'You never know, you might see someone walking up to his van armed with a gun.'

'You're full of shit.'

'Thank you, Sergeant.'

Chapter Four

'She thinks she's in CID already.' Dave Harding gestured towards a workstation on the far side of the CID Area, the top of a head just visible over the monitor. He was holding a mug of coffee in each hand.

'Did you offer her one?' asked Jane, raising her eyebrows.

'No, I bloody well didn't.'

'Nice.'

'What's she doing up here anyway? In civvies too.'

'I told her to, if you must know. We're working together on a missing person case.' Jane flicked on the kettle and picked up two mugs. 'I'm not working downstairs, so she's got to work upstairs. Is that all right with you?'

'I suppose so.'

'White, no sugar,' said Jane, setting a mug of tea down on the workstation next to Sarah a few minutes later. Sarah hadn't looked up once during that time and had no idea Jane was there.

'Oh, thanks,' she said, with a start.

'I thought your shift didn't start till ten?' Jane pulled a chair out from under the adjacent desk and sat down.

'I've been doing a bit of digging into his current cases, the ones he had on the go when he disappeared.' Sarah had picked up her notebook and was flicking back through the pages. 'The benefits fraudster is on bail and awaiting trial. She's on the system. I'm just waiting for a call back from the DWP to tell me whether the video surveillance footage was disclosed before or after our man disappeared.'

'What about the lad who had his leg blown off?'

'Ben Clifford; he settled before any video evidence was disclosed, so he probably never even knew he was under surveillance.'

'Probably,' muttered Jane.

'The whiplash claim settled, but Barry's evidence was never disclosed in that one either. Stevens, the bloke running the guesthouse, is more interesting. The defence offered him a pittance – their words, not mine – which he turned down. Then they disclosed Barry's video evidence, *before* he disappeared, and made a Part 36 Offer.' Sarah was reading from her notes. 'Whatever that means. Anyway he finally took it a few months later, just before the trial, which meant that he had to pay the costs. Something like that anyway.'

'Not a happy camper then.'

'He was claiming about two hundred and fifty thousand, with future loss of earnings and what have you. Settled for thirty, but the costs from the date of the Part 36 Offer would've come out of that. Probably left him with next to nothing.'

Go in hard, Nick had said. 'We'll start with Clifford and Stevens, in that case; and a visit to Curry Rivel. I want to see where Mercer was the day he went missing.'

'Scientific are meeting us at his flat at eleven,' said Sarah.

'Bags of time.'

◆ ◆ ◆

It was the sort of drizzle that seemed to float in the air; the stuff that hardly registers on the windscreen, and yet soaks you to the skin as soon as you get out of the car. Jane sighed. She'd left her umbrella in the back of Dixon's Land Rover. 'I don't suppose you've got a brolly?' she asked.

'No, sorry,' replied Sarah. 'Should you be getting soaking wet in your condition?'

'We'll stay in the car. I only wanted a look anyway.'

High hedges trapping mist, the branches of trees clawing their way skyward, the only sound the occasional car racing past on the main road. One of the bungalows had left their Christmas lights on all night, a small inflatable snowman lying face down on the lawn. Lights twinkled in the hedge down the side of the drive, more in the branches of a dormant apple tree.

'Hardly feels like Christmas, does it?'

'Never does in this job.' Jane was looking down at the line of dormer bungalows. 'Last year it was a woman stabbed to death on Christmas Eve over at Northmoor Green. Turned out she was pregnant.'

'That's the one the lad who lost his leg lives in,' said Sarah, clearly deciding a change of subject was called for. She was looking out of the passenger window, pointing at the first bungalow in the lane below them. 'His name's Ben Clifford; lives with his parents.'

Four bungalows set in a cul-de-sac at the bottom of a bank and parallel to the main road, backing on to open fields, a line of telegraph poles rising out of the mist beyond.

Jane had parked in a large lay-by on the main road overlooking the bungalows, an empty SUV parked at the far end, the back seats down.

'They must flood here, don't you reckon?' asked Sarah.

'Might do, I suppose; the Parrett's a hundred yards or so that way. You can see the bridge.' Jane frowned. 'What concerns me more at the moment is where Mercer could've parked to watch Clifford's bungalow without being seen. A white van would stick out like a sore thumb parked here all day.'

'Not in this lay-by,' countered Sarah. 'There's a public footpath at the end of the cul-de-sac there. You can see the stile, and the path goes off across the fields towards Langport, so dog walkers will park here. It's on the River Parrett Trail. Then you've got fishermen; Mercer disappeared on the eighteenth, and the fishing season opened on the fifteenth.'

The bow of a small boat that had seen better days was visible above the fence in the corner of the front garden; four cars parked on the drive, none of them looking as though they'd moved in a while.

Next door was tidier, the garden clearly tended even in winter.

Sarah was sitting up in the passenger seat, looking along the grass verge opposite the bungalows. 'Looks like cars park down there too. See all the tyre tracks in the mud?'

'Delivery vans, maybe.'

'There was a funeral on, don't forget, the day Barry went missing.' Sarah was flicking through her notebook again. 'That house there, so there'd have been plenty of cars here for that. It was the daughter, and the funeral tea was here as well, so that's loads of visitors probably.'

The sound of a door slamming, then a small liver and white springer spaniel appeared down the side of the cars parked in the driveway of the Cliffords' bungalow. The dog ran out into the cul-de-sac and began sniffing along the base of the fence.

'That's Ben,' said Sarah.

Jeans and a black coat, hood up, he was following the dog, lead in hand.

'Let's go and have a word,' said Jane. She slammed the car door behind her. 'Excuse me,' she said, raising her voice over the sound of a car racing past behind her. 'Can we have a word?'

Sarah was waving her warrant card in front of her.

'I'm putting him on a lead,' protested Clifford.

'Not about that.' Jane was picking her way down the muddy path that led from the lay-by to the cul-de-sac below. 'It's Ben, isn't it?'

'Heel.' He had clipped the lead on to the dog's collar and was pulling it towards him. 'Trained him myself,' he said, although the dog was taking no notice. 'Heel, you little bug—'

'We wanted to ask you about a van parked in the lay-by back in June.'

'Not that again. We had one of your lot sniffing around here months ago. There are vans in that lay-by all the time during the fishing season. They park there and walk down to the bridge.'

'This one was different.'

'How so?'

'There was a man in it watching you, and that man has since disappeared.'

'Watching me?' Ben brushed his hood back and scowled at Jane. 'No one mentioned that before. Why was he watching me?'

'It was part of your injury claim,' replied Jane. 'The defence thought you were exaggerating so they had you placed under surveillance.'

'I had my right leg blown off. How the fuck do you exaggerate that?'

'Do you remember the van?'

'No. Look, I had no idea I was being watched and I wasn't exaggerating my claim.'

'You've since settled?'

'Yes.'

'Was surveillance footage disclosed by the defence?'

'No. They made me an offer and I took it.' Ben was wrapping the dog's lead around his hand. 'My solicitor and my barrister said it was a good offer. Am I under arrest?'

'We're just following up on a missing person and asking if you recall seeing anything unusual; mid-June, so six months or so ago.'

'Well I don't. And I've got a dog to walk and a doctor's appointment to get to.'

'A man is missing,' said Sarah.

'A man who was watching me.' Ben turned for the stile at the bottom of the cul-de-sac, dragging his dog with him. 'And I'm hardly going to give a shit about him, am I?'

◆ ◆ ◆

'A bit miserable on the beach, was it?'

'Didn't get that far.'

Dixon was sitting in the porch at Berrow Church, sheltering from the drizzle, Monty on the granite seat next to him, wagging his tail.

'I saw your Land Rover from the road. We need to have a chat about your stag do,' continued Poland, lowering his large frame on to the seat opposite.

'Haven't you organised that yet, Roger?'

'Not yet.'

'Well, don't bother on my account. A curry in the Zalshah will do.'

'Mark Pearce suggested a live sex show in Amsterdam.'

Dixon wasn't entirely sure he wanted to know. 'And where are we going?' he asked, his voice filled with trepidation.

'Lynmouth.' Poland looked pleased with himself. 'There's a little hotel on the harbour – a nice meal and a few beers.'

'Perfect.'

'I didn't think Amsterdam was really *you*.'

'I haven't got a passport anyway.'

'Mind you, I can't guarantee they won't strip you naked and set you adrift in the Bristol Channel in a little rubber boat.'

'Yes, you can, if you know what's good for you.'

'How did the job interview go yesterday?'

'They kept me waiting nearly half an hour, so I walked out. I'm guessing Charlesworth was behind it; probably someone he met at his lodge.'

'David isn't a Freemason.'

'Really?' Dixon felt relieved. 'Just a bunch of tossers then. I had a lucky escape.'

'You've got another this afternoon?'

'Fords in Weston. That's a commercial property vacan—'

'Commercial property?' Poland laughed out loud – quite deliberately, Dixon thought. 'You'd last five minutes as a corporate lawyer, even less doing commercial property. Can you imagine it?'

Dixon chose silence.

'Spending your days poring over leases, worrying about rent review clauses and repair covenants and rubbish like that. You'll have your head in a gas oven in a couple of weeks. Still, it was nice knowing you.'

'Thank you.'

'Just don't do it until after the wedding. Jane'll get your pension that way and I've never been a best man before.'

'I thought about after the honeymoon, actually,' said Dixon. 'I don't want to miss a trip to the Lakes.'

'Look, you really need to—'

Dixon raised his hand, silencing Poland mid-sentence. 'Not another lecture, please, Roger.'

'All right, all right.' Poland stood up. 'C'mon, let's get this dog walked.'

'It's pissing down.'

'It's only water.'

◆ ◆ ◆

'Thanks very much for coming back to me.' Sarah rang off and dropped her phone into her coat pocket. 'That was Mrs Baynes. He didn't have cloud backup. He said it would've cost an arm and a leg using mobile data to back up video footage all day, every day, so he never bothered.'

'Good point,' said Jane. She was reversing into a parking space on the seafront at Burnham-on-Sea, opposite a grey two-storey building with sash windows and battlements.

'Don't tell me that's the guesthouse.'

'Called Beach View, oddly enough.'

The sign in the window announced there were 'No vacancies'.

'It can't be full this time of year,' said Sarah. 'And the car park's empty.'

'It'll be workers from Hinkley Point, I expect. They'll all be over there at this time of day.' Jane was gesturing across the estuary to the nuclear power station, perhaps two miles away across the murky grey water of the River Parrett, the tide in and lapping at the base of the wave return wall. The huge concrete blocks of A and B dwarfed by the building site of Hinkley Point C, a forest of cranes in the middle. Jane had tried counting them before, when she'd been out on the beach with Nick and Monty, and had given up at twenty something.

'Bloody hell! I've not seen it before, except on the telly.' Sarah was holding her phone up, using her fingers to zoom in before taking a photograph. 'That tall crane in the middle, is that where Inspector Dixon was when the firearms officer took the shot?'

'Yes.'

'All us cadets wanted to join Armed Response after that.'

'It's not all it's cracked up to be,' said Jane, stifling a sigh at the memory of Nick's blood spattered clothes; most of them had gone in the rubbish rather than the washing machine.

The sight of their warrant cards was enough – Roy Stevens kicking off before Jane had even opened her mouth.

'My solicitor said I wouldn't be bloody prosecuted and now I've got you lot on my doorstep. You'll have to wait there while I ring him.'

Jane stuck her foot out, stopping Stevens closing the door. 'Can I just ask, before you slam the door in my face, what you're talking about?'

'The defence solicitors said I'd been lying about how bad my injuries were; said they'd be reporting me for perjury.'

'They may have done, Mr Stevens, but we're not here about that, I can assure you.'

'Oh. What are you here about?' he asked, opening the door.

'Can we come in?'

Stevens stepped back into the hallway. 'Through there,' he said, gesturing into the lounge.

'Can you tell us where you were on the eighteenth of June, please? It was a Thursday.'

'We'd have had guests in, that much I can tell you. Let me get the diary.'

Jane waited, listening to the footsteps out in the hall. Then Stevens reappeared carrying a large book and flicked back through the pages. 'Here we are, eighteenth of June. My wife had a hospital appointment in the morning, so I'd have taken her over there after we'd given the guests breakfast. We stopped at the garden centre, Sanders, on the way back, I do remember that.'

Sarah was making notes.

'Look, what's this all about?'

'What about the afternoon?' asked Jane.

'There were a couple of changeovers, so I'd have done the rooms, got them ready, done the washing. Anita might remember if we did anything else in the afternoon, but I can't honestly . . .' He was flicking dry skin from his scalp and shaking his head at the same time; ended up looking remarkably like Stan Laurel. 'We do go to the cinema sometimes. She keeps a diary, come to think of it.' He stepped out into the hall and shouted his wife's name.

'Does the name Barry Mercer mean anything to you?' asked Jane.

'Him! Yes, it bloody well does. What a shitty way to make a living,' Stevens sneered. 'Good at it, though. I'll give him that.'

'What is it?' A delayed shout from his wife, somewhere upstairs.

'Bring your diary, will you. There are some police here who want to know what we were doing on the eighteenth of June.'

'Give me a minute.'

'His evidence cost you a lot of money, I imagine?'

'I cleared just under eight grand after the costs had been paid. I'm in a bad way,' he said, rubbing the small of his back. 'I have good days and bad days, but his videos made it look like I was fit as a fiddle.'

'Fiddle' being the operative word.

'How much was your claim worth, do you think?' asked Sarah.

'A quarter of a million, on paper, but my solicitors said I'd probably end up with about fifty or sixty. That was until we had a visit from Mr Cripps.' Stevens was trying to mask the venom in his voice; failing. 'That was the name he used. Cripps. It's a bloody river out on the Levels. More like bloody *Crippen*. I should've known.'

'I had a hospital appointment on the eighteenth of June.' A small voice from a small woman, standing behind Stevens. 'It's a little bit embarrassing, if you don't mind?'

'That's fine,' replied Jane.

'Then we had lunch at the garden centre and went to the cinema. Out of season, the Ritz sometimes shows old films in the afternoon. It's lovely to see them on the big screen, don't you think? That week it was *Gone with the Wind*.'

'What time did you get home?'

'No idea. My diary doesn't say. The film started at two-thirty and it's a long one. Four hours with the intermission, so that makes it six-thirty before we came out.'

'What's the significance of the eighteenth of June?' asked Stevens, turning to Jane.

'Mr Mercer is missing, Sir,' she replied, matter of fact. 'He was last heard from on the morning of the eighteenth, and we're just trying to rule out foul play.'

'You think he's dead?'

'We don't know. That's the point.'

'Well, I didn't kill him.' Stevens folded his arms and leaned against the back of the sofa. 'Not that I didn't want to at the time, but he was just doing his job. If it hadn't been him, it would've been someone else.'

Chapter Five

It had been a long night, once she'd got over the magnet fishing. A hot shower and a bottle of Pinot Grigio had done the trick, and it must have been three o'clock in the morning before she finally let him get to sleep.

The day had dragged, but then every day did. It was always the same: yelled at by Steve for being a few minutes late – 'I'll make up the time in my lunch break', 'Make sure you do' – a coffee from the machine, then it was on to his first set of tyres. Sometimes it was a puncture repair, and if he was really lucky, checking the tracking and wheel balancing too. Variety is the spice of life and all that.

A Formula 1 mechanic, Ferrari preferably, in the pits changing tyres in seconds – that had been his boyhood dream. Silverstone, Monaco; he still had the posters on his bedroom wall.

He'd got as far as Highbridge Tyres and Servicing.

Changing tyres on autopilot, daydreaming about magnet fishing, occasionally thinking about her.

A couple of minutes picking the mould spots off his Marmite sandwich, leaving oily fingerprints on the stale white bread.

Marmite because that's all there was. It was supposed to be his lunch, but today it was a late breakfast.

'Oi, shit for brains, come 'ere.' Steve was standing at the back of the garage, beckoning him.

What now?

He left his sandwich balanced on the rim of his coffee cup and trudged towards the back door, his hands thrust deep into the pockets of his overalls.

Steve was standing on the far side of the yard now, his hands on his hips, staring at the ground behind a muddy pickup. 'You've been out on the Levels again, collecting crap.'

'So what if I have?'

'Explain to me what this is?' Steve gestured to a puddle on the ground, muddy water dripping from the pickup, tinged with pink, like someone had thrown a strawberry milkshake in the back. That must be it. They'd been to the drive-through on the way home from North Curry, after all.

He looked half-heartedly into the back of the pickup, expecting to see a cardboard drinks carton in amongst his rusting treasure trove.

'It's coming from that tin box,' said Steve, keeping his distance.

A trickle of pink muddy water, snaking across the bed of the truck towards a drain in the nearside rear corner.

'You'd better open it.'

'Really?'

'It looks like blood to me.'

'It's locked.'

'Get a crowbar then.'

Lighter than it had been when he dragged it out of the Tone, he lifted the box out of the back of his pickup by the handles, holding it at arm's length. Once it was on the ground he jammed the crowbar under the lid near the lock. 'Shouldn't we just call the police?' he asked.

'Just open the bloody thing, Darren.'

Hard man Steve, seen-it-all and done-it-all ex-army Steve, was the first to vomit, not even having time to turn away.

◆　◆　◆

'They've been diverted.'

'For fuck's sake,' hissed Jane. 'What time are they coming?'

'They're not.' Sarah lowered her voice, embarrassed to be delivering bad news. 'Not today anyway.'

'It's not your fault.' Jane was parked outside Mercer's flat, drumming her fingers on the steering wheel, waiting for Scientific Services. They'd arrived late to find Scientific hadn't turned up at all. A missing person was clearly bottom of the pile. 'It had better be bloody good, whatever it is.'

'Human remains, apparently. In the back of a pickup at Highbridge Tyres, of all places. They did the tyres on my Fiesta. Cheap as chips, they are.'

'Let's get over there, just in case it's our man.' Jane climbed out of the driver's seat. 'You drive and I'll ring in; see if I can persuade Janice to assign it to me.'

The clincher was Jane's assurance that she was already on her way, although it took much of the fifteen-minute drive to the Walrow Industrial Estate to convince the managing DCI at Express Park, Janice Courtenay. 'A temporary measure anyway,' Janice said. 'A major investigation team is inevitable.'

'As long as I'm bloody well on it,' Jane replied.

She dropped her phone into her handbag and looked up, just as Sarah pulled into the car park in front of Highbridge Tyres.

The low wall at the front looked painfully familiar, and suddenly the memories were flooding back.

'Are you all right?' asked Sarah.

'Yes, fine,' snapped Jane. She glanced across the road at the remains of the furniture factory. All that was left was a pile of rubble behind a temporary steel fence, and yellow posters tied to lamp posts; planning applications in to rebuild, probably.

Several men in blue overalls were sitting on the low wall, drinking coffee and smoking; the same wall she had been sitting on that night all those months ago, chain smoking other people's cigarettes while she watched the flames climbing into the sky, people telling her that Dixon was inside, dead. The feeling of hopelessness came roaring back, as if it were happening all over again.

Maybe she would prefer it if he got a job in a law firm after all? Behind a nice, safe desk.

'Come on,' she said, blinking away the moisture that had formed in the corners of her eyes. 'Let's go and see what we've got.'

The roller doors at the front of the garage were open, several cars inside – two up on vehicle lifts, their wheels lying on the concrete floor. A Scientific Services van was parked outside the office, to the side of the main garage, two ashen-faced men in overalls sitting inside, drinking glasses of water, their eyes glazed over.

'It's in the staff car park round the back,' said the senior Scientific Services officer, Donald Watson. Dressed head to toe in white overalls, face mask on, but Jane recognised his voice mercifully. 'Suits in the back of the van. Help yourselves. Stepping plates from the corner, although that's mainly for the vomit. Those two in the office were sick everywhere.'

'You can sit this out if you'd rather, Sarah.' Jane was holding a set of overalls in her outstretched hand.

'No, thank you. I'll be fine. And if I'm not, I've just got to get used to it, haven't I.'

'You'll need large,' said Watson, turning to Jane. 'To fit over your bump.'

'Human remains, Donald?' she asked, holding the door of the van to steady herself while she pulled on the trousers.

'A head and hands. Sounds like a pub, doesn't it? I'm just popping to the Head and Hands for a beer.'

Jane grimaced. Nick would've told him to show a bit of respect if he had been there, but a humble sergeant probably couldn't get away with it. One complaint from Scientific and she'd be off the case.

'How old?'

'Six months maybe, but that's not really my field.'

'Of course not. Sorry.'

'You'll need to have a word with laddo in there,' said Watson, gesturing to the office. 'Darren Smith. He fished the box out of the Tone yesterday with his magnet and it's been in the back of his pickup ever since.'

'We'll need the dive team in that case. Where on the Tone?'

'Newbridge,' replied Watson. 'They're already on the way there; be about an hour.'

'Is there a pathologist coming?'

'No point. We'll take the box over to Musgrove Park for Dr Poland to do his bit when we've finished. It's not that big, and it'll fit in a large crate.'

◆　◆　◆

'Ready?'

A very pale looking Sarah swallowed hard. 'This'll be my first body,' she mumbled.

'Well, it's not really a body, is it.' Watson was trying to reassure. 'It's just body parts.'

'You're not helping, Donald.' Jane ushered Sarah towards the corner of the garage and the line of stepping plates leading across the staff car park at the back, privately thanking her lucky stars her morning sickness had only lasted a couple of days.

Several cars were parked facing the wall, a large tent covering the rear of the black pickup truck on the end and the ground behind it. The stepping plates led to the tent entrance, camera flashes going off inside, visible even over the brightness of the arc lamps.

The nearside of the pickup and its wheel arches were plastered in grey mud; a regular sight on the Levels in winter. It was impossible to keep a car clean.

Jane looked at Sarah and gave her best reassuring smile, then pulled up her face mask and set off along the stepping plates, listening to the young officer's footsteps behind her. No hint of hesitation: a good sign.

'In you go then.' Watson was wearing latex overshoes, which clearly exempted him from use of the stepping plates.

'You shouldn't creep up on people, Don.'

'Nearly gave birth on the spot, did you?' Mischief in his voice. Watson pushed past them and into the tent, holding the flap open and gesturing to the right. 'The plates go that way.'

The tin box was on the ground behind the pickup, near a puddle of mud and blood, the pink fluid dripping slowly from a drain. Jane was mesmerised, watching each drop gradually getting larger until it could hang on no longer.

'Strawberry milkshake, the lad called it.' Watson shuddered. 'Won't be having that for a while.'

The lid of the box was open, the lock broken, a crowbar lying on the ground next to it where it had been dropped. There was a strong smell of vomit too.

'Cornflakes and coffee,' said Watson. 'That was the manager. The young lad made it down the side of the truck before he—'

'Thank you.' Jane didn't need those details.

Sarah was breathing hard behind her face mask, her eyes wide and fixed on the box.

'It's a white male, adult; that's about all I can tell you.' Watson was leaning over the tin box. 'Well, I say *a* white male; it could be more than one, couldn't it? We won't know until we get an ID. That'll be for the pathologist, though. There'll be plenty of DNA and the teeth are intact, so an ID should be easy. Fingerprints are probably shot, mind you. Too long in the water.'

The head was resting on its side in the box, the hands unceremoniously stuffed down behind it, the remains half submerged in . . . Jane shuddered to herself, trying to lose the vision of strawberry milkshake.

'Is it Mercer?' asked Sarah.

'Impossible to tell.' Jane had seen a photograph of him, of course. 'Same hair colour – that's the best we can say at the moment.'

'Barry Mercer?' asked Watson.

'Yes.'

'I knew him, back in the day. There's the remains of a moustache, if you look closely. Barry always had a moustache.'

'What's in the back of the van?' Jane asked, before she was offered the opportunity to *look closely*.

'Junk the lad's fished out of the rivers,' replied Watson. 'We haven't been through it yet.'

'Fished out of the rivers?'

'Magnet fishing. They use a really powerful magnet on the end of a rope, chuck it in and drag it back across the riverbed.'

'What for?' asked Sarah.

'Fun.'

51

'We'd better go and have a word with him,' said Jane. 'Gets us out of there too,' she whispered to Sarah, once they were back out on the stepping plates.

'It didn't look real somehow.' Sarah pulled her face mask below her chin, sucking in gulps of air. 'More like a waxwork.'

Jane decided to spare her the lecture about anaerobic decomposition.

Darren was sitting in the office, still looking ashen-faced, when Jane and Sarah walked in, having deposited their overalls in a crate at the back of Donald Watson's van. The manager, Steve, must have recovered something of his equilibrium and was answering the telephone.

'No, I'm afraid we can't today. We're closed for the rest of the day, sorry. Circumstances beyond our control. Tomorrow should be fine.' Steve rang off. 'I've sent the others home,' he said, when he saw Jane looking at the wall out the front.

'Is there somewhere we could have a chat with Darren?' she asked.

'Use my office,' replied Steve. 'I'm just going to finish off those two cars up on the lifts. The owners will be back for them later.'

Only one chair, behind a desk strewn with paper. Darren perched on the windowsill, Sarah sitting down at the desk and getting out her notebook.

'Bit of a shock, I expect, Darren,' said Jane.

'You could say that.' He puffed out his cheeks. 'God knows what Shaz is going to say when I tell her.'

'What's your full name?'

'Darren Charles Smith. Shaz was with me when I pulled it out, helped me carry it to the truck. She's going to have a fit.'

'When was this?' Jane was pacing up and down, watching the comings and goings on the stepping plates in the car park at the back, two men in overalls carrying a large black crate.

'Yesterday. About three, I suppose. We were just downstream of Newbridge on the Tone. It's a mile or so outside North Curry.'

'We're going to ask you to come with us out there in a bit. Show us exactly where. Is that all right?'

'Will they have finished with my truck by then?'

'No, sorry.'

Darren nodded.

'So, you were magnet fishing,' continued Jane.

'Yeah, on the Tone there. Bridges are good spots; cars pull up, chuck stuff in, you know what it's like. Anyway, I thought I'd give the Tone a go. I'm usually on the Parrett; found all sorts of stuff in there.'

'How long were you there?'

'Less than an hour. It was pissing down and Shaz was getting the hump. I was on the south bank, at the bottom of the slip there. It sort of angles down at forty five degrees to the water's edge. I thought the magnet was stuck and was pulling away like. Then it just came free and in came this tin box. It might have been stuck on a tree stump or something. Anyway, it was locked, so we just dumped it in the back of the truck and forgot about it. Until Steve made me open it. He saw the blood dripping.'

'Did you find anything else?'

'A roll of barbed wire and a scaffolding clamp. Oh, shit.' Darren gulped.

'What?'

'There was a hacksaw. New too; very little rust on it.'

'Where is it?'

'I chucked it in the back of the pickup. You don't think it was used to . . .'

'We'll need to get it checked, obviously.'

'She's going to kill me.' He was staring straight ahead, seemingly resigned to his fate. 'I made her carry it.'

Jane tapped on the window of the office, opened it and called across to Donald Watson. 'A roll of barbed wire, a scaffolding clamp and a hacksaw; new, very little rust.'

'A hacksaw?' Watson turned and disappeared back inside the tent.

'Where will we find Shaz?' asked Jane, closing the window.

'She'll be at work. It's a hair salon in Bridgwater. Veronica's, it's called.'

'We'll need a statement from her, and samples for exclusion purposes.'

'Samples?'

'DNA, fingerprints.'

'She's going to love that.'

'It's just a swab from inside the mouth. Nothing to fear. We'll need yours too, but we'll pop out to the Tone first.' Jane looked at her watch. 'The dive team will be there soon.'

Chapter Six

'Sell yourself to us.'

Oh, for fuck's sake. As stupid questions go, that must be right at the top of the pile.

Dixon coughed, hand over his mouth to mask his pained expression.

It was a crappy little branch office of a crappy little law firm and they were seriously asking him to sell himself to *them*.

'I like to think my CV sells itself,' he said, silently counting to ten, just as his anger management counsellor was always suggesting.

They waited for more. And so did he.

The one on the left was the senior partner, sitting with his back to the window, visible only in silhouette. It was more of an interrogation than an interview technique. The other was the managing partner, younger and down from the Bristol office. That was above a shop too.

Dixon had done his research.

'Tell me about the vacancy,' he said, running his index finger along the inside of his collar; for something to do more than anything else, although he was getting pretty hot under it.

'It's advertised as commercial property, although there'd be more residential than commercial, if the truth be told.'

'It'd be for the successful candidate to build up the commercial side,' said the managing partner, diving in to try to rescue the situation, a veiled glare at his senior colleague. 'You'd have a fairly free rein to develop that side of the practice. It's mainly pubs, hotels and guesthouses, as you might imagine. Shops too. We have good relationships with some of the local estate agents, so it'd be down to you to get in there and get the work.'

'I think my reputation may precede me when it comes to local estate agents.' One dead, two in hospital, and two arrested for murder; Dixon hoped he might get away with the understatement.

'That was you, was it?' asked the senior partner.

'I'll need time off to attend the trials.'

'Ah.'

'That was Burnham and Bridgwater,' said the managing partner, trying to sound positive. 'And memories are short. You could start with the Weston agents and build from there.'

'Do you have much experience of commercial leases?' asked the senior partner.

'Not really,' replied Dixon, bluntly. There was no way on God's clean earth he was taking the job, so no harm in being blunt.

'I admire your honesty,' said the managing partner, 'so I'll be honest with you. You're not really here for the commercial property vacancy. We have another in our Bristol office that we thought you might be suitable for. The partner is retiring, but he'd stay on until you were settled in and had got your duty solicitor accreditation.'

'We haven't even advertised it yet.' The senior partner looked pleased with himself. 'Why are you leaving the police?'

'I was arrested and charged with murder.'

'Really?'

'Framed, as it happens, but that's just detail. It rocks your confidence in your employer.'

'I should imagine it does.'

'Thank you, gentlemen,' said Dixon, standing up. 'But it seems this was a complete waste of your time, and mine, so I'll take my leave, if it's all the same to you.'

'The crime vacancy doesn't interest you then?' asked the managing partner. 'It's a head of department role.'

'No. Sorry.'

'Shame. You'd be ideal, and there's a partnership on offer sooner rather than later. The marketing would be superb too.'

If he mentions that old gamekeeper cliché I'll swing for him.

'I can see it now: "Poacher turns gamekeeper as high-flying DCI joins Bristol law firm".'

◆　◆　◆

The small car park was full of vans and trailers by the time Jane and Sarah arrived at Newbridge on the River Tone, Darren sitting in the back seat of Jane's VW Golf. Mercifully, he hadn't been sick on the way.

They stopped on the bridge and looked down at the river, steep banks on either side, footprints in the mud on the slipway down to the water's edge where two officers in drysuits were standing, one holding a rope that disappeared into the fast flowing murky water.

'I got someone in straightaway; the light will be going soon,' called the uniformed sergeant from below. 'Is that the lad who found it?'

'Yes,' shouted Jane.

'Bring him down here. The gate's just along there.'

A Scientific Services van had arrived too, several empty crates lined up along the bank to receive any 'finds'.

'This is Darren,' said Jane, when the sergeant scrambled up the bank.

'Where were you when you found it, Darren?'

'I was standing on the end of the slipway and I threw the magnet straight across to the far bank.'

'And where did it pick up the box?'

'Right in the middle. It was stuck on something, so there may be a tree stump down there.'

'Well, there's no van down there,' said the sergeant, turning to Jane. 'We've established that much already. It's a fingertip search now. I'll be getting a couple more lads in the water for a necklace in the next few minutes.'

'Necklace?' Sarah frowned.

'Three divers roped together.'

The river was thirty yards wide at the sluice gate under the bridge, narrowing to half that beyond the end of the slipway. Deep water, steep banks; it was the stuff of nightmares, soft mud and nothing to grab hold of if you fell in. It didn't bear thinking about.

The divers would hardly be able to see their hands in front of their faces, hence the fingertips – feeling in the mud for human remains.

'Glad I never joined the dive team,' muttered Sarah.

'Me too,' replied Jane.

'One of the lads in the cadets wanted to do it.'

'Where is he now?'

'Apprentice plumber.'

'I wouldn't know what to do with all the money.' The sergeant turned to Darren. 'How far down did you go?'

'Just between the bridge and the end of the slipway there. No further than that. My girlfriend was whinging about the rain.'

'Take him back to the car, will you, Sarah,' said Jane, handing over her car keys. She waited until they were out of earshot. 'They told you about the hacksaw?'

'They did. The tin box would've sunk like a stone, but body parts have some buoyancy to them, so we'll go further down, just in case.'

'Thanks.'

'Has the hacksaw been checked?'

'Not yet. It's on the way to the lab now.'

'He's got something, Mike.' The shout came from the bottom of the slipway, where the officer holding the rope was in radio contact with the diver on the riverbed. 'He's bringing it in now,' he said, taking in the slack rope.

The full-face dive mask appeared first, the eyes behind it exhausted.

'It's hard work,' said the sergeant standing next to Jane. 'Holding station in the current and feeling in the sludge at the same time.'

The diver was struggling to stand in the mud, then he reached up and placed something on the edge of the slipway, before slipping back into the water to resume the search.

The object was wrapped in black plastic, a bin liner probably, and taped up with insulating tape.

'Looks like a thigh to me.' The sergeant let out a heavy sigh. 'Lamps everybody.'

'Can you work after dark?' asked Jane.

'It's pitch bloody black down there anyway.'

'What the hell is going on, Darren?' Sharon was sitting on the wall outside the police centre at Express Park, smoking a cigarette.

'There she is. Just give me a minute,' Darren said. 'I'll go and calm her down a bit.'

'Fat chance,' whispered Jane to Sarah. They were waiting by the car in the visitors' car park, watching.

'Knows how to handle her, he said,' replied Sarah. 'We'll soon see.'

Sharon was marching towards Darren. 'I'm minding my own business, in the middle of a cut and blow dry, when the rozzers turn up at the salon and drag me here.'

'It's fine, Shaz.' Darren's arms were outstretched for a hug, but she batted him away.

'Are we being done for magnet fishing? 'Cause if we are—'

'We found something.'

Hushed voices, but Jane was close enough to overhear the conversation.

'Give us a ciggy,' continued Darren.

'It's that tin box, innit?'

Darren nodded, the end of the cigarette bouncing up and down in the lighter flame.

'For fuck's sake, what?' Sharon's eyes were wide, pleading.

Darren took a deep draw on his cigarette, blowing the smoke out through his nose as he spoke. 'A bloke's head and his hands. They're fishing the rest of him out of the river now.'

Sharon was oddly impassive, for an all too brief moment. Then the screaming started. Darren wrapped his arms around her waist, her fists pummelling his chest. 'We carried it up the . . . and it was in the back of the van all night . . . you fuck—' She spoke through the gasps, then pulled herself away from him. 'It's all right,' she said, trying to calm herself down. 'I'm fine.'

Nobody was convinced.

There was a time you could have given someone in that state a bloody good slap, thought Jane, but not now, and not in front of a police station; probably get nicked for assault these days.

'How about a cup of tea?' she said, more as a reminder to Sharon that there were other people there.

An audience had gathered at the floor to ceiling windows on the first floor of the police centre, Detective Chief Superintendent Potter among them.

'That would be great,' said Darren.

'Get them settled in an interview room on the ground floor,' said Jane, turning to Sarah. 'A nice mug of tea each, then we'll get statements from them. The police surgeon can give her something to calm her down, if needs be.'

'I'll be fine,' said Sharon. 'Really. Just give me a minute.'

'I'll catch you up, Sarah.' Jane glanced up at the windows in the CID Area. 'The chief super's here, so I'd better go and have a word.'

A major investigation team was inevitable now, and Jane was going to make damned sure she was on it. Sarah too.

Chapter Seven

'You seem to have it all under control, Jane. Well done,' said Potter, holding open the door of meeting room 2. 'Sit down and talk to me about Barry Mercer.' Potter's pinstriped two piece trouser suit matched the highlights in her greying hair. A nice touch that. 'He's a misper you were reviewing with a probationer.'

'That's right, Ma'am,' replied Jane, sitting down on a chair she had pulled out from under the table. 'Ex-police, and there's no mention of that on the file, which seems a bit odd.'

'Is it him in the tin box?'

Jane had known that question was coming. Give the wrong answer and she'd be off the MIT, as sure as eggs were eggs. 'We don't know yet' was the truth of it, but the response to that would be 'leave it to us then'. It was a bit of a gamble without DNA confirmation, but worth the risk. 'Yes, it is, Ma'am,' she replied. 'We've made a start at his office, looking at the cases he was—'

'Have we had the DNA?'

'Not yet.' Jane grimaced to herself. 'It's my visual ID at this stage, Ma'am. From photographs.'

'And you're convinced it's him?'

'I am.'

It had bloody well better be after this.

Potter's eyes narrowed and fixed on Jane's bump, looking for any increase in size since the last time they'd been 'discussing' Jane's risk assessment. 'Remind me when it's due?'

'End of April.'

Jane knew what Potter was thinking: was it really worth another shouting match when the MIT was almost certainly going to be short-staffed anyway?

'All right.' Potter sighed. 'You'd better stay on Mercer seeing as you've made a start. You and that probationer, what's her name?'

'Sarah Loveday, Ma'am. She's a bright kid.'

'Look at his current cases, and go back three years as well. I'll get someone else to take statements from those two downstairs, don't worry about that.'

'Thank you, Ma'am.'

'You'd arranged for Forensics to go over his flat, I gather?'

'They got diverted to the tin box and now they're at the river with the dive team. I've got the keys here.'

'Let me have them and I'll sort it out.' Potter extended her hand, her fingers twitching impatiently. 'Bit of a priority now, as you might imagine.'

'Who's going to be the SIO?' asked Jane, braced for a snide remark about Dixon.

'I am.' Potter folded her arms and gave a sarcastic smile. 'Seeing as there's nobody else available.'

◆ ◆ ◆

'Is this your first death message?' asked Jane. They were standing on the doorstep of a bungalow in Heal Close, Puriton. Bay window, neatly tended rose garden, the roses all pruned low for the winter; one bungalow looks much the same as the next.

'Yes.' Sarah was standing behind her, out in the drizzle, which was falling again, not that you could really see it in the streetlights.

'I'll do the talking,' whispered Jane, someone unlocking the door on the inside.

'You again,' said Mrs Baynes. 'Have you found him?'

'We think so, Mrs Baynes,' replied Jane. 'May we come in?'

'Of course.'

Jane stepped into the hallway. 'Is there somewhere we could sit down, perhaps?'

'Er, yes.' Nervous now. 'Through here.'

They followed Mrs Baynes into the living room, and waited while she perched on the edge of the sofa.

'I'm afraid we've found a body in the River Tone, which we believe to be that of Mr Mercer,' said Jane.

'The poor sod. Did he take his own life?'

'No.'

'He'd tried before, you know; suffered from depression ever since he left the police.'

'It's a murder investigation, Mrs Baynes.'

She started to sob.

'I'll get you a glass of water,' said Sarah, heading for the kitchen at the back of the house.

Jane waited, letting Mrs Baynes cry quietly until the drink arrived.

'You'll be wanting the keys to his office, I suppose,' she said, her composure regained.

'Thank you.'

Rummaging in her handbag now. 'How did he . . . was he . . . ?' She hardly dared say the words.

'We don't know yet, Mrs Baynes,' replied Jane. 'There'll need to be a post mortem.'

'What about an identification? Presumably you'll need me to . . .' She shook her head. 'There's no one else.'

'We'll be using DNA and dental records.' Jane tried a comforting smile. 'He was in the water for some time.'

'I understand.'

She didn't – she couldn't – but people could have too much information sometimes. 'We'll need a statement from you at some point,' Jane said.

'Yes, whenever you're ready. Look, there was one of your lot, about three years ago, maybe,' said Mrs Baynes, nervously, her eyes fixed on Jane, looking for reassurance.

'Go on.'

'I never got to the bottom of what it was all about, but he cornered Barry outside a pub, gave him a right pasting.'

'Do you know which pub?'

'No, sorry.'

'Had the officer been under surveillance?'

'Barry had been watching a police officer around that time, so I always assumed it was the same bloke. Long term sick when he should've been at work. Usual story.'

◆ ◆ ◆

'We'll box up the files and take them back to Express Park,' said Jane, unlocking the front door to Mercer's office.

'Shouldn't we get Scientific to go over this place as well as his flat?' asked Sarah. She was following Jane up the stairs, trying not to touch the handrail.

'I think Mrs Baynes would've noticed if this was the crime scene, don't you?'

'Unless she . . .' Sarah clearly thought better of it. Getting on a major investigation team in her first week was a big deal and she hadn't stopped smiling since, except perhaps when they'd delivered the death message to Mrs Baynes. Keeping her feet on the ground would be the next challenge.

'Let's not get carried away,' said Jane. 'You get the current files and I'll get the old ones from upstairs.' Jane tried the switch several times, then flicked on the light on her phone. 'We'll need the computers too, to go to High Tech. I saw a couple of units under the desks. Just unplug them, will you?'

A narrow staircase in the dark would be fun carrying boxes of files; dodgy carpet too, Jane could feel it moving under her feet.

Find the files first, worry about the logistics later.

Fish and chips again, but this time the smell just made her hungry.

Three years, Deborah Potter had said, but date file opened or date file closed? That was assuming they were dated at all. Jane picked up a file at random from the line leaning against the skirting board, as if in an invisible filing cabinet. She looked at the label on the front: name and address of subject; date of bill; paid, tick. Barry's priorities were clear enough.

Date of bill it is then, thought Jane, even though that would mean more files.

She began flicking the files forwards, checking the date on the label. Only about sixty or so with the bill dated within the last three years in the end, all wafer thin, a USB stick in a plastic envelope stapled to the inside fly leaf. Two files – the last two – had been billed exactly three years ago today. Jane was holding one in each hand.

'You're not carrying that lot,' said Sarah, appearing on the landing. 'Not in your condition.'

'Thanks.' She dropped the file in her left hand on the top of the pile, glancing at the name on the file in her right as she did so.

'Oh, shit.'

Chapter Eight

A briefing was under way by the time Jane and Sarah arrived back at Express Park; the short drive from Mercer's office spent in silence, Sarah clearly knowing better than to ask.

Jane recognised all the usual suspects. Louise Willmott was there, a bit lost since Nick had left, the chief super reluctant to reassign her in case he came back. Dave Harding was there, sitting next to Mark Pearce, as always; partners in crime and beer. Nigel Cole was hovering too, presumably about to face a grilling from Deborah Potter about his missing person investigation.

A couple of others Jane didn't know, drafted in from Portishead, probably.

'How did you get on at his office, Jane?' asked Potter, when she spotted Jane and Sarah standing at the back of the room.

'I've got the files in the back of my car, Ma'am,' replied Jane. 'And his computers.'

'Let's get those up to High Tech now. Give your keys to Dave.' She turned to Dave Harding. 'See if you can rustle up a car to take the computers and then bring the files in, will you, Dave.'

'Yes, Ma'am.'

'Anything else, Jane?'

She had a file tucked under her arm, but now was not the time. 'No, Ma'am,' Jane replied.

'You'll be Sarah,' said Potter. 'Welcome.'

'Thank you, Ma'am.'

'Right then, we're a small team and we've got our work cut out. The post mortem is in the morning. In the meantime, surveillance files, Jane and Sarah. Find his van, Dave and Mark. Louise, can you take a statement from Mrs Baynes, please?'

'Er, sorry to interrupt, Ma'am. Can I have a word?' Jane needed to be the one taking the statement from Mrs Baynes, but exactly why was not for public consumption. Yet.

Potter had been a senior investigating officer often enough to know when a closed door was needed. 'You were right,' she said, closing the door of the meeting room behind them. 'It is him. Dental records are a match. We'll get the DNA tomorrow.'

'I'd like to take the statement from Mrs Baynes, Ma'am. There's a particular line of questioning I'd like to—'

'What line?'

Neither of them sat down for what was likely to be a short and animated conversation, although Potter didn't know that yet.

'I went to her home to get the keys to his office, and when I told her we'd found a body she volunteered that Barry had been watching a police officer off work on long term sick about three years ago. It was around about the same time a police officer caught up with Barry in a pub car park and kicked the shit out of him.'

'Three years ago?'

'Yes, Ma'am.'

'The same officer?'

'I don't know.' Jane took a deep breath. 'But it might explain why there's no mention of Barry being ex-police on his misper file.'

'You think someone's tampered with his file?'

'Yes, Ma'am.'

'And the same person might have gone a step further this time and killed him.'

'God, I hope not,' said Jane. She dropped the surveillance file on the table and slid it across to Potter.

'Oh, for heaven's sake' – craning her neck to read the label – 'Dave bloody Harding of all people.'

◆ ◆ ◆

'What about a virus check?' asked Jane.

'We haven't got time for that.' Deborah Potter leaned back against the table. 'Just stick it in the machine and we'll see what we've got.'

Jane inserted the flash drive in the USB port and opened the folder. Multiple videos, in sequence, all dated in the August three years before.

'Just pick one at random,' said Potter.

'According to the file he'd been assaulted while making an arrest six months earlier and was claiming a back injury.'

They watched Dave pushing a heavily laden trolley out of a supermarket – it looked like Asda in Taunton – then unloading the bags into the boot of his car. Bottles, mainly.

'Hardly riveting stuff.'

'That can't be it, surely?' Jane closed the file and clicked on another – mowing a front lawn with a petrol mower. 'He's separated now and rents a two-up, two-down near the railway station, I thought.'

'Try one more.'

Changing a tyre.

'The dozy pillock fell for the oldest trick in the book. Let the tyre down and then film them changing the wheel,' Potter said, solemnly. 'I'm going to have to report this to Professional Standards. Not only is Dave now a suspect in the murder of Barry Mercer, but there's the question of him tampering with the missing person investigation file. Nigel Cole swears blind a copy of Mercer's personnel record was on there, so where the bloody hell is it?'

'It might not have been Dave who tampered with the file.'

'Hardly matters now, does it?' Potter picked up the phone. 'Go and get him and keep it quiet. I don't want everybody to know what's going on yet.'

'Yes, Ma'am.'

Maybe Nick was well out of it, Jane thought, as she rode up in the lift to the top floor where the temporary incident room had been set up. Another brush with Professional Standards was to be avoided at all costs.

'You bloody idiot,' whispered Jane, standing over Dave Harding. He was hunched over his workstation, staring at the computer screen. Four years, they'd worked together, Dave still wearing the same crumpled suit he'd been wearing when they first met. A grafter who enjoyed his beer a little too much. Jane could imagine him giving Mercer a good pasting, but killing him? Hardly.

'The files are over there,' he said, gesturing to the workstation behind him, the realisation of what she had just said washing over him. 'What d'you mean?'

'The chief super wants to see you. She's down in the video suite, room one.'

'I didn't kill him.'

'You'd better bloody well not have done,' hissed Jane. Then she turned for the lift.

Dave looked white as a sheet by the time the lift reached the ground floor; glass walls, so the ride down was conducted in silence.

'She's got your surveillance file,' said Jane, once in the corridor and away from prying eyes. 'I didn't have a lot of choice.'

'It's not your fault.'

'She's going to ask if it was you who kicked the shit out of him at some pub or other. Just deny it; there's no way of proving it was you. Not now.' Jane opened the door of room 1 in the video suite.

'Come in, Dave,' said Potter. 'This is DC Westerman from Professional Standards. She's here to take notes of our conversation.' Potter was gesturing to an officer sitting at the table, pen in hand, ready to go. 'You too, Jane. Come in.'

'Yes, Ma'am.'

'Dave, I'm going to need to suspend you from duty with immediate effect. Is that clear?'

'It is.'

'Evidence has come to light that makes you a suspect in the murder of Barry Mercer. You're not obliged to say anything at the present ti—'

'I didn't kill him.'

'You'll also be investigated in relation to an allegation of suspected tampering with evidence in the form of Barry Mercer's missing person file.'

'Look, the bloke was watching me when I was off sick; filmed me doing this and that. I ended up with a final written warning and came back to work. There was mitigation, it's all on my personnel file. It was years ago and no big deal.'

'There's a suggestion that Mr Mercer was the victim of an assault at the time,' said Potter.

'I caught up with him at the Crossways and gave him a slap. It was something and nothing. No complaint was ever made.'

'All right, I think you've said enough, Dave,' said Potter. 'Where's your car?'

'On the top floor of the car park.'

'Give your keys to Jane and wait around the front. DC Westerman will escort you off the premises. You will be interviewed formally in due course, and in the meantime, I'd suggest contacting your Police Federation rep.'

Chapter Nine

'We found our missing person.' Jane was shouting from the kitchen, Dixon half asleep on the sofa. 'What time is it?'

'Eleven,' he replied, flicking off the TV.

'Aren't you going to ask me where he was?'

'Where was he?' – over a yawn.

'In the Tone, dismembered.'

Dixon sat up. 'That explains that then.'

'Explains what?'

'Why you missed our meeting with Jonathan. He'd come over from Westonzoyland specially.'

'Oh, God. The vicar.' Jane appeared in the doorway. 'Was he all right about it?'

'Fine. I took him for a beer in the Red Cow.'

'Dave's in deep trouble too.'

It was a fine art, thought Dixon, appearing interested when really he wasn't. Still, Jane had no doubt had a stressful day and needed to get it off her chest, so it was his job to listen, just as any loving and dutiful husband would. A glass of wine would've probably helped, but that was out of the question.

'What's Dave been up to?'

'He's a suspect and it looks like he's been tampering with the missing person file too.' Jane's sentence was punctuated by the slam of the microwave door. 'Deborah Potter's suspended him and referred it to Professional Standards. Where's the mango chutney?'

'You hid the proper stuff in the slow cooker. Here, let me.' Dixon ushered her out of the kitchen. 'You go and sit down.'

Monty followed Jane into the living room and jumped up on the sofa next to her. Dixon sighed. He was watching Jane's prawn curry on the turntable and starting to feel a bit like a house husband. Yes, it was supposed to be temporary, but he hadn't banked on another farcical brush with the legal profession.

Dave, a suspect in a murder investigation. And with PSD crawling in and out of every orifice. Dixon had that T-shirt.

'Do you want the proper stuff or the sugar free crap?' he asked.

'The proper stuff.'

Dave was a good man and a loyal member of Dixon's team. 'Putting the band back together' was a phrase he had heard several times, and Dave was definitely a member of the band. Scruffy in his crumpled suit and brown suede shoes, but loyal.

'Tell me what Dave's been up to,' said Dixon, placing a tray in Jane's lap.

'The curry's still in the plastic container.'

'I put it on a plate. What more do you want?'

'He was off sick three years ago; got beaten up making an arrest and was claiming a back injury. He basically had the spring and summer off and HR employed Mercer to check up on him. He caught him doing all sorts, so Dave got a final written warning and had to come back to work.' Jane was stirring the curry, waiting for the steam to clear. 'Anyway, he caught up with Mercer and there was a fight. Mercer came off worse by all accounts, but no complaint was ever made.'

'And that's a motive for Dave killing Mercer, cutting him up and throwing him in the river, is it?'

'Potter thinks so.'

'When's the post mortem?'

'Roger's doing it tomorrow. Making a start anyway; they still haven't found all of him and the search has been called off for tonight now.'

Dixon had been watching Monty edging ever closer to Jane's curry. 'On the floor, you,' he said, pushing the dog off the sofa. 'And the file?'

'Nigel is adamant there was reference on it to Mercer being ex-police. He says he copied his personnel record and that it was on the file. Only now it's not.'

'Has Dave admitted removing it?'

'No,' mumbled Jane, through a mouthful of curry that was still too hot. She was waving her hand across her mouth now, as if that would make a difference. 'He admitted the fight with Mercer, but nothing else.'

'Are you on the major investigation team?'

'Working with the probationer, Sarah. Potter's got us digging into Mercer's past surveillance cases.' Jane shrugged. 'That's how I found Dave's file.'

'You found it?'

'Felt a bit of a shit, really, but what else could I do? I had to tell Potter.'

'It would've come out sooner or later.'

'You haven't said what happened at your interview. Did you get the job?'

'There isn't one. Not in Weston anyway. They've got a vacancy in their Bristol office, but it's crime.'

'If you're going to do that, you might as well stay in the police.' Jane was waving her fork at him now.

'Who's the SIO?' asked Dixon, preferring a change of subject.

'Potter. She made some sarcastic remark about there being no one else available. At the moment there's just me and Sarah, Mark, Lou, and a couple of others I don't know, down from Portishead, I think. She's got me and Sarah watching the surveillance footage, so we'll be holed up in the video suite for most of the time, I expect.' She was stabbing a prawn with her fork. 'Wasn't entirely what I had in mind.'

'I bet it wasn't.'

'The team's too small. We haven't even got anybody to cover the inquest.'

'What inquest?' asked Dixon.

Jane had scraped the remains of her curry on to the plate and was holding the now empty plastic container for Monty to lick the dregs of the sauce, watching Dixon out of the corner of her eye; he could see her out of the corner of his. 'The day Mercer went missing there was a funeral going on at the house next door to the lad he was watching. The daughter had died, sadly. Turns out it's her inquest tomorrow afternoon at Taunton; accidental insulin overdose, they reckon.'

'You'll be able to get a copy of the coroner's file easily enough. That'll have all the witness statements and reports on it.'

'Yeah, we will.'

'Just speak to the coroner's officer.'

'I know.'

Dixon picked up the tray from Jane's lap and headed for the kitchen. 'I thought I might take Monty out for a walk. Fancy it?'

'No, ta. You go.'

'Might get us a Christmas tree tomorrow too. I've been meaning to do that for days.'

'We won't be here for Christmas. We'll be away on honeymoon, remember?'

◆ ◆ ◆

Dixon had stirred when the alarm on Jane's phone went off, but had quickly rolled over and gone back to sleep. He seemed to remember a peck on the cheek followed by a remark about having a nice relaxing day, or something sarky like that.

Whatever, as the kids like to say these days.

Now he was standing on the quarry-tiled doorstep of a terraced house in Bridgwater. Curtains open a couple of inches, probably because they didn't fit the window; moss growing along the windowsills – the outside, mercifully; red paint flaking off the wooden door.

He glanced across at his Land Rover, double-parked alongside Dave's car; blocking the narrow residential street too, what with cars parked on either side, but someone could always ask him to move it.

Monty was standing on the driver's seat with his front paws up on the steering wheel. They'd managed a quick walk on the beach, so no doubt the seats would be covered in sand.

He tried the bell once, nice and polite, but there was no sound at all coming from inside the house. One hand on the bell now, the other banging on the door, fist clenched. Dixon leaned over and shouted through the letterbox.

'Get up, Dave!'

'Can I help you?' said an elderly neighbour, her front door on the security chain.

'Is he in?'

'No idea, sorry.'

'I'll try again.' Dixon turned back to the door and carried on banging.

'All right, all right. I'm coming.'

The neighbour was still hovering behind her front door and the safety of the chain.

'It's all right, Iris,' said Dave, blinking furiously as he looked along the front of the terrace. 'He's my boss.'

Dixon pushed past him and marched into the sitting room, opening the curtains to reveal a coffee table almost invisible under the lines of empty lager cans.

'Have you contacted your Federation rep yet?'

'I just woke up, Sir. Give me a chance.' Dave was rubbing his eyes. He was still wearing his suit trousers, the belt undone, white shirt untucked, his jacket and tie lying on the carpet. At least he'd kicked off his shoes before nodding off on the sofa.

'Do you have any coffee in this place?' asked Dixon.

'Somewhere.' Dave swallowed hard, patting his stomach at the same time. 'A bit of a heavy night, I'm afraid, Sir.' A short trudge along the corridor and he was in the kitchen, opening the cupboards one by one. 'How do you like your coffee?'

'It's not for me, it's for you. Strong and black.' Dixon had followed and was looking for somewhere safe to sit, eventually opting for a dining chair hidden under a pile of newspapers.

'Just shove that lot on the floor, Sir,' said Dave.

'Let's hear it then.'

Dave was tapping a jar of solidified coffee against the edge of the worktop, trying to loosen the granules. He stopped, said, 'I didn't kill him.'

'I wouldn't be here if I thought you did,' replied Dixon.

'What's Jane told you?'

'About the surveillance and the kicking you gave him.'

'That's all there is to it, really.'

'Bollocks.' There was a stinging force to Dixon's voice. 'I've had enough of people wasting my bloody time, Dave. There's a history here and I want to know what it is.'

Dave hesitated.

'You don't give someone a kicking just for doing their job, and not when you were the one taking the piss. And I won't ask if it was you who tampered with the misper file, but I'm going to assume it was for present purposes. Why?'

'It wasn't. Really. We came out of police college together and were based at Filton for a time. Then our paths crossed again at Fishponds. He was a sergeant by then.'

'You're still in the police and he's not, so what happened?'

'He was falsifying evidence and I reported it. He was being investigated for gross misconduct and did a deal – left before he was pushed. I've been stuck as a constable ever since.'

'Cases?'

'There were several. All of them swept under the carpet. We're going back nearly twenty years now.' Dave leaned against the fridge, the kettle boiling behind him, his eyes fixed on the ceiling. 'He planted cannabis on one, switched a tachograph on another. When I challenged him about it, he said we both knew they were guilty, he was just making sure they got what was coming to them, for the sake of the victims. He made out like he was some sort of avenging angel.'

'Speak to your Federation rep today,' said Dixon, standing up.

'Are you going to help me?'

Dixon was making his way to the door, weaving between the empty lager cans strewn on the floor. He stopped and turned. 'What d'you think, Dave?'

79

Potter's text had arrived while Jane was having her breakfast, the remnants of her toast consigned to the bin straightaway. It was a morning that would be best faced on an empty stomach.

Cover the PM will you, please? 10am. Got a meeting at HQ. Take the new kid it'll do her good.

Now they were parked outside the pathology department at Musgrove Park Hospital, summoning up the courage to go in. Jane had caught up with Sarah in the canteen at Express Park, tucking into a bacon sandwich, and it was going to be touch and go whether she kept it down.

'Are you going to be all right?' Jane asked.

'I hope so,' Sarah replied, nervously. She had pulled down the sun visor and was looking at herself in the mirror on the back. 'I look like death warmed up.'

'You do look a bit pale,' replied Jane, hoping the understatement might cheer Sarah up a bit. 'You can wait in the anteroom if you'd rather. I won't tell Potter.'

'What about the pathologist?'

'He won't tell either.'

'I'll be fine. I've got to be.'

'There won't be much blood, and a blob of Vicks VapoRub under your nose will take care of the smell.' Jane wasn't entirely sure who she was trying to convince. 'C'mon, let's get it over and done with.'

'That way,' said the receptionist. 'Through those double doors.'

Jane could have found her way in the dark – just follow the smell of disinfectant.

'Wasn't expecting you,' shouted Poland. He was leaning over the slab, a Dictaphone in one hand and a pair of surgical tweezers in the other, his latex gloves and apron smeared with blood. 'Just aprons and masks will do. You'll not be touching anything. The VapoRub's in the top drawer of the filing cabinet.'

'Thanks,' replied Jane. She had been watching Poland through the large windows between the anteroom and the lab, collecting samples and mumbling into his recorder, occasionally stepping back to allow his assistant to take a photograph or two. They must have been there five minutes or so before Poland had spotted them.

There was no hiding after that.

A big blob of VapoRub on the top lip, mask pulled up over it. Jane smoothed her plastic apron out over her bump. 'Ready?' she asked.

Sarah nodded, slowly.

'We're still missing a few bits,' said Poland, before they had even closed the lab door behind them. 'The divers are back in the river, so we'll just have to see what they find.'

Several transparent plastic crates were sitting on the adjacent slab, containing the black plastic taken from the body parts that had been recovered from the Tone. The boxes had been sealed and labelled separately: left calf, left thigh. Jane turned away. She'd find out soon enough which 'bits' were missing.

The tin box was there too, in a separate crate.

Sarah was standing with her hands behind her back, her left hand squeezing the fingers of her right, her eyes transfixed by the sight that greeted them on the slab.

'Single stab wound to the heart,' said Poland, pointing to an incision on the torso. 'I'll need to check the depth of the wound, but any length to the blade and it would've been fatal very quickly.'

Something wasn't quite right, but it took a moment for Jane to make sense of it. 'That's his back,' she said.

'Yes, that's right.' Poland sounded surprised. 'He was stabbed in the back. He's lying on his front.'

His torso might have been, but the rest of him wasn't.

'Get some air,' said Jane, pushing Sarah towards the open window in an office on the far side of the lab.

'I think I'd better.'

'How long has he been in the water?'

'Six months is about right,' replied Poland. 'That's when he was last seen, as I understand it.'

'And the DNA's back. It's definitely Barry Mercer?'

'This is him all right.'

The severed head was lying on the slab in its correct position, although the torso was back to front. Everything else was exactly as you would expect to see it, although both feet were missing.

'Can you turn him over?' asked Jane, grimacing.

'Yes, sorry.' Poland gestured to his assistant, who walked around to the far side of the slab. 'A bit off-putting, isn't it.'

Jane turned away while they did the necessary.

'There,' said Poland, 'that looks better.'

Sarah had reappeared and was edging closer to the slab. 'I'll be fine,' she said. 'I've got to get used to it.'

'What about the hacksaw?' asked Jane.

Poland lifted up a shallow plastic tray, the shiny hacksaw lying in the bottom. 'Definitely the implement used to dismember the body. There's a match with the blade.'

Jane was leaning over, examining the black bags in the clear plastic crates.

'Ordinary household bin liners, I'm afraid,' said Poland. 'Nothing special about them. And the tape's just ordinary insulating tape. There'll be rolls of that everywhere. The hacksaw might be a goer though; not a brand I've come across before.'

'Any other wounds?' Jane was taking a closer look at the body, now the picture wasn't quite so macabre.

'Some superficial bruising, so there may have been a fight of some sort. I'll need to confirm the cause of death when I open him up, but it looks like it's going to be the stab wound. D'you want to stay for that?'

Jane ignored the mischief in Poland's voice – asking a question just to be difficult. 'An email will be fine, Roger, thanks.'

'How did Nick get on in Weston yesterday?'

'You can guess.'

'And how did you get on with the vicar?'

'I bloody well missed it, didn't I?'

'Least said, soonest mended,' said Poland.

'Quite.'

'Excuse me a minute,' said Sarah. She seemed transfixed by the dismembered body on the slab, tipping her head from side to side, before blurting out, 'Where are his feet?'

'We still need to find them,' said Poland, calmly. 'So if you could pass that on to the dive team, that would be most helpful.'

Chapter Ten

The Somerset Coroner's Court was a gothic building in the middle of Taunton, as close to going back in time as you could get – stone arches, wood panelling and that smell. It would have to be the public gallery this time, although the security guard had recognised him and hadn't questioned it when he parked in the staff car park at the back.

The usher recognised him too. 'Which one are you here for?' he asked, glancing down at his clipboard. 'I'm not expecting you, am I?'

'No,' replied Dixon. 'Can I see the list?'

There were three and Emma Carpenter was the only female; Jane had said it was the neighbour's daughter. 'Carpenter,' he said.

'That one's on next,' replied the usher. 'The family are over there' – his voice quiet – 'with their solicitor.'

'Thanks.'

Parents, and a younger sister, possibly. All of them sobbing quietly, the mother clutching a framed photograph, both arms wrapped around it tight.

'Shall I let the coroner know you're here?'

'No, thank you. I'm just here as an observer this time. I'll sit in the public gallery.'

'Oh, right. Fine.'

Dixon waited until everyone had gone in, then crept into the court and sat down at the back of the public gallery; not that there was anyone sitting in front of him. A couple of journalists were sitting in the seats reserved for the press off to his left; the family of the deceased sitting behind their solicitor, still sobbing quietly.

A uniformed police constable was there, the coroner's officer too – Dixon couldn't remember his name – and at the bench in front of them another tall man in a suit and tie, looking distinctly nervous, was sitting next to a young woman in a sharp suit, a lawyer's notebook open in front of her.

Dixon watched the coroner waving at the usher – a private conversation, lips hardly moving – then the usher approached the public gallery, leaned over and whispered, 'He wants to know what your interest is in this inquest, Sir.'

The uniformed constable clearly did too, glancing over his shoulder at frequent intervals.

Michael Roseland was the senior Somerset coroner, and their paths had crossed several times already in the little over a year since Dixon had transferred from the Met.

The family were staring at him now, disapproving glances at the ghoul in the public gallery come to enjoy the spectacle.

'Observing,' whispered Dixon in reply. 'There's a remote possibility of a connection to a current investigation.' That much was true.

'That you're involved in?'

'No.' That was true too. Misleading the coroner was not an option; not only was Dixon still a serving police officer – just – but he was also a solicitor, which made him an officer of the court.

Then the constable took his opportunity, sliding into the seat next to him. 'Anything I can do, Sir?' he asked.

'No, thank you.'

'Would you like to see the file?'

'Best not. Just observing.' Dixon hoped he'd take the hint and return to his seat next to the coroner's officer. 'Pretend I'm not here.'

'Yes, Sir.'

'This is an inquest touching the death of Emma Fleur Carpenter,' said the coroner, loudly. 'Emma sadly died on the ninth of June, the inquest was opened and adjourned on the twelfth of June, and we are now in a position to proceed. I gather Emma's family are here' – a reassuring smile in their direction – 'and that you are represented by Mr Walker of Topley and Curran. Is that correct?'

'It is, Sir,' said the solicitor, jumping up.

'I would simply remind you then, Mr Walker, that this is an inquest. We are here to determine the facts of Emma's death: who she was; how, when and where she died. We are not here to apportion blame.'

'No, Sir.'

'It may be that the question of liability for Emma's death is heard before a different court at a later date, but I will not allow any questioning today that goes to that issue. Is that clear?'

'It is, Sir.'

So the family blame someone for their daughter's death, thought Dixon. The tall bloke, probably, given that he looked as if he was about to throw up. And he was 'lawyered up', as Americans liked to say.

'Emma was eighteen at the time of her death and was a student at the University of Avon at Bristol,' continued the coroner. 'During the holidays she lived with her parents at 2 Midway Close,

Curry Rivel. I have statements on the file from Emma's parents' – another reassuring smile at the family – 'and I propose simply to read them, rather than call you to give evidence. Is that acceptable, Mr Walker?'

'It is, Sir. My clients having nothing they wish to add to their statements at this stage.'

Of the three of them, Emma's father, Andrew, had kept his composure the best, but he began to crack when the coroner was reading his witness statement into evidence. Reliving the finding of Emma's body had been the last straw.

'We can take a break, if that might assist,' offered the coroner.

'No, thank you,' Andrew Carpenter mumbled.

The coroner turned back to the statement, reading aloud. 'We arrived home at about eleven and there was no sign of Emma. She was due home from college the evening before, so I ran upstairs and checked her bedroom. She was lying in bed, the duvet over her, and just looked as if she was asleep, so I left her and went back downstairs. The dog wouldn't stop barking and I kept trying to shut him up. In the end I put him back in the car because we didn't want to wake Emma up.' He paused to allow the court stenographer to catch up, before continuing. 'By lunchtime we thought we'd better wake her so she could have something to eat. My wife went upstairs and then I heard her screaming. I ran upstairs and found my wife on the floor. I couldn't find Emma's pulse and she was stone cold, so I dialled 999.'

Oddly impassive, the statement sounded, although that was down to the police officer transcribing it more than Andrew Carpenter, probably.

'Emma's insulin pen was on her bedside table. I didn't notice at first that it was the wrong pen, only later when the duty doctor came.'

Dixon sat up. It was a situation that had haunted him since the day he was diagnosed with diabetes; sleeping through a hypo. There was no waking up from that.

'Emma was on a low dose of insulin,' continued the coroner, still reading from Andrew's statement. 'And her pen was calibrated in single units. She had been prescribed fifteen with each meal during the day and then fifteen units of a different, slow-acting insulin at bedtime. The pen I found on her bedside table was calibrated in double units, so if she turned the dial fifteen times, she'd actually be getting thirty units of insulin. It's supposed to be for those on higher doses, but someone must have given her the wrong pen when she put her prescription in.'

Dixon slid his own insulin pen out of his pocket and checked the calibration: single units. Would he notice if he was given the wrong one by mistake? Yes, he bloody well would, because he checked and double-checked it every time he gave himself a jab.

That explained the tall bloke looking nervous, though; almost certainly the pharmacist who fulfilled the prescription. He was in for a bumpy ride, whatever the coroner may have said about blame.

Linda Carpenter's statement gave much the same information about her daughter's death, the admission that Emma had taken one of her sleeping tablets almost glossed over. Then came the post mortem report. The coroner was clearly saving the best for last – either that or putting it off for as long as he could.

Cause of death was hardly controversial as it turned out: multiple organ failure, hypoglycaemia, insulin overdose.

The toxicology results, on the other hand, were noteworthy – the pathologist's own word – showing insulin levels consistent with a dose of approximately sixty units of insulin analogue, the inference being that Emma had done her injection twice by mistake. Add to that traces of benzodiazepine, possibly temazepam, and it was easy to see where the pathologist was taking the coroner.

Accidental death.

It was easy to see how it *could* happen, but the question was whether it *would*. Dixon had lost count of the number of times he'd said to Jane last thing at night, 'Have I done my jab?' And her answer was always the same: 'Dunno. Check your blood.'

'Can we have Mr Townsend in the witness box, please?' asked the coroner. 'I gather you're represented by Miss Paterson.'

'I am, Sir.'

Once sworn, the coroner took him through his witness statement. Short and to the point it was too. Yes, he had fulfilled Emma's prescription for a new insulin pen, and the records showed he had dispensed the correct item. Procedures were discussed, storage, labelling; the actual prescription was produced in evidence, absolving her doctor of any blame – the correct pen had been prescribed. And dispensed.

'Mr Walker, do you have any questions for Mr Townsend?'

'I do, Sir.'

'Please bear in mind what I said at the outset.'

Walker glanced down at his notebook. 'Do you have any idea how it is that Emma came to have the wrong insulin pen?'

'I'm afraid not.'

'Where else might she have got it from?'

'I really don't know.'

'How long have you been a pharmacist?'

'Twelve years.'

'Have you ever dispensed the wrong medication in that time?'

The coroner looked up sharply. 'Be very careful, Mr Walker.'

'It's a fair question, Sir. I am merely seeking to get to the bottom of where Sarah got the wrong pen from; if she could have got it from her local pharmacy by mistake.'

'Mr Townsend has already said he doesn't know.' The coroner's patience was being tested and he was doing his best not to bristle. 'You'd better answer the question, Mr Townsend.'

'Yes,' he said, reluctantly, and after several glances at his lawyer. 'I'd be lying if I said mistakes don't happen, but not with these insulin pens. They had to be ordered in specially for her. I remember it started when she moved into the halls of residence.'

'Do you have any more questions, Mr Walker?'

'No, Sir.'

'That's it?' shouted Emma's father, banging his fist on the desk in front of him. 'He's going to get away with it!'

'Please tell your client to calm down, Mr Walker.' The coroner stood up. 'I think it may be helpful if we took a short break. Five minutes.'

Dixon gestured to the uniformed officer. 'Let me have a look at the file, will you?' he mouthed, and he was still flicking through the statements when the family filed back into court a few minutes later. 'I need a word with the coroner,' he said to the usher. 'Before we start again.'

The only thing left to do was to record a verdict of accidental death. And Dixon wasn't having that.

◆ ◆ ◆

'If someone's killed him then it's most likely going to have been because he saw something he shouldn't.' Those had been Dixon's own words to Jane when she'd first asked his advice about Barry Mercer's disappearance and what was then just a missing person case. Now it was murder, and one of the things Mercer had seen was Emma Carpenter's funeral.

'I thought you were just observing,' said Michael Roseland, when Dixon was shown into his office.

'Are you diabetic, Sir?' asked Dixon.

'No.'

'Well, I am. And something about this just doesn't add up. No one has checked her blood glucose monitor, for a start.'

Roseland sat up. 'Go on.'

'I give myself fifteen units last thing at night – it's a single unit pen, so that's fifteen clicks when I turn the dial – and sometimes I can't remember whether I've done it. But, if I'm in any doubt, I don't just give myself another injection on the off chance and risk a hypo in my sleep. I check my blood sugar level. Emma would've done that before she gave herself another jab, leaving aside the question of whether she would have noticed the pen was the wrong one. I would notice; the single dose pen is green and the double dose is blue. And you certainly wouldn't take a sleeping tablet without checking your blood first.'

'Are you suggesting there's been foul play?'

'I really don't know, but it can't be ruled out based on the evidence I've just sat through.'

'You mentioned a current investigation to my usher?'

'A murder. It's not my case, though.'

'Whose case is it and why aren't they here?'

'I'm not sure they know there might be a connection yet, Sir. It's still early days. A private detective has been murdered.'

'The body parts in the Tone? I was notified yesterday.'

'He was a surveillance expert and had been watching the house next to the Carpenters' on the day of Emma's funeral.'

'What d'you want me to do?'

Dixon knew there was only one answer to that question and what the coroner would do next, but he'd never *really* wanted to go back to the legal profession anyway. 'Adjourn,' he replied.

'But it's not your case?'

'I'm still on leave, technically.'

'I'd better run this past David Charlesworth.' Roseland leaned forwards and dialled a number on his phone. 'Can I speak to the ACC, please. It's Michael Roseland, Somerset coroner.'

'Putting you through.'

'Charlesworth.'

'David, you're on speakerphone. It's Michael Roseland; I've got a DCI of yours here asking me to adjourn an inquest. As you know, a formal request for an adjournment should come from the senior investigating officer but it's not his case. He says he's on leave.'

'Nick Dixon?'

'That's right.' Roseland was watching him listening to the conversation. 'He seems to think there may have been foul play and it's connected to that body in the river the dive team found yesterday.'

'Nick?'

'Yes, Sir.'

'Are you sure you're ready to come back?'

'Yes, Sir.'

Charlesworth hesitated. 'And you're sure this is the right case?'

'Barry Mercer was watching the house next door on the day of the dead girl's funeral.'

'All right. Take over as SIO with immediate effect. I'll let Deborah Potter know. Is that good enough for you, Michael?'

'It is,' replied Roseland. 'Although her father isn't going to like it.'

Chapter Eleven

'Are you responsible for this?' Fists clenched, steaming towards Dixon in the foyer of the Somerset Coroner's Court. 'I ought to knock your bloody block—'

'I wouldn't do that, if I were you, Sir,' said the uniformed police constable, stepping in, his arms outstretched.

'Who the hell does he think he is?'

Carpenter's wife was tugging on the sleeve of his jacket, still clutching the framed photograph of Emma to her chest in her other hand. 'Don't, Andrew! He's a police officer. I've seen him on TV.'

Andrew Carpenter crumpled. 'A police officer?'

Dixon reached into his inside jacket pocket and pulled out his warrant card; something he thought he'd never be doing again. Good job Jane had kept it.

'This is Detective Chief Inspector Dixon,' said the uniformed officer.

'I just wanted this sorted out,' said Mr Carpenter, shaking his head. 'For these two more than anyone else.' He put his arms around his wife and daughter. 'We need to move on and we can't do that with this hanging over us.'

'You mentioned in your witness statement that Emma was careful with her diabetes. How careful?'

'Very,' replied Mrs Carpenter. 'She always checked her blood and watched her diet, and she always got a gold star for her blood glucose readings at her check-ups.'

'I wish I could say the same,' replied Dixon.

'You're diabetic?'

'I am, Mrs Carpenter.'

'Then you understand.' She stepped forwards, tearing herself from her husband's grasp. 'Something about this isn't right and he just keeps telling me I'm imagining it.' A nod over her shoulder. 'There's no way she'd have done her jab and taken a sleeping pill without checking her blood first. And no way she'd have done a second jab either.'

'Where's her blood testing kit?'

'We've got it at home,' replied Mr Carpenter. 'I don't understand why these questions weren't asked before?'

'I've said all along this was no accident, and there's no way she'd have taken her own life either, before you say that. She had a family who loved her and everything to live for.' Mrs Carpenter held the framed photograph up in front of Dixon. 'Look at her. Does that look like a girl who'd take her own life?' The photo had been taken using a selfie stick in her outstretched hand, Emma sitting cross-legged on a surfboard on the beach, beaming at the camera. 'She used it as her profile picture on Facebook.'

'Where was it taken?' he asked.

'Croyde.'

That explained the wetsuit.

'There was no suicide note either,' said Mr Carpenter, a noticeable tremble in his voice. 'They usually leave a note, don't they?'

Sixty units of insulin and a sleeping tablet. It was as good a method as any. Painless. Dixon hadn't entertained the possibility that Emma had killed herself, but if she had, that would make Mercer's disappearance on the day of her funeral a coincidence. And Dixon didn't believe in coincidence.

Either way, now was not the time.

'Can I suggest that you go home and I will come and see you later today. All right?' A reassuring smile, as if the Carpenters hadn't been on the receiving end of enough of those already today.

Mrs Carpenter was staring at Dixon, her eyes burning into his. 'You don't think she killed herself, do you?'

'I really don't know. All I can say is that the evidence before this inquest is inconclusive as it stands at the moment.'

'And if it really wasn't an accident . . .' Mrs Carpenter's eyes glazed over. Lost in her thoughts.

'Later today,' said Dixon, taking her hand. 'I promise.'

◆ ◆ ◆

Deborah Potter was perched on the edge of a table, in front of the whiteboard on the top floor of the police centre at Express Park. The board was gradually being populated with information about Barry Mercer, arrows connecting people and places, photos stuck on with Sellotape, names and dates in Louise Willmott's handwriting. It was usually Jane's job, so it made a nice change to have been out and about, even if it had meant attending the post mortem.

'I'll make us a tea,' said Sarah, heading for the kettle.

'Anything interesting?' asked Potter, turning to Jane.

'Single stab wound to the back, Ma'am,' she replied. 'Left side, penetrated the heart. Death would have been almost instantaneous. The body was then dismembered with the hacksaw we recovered from the back of the pickup.'

'Well, at least we don't have to worry about the first seventy-two hours.' Potter was holding an arm of her reading glasses between her teeth. 'That was six months ago.'

'Are we getting any help?' asked Jane.

'There are eight coming from Portishead tomorrow, but that's going to be it, I'm afraid.'

'Eight?' Jane dropped her handbag on a workstation. 'We're a man down as it is, with Dave suspended.'

'That's just the way it is,' replied Potter. 'It's practically a cold case anyway.' Her phone pinged on the desk next to her, a smile creeping across her lips as she read the email, holding her phone at arm's length. 'Anyway, it'll soon be someone else's problem,' she said, slipping on her reading glasses and tapping out a reply with her index finger. Then she stood up and clapped her hands. 'Everybody.'

Clearly an optimist; today anyway. 'Everybody' meant Jane and five others at the moment. And three of them were down in the video suite watching traffic camera footage.

'You're getting a new SIO,' continued Potter. 'He's on his way now. Brief him when he gets here, and good luck.'

'Who is it?' asked Jane.

'You'll find out soon enough.' Potter headed for the top of the stairs. 'And you, new girl.'

'Yes, Ma'am,' replied Sarah.

'Enjoy the ride.'

◆ ◆ ◆

Dixon parked in the visitors' car park and looked up at the floor to ceiling windows of the police centre. He'd done the same when he'd been walked out to the security van in the cage at the back of the building, the day of his court appearance.

That time, umpteen faces had been pressed to the glass, trying to get a view of the DCI in handcuffs, charged with murder.

This time there was only Jane, her grin visible even from the car park. At least she resisted the temptation to wave.

The receptionist was out from behind his desk in a flash, holding the front door open for him. 'Well done, Sir,' he said.

'Thank you, Reg.'

'You bloody showed 'em. I knew you'd be back. Never doubted it for a minute.'

The applause started when he appeared at the top of the stairs and was walking along the landing past the CID Area, officers standing up from behind workstations and cheering. More in uniform and civvies standing and banging on the windows of the canteen.

It was a small crowd waiting for him on the second floor, but then it was a small team. He'd been warned about that.

A hug from Louise. 'Glad to have you back, Sir,' she said.

'This is Sarah Loveday,' said Jane. 'The probationer I was telling you about. It's her case, really.'

'Glad to have you aboard,' said Dixon. 'Where are the others?'

'Mark's got them down in the video suite, Sir,' replied Sarah. 'They're watching the traffic cameras for Mercer's van.'

'The chief super did say there'd be eight more down from Portishead tomorrow.' Louise was trying to be helpful.

'Who went to the PM?' Dixon asked, standing in front of the whiteboard, his hands thrust deep into his pockets.

'We did,' replied Jane.

'Let's have the others up here,' said Dixon. 'Then we'll make a start.'

'Someone from Personnel was looking for you,' whispered Jane, while Louise rang down to the video suite. 'That's how I knew you were our new SIO. They wanted you for your Return to Work interview.'

'Return to Work interview, my arse.'

'I told them you'd be too busy.'

'Thank you.'

'I'm guessing you went to see Dave?'

'We need to sort this out quickly, before the silly sod drinks himself to death.'

'You're back,' said Mark Pearce, appearing at the top of the stairs. 'Thank fuck for that.'

Dixon didn't recognise the two officers who had followed Mark up the stairs.

'I've got a couple of PCSOs helping me with the video footage,' continued Mark, with a glance over his shoulder. 'Rachel and Rich.'

'And eight more is all Potter could spare?'

'She said it was almost a cold case.' Louise took a swig from her mug and shuddered. 'About as cold as this coffee.'

'All right.' Less than an hour into his return to work and Dixon was already going to be sticking his neck out; such a small team meant that lines of enquiry had to be prioritised and others parked for the time being. And that's what SIOs did – stick their necks out – according to Charlesworth. Maybe Dixon should have gone to his interview with Personnel after all? 'We're going to be working on the basis that Barry Mercer was killed because of something he saw on the day he disappeared; the day of Emma Carpenter's funeral.'

'DCS Potter's got us going back through his cases for the last three years.'

'Park that for the time being, Jane. Focus on the case he was working on that day – that's Ben Clifford and his personal injury claim. We'll need Mercer's file, and I want to see any footage he'd got from previous days.'

'The claim has settled.'

'Get the defence solicitor's file too, in that case. And I want to know everything there is to know about Emma Carpenter. Mercer was parked outside her family home throughout the afternoon of her funeral tea and disappeared that same day.'

'It was her inquest earlier,' said Jane. 'I spoke to the officer in the case and he said it was likely to be a verdict of accidental; not enough evidence for suicide.'

'I went to the inquest and it was neither,' replied Dixon. 'It's been adjourned and I'm going to see the parents a bit later. Lou, you're with me.'

'Yes, Sir.'

'Rachel and Rich, can you stay on the traffic cameras, please? Find Mercer's van. Mark showed you how to do it?'

'I did, Sir,' replied Mark. 'We were working on the cameras in the middle of Curry Rivel to begin with. Then it's the A358 and the A361. A bit like finding a needle in a haystack, mind you.'

'Stick at it. If we find his van, chances are we find his killer. You might as well go and crack on with that now.'

Dixon waited until the two community support officers had reached the bottom of the stairs.

'Now we come to the confidential bit,' he said. 'And Mark, this is for you. There's a history between Dave and Barry Mercer. Were you here when Dave was off long term sick?'

'Was it Mercer who caught him taking the piss?'

Dixon nodded. 'Dave denies tampering with the missing person file, though, which means that someone else did and I want to know why. You'll need to be discreet, and Professional Standards may get in your way because they're going to be investigating Dave, but I want a look at the cases that Mercer and Dave worked on together at Fishponds.'

'Yes, Sir.'

'Any crap from Professional Standards and you refer them to me.'

'I'd pay good money to watch that.'

'Right then, Lou, let's go and see Mr and Mrs Carpenter.'

Chapter Twelve

The framed photograph of Emma was back where it belonged, taking pride of place in the middle of the mantelpiece, Mrs Carpenter gently rubbing her fingerprints off the glass with a tissue, as if she hadn't done so ten times already.

It was a large dormer bungalow; neat and tidy, the usual framed photographs on the walls in the hall – both daughters at various ages, at least two dogs, family holidays. Several small trophies in a glass-fronted display cabinet too. Diving, judging by the figure on top of one.

'They're Emma's,' said Mrs Carpenter, her voice oddly abrupt. She hadn't spoken since she'd opened the front door and announced that her husband was out with the dog. They'd gone along the river, apparently; fifteen minutes at most. Her younger daughter had then been despatched to her bedroom to watch something on her iPad.

'Is anyone else in the family diabetic?' asked Dixon, when he'd finished looking at the photographs on display.

'Is that relevant?'

She'd lost her daughter, and seen the inquest adjourned, so was bound to be a little defensive. 'It would help to know whether there was someone in the family more experienced at managing diabetes.'

'I am,' said Mrs Carpenter. 'My mother was too. So, yes, I gave it to her, as my husband has taken great delight in pointing out more than once.'

'It's not your fault.'

'It was my sleeping tablet, wasn't it?'

'You'd been able to help Emma manage her diabetes?' asked Dixon, changing the subject.

'Yes. I'd drummed it into her, how important it is. Was.'

'How old was she when she was diagnosed?'

'Fourteen.'

Going through the teenage years as a diabetic was something Dixon had been spared, not that he'd ever had much of a sweet tooth. And he'd been too busy rock climbing to go drinking.

'Were you on the same insulin?'

'No.'

'You said you have her blood glucose monitor?'

'You want to take it, I suppose?'

'Yes, please.'

'She was getting one of those wearable monitors that connects with your phone, but it hadn't happened yet. Have you got one?'

'They wouldn't let me have one,' Dixon replied, rubbing the tips of his fingers with his thumbs. 'I don't check my blood often enough to be eligible.'

'You really should.'

'I know.'

Dixon and Louise listened to Mrs Carpenter's footsteps on the stairs, the sound of a drawer opening, then keys in the front door.

'Whose is that bloody Land Rover parked across our drive?' asked Mr Carpenter, slamming the front door behind him, his border terrier already in the living room, sniffing Dixon's shoes.

'That police officer, Andrew. He's in the living room.'

'Oh.'

'I'm just getting Emma's blood testing kit.'

'So,' said Mr Carpenter, throwing his coat over the banister. 'If it wasn't suicide, or an accident, what was it? And why weren't these questions being asked before?'

'I really don't know yet,' replied Dixon. 'But I intend to find out.'

'You really think it was murder?' Carpenter was watching the bottom of the stairs, his voice hushed. 'She'll never cope with that.'

Footsteps on the landing.

'Where were you the night Emma got home?' asked Dixon.

'We'd been to stay with my wife's parents for a couple of nights. Emma was due back from college, so she got the train to Taunton and a taxi from there. I'd usually fetch her from the station.'

'What time did she get back?'

'I don't know exactly. She'd have got the seven-thirty-two out of Temple Meads. That's the train she always took.'

Mrs Carpenter handed a small black pouch to Louise. 'Here's her blood testing kit.'

'Had she taken your sleeping pills before?' asked Dixon.

'Not that I know of.' She shook her head. 'I'm not even sure it was one of mine. It was an old prescription, probably past its use-by date. It was in the cabinet under the sink in our en-suite. I didn't even know she knew they were there, to be honest.'

'Was she a drug user?'

'Certainly not!'

'No, she bloody well wasn't,' said Carpenter, putting his arm around his wife. 'Not all students are, you know.'

'What was she studying?'

'Fine Art. It was called West of England Polytechnic when I was there, but they get to call it the University of Avon now.'

'She was in her second year,' said Mrs Carpenter. She was fishing for a paper tissue she'd stuffed up the sleeve of her cardigan. 'We're wondering why we weren't asked any of these questions when we gave our statements originally?'

'It's just routine, Mrs Carpenter,' replied Dixon, dodging the question, or trying to anyway. The truth of the matter was assumptions had been made by an incompetent investigating officer, but he could hardly admit that.

'Now, I know that's not true.'

'Can I see her room, please?'

'I'll show you,' said the husband. 'Follow me.'

The ceiling sloped to a dormer window that looked out over the fields at the back of the bungalow. 'It's exactly as she left it.'

'I haven't even changed the sheets.' Mrs Carpenter had followed them up the stairs and was standing in the doorway.

'Is that her current computer?' asked Dixon, gesturing to a laptop that was sitting on a small desk, where Emma would've done her school homework, probably.

'D'you want to take that as well?'

'Please.'

Mrs Carpenter picked it up and slotted it into a laptop case that had been on the floor under the desk.

Only one poster had survived from her early teenage years: a large picture of One Direction on stage somewhere, stuck to the wall above her bed with Blu Tack. The remaining wall space was covered in photographs, the smaller ones framed, others pinned onto a corkboard above the desk; some that were larger had been stuck on the wall with more Blu Tack and were curling at the edges.

'It's street art, in case you were wondering,' said Mr Carpenter. 'Art with a silent "f", I used to call it. Drove her mad, that did.' He blinked away a film of moisture; gone as quickly as it had appeared. 'She took the photos as part of her art project.'

Some were in colour, but most had been taken in black and white. Dixon recognised the underpass on the M32 motorway, the Bearpit in the middle of Bristol, the side of the Victoria Hotel in Burnham-on-Sea. More that he didn't recognise, some with the artists at work, spray can in hand, hoodies covering faces.

'Did Emma paint any of these?' he asked.

'No,' replied Mrs Carpenter. 'She did do some. There's a rucksack in the bottom of her wardrobe with spray cans in it.' She waved away a protesting glare from her husband. 'They'll find it soon enough if they look. But she was mainly studying street art as part of her degree project. She did have a friend who did a lot of it, but I can't remember his name. It was something weird, with a "z" on the end of it.' Mrs Carpenter stepped forwards, pointing at one of the photographs. 'He did that one, and it was never "graffiti", always "street art". That would get you in trouble too.'

'I suppose you would've nicked them, if you'd seen them?' asked Mr Carpenter, a sharp edge to the mischief in his voice.

'If it's done with the consent of the property owner, then no offence has been committed,' replied Dixon, giving the obvious answer to what felt an odd question. 'Otherwise, it's criminal damage contrary to section 1 of the Criminal Damage Act 1971.'

The style of some of the images looked familiar too, not that Dixon was an art expert, let alone a street art expert. Definitely stencilled, that much was obvious; the subject painted in black and white with a single burst of colour providing a focal point. He'd seen similar in Burnham and Bristol. And on the TV news; the artist was well known to say the least.

'They're by Van Gard, surely?'

'That's right. She was studying Van Gard as part of her art project. She said she knew who he was, but we didn't believe her. After all, he's anonymous, isn't he?'

'You held her funeral tea here, I believe?' asked Dixon, when they were halfway back down the stairs.

'Er, yes, we did,' replied Mr Carpenter, clearly surprised by the change of direction. 'It was at Taunton Crematorium, then we came back here.'

'Were there many?'

'Yes, lots,' replied Mrs Carpenter, clearly taking some crumb of comfort from it. 'Friends from college in Taunton, Bristol too. Teachers, her tutor, there was quite a crowd.'

'Maybe thirty or so came back here for a drink,' said Mr Carpenter, a hint of a smile at the memory.

'Was there a charity collection?'

'Children's Hospice South West. Emma used to do fundraising swimathons for them, so we thought she'd like that.'

'Can you let DC Willmott here have a complete list of names, please? While you're doing that I'd just like to nip back upstairs, if I may.' Dixon was already taking the stairs two at a time when he finished his sentence, leaving the Carpenters no time to object.

Louise had taken the hint too. 'Right, just fire names at me and I'll scribble them down as fast as I can.'

The bedside table was where he kept his. Emma's had three drawers, the bottom one the deepest; two boxes of spare needles, several smaller boxes of testing strips, a bag of Jelly Babies – Dixon used fruit pastilles, but the effect was the same. The only thing missing was the spare injecting pens. Every diabetic had a spare pen in their bedside table.

Dixon had three.

'Find what you're looking for?' asked Mr Carpenter. He had tiptoed up the stairs.

'She hasn't got a spare insulin pen,' replied Dixon, with no hint of apology in his voice.

'Really? She usually had a couple, I thought. Are you seriously suggesting someone came in here and killed our daughter?' Mr Carpenter asked, his voice brittle.

◆　◆　◆

'If Van Gard wants to spray paint my house, I'll even get it rendered for him specially,' said Louise. 'Then I'll chip it off and flog it at auction.'

Dixon was sitting in the driver's seat of his Land Rover, outside the Carpenters' bungalow. He was studying the photograph of the piece of street art painted by Emma's unidentified friend; a hand outstretched, with a lighthouse growing out of the back of it. 'What d'you make of that?' he asked, handing the photo to Louise in the passenger seat.

'Nothing.'

'Me neither. We'd better find out who he is and speak to him, all the same.' Now Dixon was watching the house next door, a young lad with a slight limp leaving with a springer spaniel on a lead. 'That'll be Ben Clifford.' He started the engine when Clifford turned towards them. 'Prosthetic legs must be good these days.'

'You should watch the Paralympics,' said Louise, turning in her seat to watch Clifford as Dixon drove out of the cul-de-sac. 'Don't you want to interview him?'

'I want to see the solicitor's file first. Let's get Emma's laptop to High Tech, CCTV at Taunton railway station the night she arrived home – taxis obviously. And get a list of donations at her funeral, in case they've forgotten anyone.'

'Do you really think Emma's death has got anything to do with Barry Mercer?'

'Humour me.'

Chapter Thirteen

'Everybody else has gone home,' said Jane, with a tired glance over her shoulder. 'The two PCSOs had been on duty since six this morning. Mark since eight.'

Dixon looked around the deserted incident room, all of the workstations empty. Jane was standing in front of a second whiteboard that had been set up, the name 'Emma Carpenter' written at the top. Several photographs had been stuck on, all of them ones Dixon had seen at the family home.

'We saw Ben Clifford taking his dog for a walk,' said Louise. 'Hardly limps at all.'

'I've got the surveillance footage taken by Barry in the days before he disappeared. He'd been watching him for five days,' said Jane. 'It's all on a flash drive.'

'All right, let's watch that. You go, Lou, and be back here for eight.'

'Yes, Sir.'

The video suite was deserted too. Dixon slid the sign to 'Occupied' and held open the door for Jane. 'Have you watched any of it?'

'Not yet. I've not long had the flash drive back from High Tech.' She switched on the computer and the two screens. 'How did you get on with Emma Carpenter's parents?'

'They're wondering what it's all about and I can't give them any answers.'

'The defence solicitors are sending over a complete copy of their file by courier in the morning,' said Jane. 'But they confirmed that the case settled *before* Mercer's footage had been disclosed. They made a Part 36 offer and it was accepted, whatever that means.'

'Let's say they make an offer of a hundred thousand pounds, and they say "this offer is made pursuant to Part 36 of the Civil Procedure Rules". If the claimant accepts it, that's case closed and the defendant pays all the costs up to that point. If the claimant fights on and is awarded less than a hundred thousand, then he has to pay all the costs incurred by both sides after the date the Part 36 offer was made. That could be thousands, more if the case goes to trial, and that would take a sizeable chunk out of his award.'

'That's what happened to Roy Stevens. They said it was quantum only in Clifford's case.'

'That just means liability had been admitted; the defendant had accepted the accident was his fault. All that's left to argue over after that is how much the claimant gets.'

'Here's the first one,' said Jane, clicking on a file on the screen. 'There's only three days' worth, filmed over that week in June.'

'When you think Mercer probably waited all day for this footage.' Crutches this time – learning to use a prosthetic leg, by the looks of things. In the early stages of weight-bearing on it, possibly, thought Dixon. 'He must've been bored out of his mind.'

'Clifford played a lot of football, apparently,' said Jane. 'He played for Curry Rivel and was very active before the accident. The letter of instruction from the solicitors to Mercer talks about an exaggerated claim for Smith and Manchester damages, whatever that is.'

'It's a lump sum to compensate for the disadvantage you're now at on the open labour market. He was joining the cast of *Riverdance*, I suppose,' Dixon said, quickly kicking himself that he'd said it out loud.

'Wow, where did that come from?' snapped Jane, with a glare. 'You cynical sod.'

'Six months in the litigation department when I was a trainee, acting for insurers defending claims just like this.'

'You did personal injury work?'

'Some.'

Clifford had climbed into the passenger seat of a taxi with some difficulty, the footage stopping and then starting again outside the doctor's surgery in Curry Rivel. 'That explains the crutches,' muttered Dixon. 'Lay it on nice and thick for the doctors, then it's in your medical records, isn't it?'

'Let me tell you, if I'd had my leg blown off, I'd bloody well lay it on thick and make damned sure I got every penny I was entitled to.'

'And more if you could?'

'And more if I could.' With an emphatic nod.

'Let's try the next file.'

Brean Golf Club, filmed with a telephoto lens from the country lane behind the course. Red flags fluttered gently in the breeze, golfers coming and going; Clifford was driving a buggy, his clubs on the back, crutches resting on the passenger seat next to him.

Wearing long trousers, his right foot at an odd angle.

'He's got his left foot on the pedals,' said Jane.

'There are only two on a golf buggy, so he can get away with it – accelerator and brake.'

Clifford stopped at the next tee and made his way to his bag of clubs, holding on to the buggy for support. Then, using his golf club as a walking stick, he hobbled up on to the tee. Getting the ball on a tee peg was a bit of a struggle.

'I admire him for trying,' said Jane.

A good clean hit, down the middle of the fairway too, but Clifford lost his balance and ended up sitting on his backside.

'When I spoke to Mercer's secretary and she said he'd caught him playing golf, this is not what I was expecting.'

'It reminds me of Douglas Bader in *Reach for the Sky*,' said Dixon.

'Have I seen that one?'

'I've got it on DVD.'

The last file was dated the day before Mercer disappeared and included a three-minute sequence during which Clifford walked fifty yards without crutches. Just.

'I can see why the defence didn't disclose it,' said Dixon. 'He hardly walks with a limp now, but I should imagine that's all the practice he's had. How much did the claim settle for?'

'Three hundred and thirty thousand, plus costs.'

'I'll go and see Clifford in the morning,' said Dixon, pulling the flash drive out of the computer. 'When are Scientific going into Mercer's flat?'

'In the morning. I said I'd meet them there at nine.'

Separate cars on the way home, Dixon resisting the temptation to stick the blue light on top of his Land Rover – the Red Cow stopped serving food at nine. Jane arrived ten minutes later with Monty in tow.

'I think he's got used to having you around,' she said, watching the dog curling up in front of the fire. 'He's torn his bed to shreds. Separation anxiety, they call it.'

'I get that whenever we're apart.'

'You soppy sod.' Jane took a sip of tonic water. 'How does it feel to be back in the saddle? I heard the cheer when you walked along the landing.'

'That's just because I got the better of Professional Standards.'

'Let's hope Dave can do the same,' replied Jane. 'How was he?'

'Hungover, which is saying something.'

'Did he admit tampering with Mercer's file?'

'No, and I don't think he did. Why would you, in Dave's position?'

'Potter thinks it was to stop it coming out that Mercer had been a copper.'

'And why would that make a difference to Dave?' Dixon took a swig of beer. 'If he's a suspect in Mercer's murder, which he isn't, it's because it was Mercer who'd filmed him faking a bad back and they'd had a bust-up at the Crossways. Not because they'd worked together years ago in Bristol. Potter didn't know about that when she suspended him.'

'There could be something else.'

'Or some*one* else.'

Two portions of fish and chips approaching from the kitchen forced a change of subject. 'It's nice to see the cogs going round again,' said Jane. 'I thought for a while your brain was going to mush, watching the same old films over and over. I'm assuming you're back for good?'

'How are you getting on with the new probationer?'

'Sarah. She's a bright kid.'

Dixon waited until Rob was safely back behind the bar. 'We've got Mercer's missing van to find, and Ben Clifford worked at a car breaker's yard. Hardly rocket science, is it?'

'What d'you want me to do?'

'Send Sarah in there, in uniform so she's wearing her body-cam. Looking for a missing van, just checking with car breakers in the area, that sort of stuff. Get her to have a good look around, but get her to make sure they know it's just routine. I don't want them to think we suspect that's where Mercer's van ended up.'

'Do we suspect that's where his van ended up?'

'Get her to ask what happens to the vehicles when they've been crushed.'

'They'll go for recycling somewhere.'

'And keep an eye on the place after she's left. See if they try to dispose of anything.'

'Where will you be?'

'Talking to Ben Clifford. Lou's told him to expect us in the morning.' Dixon was talking with his mouth full. 'I'll want to see her bodycam footage.'

'She's got her head screwed on the right way. She'll do that without breaking sweat.'

'Good.'

'We delivered her first death message yesterday, telling Mrs Baynes that we'd found Mercer's body.'

'His secretary?'

'Yeah, I know, not a close relationship, but it still counts as a death message all the same.'

'Does it,' said Dixon, idly.

Jane was still talking, but Dixon had stopped listening. Something about Sarah and inviting her to their wedding reception. He had moved on; out on the beach with Monty, a cold north wind and the rain pelting down, taking shelter in the entrance to the gents at Brean. They'd been locked, the heavy steel door closed and padlocked, but the wall offered some respite from the driving rain. He remembered the water pouring over the guttering, the downpipe blocked by sand, probably.

And the graffiti on the wall.

'Let's go,' he said, bolting the last of his chips.

'Where?' demanded Jane, but he was already on his way to the door, Monty trotting along behind him.

Dixon held open the passenger door of the Land Rover, allowing Jane to climb in, still holding the last of her battered fish in her fingertips. 'Nothing like a quiet meal out. And you can stop that.' She was trying to put on her seatbelt and stop Monty eating her fish at the same time; not easy with greasy fingers. 'Where are we going?'

'Brean.'

'Not for a walk at this time of night.' Jane sighed. 'Can't you just take him in the field behind the . . .' She gave up, knowing well enough when Dixon was deep in thought.

Coast Road at sixty miles an hour, blue light flashing. It was dark, a cold and clear night. Jane leaned over into the back of the Land Rover, feeding the last few flakes of her fish to Monty.

The road at Brean narrowed, the verges covered in sand that met in the middle of the lane. Four wheel drive essential at this speed.

Dixon swung into the beach entrance at Brean and stopped in front of the toilet block, his headlights on full beam. Single storey with a flat roof, the walls painted cream, the black steel doors of the gents and ladies both padlocked. The huge steel gate across the beach slip had been closed too; a sure sign of a high tide.

'What are we looking at?' asked Jane.

The painting of an old man sitting on a stool and holding a bright red balloon – the one that everybody thought was a Van

Gard – had gone. Painted over and replaced by the figure of a girl stencilled on the cream wall, sitting cross-legged on a surfboard, just above the sand that had collected against the side of the building like a snowdrift.

The burst of red this time coming from a syringe in her arm, a trickle of red paint from the needle running down the wall to a puddle in the sand.

'We're looking at Emma Carpenter's death message.'

Chapter Fourteen

The bundle was five inches thick, in a dog-eared yellow folder; correspondence, court documents, witness statements, medical reports, engineers' reports. 'They sent the original and kept the copy,' Louise had said when she'd handed it to him.

Now they were sitting in Dixon's Land Rover on the outskirts of Curry Rivel, in a lay-by further along the main road, out of sight of the Carpenters' bungalow.

'I don't know how you get through it so quick,' said Louise.

'It helps if you know what you're looking for.'

The morning's briefing had been short, followed by twenty minutes flicking through the solicitor's file, and now on to see Ben Clifford. If there was one thing Dixon did know, it was his way around a solicitor's file. He climbed out of the Land Rover and walked along the grass verge into the cul-de-sac, then down the drive between the hedge and the cars; only the car at the front looking like it had moved in years.

Shards of broken glass leaning up against the wall at the side of the house; a laundry basket full of empty wine bottles. And a tumble dryer, the door open, the plug ripped off the end of the cable.

'He lives here with his parents,' said Dixon. 'But he's over eighteen, so we'll speak to him alone.' Movement behind the frosted glass, so he took his index finger off the doorbell. Barking too. 'It's just a springer, don't panic.'

'You'll be the police,' said the man who opened the front door, white T-shirt pulled tight over his beer belly.

'Yes, Sir,' replied Dixon. 'Here to see Ben. My colleague did ring.'

'I'll sit in, if that's all right. I'm his father.'

'No, Sir. I'm afraid not. Ben is an adult and we'll speak to him alone.'

The man puffed out his chest, half-heartedly squaring up to Dixon, before thinking better of it. 'Is he in trouble?'

'Not as far as I'm aware, Sir.'

'All right. This way.'

Ben was bending over, clipping a lead on the same dog Dixon had seen the day before. 'I was just going to take Tyson out for a walk,' he said.

'We'll talk while we walk in that case,' replied Dixon. 'There's nothing I enjoy more than walking a dog.'

'You got one?'

'A Staffie.'

'What am I supposed to have done?'

Ben's father was hovering in the doorway of the utility room, so Dixon gestured to the back door. It was either that or have to walk back through the house, past the piles of newspapers and bags of dirty laundry.

Dixon waited until they were back out in the lane. 'Do you remember about six months ago, speaking to a uniformed officer about a missing person?'

'Yeah. The sod was watching me, although they never mentioned that at the time. Some of your lot told me about him a couple of days ago. He was last seen parked up there,' Ben replied, pointing to the lay-by at the top of the steep grass bank opposite his house. 'Filming me from a van.'

'It was the day of Emma's funeral.' Dixon was following Ben along the lane towards the stile in the fence at the end, Louise alongside him. 'Did you go?'

'I did, but my parents didn't. I was at school with Emma, but they didn't really know her.'

'And d'you recall seeing the van? Either that day or in the week leading up to it?'

'I may have done, but it didn't register with me if I did. There's all sorts in that lay-by. We even get fishermen sleeping in their vans.' Ben let his dog off the lead and it squeezed under the stile as he climbed over it, a little stiffly perhaps, his prosthetic leg hardly noticeable at all.

'Surely your solicitors warned you that you might be watched as part of your personal injury claim,' asked Dixon.

'Yeah, they did.'

'Well, I've seen the film. You were playing golf at Brean and ended up flat on your backside.'

The path followed the river, long and winding out across the Levels, the wet grass flicking at Dixon's trousers. Wellies would have been the order of the day, if he'd thought about it. Louise could've done with some too.

'I've improved a bit since then. Not much, though.'

'Douglas Bader got down to a single-figure handicap, and he'd lost both legs.'

'Who's Douglas Bader?'

'Google him.'

'I will.'

'You were still on crutches in most of the footage, which tallied with your witness statement, so the defence never disclosed it. It helped you more than it helped them, hence the Part 36 offer.'

'My barrister said it was a reasonable settlement and my dad said I should take it, so I took it. I'm going to use it to get my own place. I'd had an interim payment, which paid for some physio and my new leg.'

'You hardly limp at all.'

'It's taken a lot of work but I'm getting there.'

'There was no psychiatric report,' said Dixon. 'Most people would have been claiming post-traumatic stress disord—'

'Shit happens, doesn't it?' Ben shrugged. 'They did ask me if I wanted counselling and that, but I thought bollocks to it. You just get on with it, don't you. I remember the bang, and I looked down and my leg was on the ground. Then I just fell over. There was no pain, I just fell over. Can't say I've ever had phantom limb pain, either. Been very lucky.'

'Lucky?' Louise clearly hadn't been able to stop herself.

'Yeah, I reckon. Like I said, shit happens. If the bit of fire extinguisher had been a couple of feet higher it'd have taken my head off, let alone my leg.' He took a mouldy tennis ball out of his coat pocket and threw it into the deep grass. 'That'll keep him busy for a minute or two.'

'Are you going back to work?'

'Back to college. I'm doing an IT course.' Ben stopped and turned. 'So, you're still looking for this missing person then, the surveillance bloke?'

'He's not missing anymore. We found his body in the Tone and it's now a murder investigation.'

'Well, I didn't kill him.'

'You're a witness, Ben, that's all.' Dixon looked up at the dormer windows of the bungalows behind him, just visible over the high hedges along the rear boundary. That feeling of being watched, perhaps. And there they were. The Carpenters in one dormer window and Ben's parents in the next door window.

The full set.

'Where were you the night Emma died?'

'At home. We all were. Watching some crap on Netflix, I expect. I remember the ambulance outside the next day, and we could hear them crying, but that's all, really. I never saw her arrive home or anything like that.'

'Or anyone else?'

'No. Sorry. I'm not being much help, am I?'

'Can I help, lamb?'

The man towered over Sarah. It didn't help that he was standing on the first step at the entrance to the Portakabin.

'We're just checking with local car breakers—'

'We're not a car breaker,' interrupted the man. 'We are a properly regulated Authorised Treatment Facility.'

'That breaks cars?'

'Yeah.' He gave a toothy grin, although it was more of a missing-toothy grin.

'We're looking for a white Vauxhall Combo.'

'The nearest Vauxhall garage is on the edge of Taunton, lamb.'

It wasn't the first time, and it wouldn't be the last. Somebody should've told this tosser it was the twenty-first century, thought Sarah. 'I'm not your *lamb*, but I am looking for a white Vauxhall Combo. The owner is missing and we'd like you to check your records, to see if the van came through here, please.'

'Now?'

'It's either that or I can check your records for you.'

The man disappeared inside the Portakabin, Sarah following him. The DCI wanted footage of everywhere on her bodycam, so best foot forward.

'Oi, I didn't invite you in.' The man was flicking through the pages of a desk diary.

'You didn't tell me I couldn't come in.'

'Registration number?'

'BL08 ZVN,' replied Sarah. She was circling the dank and smoky office, a few beams of light forcing their way through Venetian blinds that were hanging at an odd angle. She pulled the cord of one, but it wouldn't budge.

'A Combo, you say?'

'I didn't think smoking was allowed in the workplace anymore,' said Sarah.

'It's my private office. No one else comes in 'ere.'

A small armchair was positioned in front of an electric fire, an out of date and outdated calendar hanging on the wall above the fireplace. An old chest of drawers with a set of scales and a box of padded envelopes on top. Sarah made sure to point her bodycam at the camp bed set up in the far corner, behind the desk, a duvet hanging over the side and trailing onto the floor.

'Are you sleeping in here?' she asked.

'Only temporary,' replied the man. 'No, there's nothing. No Combo van has been through here for ages. Plenty of Transits and stuff, but we've not had a Combo.'

'May I check?'

'Be my guest, lamb.'

A dog-eared, coffee-stained desk diary, each page a list of registration numbers; ten or fifteen, sometimes more. Sarah turned back to the beginning of June and scanned each page in turn.

'Are you going to be much longer?'

'I don't want to have to come back and disturb you again, do I?' she replied, ignoring the huffing and puffing.

A sarcastic 'Satisfied?' greeted her closing the diary.

'Yes, thank you.' High Tech might have been interested in the computer, although they'd have to have worn hazmat suits. The keyboard was stained and covered in crumbs, the screensaver only just visible through the thick layer of dust. 'May I have a look around the yard? Sorry – facility.'

'I'll have to come with you and you'll have to wear this.' He lobbed her a hard hat.

'What about you?'

'My premises, my risk.'

Lines of cars were waiting to go under the crusher. No vans, though.

'We strip them down,' said the man, trudging along behind Sarah. 'Take out all the pollutants, fuel, oil, filters, brake fluid, stuff like that – tyres off too – then we flatten what's left in the crusher and bung them over there.'

'Then what happens to them?'

'Once a week we have a collection and the crushed cars go off to be recycled. They go through a big machine that shreds them and sorts the metal from the plastics and the fabrics, and Bob's your uncle. The tyres go off to be recycled too.'

'If the cars are stripped down before they go in the crusher, then what happened to Ben Clifford?'

'You know about that?'

'He's a friend of a friend.'

'There was a fire extinguisher in the glove compartment and the silly sod missed it. It was his own fault, really, but the insurers settled his claim anyway. They didn't listen to a word I said, decided our procedures were to blame – lack of risk assessments, training, stuff like that. Some flash solicitor came to see me from

Bristol, and he said the judge would see a young lad who'd lost his leg and an insurance company's chequebook, that he'd find a way to award him some money, so they settled it. He's doing all right by all accounts. Off to college, I think.'

'I bet your insurance premium went up.'

'And the rest. There's a pressure release valve on a fire extinguisher and it failed, so my insurers were trying to get some of the money back from the manufacturer. Don't know how that finished up, but it's costing me about a grand a year in extra premium. That's all I know.' There was an odd clicking sound when he spoke – a loose dental bridge, possibly. 'I felt sorry for Ben, I really did. And when it happened . . . I've never seen anything like it.'

'Where was he standing?'

'Just over here, lamb,' said the man, setting off across the yard. 'We screen the car crusher with a wall of these old ones crushed into cubes, and there's a narrow gap, see?' Pointing 'The shard of metal flew through that gap and hit him standing about here. What are the chances of that, I ask you?'

Sarah walked along the lines of flattened cars stacked one on top of the other. There were several white ones, but no Vauxhalls – not that she'd ever really been a car enthusiast, but the badges were obvious.

'Any of these from June?'

'Nah, June's will be long gone.'

'Well, thank you very much, Mr Higgs, you've been very helpful.'

'It's my pleasure, lamb.'

Chapter Fifteen

'That was Jane.' Louise was plugging her phone back into the charging cable sticking out of the power socket in Dixon's Land Rover. 'She's spoken to the beach warden and he says it appeared the week after half-term. He had a couple of days off after the rush and noticed it when he got back on the tenth. Emma died on the ninth.'

'Anything else?'

'Sarah's been into the car breaker's and had a good look around. The records confirm no vans fitting the description, blah blah, but then you'd expect that, wouldn't you?'

'You would.'

'She's got some good footage of the place on her bodycam. Said the owner's a berk; kept calling her "lamb", apparently. Sleeping in his office too. Oh, and the ACC was looking for you.' Louise was looking over her shoulder, trying to read a sign on the wall. 'I think this is a loading bay, isn't it?'

'The campus is closed for Christmas,' said Dixon, switching off the engine. 'Well, at least no one can accuse it of being a red-brick university.'

'What's a red-brick university when it's at home?'

'One of the new ones. Snobs look down their noses at them.'

'Snobs like you, I suppose?'

'Hardly.'

'You must've gone to either Oxford or Cambridge?'

And there it was again. A flashback to a part of his life that he'd boxed up and put away; a chapter only recently closed for good, or so he had thought. A fiancée disappeared, her killer apprehended seventeen years later. At least he'd had the decency to plead guilty. Dixon had been there, sitting in the public gallery with Fran's parents. A whole life tariff too.

Justice, of sorts.

He sometimes wondered what Fran would think of Jane, but Fran had liked everybody and everybody had liked her, so they'd have got on. No doubt about that.

No, he hadn't gone to Oxford or Cambridge. Unless you included the tutorial college where he'd gone to resit his A levels; that was his five months 'up at Oxford'.

He'd failed all the exams at the end of the first year of his degree too; an unwelcome interruption to what was supposed to have been a long hot summer working in a pub in the Lakes. And the night that turned it all around, drinking into the early hours with Paul – never seen him before or since – but after that he'd hitch-hiked home from Wasdale and got on with it; never failed another exam since.

'So, which one did you go to, Sir?' asked Louise. 'Oxford or Cambridge?'

'Neither,' he replied, sliding out of the Land Rover, his tone telling Louise it was not a point to be pressed.

Concrete steps up to the obligatory floor to ceiling windows, a pillar of light brown brick in between each. The reception desk inside was unoccupied and the lights were off, even in the vending machines against the far wall.

'Looks closed,' said Louise. 'He did say he'd be here when I rang. Just knock and the caretaker will let us in.'

Dixon tried the door, rattling it loudly. Then he banged on the glass with the flat of his hand.

The bundle of keys on the end of the chain looked more like some sort of medieval weapon, the man twirling it as he walked along the corridor towards them. How anyone was supposed to tell which key was which was beyond Dixon.

The man stopped behind the front doors, gawping at them through the glass. 'Denton Miller, Facilities Manager', according to his badge. The hair on his head had been shaved shorter than his beard – more recently too – which seemed an odd way round, at least to Dixon. Jeans and a green fleece with the UA@Bristol logo on it: a red square with the wording in white.

Imaginative.

'We're closed for the holidays.'

Dixon was ready for that and slammed his warrant card against the glass. 'We're here to see Mr Ratcliffe. He's expecting us.'

Bolts top and bottom, then the correct key selected first time to unlock the doors.

'The art department is along the corridor, this way,' said Miller, pointing. 'I'll need to come with you.'

'Facilities manager and security guard? You should ask for a pay rise. And you can always call the police if we steal something.'

Miller grunted. 'Please yourself. My office is over there when you want me to let you out.'

'Thank you.'

Dixon and Louise walked along the corridor, Louise looking in the windows on either side; meeting rooms on the right, the library on the left. Dixon was listening for Miller's footsteps behind them, the nosy bugger loitering in the foyer, watching their every move.

'I'm starting to feel I missed out,' said Louise, as they walked past a noticeboard filled with gig posters.

'What on?'

'Three years of partying by the looks of things.'

'And a wagonload of debt.'

'Yeah, I haven't got that. If you had your time again . . . would you . . . ?'

'No. It got me on the fast-track programme, but that's all I've got to show for it.'

'You're a solicitor, surely?'

True, and it gave him a certain freedom. One thing he had learned in recent days though: if he was going to get a job as a solicitor, it wouldn't be doing criminal work. The equivalent of a proctologist in the medical profession.

The art department was on their left, the south side of the building, steel girders replacing the brick pillars to maximise the light; artists did need light, which made graffiti all the more interesting, given that most of it was done in the dark.

There was no partitioning either, the art department a large open space with workbenches all around the outside. Several sculptures were standing in the middle of the room, covered with sheets; easels too, some with canvases, some without.

Three goldfish-bowl offices were situated at the far end, only one of them occupied.

'That'll be Malcolm Ratcliffe,' said Dixon, watching the man getting up from behind his desk as Louise walked along the line of paintings mounted on the wall, her hands behind her back in full art gallery mode. Anyone would think she could make head or tail of what she was looking at.

Dixon certainly couldn't.

'You'll be the police,' said Ratcliffe, hovering in the doorway of his office.

'Yes, Sir.'

'Here about poor Emma. I went to her funeral.'

'I know,' replied Dixon, watching for any reaction.

'This is her stuff over here.'

Dixon followed Ratcliffe over to the far wall, where a series of paintings had been mounted on display boards.

'The students put them up after she died and we've left them here as a sort of tribute to her, I suppose.'

It looked more like a shrine.

'Her parents are collecting them in between Christmas and New Year.'

It was definitely 'modern' art, Dixon was sure of that much. But 'fine'? Apart from that, he had no real idea what it was he was looking at. Blocks of colour, shapes – mostly square. He tried to hide his frown.

'I can see you're what we call a traditionalist,' said Ratcliffe. 'You like to be able to recognise what you see in a painting.'

'It goes with the territory, I'm afraid, Sir,' he replied. 'I like to be able to explain what it is I'm looking at.'

'And therein lies the challenge of contemporary art. It's about visualising ideas; the artist is challenging you to explain what you see.'

'In the police, we'd call that a LOB.'

It was Ratcliffe's turn to frown.

'Load of bollocks,' offered Louise.

'Charming. Look, I wouldn't say this to anyone else.' Ratcliffe's voice was low even though only Dixon and Louise were within earshot, his eyes furtive too. 'But Emma wasn't what I would call very talented. Her work on her street art project was superb and I suggested to her several times she might be better suited to the Art History course, but, no, she wanted to do Fine Art.'

'Tell me about her project,' said Dixon, still squinting at the paintings.

'She was studying the evolution of the Bristol street art movement. From the early chalk slogans in Redcliffe Caves – that was her first module – right up to the suffragettes chalking the pavements. Next year was to be the present day street art you see all around you. She was out there, getting to know the artists, really immersing herself in the street scene. She worked part time in the Subway Gallery too. We sell spray paint and what have you.'

'*We?*'

'My wife runs it, really. I'm too busy here.'

'You'll be familiar with the street scene in that case, Mr Ratcliffe?' asked Dixon.

'Not terribly, if I'm honest. Sculpture's more my thing, I'm afraid. I know a little about it, mainly from Emma's project – and other students have looked at it in the past, of course. I have a colleague who knows about it. She teaches a module on the subject, actually.'

Dixon raised his eyebrows.

Ratcliffe took the hint and turned to Louise. 'Her name's Trudy Lister. She's got a flat in Clifton; off The Avenue, 87c. I've dropped her up there often enough from my taxi. Do you want her number as well?' he asked, fumbling in his back pocket for his phone.

'Thank you, Sir.'

Ratcliffe was holding his phone out to Louise, who was scribbling down a number.

'It was Emma's inquest yesterday, wasn't it?' he asked.

'Did you give a statement?'

'I wasn't asked.' Sliding his phone back into his pocket. 'I had a student take their own life a couple of years ago and that was terrible; jumped off the top floor of the Trenchard Street car park. I gave a statement then, but wasn't asked this time. I don't think there was any suggestion that Emma killed herself. Certainly not as far as I'm concerned, anyway. Happy, bubbly. She had no reason to, as far as I'm aware.' He hesitated. 'No, I thought it was accidental. We all did.'

'The inquest was adjourned, Sir,' said Dixon. 'At my request.'

'Can I ask why?'

'Because I'm not satisfied it was an accident.'

'Really? What was it then?'

'A tragedy. We've got her laptop, so I'm guessing her project and notes will be on that?'

'Er, yes. I'm not sure where else they'd be. I've got the completed modules as her tutor, so I can email them to you, if you like, but they should be on her laptop.'

Dixon remembered his own tutor. A meeting when he'd first arrived – 'Pastoral care. If you ever need any help, my door's always open' – never saw him again after that.

Twat.

'What did being her tutor involve?'

'Not a lot, to be honest. I had and have much more interaction with some of my other students; some need more support than others. I was working with her on her project, of course, for delivery in her final year, but she was studying Creative Analysis with Trudy and Developing Practice with Dom – that's Dominic Meek.' Ratcliffe was watching Louise writing the names down. 'You'll want to speak to them, I suppose?'

'We will, Sir,' replied Dixon. 'Where did she live when she was in Bristol?'

'She was in halls of residence for the first year, then last year she was sharing a flat with Evie Clarke in Montpelier. Evie will be at home for the holidays now, of course.'

'Where's that?'

'She lives on the edge of the Cotswolds, I think. Burford or somewhere like that.'

Dixon slid an envelope out of his inside jacket pocket. 'These are copies of some photographs on Emma's bedroom wall at home. Do you recognise any of these places? That one's the M32 underpass.'

'Yes.' Flicking through the black and white photos. 'These are good. Really, really good. She should have been on the photography course.' He handed a photo to Dixon. 'That's the subway at Bedminster. A well known spot for street art, but the drains are always blocked so you'll need wellies. Those are the Bearpit, but I'm sure you know that.'

'And this one, Sir,' said Dixon. 'Do you know the identity of the artist?'

'Not seen that one before, but the "SZ" tells me it's Slime Zee. He's well known around Bristol. His real name is Sebastian Cook.' Ratcliffe gave a theatrical roll of his eyes. 'Used to be a student here, I'm afraid to say.'

◆ ◆ ◆

'Shall I give him a shout?' asked Louise, when they got back to the foyer.

'I'll do it.' Dixon gave a sharp bang on the door, then pushed it open. 'You were going to let us out,' he said, watching Miller sit up sharply. He had been slouched behind his desk, his feet up on the radiator, watching something on his computer.

'The cricket highlights from Oz, if you must know,' he said, defensively. 'There's a very strict policy about what we can and can't watch.'

'Pleased to hear it,' replied Dixon, not taking the hint to leave despite Miller gesturing to the door. 'How long have you been the caretaker here?'

'Facilities manager, if you don't mind; and I've been here a couple of years.'

'And how well d'you know the students?'

'Some I know – them that speak to me. Most don't know I exist and some look through me as if I don't. You get used to it.'

'What about Emma Carpenter?'

'The one who died?'

'She was a fine art student; second year.'

'They're a weird bunch, the art students. And the lecturers aren't much better,' Miller said, clearly struggling to muster much enthusiasm. 'Well and truly up their own arses. I can't make head nor tail of most of it. Creative Analysis bollocks. It's just teaching them to justify why their pictures are shite. No bloody talent, that's why.'

'D'you paint?'

'Walls, when they need it. White emulsion. Look, some of them are good, bloody good, but most . . .'

Dixon was looking around the room: small and grubby, tins of paint on the windowsill, brushes wrapped in kitchen roll. A toolbox on the floor by the radiator. The cupboard was ajar, revealing a vacuum cleaner, carpet shampooer and a bucket full of mops. There was a sink in the corner too, a dirty towel hanging over the edge. Various bottles of detergent were standing in a plastic crate, with damp cloths screwed into balls.

'I use that for the graffiti in the loos,' said Miller. 'Street art, my foot. You wouldn't believe some of it. You'd have thought they'd have grown out of it at school.'

'You would.' Dixon smiled. 'Although we get our fair share of it in the police station, don't we, Constable?'

'Not in the ladies, Sir,' said Louise, playing along. She'd worked with Dixon long enough to know.

'You didn't say whether or not you knew Emma Carpenter,' he said, his tone suddenly sharp.

'Didn't I? Oh, sorry,' replied Miller, taking the sudden change of tack in his stride. 'No, I didn't know her, I'm afraid. I must've seen her around, but I can't recall ever having spoken to her. We may have passed the time of day, I suppose.'

'What about the lecturers, how well d'you know them?'

'Some of them very well. I have to liaise with the heads of department if there are any building-related issues, so I know them. Some of the others too, although it's usually when they're complaining about something.'

'And Malcolm Ratcliffe?'

'He was the only one who came over from the old campus. Been here years, he has.'

'Right, well, thank you, Mr Miller. If you could let us out now.'

The keys again, twirling them as he walked. 'I take it you suspect foul play if a DCI is involved?' asked Miller.

'We're keeping an open mind.'

'I'll keep my ear to the ground, and if I hear anything I'll let you know,' said Miller, tapping the side of his nose with his index finger. 'I can be your man on the inside.'

'Like the college porters in old episodes of *Inspector Morse*,' said Dixon. 'Nobody knows more about what's going on.'

Chapter Sixteen

'Can I ask you something, Sir?' Louise had turned to face Dixon, the seatbelt locking tight across her shoulder.

'Go ahead.'

'When did you become such a cynic?'

'I'm not cynical, I'm angry. There's a difference,' he replied, pulling on the handbrake outside the block of flats in The Avenue. 'It started when I was arrested for murder. By the time I was charged, I was bloody livid. Fury came next, sitting through my bail application after a night in the cells.'

'Yeah, but—'

'You were watching from the window when I was led out to the van in handcuffs.'

'Nobody thought you'd done it.'

'Which makes it worse, not better.' Dixon switched off the engine. 'And then there's the lost promotion.'

'That you didn't want.'

'Are you telling me you want a transfer?'

'No. Of course not.'

'It'll pass. Anger always does.'

'It's what it leaves behind that worries me,' muttered Louise.

'C'mon, let's go and see Emma's street art lecturer, shall we? I haven't had a good laugh in ages.'

87c was the rear garden flat, entrance down the side, according to the arrow on the wall. It was a large building, converted into flats at some point; doubtless a very grand residence once – something out of *Downton Abbey* perhaps – with large bay windows and a horse-drawn carriage waiting out front. 87c would have been the tradesmen's entrance, probably.

'Trudy Lister?'

'Malcolm rang me and told me you were coming,' replied the woman, turning away mid-sentence. 'Come in.'

She had gone before Dixon and Louise were through the front door, Dixon taking a moment to look at the photographs on the walls, all of them depicting Bristol street art and all of them in black and white. The only colour came from several Upfest posters, announcing the annual urban paint festival, each poster carefully framed and mounted on the wall. Long corridors had their uses.

'Through here,' came the shout. 'I'm guessing you're looking at them through police officers' eyes,' said Trudy when Dixon and Louise appeared in the doorway of what should have been the living room. There was a fireplace, but not much else in the way of traditional living room furniture.

'That would be because we are police officers,' replied Dixon. 'That's not to say we don't recognise the skill involved.'

'Skill, as opposed to talent?' She had pulled her goggles up on to the top of her head, sweeping her frizzy hair back off her face to reveal clean patches where they'd been, the rest of her face spattered with red paint spray.

Dixon had been there, and it hadn't been paint. He had chosen his words carefully, and Trudy had spotted it straightaway. Time for a little jousting.

'Is there a difference?'

'Of course there is. Skills can be taught.'

'Isn't that what you do?' Dixon was doing his best to sound sincere. 'Teach street art?'

'I lecture *about* it. They learn to hone their own artistic talent, however that may manifest itself, in the Professional Development modules. Students are encouraged to go wherever their artistic talent takes them.'

'Even if that means subways and underpasses?'

'Certainly not! We have an absolute ban on illegal street art. Anyone found doing that is off the course immediately.'

Several large easels had been set up facing the back windows of the garden flat, stencils taped to canvases, the floor beneath them covered in dust sheets and aerosol cans.

'Isn't using a stencil tantamount to cheating?' Dixon asked, making sure that Trudy noticed his frown. 'Painting by numbers.'

'It's a valid artistic style,' she replied. 'It's been around a while, but Van Gard put his own twist on it and made it mainstream over twenty years ago; illegal sites require speed, Inspector. In and out as quick as you can, "and before the pigs arrive", was the reason for it. Sorry, I'm quoting his words.'

'You know this artist, Van Gard?'

'Nobody does. He's anonymous. I'm sure I must have seen him around without knowing it was him.'

'Has he sacrificed any of his artistic integrity in the pursuit of commercialism?' asked Dixon. 'He makes a lot of money selling his art these days, doesn't he?'

'You do surprise me, Inspector. I hadn't expected such an erudite question from a police officer.'

He'd surprised himself, but he wasn't going to tell her that. Louise too, judging by her stifled chuckle behind him.

'He's had to compromise on the setting very often, so the art can be sold. That affects context, and often the biting satire that he intended is lost. Size too; you'll seldom see him cover the side of a building, although that may be because it takes too long, of course.'

'Are any of the pictures in your hall of artworks by Van Gard?' asked Dixon.

'No, they're all mine.'

'Even the ones from the Bedminster subway?'

'Allegedly.' Trudy's eyes flicked to Dixon, hoping he saw the funny side. 'Can I take the fifth?'

'You've been watching too much American TV. Not that I see a TV, mind you.'

'There's one in the spare bedroom. I use that as my lounge, although I don't get much time for watching TV.'

'What about Slime Zee?' Dixon handed Trudy the photograph taken from the wall in Emma Carpenter's bedroom. 'Do you know him?'

'Seb Cook. He's one of my old students,' she said. 'Not his best work. It's on the side of a pizza place in Charlotte Street, I think.' She shook her head. 'What does it tell you?'

'That somebody's got a lighthouse growing out of the back of their hand.'

'Interesting, if a little obvious. Remember, the gift of art is in how people react to it – so react. Don't just say what you see. This isn't *Catchphrase*. The artist is challenging you to interpret it.'

Dixon had done enough of that lately, parked outside the toilet block at Brean beach, interpreting Emma Carpenter's death message.

'I'm more concerned with finding him.'

'He's a DJ on the club scene at weekends and works behind the bar at the Fleece during the week. Lives in St Pauls somewhere, I think. His father's a banker, not that I'd hold that against him.'

Time for a question Dixon knew the answer to. 'Did you go to Emma Carpenter's funeral?'

'Malcolm and I went to represent the university. He was her tutor too, so had the closest relationship with her, but she'd been a student of mine for a year, so I thought I ought to go.'

'He said her project on street art was going well?'

'It was more of a historical project so far, so I hadn't been involved. She'd covered the early graffiti and then the protest movement. She was going to be looking at the contemporary stuff this year, which is when I would've been able to help her more.' Trudy's face had softened. 'Sadly it was not to be.'

'Was she a good student?'

'Not standout, to be honest. Average. Malcolm thought she was doing the wrong course and that Art History would've been better for her. Her street art project certainly had potential and she'd even talked about publishing it. She was really immersing herself in the contemporary scene, doing her research. She was quite friendly with Slime Zee – not romantically involved, though. I wouldn't want to give you that impression.'

'Was she popular?'

'Yes, I think so. I'm not aware of any fallouts.' Trudy sat down on the arm of an old chair and lit a cigarette. 'Look, she wasn't suicidal, so we all assumed it was accidental, to do with her diabetes.'

'It's certainly possible,' said Dixon. He was scrolling through the images on his phone, looking for the best one. The only pictures he'd got had been taken at night. Scientific would be there now, taking more and better photographs of the toilet block, but for now, this one would do. 'You're the expert in artistic interpretation?'

'I suppose so.'

He handed Trudy his phone. 'Interpret that for me.'

'That was a bit brutal.'

'Bollocks.' Dixon took a deep breath and exhaled through his nose, still staring at the image on his phone. 'If it had been a tribute to a dead friend then the artist would've painted Emma injecting herself. Who do those hands belong to, holding the syringe? They're not Emma's. That must be significant.'

'I agree,' said Louise. 'Trudy did at least give us a list of people who she thought might have done it.'

'I notice she didn't put her own name on the list. She uses stencils, doesn't she?'

'She was at an awards dinner on the night Emma died. And yes, of course I'll check.'

'All that gushing about a single burst of colour in a black and white image, as if that's anything new. *Schindler's List* was made thirty years ago.'

'Not seen it, I'm afraid.'

'You should. Everybody should.' Dixon was staring out of the window. 'It's shot in black and white and there's a little girl in a red coat.'

'Yes, hello,' said Louise, her phone to her ear. 'I'm trying to get hold of Sebastian Cook. Seb, yes. Is he in this afternoon? Starts at six? Right, thank you. D'you know where I might find him? Thanks very much.' She rang off. 'That was the Fleece. He'll be at the recording studio, they said. Back Row Records. Give me a minute and I'll google them.'

Dixon started the engine.

'They're the other side of the river, down behind the railway lines. It's a new unit along Mead Rise, probably to drown out the noise.'

Dixon parked in the car park in front of the unit fifteen minutes later, the drive conducted in perfect silence. The windows and doors were tinted, no signage to tell them they were in the right place. 'Are you sure this is it?' he asked.

'It's the right address. I used the satnav on my phone.'

'You go in the front and I'll go round the back. There's bound to be a back door. And I bet you a tenner he's got his baseball cap on back to front.'

It turned out to be a fire door, so it would open outwards when the time came – a sharp kick to the release bar, probably. Dixon took a step back and waited.

'The filth, Slime mate, looking for you!'

Running.

Then the metallic clank of the fire door opening.

'Ah, there you are, Seb,' said Dixon, sitting on the wall at the back. 'We just wanted to talk to you about Emma. You're not under arrest, you've done nothing wrong and you're free to go whenever you wish.'

The boy's eyes were dilated, darting from side to side. Baggy jeans with the crotch down by his knees; if he tried to run he wouldn't get very far anyway. And his padded jacket was already down over his shoulders. No hat, though, which was a shame.

'She's dead.'

'She is, and I want to know how and why.'

'They said it was an accident.'

'Who's *they*?'

'The word on the street, you know. Just rumours, like.'

Seb turned to see Louise behind him in the corridor.

'That's my colleague and she's not going to arrest you. All right?' Dixon gestured to the wall next to him. 'Come and sit down and stop farting about. This is important.'

'Yeah.' Seb did as he was told, sitting at arm's length, his eyes fixed on the fence at the back of the yard.

'How well did you know Emma?'

'She was always hanging around, like. I met her at Upfest last year, the paint festival. Me and a few others was doing a mural in Montpelier and we got chatting; studying the street scene at the uni or something, she said. She did a few afternoons in the gallery, as well – never buy your paint online, it leaves a paper trail.' Seb gave a nervous grin. 'She knew my old lecturer, Trudy, so I thought she must be all right. I introduced her to a few people and she took photos. She was always taking photos.'

'She was doing a project on Bristol street art.'

'I said I'd help her.' Eyes still darting. 'She was always hanging around the Fleece, and she'd turn up at the Island and the Attic Bar when I was doing a gig.'

'Were you in a relationship?'

'No, mate. Not my type. I did like her flatmate, though, if you know what I mean?'

'Were you in a relationship?'

'With Evie, yeah.'

Dixon handed Seb his phone. 'Do you know who painted that?'

'It's a stencil, so it could've been any one of ten people. More, maybe.' He tipped his head. 'That's supposed to be Emma, innit?'

'I believe so. It's on the toilet block at Brean beach. Do you know anyone who goes down that way?'

'There are a few. Street art is big in Burnham and Highbridge. There's a festival down there every year that we all go to. I done one on the side of a pub down there last year.'

'If I told you that I thought Emma had been murdered, what would you say to that?'

'That someone done her in, like?'

'Yes.'

'I'd think you were nuts, mate. Who the fuck'd do a thing like that?'

'You tell me.'

'Not me, that's all I know.' Seb fell silent, breathing deeply through his nose.

Dixon waited.

'All I know is she was going to try and find out who Van Gard is. It was going to be the big part of her project, unmasking him. I tried to talk her out of it. Nobody knows, and if he wants to keep it that way, good luck to him, but no, she was going to out him good and proper.' Seb was up and running before Dixon could react. 'Gotta go, sorry.'

'Let him go,' he said, when Louise started to give chase.

'Unmasking Van Gard.' Louise was leaning over, her hands on her hips, puffing hard even though she'd only run twenty yards. 'Maybe Van Gard doesn't want to be unmasked?'

'Quite.'

Chapter Seventeen

'Got a minute, Nick?' Deborah Potter was holding one arm of her glasses between her teeth, her smile clearly forced.

Dixon knew an ambush when he saw one. Charlesworth was sitting in the far corner of meeting room 2 reading something on the table in front of him: a Policy Log – obvious even at five paces, through the glass partition and upside down.

He knew what was coming and it would be yet another test of his anger management skills. He had counted to ten silently twice by the time Potter closed the meeting room door behind him.

'I've had a call from the vice chancellor of UAB, Nick,' said Charlesworth, looking up. 'He's wondering why you seem to think one of his students has been murdered.'

'I'm wondering the same thing.' Dixon slid a chair out from under the table and sat down, aware that he hadn't been invited to do so but damned if he was taking a dressing down standing up, like some schoolboy in the head's office.

'You don't give a reason in your Policy Log.'

'Yes, I do.'

'Not a compelling one.'

'Does it need to be compelling? I'm exploring a line of enquiry – that Mercer was killed because of something, or someone, he saw at Emma Carpenter's funeral.'

'You're causing her family a lot of upset, I gather.'

'I know that.' Dixon folded his arms. 'It's bound to be upsetting to find out there's a possibility your daughter was murdered. Either way, the evidence before the inquest is incomplete and inconclusive. The family understand that and so does the coroner.'

Eight, nine, ten . . .

'Look, Nick.' Potter was still sucking the arm of her reading glasses. 'You've got a man whose been stabbed in the back, dismembered, and his remains thrown in the river. Surely that should be the focus of your investigation?'

Not even bothering with good cop, bad cop. Nice.

'It should and it is. I'm the SIO of a major investigation team and I've delegated. I've got people looking for Mercer's van, people going back through his surveillance files, Scientific are in his flat, his computers have gone to High Tech.'

'Yes, but—'

'I've got people following up on the hacksaw, trying to find where and when it was purchased. Roger Poland's still doing his bit. The dive team are coming back at the end of the week to try again – we're still missing his feet and the murder weapon.' Dixon was reeling it off, his voice flat. 'Then there's CCTV and number plate cameras. I've got three people on them. Have I forgotten anything?'

Charlesworth drew breath, but not quickly enough.

'I've spoken to Ben Clifford myself and eliminated him from the enquiry,' continued Dixon. 'There's been an informal look around the car breaker's yard and I've still got to look at the body-cam footage from that.'

'It should be the focus of *your* investigation,' said Charlesworth, his tone conciliatory. 'You're the one who'll find his killer, no one else.'

Dixon opened the photograph of the stencilled painting of Emma Carpenter's death message on his phone and slid it across the table. 'That was painted on the wall of the loos at Brean shortly after Emma's death.'

'It's a depiction of what happened, surely?'

'If it was a depiction of an accidental overdose, she would be holding the syringe.'

Charlesworth was sucking his teeth. He glanced at Potter, who remained impassive, anxious not to commit either way. Then he turned back to Dixon.

There's more?

'I've had a complaint from Superintendent Carlisle. You may remember him?'

Tempting, but Dixon wasn't taking the bait.

'Professional Standards are investigating an allegation against David Harding that he tampered with Barry Mercer's missing person file,' continued Charlesworth, 'and Carlisle tells me you've already requested all of the files that Mercer and Harding worked on together at Fishponds. Is that right?'

'It is.'

'PSD need them.'

'PSD can't have them.'

'Yes, but—'

'If you'd like me to, Sir, I'm more than happy to ring Superintendent Carlisle and explain it to him myself.'

'I'll bet you are.' Potter gave a mischievous grin.

It had been Carlisle who had arrested Dixon for murder, and six weeks since that day on the beach when the whole thing had unravelled in spectacular style. No apology, or even an acknowledgement that Professional Standards had got it wrong, had been forthcoming in the weeks since, but Dixon knew their paths would cross again. That it was happening so soon was a bonus.

'What's so important about the old files?' asked Charlesworth, struggling to contain his exasperation. 'I'm just trying to act as peacemaker here, between you and PSD. Keep you apart, at least.'

Dixon turned to Potter. 'Did you or did you not designate Dave Harding a suspect in the murder of Barry Mercer?'

'I did, because of his surveillance of Dave, and he admitted they had an altercation.'

'In that case I need the files. Dave and Mercer have a history and I need to investigate it. If Carlisle wants to obstruct a murder investigation that is entirely a matter for him, and not without its consequences.' Dixon slid his hands into his pockets, if only to stop himself rubbing them together.

'Is it really the focus of your investigation?' asked Charlesworth.

'It's a line of enquiry that needs to be eliminated.'

'Leave it to me then.' Charlesworth swallowed hard. 'I'll deal with it.'

'I can arrange for PSD to have copies of the files, if that's any use, Sir. I can hand deliver them myself to Superintendent Carlisle and even insert them in his—'

'There's no need for that, thank you.'

Dixon stood up; the meeting was over, at least as far as he was concerned. 'Let's be clear about this,' he said. 'Barry Mercer's missing person file was tampered with by someone in this building. I want to know who and why.'

'We'll be back in an hour' may have been a bit optimistic.

'What does he want to talk about?' Jane had asked on the drive out to Westonzoyland in Dixon's Land Rover.

'Life, the universe and everything,' Dixon had replied.

'God, you mean?'

'Him as well. We're getting married in a church, aren't we?'

Now they were sitting in the front row of the pews, Reverend Jonathan Philpott sitting on the steps in front of them. Dixon had resisted the temptation for another turn around the Battle of Sedgemoor museum at the back of the church; he already knew all he needed to know about that.

'It's very good of you to agree to marry us, Jonathan,' he said.

'It's just a shame there's no vicar in Brent Knoll at the moment.'

'Not really. We'd rather have someone we know.'

'So, let's cut to the chase,' said Jonathan, rubbing his hands together. 'I know you're busy. Tell me about your relationship with God. What about you, Jane? Do you believe?'

'Yes, I do.' Her face flushed. 'I can't pretend to be a regular churchgoer though, I'm afraid. Births,' she said, patting her abdomen, 'deaths and marriages, really. Sorry.'

'Don't be. Some people don't even manage that. And what about you, Nick?'

'We have an understanding,' Dixon replied. 'Me and God.'

Jonathan waited for an explanation, just as Dixon would have done.

'He makes the mess and I clear it up. I'm sorry to sound cynical, Jonathan, but when you've seen what I've seen . . .'

'That tells me you believe he exists, anyway.' The vicar gave a warm, understanding smile. 'How about people make the mess and God sends you to clear it up?'

'Don't tell him that,' said Jane. 'It makes him sound like God's gift!'

'Maybe he is? Maybe you all are? Look at what you did for my parishioner, Daniel Parker. Two life sentences for murders he didn't commit. I prayed with him on my prison visits. And God answered. He sent you.'

'Daniel was lucky.'

'I don't believe that for a minute,' replied Jonathan. 'How's the sternum?' he asked, rubbing the tips of his fingers up and down his breastbone.

'You heard about that?'

'Lucy told me. You deliberately walked into a crossbow bolt at point blank range. Tell me, why did you do that?'

Dixon was starting to think that a vicar they knew might not have been such a good idea after all. Jonathan had taken Daniel Parker in when he had been released from prison, much to the consternation of some of the residents of Westonzoyland. Then he had supported Daniel through the battle to get his son back, found them a place to live in the village. If ever there was a God's gift . . .

And Jane's half-sister, Lucy, being in a relationship with Daniel's son, Billy, gave the vicar a direct line into their family.

Family. I suppose it is, thought Dixon.

'How's Daniel doing?' he asked, trying a change of subject.

'Well,' replied Jonathan. 'Everything changed for him when you caught the real killer. The council agreed to end the care proceedings and Billy came to live with us at the vicarage for a time. Then, and this made my eyes water I can tell you, when they moved into their little place in Macey Close they had over a hundred "welcome to your new home" cards, some of them anonymous. People were leaving gifts on their doorstep for days; furniture was donated, they had five kettles and a couple of toasters. The community really rallied round; it was lovely. And it was all thanks to you.'

'Lucy seems happy with Billy,' said Jane.

'And settled. You came into her life at just the right time,' replied Jonathan.

'God sent us, I suppose?' Dixon kicked himself that he had said that out loud.

'You tell me,' replied the unflappable Jonathan.

A chance encounter at their mother's funeral; neither Jane nor Lucy had known the other existed. Jane had been adopted at birth, Lucy in and out of foster care all her life; all fifteen years of it, up to that point nearly a year ago. It had been a crossroads for Lucy, no one would dispute that, and now she was at college and a police cadet. It could so easily have gone the other way.

'She tells me you're struggling, Nick.'

'She talks too much.'

'He's angry,' offered Jane.

'Daniel Parker spent fifteen years in prison for crimes he didn't commit and yet he carries no anger, no bitterness. He's at peace with it,' said Jonathan. 'He sees it as a test that he passed. He's moved on, and you need to do the same.'

'A colleague of ours paid for that with his life.'

'A colleague of yours sacrificed himself to save others. John, chapter fifteen, verse thirteen: "Greater love has no one than this: to lay down one's life for one's friends."' Jonathan stood up. 'It was a test, Nick, and you passed. Move on. And now your phone's buzzing in your pocket. I'm guessing there's somewhere else you need to be.'

It was a short telephone conversation, over before Dixon and Jane reached the Land Rover, which was parked in the road outside the churchyard.

'We're on our way. Speak to Emma's housemate and get the local lot to take her into protective custody,' he said, before ringing off.

'Where are we going?' asked Jane, climbing into the passenger seat.

'Junction 3 on the M32. Slime Zee's dead. Looks like he jumped from the bridge and was hit by several cars on the carriageway below.'

'Jumped, or was pushed?'

Chapter Eighteen

Driving down the hard shoulder, blue light on the roof flashing, Dixon had gone the long way round and was heading south on the M32, past two lines of traffic being diverted off the motorway at junction 2.

Their warrant cards at the ready, the patrol cars moved and suddenly they had the motorway to themselves, the traffic blocked in both directions. Dixon had already given an instruction that it was to be treated as a crime scene, much to the consternation of the officers tasked with keeping the traffic moving.

It also meant the new crime scene manager would be there. Hari Patel and his clipboard.

'Just remember,' said Jane when they were climbing out of the Land Rover. 'It was a test and you passed.'

She obviously liked that little pearl of wisdom; no doubt he'd be hearing it again.

Streetlights merged with blue lights, car headlights and arc lamps up on the bridge and on the carriageway below, to cast an eerie glow across the road – deserted apart from police vans and a solitary ambulance. And several cars parked on the bus lane further down; the poor sods who'd hit him, probably.

'DCI Dixon?' said an officer in a hi-vis jacket.

'Yes.'

'The crime scene manager is up on the bridge.'

'Thank you.'

'It's a bit of a walk from here, I'm afraid. The slip road that side is your best bet; it's the shortest.' Gesturing to the northbound carriageway. 'Just hop over the crash barrier.'

The southbound hard shoulder had been turned into a nearside bus lane, a Scientific Services tent set up about a hundred yards down from the bridge.

Dixon looked up at the railings on the bridge above. Six feet high, possibly, for obvious reasons. Easy to climb over, but not so easy to throw someone over. A Scientific Services officer in overalls was checking the railings for fingerprints, another was on his hands and knees, both under the watchful eye of Hari, identifiable from this distance only by the clipboard.

Their paths had crossed once before and it hadn't gone well, saved only by the lack of sarcasm in Hari's voice when he had referred to Dixon as 'the boy wonder'.

Dixon would make an effort.

They walked along the carriageway, careful to avoid the skid marks and blood that had been marked out with spray paint on the tarmac, arriving at the tent that had been set up on the bus lane just as the Bristol pathologist, Leo Petersen, emerged. 'Not a pretty sight, I'm afraid,' he said. 'He was hit by three cars. Killed instantly, multiple catastrophic injuries.' His sentence was punctuated by camera flashes going off inside the tent.

Dixon sighed. 'I'm guessing you're not going to be able to tell whether he was thrown or jumped?'

'Hari told me that's what you were thinking and I'll certainly check, but any injuries from a struggle will be masked, I'm afraid, unless we get very lucky. See for yourself. Just stick to the stepping plates.'

Dixon lingered long enough to check it was the same lad he had been speaking to earlier that day; not easy when his skull had been crushed, still less so through the tyre marks and the blood. He thought about trying to make sense of Slime Zee's limbs, which were at peculiar angles, twisted and mangled, but decided against it, turning away quickly.

'Is it him?' asked Jane, when Dixon emerged. She had waited outside the tent.

'It's the same lad I was talking to earlier. Sebastian Cook, to give him his proper name.'

'There was ID,' said Petersen. 'Hari bagged it up.'

It took them a few minutes to clamber over the concrete barrier of the central reservation and then walk up the northbound off slip, Dixon looking at the graffiti on the walls, random 'tags' and the odd slogan about the Tories, the expletives painted over by the council, probably. 'Kev, ring Dad, innit!' had been scrawled in red letters three feet tall, followed by 'Kev rang Dad!' and a smiley face.

'The proper street art's down in the underpasses,' said Hari, watching them approach from the top of the off slip. 'That's just kids tagging, like a dog marks its territory.' He greeted Dixon with a warm smile. 'Glad to see you beat the rap.'

Another one watching too many American films.

'Thank you.'

'There's not much to see, I'm afraid. I know you think he may have been pushed, but we're going to be hard pressed to prove it. Scientifically anyway.'

'No CCTV?' asked Jane.

153

'It's a blind spot.' Hari was gesticulating with his clipboard. 'There are cameras everywhere, even one under the bridge that shows him landing on the carriageway, but there's nothing up here. This middle section here' – pacing it out – 'about five yards, is a blind spot.'

'Is there footage of him walking on to the bridge?'

'Alone, yes. He came along Easton Way.'

'Is it possible to get up here without being seen on camera?'

'Yes, if you climb up through the vegetation from down there.' Hari was pointing to the area of parkland in the middle of the roundabout.

'Are there cameras down there?'

'I'll check.'

'And I want photographs of every single piece of street art down there – underpasses, the lot, please.'

'We can do that. Might be best to wait for daylight.'

'Are those treehouses?' asked Dixon, squinting at square objects in the branches of the larger trees, the upper branches level with the roundabout.

'Uniform checked them and they're empty.'

Dixon was standing next to the railings. 'I'm six foot, so these must be—'

'One point five metres,' said Hari.

'Anything on the ground over there?' Three arc lamps had been set up, their lights shining on the pavement at the point above the blood staining the carriageway below.

'No blood. A few scuff marks, but then you'd expect that even if he climbed over under his own steam.'

'What did he have on him?'

'I've got a crate in the back of my van.'

Several evidence bags. The contents of his pockets: a wallet, hand rolling tobacco, Rizlas, a lighter, keys and a few coins. A small rucksack. 'These were in it,' said Hari, picking up an evidence bag containing four aerosols. 'We found a couple of others in the road, so I'm guessing they'd been in his pockets. Here.' Holding up another evidence bag, the cans inside dented. 'He might have been trying to paint the bridge and just fell, you never know. You sometimes see stuff painted where the motorists can see it, don't you?'

'And he just happened to pick the blind spot?'

'You wouldn't want to be caught on film doing it,' said Jane.

'In which case you'd be out in the early hours, surely,' said Dixon. 'What time was it?'

'Just before seven,' replied Hari.

'The rush hour's not long over at that time of day. Cars everywhere,' said Dixon.

'Where's the DCI?' The voice sounded out of breath.

'Here.'

'Guv,' said the officer, running over. 'Someone's come forward who was travelling northbound on the M32, says they looked up at the bridge and saw two people. He thought they were fighting. We're getting a statement from him now.'

◆　◆　◆

Dixon was turning off the M5 at junction 11A before Jane finished the telephone calls.

A team of three, led by Mark Pearce, was on its way to the Bristol CCTV control room with instructions to find and track the second figure on the bridge – the description given by the motorist who had come forward was good, but not great, unfortunately.

Jane's father was on his way to their cottage in Brent Knoll to pick up Monty, and a room had been booked at the Cirencester Premier Inn. It wasn't terrifically close to Burford, but it would have to do. It was on their way home anyway.

'Do you think we should book two rooms?' Jane had asked.

'I think we're way past that, don't you?'

'Yeah.'

The longer telephone call had been to the Gloucestershire Police, Dixon's knuckles whitening as he listened to Jane's end of the conversation.

'Evie Clarke, yes. What d'you mean *missing*?' Jane's hand had been firmly planted across her forehead while she repeated the information for Dixon's benefit. 'Left the Mermaid after her shift behind the bar last night . . . walking distance but she always drove when it was dark . . . picked up just before midnight on a traffic camera on the A40 roundabout . . . only half a mile at most from there . . . no sign of her or her car after that.'

'Escalate it,' Dixon had said.

To be fair to him, the detective sergeant to whom Jane's call had been transferred had not needed much persuading – the missing person file was already on his desk for review. 'You're about forty-five minutes away. Detective Inspector Coates will meet you there.'

First Emma Carpenter, and now her flatmate. Sebastian Cook too; they were still scraping him off the M32. The connection between the three of them was street art, but what was the connection with Barry Mercer? Was there one? Maybe not.

Maybe he'd just been parked outside the wrong house at the wrong time.

It was gone ten o'clock by the time they pulled up outside Evie Clarke's house in Signet End, Burford, an unmarked car with a blue light on the roof already parked across the drive. Lights were on inside the house, the curtains on the ground floor open; figures moving about, watching and waiting.

'DI Coates, Sir,' said a man striding towards them across the block-paved driveway, weaving his way between the parked cars.

'I've spoken to the family and told them you're on the way. I've not told them why, I'm afraid.'

'What checks have you done?' asked Dixon.

'The usual.' Coates's voice was hushed, conscious of the family watching him from the window. 'Her phone's switched off. Last ping was a mast in Burford at six yesterday, so it looks like she switched it off when her shift started and never switched it back on. No movement on her bank account, nothing like that. We've checked family and friends – no one's heard from her – and we're checking traffic cameras for sightings of her car, widening the search area. Checking with her boyfriend too. He's a lad from Bristol, apparently. We've left messages for him, but he's not come back to us so far. I was planning to go down and see him tomorrow if he doesn't get back to us before then. His name's Sebastian Cook.'

Chapter Nineteen

Mr and Mrs Clarke were standing on the doorstep holding hands tightly, a teenage boy loitering in the hallway behind them. The door was open, light streaming out into the drive.

Cotswold stone, the trees in the front garden perfectly pruned, evergreen hedges trimmed. A Jaguar was plugged into a socket on the outside of the double garage.

'Mr and Mrs Clarke,' said Coates, 'this is Detective Chief Inspector Dixon and Detective Sergeant Winter of Avon and Somerset Police.'

'Have you found her?' demanded Mr Clarke.

'May we come in?' asked Dixon, knowing the best way to avoid answering a question was to ask another.

'Yes, of course.'

The fireplace in the living room was Cotswold stone too.

'This is our son, Nathan,' said Mrs Clarke. 'And this is Evie.' She handed Dixon a framed photograph from a bookshelf.

'We've got a copy of that one, Sir,' said Coates. 'She uses it on her Facebook profile. It's on the system.'

At a dining table somewhere hot, smiling at the camera, a cocktail in one hand and the camera in the other; a selfie then. Short dark hair and a nose stud. Whoever she was sitting with had been cropped out.

'She did the gap year thing,' said Mrs Clarke, pulling a paper tissue from her sleeve. 'That was taken in Thailand. There was a whole group of them backpacking. We'd never have let her go on her own.'

'When did you last see her?' asked Dixon.

Mr Clarke sighed, loudly. 'We've been through all this twice today already,' he said. 'Will someone please tell us what is going on?'

'She left about quarter to six yesterday to go to work. She's behind the bar at the Mermaid, in her holidays, for a bit of extra money, you know. "Bye, Mum," she said, and that was it. She was gone. We didn't even notice until this morning that she wasn't here. I usually wake her up about ten if she's not up by then anyway.' Mrs Clarke was sitting on the edge of the sofa, next to Jane. 'Students.' She shrugged. 'She's studying Fine Art at the University of Avon; in her final year. She loves it.'

'What about that boyfriend? Have you spoken to him yet?' Mr Clarke wrapped his left hand around his right fist, knuckles whitening. 'Sebastian Cook, all squeaky clean when he turns up here to meet the gullible parents, but I looked him up on the internet. *Slime Zee*, with his baseball cap on backwards, spraying walls with graffiti. Big in the so-called *club scene*, apparently. Let me tell you, it's the last time he crosses the threshold of this house.'

'He's dead, Mr Clarke,' said Dixon, not trying to soften the blow. 'He fell from a bridge over the M32 just before seven o'clock this evening.'

'Oh God, no.' Mrs Clarke began sobbing quietly.

'Had Evie talked to you about Emma Carpenter at all?'

'A lot. They were best friends. Emma came here several times and they shared a flat in Montpelier, a little two-bedroomed place above a corner shop; they were both in the second year on the Fine Art course then.' Mr Clarke was pouring himself a whisky. 'Why, was she murdered as well?'

'The evidence is inconclusive, although this was painted on the wall of the public toilets at Brean shortly after her death.' Dixon handed his phone to Mr Clarke, showing him the stencilled image.

Clarke stared at it for a second or two, then passed the phone to his wife.

'D'you think Evie's dead?' Mrs Clarke looked up, blinking away the tears. 'Is that what you're saying?'

'I think we need to find her sooner rather than later,' replied Dixon.

'Dead or alive.' Clarke was talking to himself as much as anything, gulping his whisky.

'Rest assured, we're doing everything we can,' said Coates.

'Where's her computer?' asked Dixon.

'In her room. She was working on her project. Emma's was on street art and Evie is doing hers on street art *installations*.'

'What . . . ?' Coates clearly wished he hadn't asked.

'It's sculptures – *things*, as opposed to paintings – that pop up here, there and everywhere. That's Evie's thing, sculpture. Good at it too.'

'Can I see her room?'

A child's bedroom; the child had grown, but the room hadn't, the wallpaper still pink, a Barbie doll sitting on top of the books on the shelf. One Direction posters again, and some black and white photographs of statues in various stages of completion. Dixon recognised the studio at UAB.

'Those were taken by Emma,' offered Mrs Clarke. 'It's Evie's work though.'

A child's desk, marks in the varnish where stickers had been peeled off. Dixon had seen it all before.

An iPad on the bedside table.

'Has Evie ever mentioned an artist by the name of Van Gard?'

'Part of her project was about him. He does installations as well as paintings. He did one at a model village in Torquay or somewhere. She went down there and got photos of it before they moved it.'

'Went for four hundred thousand at auction,' said Mr Clarke. 'It was an Airfix tank with the words "peace keeping-force" written on the side in blue ink, graffiti-style – "peace", question mark, with the "keeping-force" hyphenated. Beats me. He bungs it in the model village and suddenly it's worth thousands. Makes a lot of money, does Van Gard. Some of his pieces have sold for over a million.'

'Can I take her laptop?' asked Dixon.

'What for?'

'I'd like to get our High Tech team to have a look at it; see a copy of her project and any photos that might be relevant. Emails, social media. So much of our lives is digital these days.'

'Yes, take it.' Clarke picked up the laptop and handed it to Dixon. 'Anything if it helps you find her. You'll want her iPad too, I expect,' he said, handing it to Jane.

'Does she know who Van Gard is? His identity.'

'That was going to be the centrepiece of Emma's project – tracking down Van Gard and catching him in the act. She wanted a series of photos of him at work, or better still film of him at work, and then she was going to confront him on camera.'

'*Confront's* the wrong word, Ian,' said Mrs Clarke, correcting her husband. 'It wasn't like that. She thought his work was wonderful – they both did. Emma just wanted to be the one to reveal his identity to the world. She came to stay for a few days at Easter, and I remember talking to her about it.' Mrs Clarke nodded. 'Didn't we, Ian?'

'I remember saying to her, I said what if he doesn't want his identity to be revealed? He makes a lot of money out of being anonymous; his artwork sells for millions and his anonymity is part of the mystery, the mystique. Take that away and what have you got? A plastic tank with paint on it and a few stencils on a wall. They're ten-a-penny these days. Everybody's doing it.'

Mrs Clarke sat down on the single bed and picked up a teddy bear that had been leaning against a pillow. She held it tight to her chest and looked up at Dixon, her eyes welling up. 'She's alive, I know she is.'

'We'll find her, Mrs Clarke,' said Dixon.

'If she was dead, I'd know.' She turned to Jane. 'You're going to be a mother. You'd just know, wouldn't you?'

'I think so,' said Jane.

Mr Clarke sat down next to his wife and put his arm around her shoulders. 'Dead or alive,' he said. 'We must have her back.'

Coates's text arrived on the stroke of midnight, just as Dixon and Jane were checking into the Premier Inn on the edge of Cirencester.

Found her car lay-by north of Chadlington. No sign Evie.
Checking traffic cameras.

'Doesn't sound good, does it?' Jane was leaning over, reading the message on Dixon's phone as they waited at the reception desk.

He could have done without the telephone call from the duty superintendent at Gloucester. That had been twenty minutes wasted, sitting in his Land Rover outside the Clarkes' house; keeping his voice down in case the family overheard. Dixon couldn't remember the officer's name, but his opening line had set the tone: 'Look, what's all the fuss about?'

Coates had been decent enough to warn him – the 'duty super' was well known for it, apparently. Another line Dixon would remember was 'We don't appreciate officers from other forces, coming up here, telling us what to do.' That was a belter, that one.

Jane had been leaning across from the passenger seat, listening in, and had dug her elbow into Dixon's ribs before he had a chance to draw breath. It had given him the moment he needed to frame his reply.

'Evie's flatmate is dead in suspicious circumstances and her boyfriend has been murdered. I wouldn't want to be in your shoes explaining to Evie's parents that when their daughter went missing, you went back to bed.'

That had done the trick.

'We'll need a team up here first thing in the morning to liaise with the Gloucester lot; make sure they're taking it seriously.' Dixon was jabbing the lift button with his thumb.

'We're not staying up here?'

'No point. It's a threat to life now, so Gloucester *should* be throwing the kitchen sink at it. The best thing we can do is go home and feed in information as we find it.'

'What information?' asked Jane, frowning.

'The key to this is down there, not up here.' The other option was just to ignore the question, of course. 'See if Mark's finished at the CCTV Hub, and he can come up here tomorrow if he has.'

Jane was tapping out a text message as they rode up in the lift. 'You haven't got your night insulin,' she said.

'I'll live.'

'Or your blood testing kit.'

'What happened to proper bloody keys.' Dixon was waving the card in front of the sensor and rattling the door handle at the same time.

'Here, let me,' said Jane, snatching the keycard from him and opening the door. 'So, what happens tomorrow?'

'We finish Emma's project for her.' Dixon kicked off his shoes, before collapsing on to the bed. 'And find Van Gard.'

Chapter Twenty

'Yeah, but' – Sarah shook her head – 'people have been trying to do that for years, Sir. Loads of journalists, there was even a documentary on TV. *The Hunt for Van Gard*, I think it was called. You might find it on YouTube.'

The briefing had broken up by eight-thirty, all except Louise, Jane and Sarah despatched to continue the investigation the old-fashioned way – knocking on doors, interviewing witnesses, watching hours and hours of traffic camera footage. Not to mention Mark and his small team, still ensconced in the Bristol CCTV Hub.

'Find Van Gard and we find Evie. It's as simple as that. Alive, God willing,' Dixon said.

'That's assuming you're right about Emma Carpenter.' Louise, sticking her neck out.

'Any doubt about that went out the window when Seb Cook was murdered,' replied Dixon. 'And now Emma's flatmate has gone missing. We need to know what it was at Emma's funeral that got Barry Mercer killed.'

'So, how do we find him?' asked Jane. 'Or her.' Hastily correcting herself. 'We don't even know if Van Gard is male or female, do we?'

'Loads of people have tried,' said Sarah. 'Like I said there's even a TV docu—'

Dixon raised his hand, silencing her mid-sentence. 'We are highly skilled CID officers with access to tools that journalists don't have. Mobile phone mast data, for a start. It's also a murder investigation with a threat to life abduction ongoing, so anyone refusing to talk to us is likely to get themselves arrested for obstruction.'

'You have a plan?' Jane asking a question she knew the answer to, possibly. It had been a long drive south that morning, most of it in silence, Dixon deep in thought.

'Everyone who was at Emma's funeral has been spoken to and a statement taken. We have their mobile phone numbers, so I want them checked to see if any were in the vicinity of Emma's house on the night of her death, junction 3 on the M32 last night, and Burford the night Evie disappeared.'

'All of them?'

'Expedited.'

'That's going to cost an arm and a leg.'

'I'm authorising it, and Charlesworth will back me up if anyone questions it.'

'Anything else?'

'Chase up Emma's laptop at High Tech. I want to see her project and any research relevant to it. Photos too. She must have been getting close, otherwise why kill her?'

'Don't you think we might be in danger of overcomplicating things a bit, Sir?' asked Louise, nervously. 'She could just have been having an affair and someone is killing to cover it up. It's possible, surely? And Barry Mercer might just have seen something he shouldn't – a kiss or something.'

'Then why the death message on the side of the toilets at Brean?'

'I don't know.'

'Neither do I,' replied Dixon. 'So we keep digging. We'll need another whiteboard too, Jane, please, with everything on it we know about Van Gard; any images from Emma's laptop.'

'Me?'

'Thank you.'

'Answer me this then.' Louise was looking puzzled. 'If you're right, why didn't Emma's killer take her laptop?'

'It was supposed to be an accidental death, and he or she is far too smart for that.'

Jane's text message arrived before Dixon had reached his Land Rover on the top floor of the car park.

> *Are you doing this deliberately to keep me out of harm's way?*

He tapped out a reply while he was waiting for the electric gates to open.

> *Yes. Nx*

It didn't take long, but the gates did, giving him time for second thoughts and a chance to sweeten the pill.

> *I need a capable senior officer in charge of the incident room. Nx*

> *Bollocks. Jx*

'Where are we going?' asked Louise.

'The auction house that sells his stuff,' replied Dixon. 'A Van Gard sold a month ago for one-point-two million. I want to know where they got it from and where the money is going.'

A full car park was not a good sign.

'Must be a sale on,' said Louise.

Dixon counted two Bentleys and an Aston Martin in amongst the Jaguars and Range Rovers – none of them black with tinted windows, mercifully. He left his Land Rover in the far corner of the car park, blocking in two Volvos in the staff car parking area.

'The sale room is that way, Sir,' said the receptionist – a young lad in a blazer and tie; trainee auctioneer, probably. 'Have you registered with us online?'

'Who deals with the Van Gard sales?' asked Dixon, with a wave of his warrant card.

'Those are handled by Mr Hearne, but he's busy this morning, I'm afraid.'

Dixon glanced at the sign above the double doors: 'Hearnes, Rampton and Woodruff, auctioneers since 1876'.

'Where will I find him?'

'He's conducting the auction in the sale room now, I'm afraid. Fine art and collectibles today.'

'Anything by Van Gard?'

'Lot sixty-one. There's a picture in the sale catalogue, if you'd care to buy one?'

'Buy one?'

'They're five pounds.'

'I'm in the wrong business,' muttered Dixon under his breath. 'Seller's commission, buyer's premium; you get it at both ends and then charge for the catalogue on top?'

'Industry standard practice,' the receptionist said defensively; a well-rehearsed response to an often-asked question, Dixon felt sure.

'What is the Van Gard?'

'It's an installation.'

Dixon couldn't quite get used to the word 'installation' describing art. The last thing he'd installed had been software on his laptop. And a plumber had come and installed a new boiler.

'A satirical piece – *Harvesting*, it's called.'

Dixon looked at the picture in the open auction catalogue on the table in front of him. 'What d'you make of that, Constable?' he asked, turning to Louise.

Silence.

'No, me neither.' He glanced up at the ticker above the double doors, the sign reading 'Lot 33'.

'It'll be about an hour before we get to it.' The receptionist had correctly anticipated Dixon's next question.

'Do you have a list of everyone in there?'

'They have to register to bid, yes, but I'm not sure I can . . .' His voice tailed off as Dixon's frown deepened. 'I'd need to check with Mr Hearne, and he's tied up.'

'Let's get him out here then,' said Dixon.

'I can't do that!'

'Is there another auctioneer on site who could take over from him?'

'Well, there's—'

'Do it. And do it now, please.'

The young trainee disappeared through a side door just as the ticker changed to 'Lot 34', then the double doors flew open, a small crowd making for the coffee machines on the far side of the foyer; all percolators and small packets of biscuits. Cups and saucers too.

Dixon stepped into the back of the sale room. Plush carpet, rows of red velvet chairs either side of the central aisle, some still occupied by those preferring to sit out the coffee stampede.

A large man was striding towards him, leaving the trainee on the platform. Greying moustache, red face and matching corduroys. 'This way,' he said, marching past them without waiting for an explanation.

An equally large door at the top of the stairs, the name 'Richard Hearne' in gold lettering. A leather topped desk, large conference table. Oil paintings on the wall – there was no street art here.

'Make it quick, will you?' snapped Hearne, slumping down in an armchair behind his desk. 'I said there'd be a ten minute break. That's all. It'll be tight as it is today.'

'It's a double murder investigation, Sir,' replied Dixon. 'There's also a third person, a young student, missing.'

'What's this got to do with me?'

'You – nothing, hopefully, Sir. We're making enquiries about the artist known as Van Gard. We have a number of questions and are keen to trace him or her. We were hoping you might be able to help.'

Hearne hesitated.

'I can come back with a warrant, if that would assist?'

'There's no need for that. I can't help you much anyway, even if I wanted to.' He leaned forward and picked up a partially burnt cigar off the ashtray. 'I suppose you'll arrest me for smoking in the workplace,' he said.

'Either that or accessory to murder, perhaps.'

'Now, hang on a minute.' Hearne dropped the cigar in the bin beside his desk. 'Van Gard is wanted for murder?'

'At the moment we are hoping he or she can assist with our enquiries.'

Hearne pressed the intercom buzzer on his phone, the door quickly opening behind Dixon. 'Get Rupert to take over the sale,' said Hearne to the woman hovering in the doorway. 'I'll be down for lot sixty-one.' Then he slouched back into his chair, pausing until the door closed again. 'Van Gard is male, I can tell you that much.'

So could Dixon, given the strength involved in lifting Cook over the railings on the motorway bridge.

'We get our instructions from a firm of solicitors in Whiteladies Road,' continued Hearne, an impatient edge to his voice. 'I've never dealt with or spoken to Van Gard myself. No one here has. The money we send to an offshore company in the Cayman Islands. I can let you have the banking details, and the solicitor's details as well, but apart from that I'm not sure I can be much help. We sell the artwork, take our commission, and send the balance where the solicitor tells us. It's as simple as that, really.'

'How d'you know Van Gard is male?'

'The solicitor let it slip once – in conversation, you know. Just said "he".'

Dixon glanced at Louise's notebook, open on her knee.

Hearne took the hint. 'The firm is called Fords. They have a Weston office too, but we deal with the Whiteladies Road office; a Mr Crosby.'

'How do Van Gard's artworks get here?'

'We collect them from the Fords office. We've got a van that does the rounds.'

'How often?'

'We do sell quite a few Van Gards. We've got a bit of a reputation for it now. Sometimes the sales are for him direct, but more often it's for the people who've got his artwork. A painting appears on the side of their house overnight, they remove it and sell it. I mean, wouldn't you?' Hearne laughed. 'Occasionally you get twits who don't know what they've got and paint over it, but most check first. We get emails with photos from time to time, but Van Gard puts them on his website if they're originals. That's how we authenticate them. They're stencils, and everybody's at it these days.'

'Is this a Van Gard?' asked Dixon, handing Hearne his phone, Emma Carpenter's death message on the screen.

Hearne used his fingertips to zoom in on the image. 'No, the shading is all wrong. Very basic, I'd say.'

'What about his installations?'

'We've sold a few of those too. The last one was the tank he left at the model village. They replaced it with a replica and sold the original; went for four hundred thousand from memory.'

'And the model village got the proceeds of that?'

'Yes.'

'What about today's?'

'That's come direct from Fords, so it's a sale on behalf of the artist himself. *Harvesting*, it's called. Don't ask me why.'

'Is there a reserve price?'

'Never is with a Van Gard. The estimate is three hundred thousand, but it'll go for more than that. We've had a lot of interest online. He's becoming more popular, if anything. There's been a lot of media coverage – speculation about his identity too. It's a shame.'

Dixon had sat down on a leather chair in front of the desk, but stood up, taking a moment to look at the paintings on the wall. 'What is?' he asked, examining a pair of small figurines on the mantelpiece.

'His anonymity is part of the attraction, but with you lot on his tail it's bound to come out now, isn't it?' Hearne was making no effort to hide his disappointment. 'Journalists have tried, we've even had them in here working for us undercover – hidden cameras, the lot, would you believe it – but they've never got close. Still, all good things must come to an end.'

'Why an end?' asked Louise.

'Once his identity is known, the bubble will burst, I suspect,' replied Hearne. 'A Van Gard suddenly becomes a Joe Bloggs from Bristol, or wherever. Hardly the same is it?'

'Can we see *Harvesting*?' asked Dixon.

'You're not going to confiscate it to check for DNA, are you?'

'No, Sir.'

'Sorry, I've been watching too much true crime on Netflix.'

A stack of miniature haybales and a toy combine harvester, the words 'scorch dearth' spray painted in tiny lettering on the side, graffiti-style.

'What does it say to you, Inspector?' asked Hearne.

'Nothing,' replied Dixon. 'But then I've never been good at cryptic crosswords either. It's not the way my brain is wired, I'm afraid, Sir.'

'This is where the viewing takes place,' said Hearne. It was a large room, double doors opening outwards into the sale room. Huge shelves were stacked with various items for auction, each carefully labelled, a small sticker somewhere on every item. 'We open for three days before each sale so people can come and have a close look at what they're going to be bidding on. It's all catalogued, and online too.'

'And there was a lot of interest in this piece, you said.'

'Mostly from abroad, I think.'

'Do people register for the viewings as well as the sale?'

'They do,' replied Hearne. 'I'll get you both lists.'

Panes of one-way glass in the doors allowed Dixon a look at the faces in the sale room without being seen. Lines of faces, some looking down at phones or the auction catalogue, some with their eyes closed. Someone was bidding in the room, but Dixon couldn't see who, the lot a watercolour of a moorland scene somewhere.

He was working his way along the back row, trying to get a look at each face, when she looked up.

Chapter Twenty-One

The changeover took a moment, allowing Dixon and Louise to slip in the back of the sale room as Hearne stepped up on to the podium for the auction of lot 61.

The vacant chair was useful. No need to tower over her. 'Hello, Miss Lister,' said Dixon, sitting down. 'Fancy seeing you here.'

She sighed. 'Only a police officer would find a fine art lecturer at a sale of fine art and collectibles interesting.'

'Come here often?'

'Yes, actually.' She folded her arms. 'We all do.'

'You heard about Evie Clarke, I take it?' whispered Dixon.

'We had a staff meeting this morning.'

'Did you know her?'

'I was her tutor, and someone is coming to take a statement from me this afternoon.'

'Right then, ladies and gentlemen,' said Hearne, up on the podium. 'Now we come to lot sixty-one, *Harvesting*, an installation by Van Gard, which has been verified by us in the usual way. Can I start the bidding at three hundred?'

It was brisk; two bidders in the room and one online, judging by the arm being raised by someone sitting at a computer behind the podium.

Increments of one thousand pounds quickly rose to five thousand and then ten, the bidding eventually slowing at five hundred and thirty thousand.

'Sold, at five hundred and thirty thousand pounds; online bidder number three-two-one.'

The bang of the gavel coincided with the smallest of flashes, a tiny flicker of flame rising from the miniature haystack of lot 61. Some audience members gasped, others reached for their phones, as the hay disappeared in a ball of flame that burned out before the first fire extinguisher arrived on the scene, Hearne holding his assistant back before he blasted the installation with a jet of foam.

'It's gone out by itself,' he said. 'There's no need for that.'

There was not even enough smoke to set off the alarms – the charred remains of the tiny haystack smouldering on the table next to the podium.

Some of the gasps had turned to laughter, the losing bidders looking unusually relieved.

'That'll add to its value, if anything,' said Trudy. 'Scorch dearth. Van Gard is brilliant.'

'Do you know him?' asked Dixon.

'Sadly not, but I never miss a sale. You never know what's going to happen.'

'Emma Carpenter knew him.'

'Did she?'

'It's why she was killed. It's why Slime Zee was killed too. And it's why Evie Clarke has gone missing.'

'And you're going to find him, I suppose.'

'We are.'

Dixon was sitting in his Land Rover, still blocking in the two Volvos, flicking through the lists that Hearne had given him. Several names appeared on both, but only a handful had gone to the viewings and not the sale; several names Dixon recognised from UAB, including Emma's tutor, Malcolm Ratcliffe.

'I wouldn't want to be one of the lawyers trying to sort that out,' said Louise, sitting in the passenger seat.

'There's nothing to sort out, just like Hearne said,' replied Dixon. 'Once the gavel falls it belongs to the buyer and it's his risk.'

'They've got to hope what Trudy Lister said is true, that it's gone up in value.'

'It bloody well won't by the time we've finished with Van Gard.'

'I'm still not seeing it, I'm afraid, Sir.' Louise spoke quietly, unsure of her ground. 'There just seems a lot of guesswork in it.'

'Go on.'

'We're making an *assumption* that Mercer's murder is connected when it might not be. We've got no evidence that Emma was murdered, or that the painting on the side of the bogs at Brean is her death message. It might not be her at all.' Louise's voice was gathering momentum. 'Look, I accept it's likely Evie's disappearance is connected to Seb Cook's death, because they were boyfriend and girlfriend, but that's it, surely? That's the only meaningful connection we have.'

Louise had a point, and she seemed determined to press it home.

'I just think you're barking up the wrong tree, Guv.'

Guv? She'd never called him that before either.

'You've never gone out on a limb like this before,' she continued. 'There's a connection, we just don't know what it is yet.'

'Then we should concentrate on finding it, surely? Because from where I'm sitting, we're coming at it from the wrong end. We've decided Van Gard is the killer and—'

'I've decided.'

'All right, you've decided Van Gard is the killer and you're bloody well going to prove it. You even told Trudy Lister, so it'll be all round UAB before you can say Jack Robinson.'

'I want him to know we're coming for him.'

'We can always arrest him for arson, I suppose.' Louise had turned in her seat and was staring out of the passenger window. 'This is not easy for me, Sir, but since you've got back it's almost like you're not thinking clearly anymore. I'm sorry, but I think you've got it badly wrong this time. And I'm not the only one.'

'Are you here on official business, or have you changed your mind about the job?' The managing partner gave an apologetic smile, the answer obvious to a question he knew he shouldn't have asked. The warrant cards had left no real doubt.

Dixon tried to ignore Louise's quizzical look. 'Official business,' he said.

They were standing in the reception area at the Bristol office of Fords Solicitors in Whiteladies Road, his Land Rover parked in the taxi rank outside, blue light on top to see off any traffic wardens.

It wasn't as bad as Dixon had thought, but bad enough. A glass door in between a newsagent's and a dry cleaner's; old legal cartoons with dots of mould hanging in the stairwell – overweight barristers and sleeping judges. The same ones had been on the wall in the conference room at the firm he had trained at, only without the mould.

A list of the partners in the firm was hanging on the wall behind the reception desk, next to their employer's liability insurance certificate and Lexcel accreditation. The receptionist was keeping her head down behind her computer, the phone ringing out on the desk; too busy trying to listen to what was going on, probably.

There's nothing like a bit of office gossip.

Louise had spent five minutes trying to talk him out of it, to be fair to her, and phrases like 'We've got no evidence' and 'We're going to look like a right bunch of idiots if you're wrong' were still ringing in his ears. 'Are you sure you want to do this?' had been her last effort, just as he was ringing the intercom at the front door. The mention of the word 'police' had been enough to see to it that the managing partner was in reception to greet them when they reached the top of the stairs.

'We'd like to speak to whoever acts for Van Gard,' said Dixon.

'And how do you know that anyone here does?'

'We've got two murders and a missing student. We have reason to believe that Van Gard may be able to help with our enquiries and we need to speak to him as a matter of urgency.'

The managing partner folded his arms. 'I'm sorry, we can't help you.'

'Can't or won't?'

'You're a solicitor. I know, I've seen your CV, so you'll have heard of client confidentiality and legal professional privilege. I'm hoping those are familiar concepts?'

'We know you act for him.'

'I can neither confirm nor deny that, I'm afraid.'

'This is a double murder investigation.' Dixon was fighting the urge to pace up and down – that and wipe the sarcastic look off the managing partner's face.

'Do you have evidence that Van Gard has committed a crime?'

Dixon hesitated. 'No,' he said, reluctantly.

'Any evidence that Van Gard is about to commit a crime?'

'No.'

'Then we are under no professional obligation to assist you in any way at all. In fact, to do so would put us in breach of our duty of client confidentiality. Our solemn duty.'

◆ ◆ ◆

'That went well,' said Louise, the door slamming behind them. 'And what did he mean, "Have you changed your mind about the job?"'

'I went for an interview at their Weston office.'

'You're leaving the police?'

'Let's try the production company that made that documentary. They spent weeks trying to find out who he is, so maybe they know something they didn't broadcast?'

'You're staying on Van Gard?'

'We are.'

Dixon was in the newsagent's buying chocolate when Louise caught up with him a few minutes later. 'You all right, Sir?' she asked.

'Blood sugar's a bit low,' he replied. 'Well?'

'They're based in Swansea, but the documentary was produced and directed by Danielle Kemp. She's in Bristol today, over at UAB as it happens.'

'Doing what?'

'She's a guest lecturer on the Filmmaking course.' Louise looked at her watch. 'She's there now.'

Turquoise was an odd choice of colour for cladding – the building looking more like a spaceship than anything else. Still, at least there was a parking space and a small canteen.

The back wall of the lecture theatre was glass, the seating tiered down to the front where a woman was pacing up and down, occasionally turning to gesture to a presentation slide on the screen behind her.

'That's Danielle,' said a familiar voice to Dixon's left. He turned to find Malcolm Ratcliffe sidling up to him. 'One of my old students and now a documentary filmmaker. Very talented she is, too.'

'Is Evie Clarke a student of yours?' asked Dixon.

'She is. I've already given a statement,' replied Ratcliffe. 'Your lot are over at my department now, interviewing everybody. She's one of our better students, to be honest, and I hope to God she's all right.' Ratcliffe frowned. 'What's your interest in Danielle?'

'My interest is in Van Gard, and Miss Kemp made the documentary.'

'Never found out who he is, if that's what you want to know.'

'Doesn't everybody?'

'She's finishing in five minutes,' said Ratcliffe. 'She'll use the side door, along the corridor and down the first flight of stairs. You can't miss it.'

Dixon pushed open the door a crack to find Danielle Kemp standing down at the front of the lecture theatre, surrounded by students firing questions at her, more waiting their turn to do the same thing.

'Go and rescue her,' said Dixon, watching from the side door as Louise stepped forwards with her warrant card at the ready.

'Thanks for that,' said Danielle, her relief evident. 'Most of them are just after a placement with my production company.' She was stuffing her laptop into a bag slung over her shoulder, the cable still dangling from a side port. 'And it can get a bit tiring.'

'Tea?' asked Dixon, gesturing to the canteen.

'Just a boiled water for me.'

Tall, dangerously thin, with short dark hair; jeans and a baggy pullover.

179

'You were a student here, I gather,' said Dixon. Small talk would do until Louise got back with her notebook, and the teas.

'Fine Art.' Danielle took a fruit teabag from her laptop case, then slung the case over the back of her chair. 'I should've done Filmmaking, as it turned out, not that it would've done me any good.'

Dixon waited.

'I got into documentaries quite by accident, really. My ex – he worked in film editing, then he wanted to set up on his own, so we did it together and it just went from there.'

'You described him in the past tense.'

'He's dead now, I'm afraid. Motorcycle accident.'

'I'm very sorry.'

'It was a long time ago.' Danielle reached up and took a cup and saucer from Louise. 'Thank you.'

'We wanted to ask you about Van Gard,' said Dixon. 'Whether you found out who he was?'

'We got just about as close as anyone has, I think, which is not really close at all, to be honest.' She was dunking her fruit teabag, the water turning a disturbing shade of yellow. 'I left the film open deliberately, but the reality is I've got no idea who he is. No one has.'

'Rumours?'

'Lots of them; all of them unfounded. You've seen the film?'

It had been a long night, watching it on his phone.

'We explored a few of the rumours, spoke to a couple of suspects whose names came up more than once, but nothing. I'm sure plenty of people in the street art scene must know who he is, but they keep it a closely guarded secret. He's one of them, after all, isn't he? One of the legendary figures, and they're a secretive bunch at the best of times.'

'You got some of them to speak to you, I saw.'

'Only by hanging around for ages and earning their trust. And even then they gave precious little away.'

'Tell me about the photo,' said Dixon.

'It was a grainy image, taken at night on a phone, that was *supposed* to be him. It could've been bloody anybody.' Danielle gave a self-pitying sigh. 'It was all I came up with in nearly a year of research. And he had his back to the camera. Hardly going to win me a BAFTA, was it?'

'Where was it taken?'

'Gordano Services, apparently. There is a Van Gard there, on the back of a kiosk; just a small one of two mice playing tug-of-war with a banana skin. It's on his website. Sorry, I thought you were going to be asking me about Evie Clarke. Aren't you trying to find her?'

'We are,' replied Dixon.

'I didn't know her, I'm afraid. She's not on the Filmmaking course. I've heard about it, though. This morning.'

'Does the name Emma Carpenter mean anything to you?'

'Yeah, it does.' A sip of tea. 'She contacted me claiming to know Van Gard's identity. It was after we'd finished shooting and the film was in post-production, but I met up with her anyway. It was a waste of time in the end, because she wouldn't give me any specifics; saving it for her thesis, apparently. She showed me a couple of photos on her phone and that was it. I just thought she was after a job, to be honest.'

'The photos were no good?'

'Distance shots, back to the camera, usual stuff. We used one of them, with her permission – the Gordano shot. It's the image you see in the film. Then the next thing I hear she's died of an accidental overdose. Poor kid.'

'Who told you it was an accidental overdose?'

'It's common knowledge, surely? I can't remember who told me. Isn't her inquest coming up soon anyway?'

'It's been adjourned,' said Dixon, emptying a sachet of sugar into his tea.

'Why?'

'Because I'm not satisfied it was an accident.'

'Suicide, you mean?'

'Emma Carpenter was Evie Clarke's flatmate. They shared a flat in Montpelier.' Dixon left that one hanging.

'And now Evie's disappeared.' Danielle's voice was hushed.

'She has. And her boyfriend was thrown off a bridge over the M32 last night, about seven o'clock. They were looking for Van Gard, and I think they got closer than you, which is why they're either dead or missing.'

'The Van Gard I know wouldn't do that,' protested Danielle. 'Not that I know his identity,' she added, hastily. 'Just his reputation. He's an artist. He's done peace protests, for heaven's sake.'

'I want names,' said Dixon.

'I don't know his name.'

'If you had to guess. Names that came up more than once in amongst the rumours.'

'I checked them out. They were discredited. I ended up thinking I was being misdirected. None of them came to anything.'

Dixon slid Louise's notebook in front of Danielle and handed her a pen.

'List them for me, please.'

Chapter Twenty-Two

'Let's try the Subway Gallery.'

Satnav again, Dixon parking in a bus stop this time.

It looked like an art gallery, the walls covered with framed prints in the street art style; definitely no gilt here. Lines of them; brightly lit, with twinkling Christmas lights draped around the frames. A selection of Christmas cards too, and more prints in a rack waiting to be framed.

The far wall was hidden behind shelves holding spray cans and ink pens of every shade known to the street artist; a student-aged girl standing at a counter, her back to the window, encasing a framed print in bubble wrap.

A bell jangled above the front door when Dixon pushed it open; the girl turned and looked at him, then went back to wrapping the black frame.

'Can I help you?' A glossy magazine hastily shut and dropped on a desk, the woman appearing through an open door at the back of the gallery.

'We're just looking,' replied Dixon, Louise hastily thrusting her warrant card back in her pocket behind him.

'There are more upstairs,' said the woman. Mid-forties, maybe. Black trouser suit, white blouse; a little too much make-up. 'We've got an exhibition on – the Stokes Croft Community Art Group.'

'Do you have anything by Van Gard?' asked Dixon.

'There are several prints you can choose from in the rack, and Sam will frame them for you.'

'I was looking for an original, really.'

The woman stifled a laugh. 'You'd need to try the auction house, in that case. We've only got this one, and it's not for sale, I'm afraid,' she said, gesturing to a small black frame screwed to the wall behind her.

Dixon walked over to take a closer look. Stencilled – a little old man sitting hunched on a three-legged stool, much like the version that used to be on the side of the public toilets at Brean, but the red balloon in this one was replaced by a satellite dish fluttering on the end of a cable.

'It was here when we took the gallery on,' continued the woman. 'So we just left it there.'

'And you've not been tempted to sell it?' asked Dixon.

'We're not entirely sure we own it.' The woman stepped back to admire the picture. 'The previous owners said Van Gard had lent it to them, but he's never been back to claim it, so there it stays.'

'Do you know Van Gard?'

'If I had a pound for every time I get asked that.'

Time for warrant cards.

'You'll be Wendy Ratcliffe?' asked Dixon.

'I am. And no, I don't know who Van Gard is, I'm afraid.' She took a folded ten-pound note out of her pocket and handed it to Sam. 'Go and get us a couple of coffees, there's a good girl. My usual.'

Dixon waited until the door closed behind Sam, watching her run off along the pavement. 'You own the gallery?' he asked, turning to Wendy.

'My husband and I bought it ten years ago. I run it more as a hobby than anything else, and we have art students here part time to help out, like Sam. I'm only here three afternoons a week.'

'Who picks the art you sell?'

'I do. I know what sells and what doesn't. There are a few by some of my husband's students. A couple of Trudy Lister's; you've met Trudy, I'm guessing?'

'We have.'

'I was sorry to hear about Emma. She never had the greatest control of her diabetes; had a couple of hypos when she was here and I had to nip to the newsagent's for a Mars bar.'

'How long did she work here?'

'A year or so, during term times. I always make sure we have a couple of local students, like Sam, to cover the holidays.'

'What about Seb Cook?'

'The famous Slime Zee. Very talented. This is one of his,' she said, walking over to the side wall and gesturing to a framed painting. 'I told him it was a stupid name and would affect his sales, but he didn't care.'

'You know he's dead?'

'My husband told me.'

A pelican, wings outstretched, painted in all sorts of bright colours that made it look more like a parrot.

'Did you know him well?'

'Not really. He brought a couple of paintings in and asked if we'd sell them. The artists own the paintings, you see; we just take a commission when they sell. Only that one was suitable, and it's still there, as you can see.'

'When was this?'

'A year ago, maybe. There'll be a note in the book, if you'd like me to—'

'There's no need, thank you,' interrupted Dixon. 'Does the name Evie Clarke mean anything to you?'

'No. Should it?'

'Evie has gone missing. She's another of your husband's students.'

'He never said, but the name doesn't mean anything to me, I'm afraid. She's not worked here.'

'Did Emma ever discuss her project with you?'

'No. Was it anything interesting?'

'Street art; she was going to reveal Van Gard's identity.'

'Plenty have tried. Danielle somebody was the last one doing the rounds, from a TV company in Wales. She came in here several times, sniffing around.'

'And what did you tell her?'

'Same as I've told you. I've got no idea who he is. I'm just waiting for him to come in and collect his painting.'

Jane and Sarah had done a good job of the Van Gard whiteboard, so much so that Potter and Charlesworth had taken up residence in front of it, by all accounts.

'They've been here ages,' Jane had said, when Dixon emerged from the door to the car park.

The visit to Evie's flat in Montpelier had been brief and not entirely fruitful either. 'There's nothing here,' Donald Watson had said, the senior Scientific Services officer stripping off his overalls. 'See for yourself.'

And he had been right. A few posters on the walls, but everything else had gone home with Evie at the end of term.

Her current flatmate had gone home for Christmas too. To Belfast, safe and sound.

'Ah, there you are,' said Charlesworth. 'What's all this?'

Jane and Sarah had made copies of the most recent artworks from Van Gard's website and pinned them to the whiteboard with places and dates scribbled underneath. Dixon had been trying to get a look at it from a safe distance.

'What about the website registration?' he asked Jane.

'Private,' replied Sarah.

'Well?' demanded Charlesworth. 'And what's with this phone data request? That'll cost a pretty packet.'

Dixon was bristling and ready for what was coming. If even Louise was beginning to doubt him, it was inevitable others would too, and sooner rather than later. 'Everything that can be done, is being done,' he said, coldly. 'Gloucestershire are on it too.' He gestured to the whiteboard. 'This is one line of enquiry that I'm exploring. It's my belief that if we find Van Gard, we find Evie. Emma was going to unmask him; maybe she was getting too close, which is a possible motive for her murder—'

'If she was murdered.' Potter and her two pence.

'—the murder of Sebastian Cook and the disappearance of Evie Clarke,' continued Dixon, without drawing breath.

'Mobile phone mast data on everyone at Emma's funeral?'

'Not everyone. We're not doing her family, or the neighbours.'

'Why not?' Charlesworth was building up a head of steam. 'Surely her granny's a suspect too. Why not check her mobile phone? Why not the postie while we're about it?'

. . . eight, nine, ten.

'Let's take this in a meeting room, Sir,' said Dixon, calmly.

Dixon waited until Potter closed the door behind them.

'What are you waiting for?' asked Charlesworth, sitting on the far side of the round table.

'An apology.'

'What the bloody hell for?'

'I am a detective chief inspector and I am the senior investigating officer in charge of this investigation. By all means remove me if you wish, but if you ever speak to me like that again in front of my team—'

Charlesworth raised his hand. 'You're quite right, of course,' he said, his face flushed. 'That was unforgivable, and I apologise. My point stands though. Put some junior detectives on it, by all means, but it should not be *your* focus. We've had this conversation before.'

'Mercer was killed because of—'

'Something he saw at Emma's funeral. We know, Nick,' said Potter.

Maybe they were going to try good cop, bad cop this time?

'Or someone,' Dixon said.

'We get it.' Charlesworth leaned back in his chair. 'Look, media interest in this case is growing fast, and I've asked our head of corporate communications to organise a joint press conference with the Gloucestershire force as soon as possible. It would be nice if we had something to tell them.'

Vicky Thomas was going up in the world. Press officer to head of corporate communications. Still, giving her a posh new job title was better than a pay rise.

'You are the SIO,' continued Charlesworth. 'And you have my absolute confidence.'

'We just struggle to see where you're going with this one,' said Potter. 'That's all.'

'And, whether you know it or not, you've staked your reputation on it.'

A knock, then the door opened slowly.

'Excuse me, Sir,' said Sarah, poking her head around the door.

They must have drawn lots for it, thought Dixon.

'You really need to see this, I'm afraid,' she said, holding a piece of paper towards Dixon in her outstretched hand.

'What is it?' demanded Charlesworth.

Dixon was staring at the photograph, printed in colour, the paper curled at the edges under the weight of the ink.

'When was it taken?'

'The last few minutes. Mark Pearce just emailed it over. They think the painting was done overnight, but it's only just been spotted. There's a puddle of red paint on the carriageway underneath it too. Mark's gone back to the CCTV Hub to see if he can see anything.'

Dixon slid the photograph across the table to Charlesworth and Potter.

'Send a copy to Petersen, the Bristol pathologist, will you. Ask him if he can see a corresponding injury on Seb Cook.'

'Yes, Sir,' replied Sarah.

The door closed behind her as silently as it had opened.

'Where is this?' asked Charlesworth.

'The M32. Junction 3,' replied Dixon. He had stood on the exact spot the night before. 'It's a CCTV blind spot.'

'Bloody well would be, wouldn't it,' said Charlesworth. A stencil; probably wouldn't have taken more than a couple of minutes. Reaching down through the railings even, spraying it upside down, although the artist could have climbed over; a harness and short length of rope, a couple of slings perhaps, to avoid the fall on to the motorway below. 'I'm guessing it's supposed to be Cook.'

Dixon resisted the temptation to award him this week's prize for 'stating the bleeding obvious'.

A black and white image stencilled on the road bridge, visible only from cars on the carriageway directly below: a man falling – a dash of colour, blood red, on his forehead.

Chapter Twenty-Three

'What did they want?' asked Jane, when Dixon walked back along the landing. The door of the meeting room had closed behind him, so no doubt his ears would be burning for the next few minutes.

'Usual crap,' he said, still staring at the printed picture.

'Sebastian Cook's death message. Makes you wonder why there hasn't been one for Barry Mercer, doesn't it?'

Jane had made a good point and, at face value, it was telling evidence his murder wasn't connected to the others. It was a good job Potter and Charlesworth hadn't tumbled to it as well. 'Get on to the Environment Agency, will you. Get them to keep an eye out at pumping stations, bridges and sluices. Tell them to ring us if they spot any new graffiti.'

'Here's a copy of the first part of Emma's thesis,' Jane said, dropping a wad of paper half an inch thick on the table Dixon was sitting on. 'I've copied her research material too. Her photos are on a flash drive High Tech sent over; too many to print off. Ink's expensive, apparently.'

'Have you had a look at them?'

'Couldn't see anything, to be honest. There's a whole folder of street artists at work. I checked them against the Van Gards that have been authenticated on his website and there are no images of anyone painting one of them.'

'That would've been too easy.'

'No news of Evie yet.'

Dixon wasn't entirely sure whether Jane was asking him or telling him. Either way, she was right.

'I've got the flash drive in my computer,' she continued, 'if you want to have a look.'

'Lou thinks I'm barking up the wrong tree,' Dixon said, watching for her head popping up from behind a computer.

'I say go with your gut. You've never been wrong before.'

'Let's have a look at these photos then.'

Jane was standing behind Dixon, watching him click on the photographs one by one. 'What's in her thesis?' he asked.

'Nothing really. The draft is the old stuff, don't forget. She was getting on to contemporary street art this year.'

'And her research?'

'Old news articles on graffiti, Upfest stuff, documents and posters copied off the web. A couple of ebooks on the Bristol street scene. Nothing exciting.' She leaned over his shoulder, pointing at the screen. 'That's a Van Gard,' she said. 'On the side of the container. Done in May this year, according to his website.'

A three dimensional open window stencilled on the side of the rusting yellow shipping container, a child dressed in rags gazing out; a single tear the splash of red this time.

'It's called *Housing Crisis*,' continued Jane.

'And where is it now?'

'In an art gallery in Edinburgh. The container sold at auction for eight hundred thousand, and they just cut it out.'

'Mast data's in, Sir,' shouted Sarah from a workstation on the other side of the room. 'I've forwarded you the email.'

'What does it say?' At least four people in unison.

'No match, I'm afraid. None of the mobile phone numbers we checked pinged any of the masts close to Emma's on the night of her . . . on the night she died, or junction 3 on the M32.'

A walk on the beach with his dog would've been good right about now. Some time to think. It was not the news he had been hoping for, and it couldn't have come at a worse time, what with Charlesworth and Potter still in the building.

One last throw of the dice.

Dixon opened a web browser on Jane's computer. 'What's his website address?'

'Van Gard dot com,' replied Jane. 'Hyphenated.'

He clicked on 'Authenticated artwork' and scrolled down through the thumbnail images, clicking on the shipping container. '*Housing Crisis*, Avonmouth Docks, seventeenth May, four a.m.; unsigned stencil,' said Dixon, reading aloud. 'So, you've watched enough TV to know we can trace a mobile phone signal, and you leave your phone at home when committing a murder. Right?'

'I would,' replied Sarah.

'You might not leave your phone at home if you're going out to paint the side of a shipping container.' Dixon stretched his shoulders, his hands behind his head. 'The owner sure as hell won't complain, so you're unlikely to find yourself on the wrong end of a criminal damage charge, are you? Run the numbers again, Sarah, and let's see if any of them pinged the masts at Avonmouth Docks in the early hours of seventeenth May. Try that installation at the model village too.'

'Check everybody?' asked Jane. 'Again.'

'All of them.'

'But isn't Van Gard supposed to be male?'

'We don't know that for sure.'

'We won't get them back till the morning now,' she replied. 'It's nearly nine as it is.'

'You go. Get some rest and be back here by eight. All of you. Get some rest.'

'What about you?'

'I've got some reading to do.'

Dixon parked in the car park of the Red Cow, opposite the cottage, hoping the rumble of his diesel engine wouldn't wake Jane. At least Monty was with her parents, so there'd be no barking to herald his arrival home. Shame that, though; it was a clear night and perfect for a walk up Brent Knoll.

The pub was closed and he'd be long gone before it opened the following day anyway, not that Rob would mind him using their car park.

It was just after two in the morning and the streetlights had long since gone off. It had been a long night, spent catching up with the multitude of statements that had been taken and logged on the system, Roger Poland's post mortem report on Barry Mercer, CCTV clips, Scientific Services reports. He'd flicked through Emma Carpenter's thesis too, not that he didn't trust Jane; it was just his way.

Read everything.

Updating the Policy Log had taken longer than usual. Or rather he'd taken more care over it than usual, the knowledge that it might come back to bite him all too front and centre this time.

There had been umpteen statements at the Gloucestershire end of things too, sightings that had been followed up, grainy traffic camera footage to watch. Evie Clarke was still out there somewhere, and a late telephone call to her parents had not been easy. No need to apologise, they said. They hadn't slept since she'd gone missing and were unlikely to do so until she came home. The doctor had prescribed some sleeping tablets but they had no intention of taking them.

Her mother remained convinced that Evie was still alive, though, and that was good enough for Dixon.

Barking up the wrong tree was a thought, all the same.

The light came on in the kitchen before he had even slid his key into the back door lock.

'What time d'you call this?' demanded Jane, opening the door, leaving him holding his key in mid-air. 'You'll be no bloody good to anyone if you don't get some sleep.'

'What about you?'

'I waited up for you.' She took his hand and pressed it to her abdomen. 'I felt her kick.'

'Her?'

'Just a feeling I get.'

◆ ◆ ◆

Home by two; back at Express Park by eight. Jane had driven, leaving Dixon to eat his toast in peace, sitting in the passenger seat. There wasn't even a dog in the back this time, pestering him for a crust with Marmite on it.

'Monty's fine,' Jane had said, spotting him glancing over his shoulder. 'Dad said he's going to take him to the beach later.'

'Tell him—'

'I've told him to watch out for other dogs, and to keep him on the long line. Don't worry.'

Monty was soft as a mop, it was just that he didn't look it. Anything but, and other dogs seemed to want to try their luck from time to time; even the smallest of terriers. Still, Jane's adopted father was up to the task.

It had been a short night, and a night of questions. Lying awake, staring at the ceiling, listening to Jane's breathing, their heads on the same pillow. This time next week they'd be husband and wife. It would have been nice to have had a moment to enjoy it, instead of being thrown into a multiple murder investigation. And he hadn't dared mention what might have to happen if it wasn't over before the big day.

Jane knew the score, though.

The questions had come thick and fast, all of them without answers. Yet. But the biggest one – the one that was still bugging him when he woke up – was why the death messages?

It was an assumption that they were death messages at all. They could conceivably be the work of some street artist trying to immortalise the scene. Maybe even someone who knew Emma and Slime Zee?

Bollocks.

If that was right, why paint the separate pair of hands administering Emma's injection, and why paint the blood on Seb Cook's head as he fell? No, someone was sending a message.

Either to help, or to taunt. But which was it?

'Someone from PSD has been on the prowl, Sir,' said Sarah, when Dixon walked into the incident room.

'What the hell do they want at this time in the morning?' hissed Jane.

'Trying to catch us off guard,' replied Dixon.

'They were after the files Mark requested from Fishponds. I pleaded ignorance.' Sarah looked sheepish.

'Telling porkies to PSD already. You'll go far,' said Louise, with a wink.

'Thank you.'

'Have we heard from Mark?' asked Dixon.

'He's staying up in Gloucester,' replied Louise. 'A couple of sightings of Evie, but nothing concrete.'

'And where are the files from Fishponds?'

'I stuffed them in the bottom of that filing cabinet, Sir,' Sarah said, enjoying the moment. 'There are only six. Thin ones, all traffic cases; a couple of drink driving, a causing death by dangerous driving, a hit and run that turned out to be deliberate so it ended up as a GBH – that's the thickest file – drug driving and taking without consent.'

The movement was sharp, Sarah snatching the phone off her desk almost before it rang. 'Give me a sec,' she said, placing her hand over the receiver. 'Environment Agency, Sir. New graffiti on the side of the pumping station at Midelney.'

'Tell them we're on our way.'

'I'll go,' said Jane, talking over Sarah.

'They'll leave the gate open by the bridge,' said Sarah, ringing off. 'Turn left and follow the access road.'

'I need you here, Jane, please,' Dixon said, turning for the door. 'Lou, chase up the new mobile phone data, will you?'

Louise sat back with a heavy sigh.

'Sarah, with me.'

'Why me?' asked Sarah, when she eventually summoned up the courage to say something. Dixon hadn't thought he was that intimidating, but had welcomed the silence anyway; a chance to think.

'Jane's running the incident room.'

'What about Louise?'

'You took the call.'

Left on to the gravel access road, a river parallel to them, down a steep bank, murky water overflowing on to the fields on the far bank. The concrete and glass block of the Midelney pumping station just visible in a clump of trees ahead as Dixon weaved along the track to avoid the water-filled potholes, not that he needed to bother in a Land Rover.

'My father used to bring my brother fishing out here when he was younger,' said Sarah.

'What about you?'

'My mum used to take me to netball, even though I hated it.'

The fields on the left were flooded too, trees sticking out of the water like the mast and rigging of a sunken yacht. Dixon had seen one of those the last time he'd visited Burnham Yacht Club, only this time the water was a foot deep; up to the first rung on the five bar gate. No cattle either, so the farmer had had plenty of warning.

Over the bridge, and he parked under the trees next to the Environment Agency van.

The steel door of the pumping station was open, a man in a blue coat sitting at a control panel inside visible through the large windows. Sitting eight or ten feet above the water, the pumps were silent, the water calm but for a light wind-driven ripple.

'Hello?'

'Police is it,' said the man, swivelling round on what looked more like a bar stool.

'Yes.'

'Crikey, that was quick. It was all day before one of your lot came when Huish Episcopi was broken into. And it's a Saturday.'

Dixon thought it best not to tell him that burglary non-residential was just about the lowest of low priorities. Right down there with graffiti, although that had changed in the last couple of days. 'What've we got?' he asked.

'A detective chief inspector.' The man was scrutinising Dixon's warrant card. 'You must think it's serious then.'

'I won't know until I see it.'

'This way.'

They followed the man back out of the control room and across the walkway above the water. 'We switch the pumps off when the spillway starts to flood,' said the man. 'It looks pretty alarming, but those fields are supposed to go first. Protects everything else.'

That explained the absence of livestock.

'The weather forecast's good, so it'll soon drop.'

It looked like a carport on the side of the pumping station, and appeared to serve no useful purpose – not one that Dixon could see anyway, except as a blank canvas, perhaps.

'We had a message to check for graffiti, and when I went for a walk around, there it was. It's on the outside wall.'

'How long's it been there?' asked Dixon.

'No idea. Could've been there months, I suppose. We're only seeing it now because the stinging nettles are dying back. I certainly don't remember seeing it before,' he said, standing back to admire the image, his hands on his hips.

Someone trying to help, or someone trying to taunt the police . . .

'Looks like you were right, Sir,' said Sarah.

Stencilled in black on the light grey wall, a severed right foot, shoe still on, the splash of colour this time blood dripping from the stump as it stamped on a camera with a zoom lens. There were even shards of broken glass from the lens flying through the air painted on to the weathered breeze block wall.

The image was small, no more than three feet high, partially hidden behind a clump of dying stinging nettles. Dixon brushed the nettles aside, revealing a trickle of red paint running down the wall to a puddle on the ground, underneath the severed foot.

'Have you seen anyone loitering around the pumping station?' asked Dixon.

'Not really. There's usually a bloke fishing out on the Parrett. Looked like he was dead baiting for pike when I saw him yesterday. He's always here – more often than I am – and may have seen someone. It's a popular spot. He's got a green Daihatsu Fourtrak and parks in the lay-by out on the lane. I've seen it before, and there's a PACGB sticker in the back window, so it must've been him.' He added, 'Pike Anglers' Club of Great Britain,' in response to Sarah's frown.

'What's that drain down there?' asked Dixon, pointing to the water underneath the pumping station. It wasn't flowing, so he assumed it was a drain rather than a river.

'The Southmoor Main Drain. That's what we pump into. You drove out along the River Isle, and that meets the Parrett over there about fifty yards.'

Dixon looked down into the water. On the other side of the pumping station it had been murky and flowing fast. This side it was gin clear and deep. Too deep to see the bottom.

Any doubt that Barry Mercer's murder was connected to the murders of Emma Carpenter and Sebastian Cook had gone. It was his foot – his missing foot – stamping on his own camera.

Not that Dixon had doubted it for a minute, but others had. Plenty of them.

'We'd better get Scientific Services down here, Sarah. And the dive team.'

'Yes, Sir.'

'When will you be switching the pumps back on?' Dixon asked, turning to the man from the Environment Agency.

'I was just setting the timer now to bring them on at midnight for the high tide.'

Dixon shook his head. 'I have reason to believe there might be human remains—'

'I'll need to ring my supervisor in that case.'

'You do that.'

Dixon watched the man scurry off across the walkway towards the control room, as he slid his phone out of his jacket pocket. He took a photograph of the stencilled image and sent it to Jane, then tapped out a follow-up text message:

Barry Mercer's death message.

'Delivered' changed to 'Read' almost immediately, but there was no speech bubble. Then his phone rang.

'You were right then,' said Jane.

'About Mercer, yes.'

'Are you getting the dive team out?'

'Sarah's doing it now.'

'We've had the mobile phone results back and there's a hit. I'm sending the list over to you now.'

'List?'

'Well, I say *list*, there's only one number on it; it's hitting masts at both sites, perfectly triangulated each time – the model village and Avonmouth Docks.'

'Do we know whose number it is?'

'You do.'

Chapter Twenty-Four

'Enjoy the ride, she said.' Sarah was smiling to herself in the passenger seat of Dixon's Land Rover as they cruised past the block of flats in Clifton.

'Who said?'

'The chief super.'

'Chase up Scientific Services. They need to be here, ready to go in as soon as we pick him up,' said Dixon, pulling up around the corner.

'Yes, Sir.'

It was a large double-fronted block with bay windows overlooking the Downs, and a grand flight of steps up to a communal front door. Dixon had counted four buzzers as they drove past; large flats, then. Stone cornicing, hidden from the road by a high hedge that didn't offer much of a screen in the depths of winter.

Dixon hadn't had a chance to get a look at the cars in the gravelled car park at the front of the block, apart from the white Tesla that was plugged into a socket on the wall at the side of the steps.

'Scientific are five minutes away,' said Sarah, sliding her phone into her pocket. 'They're bringing the search warrant.'

'That's near enough.' A three-point turn and Dixon parked across the driveway, blocking the cars in. Two Teslas at the end, an Audi and a Mercedes.

'Don't we need someone covering the back?' asked Sarah. 'There'll be a fire escape. There must be.'

'You've been watching too much TV,' said Dixon, his index finger on the buzzer. 'We're not arresting him, just bringing him in for a chat, helping us with our enquiries.'

The Entryphone crackled into life. 'Yes.' A woman's voice.

'Mrs Ratcliffe?'

'Yes. Who is it?' Impatient.

'Detective Chief Inspector Dixon. I was hoping to have a chat with your husband.'

'You again. We're about to eat.'

'I have a dead student, a dead former student, and a missing student.'

'Of course, sorry. You'd better come in.'

Sarah was already holding the door, ready for when the lock buzzed.

Dixon resisted the temptation to take the stairs two at a time, conscious that Malcolm Ratcliffe was leaning over the balustrade above them watching them climb up towards him.

'How can I help?' he asked, when Dixon and Sarah arrived on the landing. His brow was furrowed; genuine concern, clearly.

'We'd rather talk inside, if that's all right.'

'Yes, this way.'

It was more of an apartment than a flat. Plush carpets and rugs, a selection of paintings hanging on the walls in the large hallway; oil paintings in gilt frames mounted next to street art in metal frames, the contrast striking.

Dixon and Sarah followed Ratcliffe into the living room, Dixon walking over to the bay window and looking out across the Downs. The last time he had seen them had been in the dark, being carried across the open ground to a waiting ambulance. Still, at least Jane had been allowed to walk by the stretcher, holding his hand, a set of body armour with a crossbow bolt sticking out of it in her other hand.

He turned away from the window – it never did to dwell on these things – just as the Entryphone buzzed again. 'That'll be our Scientific Services team, Mr Ratcliffe,' he said. 'If you would be so kind as to let them in. They're here to execute a search warrant.'

'A search warrant?' Bristling now. 'Am I under arrest?'

'No, Sir,' replied Dixon. 'We were hoping you would accompany us to the station voluntarily, where you will be interviewed under caution.'

'What the hell does that mean?' asked Wendy Ratcliffe. She had taken up position in the doorway of the living room, and Dixon wasn't entirely sure whether it was to keep an eye on him or on her husband. 'What's he done?'

'We're not sure that he's done anything, Mrs Ratcliffe. We just need him to answer some questions.'

Dixon was taking in the room: an old leather Chesterfield in front of the fire, armchairs either side. Nothing modern about it, except perhaps the television, but even that was in a walnut display cabinet.

'At the police station?' The colour draining from Ratcliffe's face.

'Yes, Sir.'

'Which one?'

'Bridgwater.'

'And what questions? You suspect me of something, so what am I supposed to have done?'

'It is my belief, Sir, that you are the anonymous artist known as Van Gard.'

'Don't say anything, Malcolm.' Wendy stepped forward and took her husband's hand. 'You're not under arrest. You don't have to say anything at all.'

'Is that right?' he asked.

'If you don't come with us voluntarily then you will leave me with no alternative but to arrest you.'

'What about my solicitor?'

'You will be entitled to have your solicitor present when you are interviewed.'

'Interviewed?'

'Under caution, as I said.'

Ratcliffe sat down on the arm of the sofa. 'I might as well go voluntarily then, if you're going to arrest me if I don't. Can I ring my solicitor?'

'Go ahead. Ask him to meet you at Express Park. You'll be there in about an hour.'

The buzzer again, on the wall out in the hall.

'I'll go,' said Sarah.

Four uniformed officers accompanied Donald Watson into the hallway, large aluminium cases dropped on the rug.

'Here's the warrant,' said a uniformed officer, handing a brown envelope to Dixon.

'These officers will accompany you to Express Park, Mr Ratcliffe.' Dixon handed him the search warrant. 'Your solicitor may wish to see that as well.'

'And what am I supposed to do while all this is going on?' demanded Wendy.

'You're welcome to stay, or perhaps you have a friend nearby you could visit?'

'I'll stay.'

Watson waited until Ratcliffe had been led away, Mrs Ratcliffe darting into the kitchen to switch off the oven. 'What exactly are we looking for?' he asked, making sure his voice didn't carry beyond the open door.

'Evidence that Malcolm Ratcliffe is the artist known as Van Gard. Emma Carpenter, Seb Cook and Evie Clarke were all actively engaged in an attempt to reveal his identity.'

'And he killed them to keep them quiet?'

'Yes.'

'What about Mercer?'

'He saw Ratcliffe at Emma's funeral.'

'So what?' Watson was standing on one leg, pulling on a set of overalls. 'You'd expect to see her tutor at her funeral, wouldn't you?' Watson straightened up, smirking at Dixon. 'You're barking up the wrong tree this time.'

'He obviously hasn't seen the side of the pumping station, Sir,' whispered Sarah.

'Let's just concentrate on the search, shall we,' said Dixon. 'And let's make sure we check behind all the paintings for a safe. All right?'

Dixon started in Ratcliffe's office, the furniture modern and minimalist: glass desk, chrome and black leather chair, the art on the walls all contemporary. Nothing by Van Gard, but then that was to be expected, perhaps. A small glass corner display cabinet was mounted on the wall at head height, various trophies and cups front and centre: cycling, a martial art of some sort, there was even a Ten Tors medal. Dixon had one of those somewhere.

Sarah was lifting the paintings and photographs off the wall one by one, peering behind them before replacing each carefully. 'Here we go,' she said, lifting a painting off the hook and leaning it up against the wall at her feet. 'Here's your safe.'

Small, with a combination lock.

'Go and ask Mrs Ratcliffe if she knows the code, will you?'

Dixon picked up the painting that the safe had been hidden behind. Pastel, possibly, or acrylic, not that Dixon was an expert; a painting of a red panda's head, paint trails trickling to the bottom of the canvas like blood. A casual glance and you'd be forgiven for thinking the animal's head had been severed. Maybe that was the impression the artist was after?

Nice.

'She said she didn't know it was there,' offered Sarah, unaware that Wendy was following right behind her.

'That's because I didn't know it was there,' she snapped. 'And I've always hated that painting. It's by a lecturer at the college, Trudy Lister. They were students together for a time; she was doing her finals when he was in his first year – something like that anyway. I can't begin to imagine what she was thinking of, it's revolting. I refused to have it in the gallery.'

'Get a message to the car Mr Ratcliffe's travelling in, see if he'll give us the code,' said Dixon. He was standing behind the desk, opening the drawers of a small steel cabinet, nothing much catching his eye. He reached into the top drawer and took out an old Swiss Army knife.

'Let me, Sir,' said Sarah, snatching the knife out of his hand. 'I saw this on a TV programme once, one of those American true crime things on Netflix. There was a case where a code was etched on to the blade of one of these.' She opened the blade. 'Oh.'

'Just ring the car.'

'Yes, Sir.'

Dixon was standing in the kitchen staring at a row of twelve small hooks with bunches of keys, carefully labelled, hanging on them, when Sarah reappeared. 'He gave us the code, Sir, and Mr Watson opened the safe.' She paused, before delivering the punchline: 'There's nothing in it.'

'Nothing at all?'

'No. Empty.'

'Where's Mrs Ratcliffe?'

'She was in their bedroom – keeping an eye on the Scientific lads, I think.'

'Get her, will you.'

He was still staring at the bunches of keys when Wendy appeared in the doorway.

'Talk me through all these keys, please, Mrs Ratcliffe,' said Dixon. 'What are they for?'

'They're clearly marked.'

'Not all of them.'

'Really?' She took the set down off the first hook. 'These are the keys to our holiday cottage in Padstow. And these are the spares,' she said, sliding another bunch off the adjacent hook. 'It's let out and we haven't been for years.' She pointed at the next two sets. 'These are spare car keys, mine and Malcolm's.' Then another. 'This is the garage. We've each got one of those on our car keys as well. It's electric.'

'What about this one?'

'That's the basement. It's communal and the gas and electricity meters are down there.' She shuddered. 'Malcolm always does the readings. I won't go down there.'

'And this one?' Dixon lifted a single key off a hook. It had been hung on the rack underneath the jumble of basement keys, a single key on a split ring. Small and without a label.

'I've got no idea what that one's for,' she said, frowning. 'I've never seen it before.'

Chapter Twenty-Five

Standing room only in the video suite, apparently, all eyes fixed on the feed from interview room 1; not that they didn't have better things they could and should be doing.

Trevor Crosby from Fords had driven down from Bristol; Dixon thought it best not to mention he had been offered his job. Almost.

The wording of the police caution had come as no surprise to Ratcliffe, either that or he was a good poker player. It was a shame, really. '. . . harm your defence . . .' and '. . . later rely on in court . . .' usually got a rise, but not this time.

'This interview is being audio and visually recorded on to a secure digital hard drive. Identify yourself for the recording, please.'

'Malcolm Fitzpatrick Ratcliffe.'

'Trevor Crosby, partner in the firm of Fords Solicitors, representing Mr Ratcliffe.'

'Detective Constable Louise Willmott.'

'And I am Detective Chief Inspector Nicholas Dixon.'

At least they'd got the interview room with the table.

'Now then, Malcolm,' continued Dixon. 'We have some questions—'

'Let me stop you there,' interrupted Crosby. 'I have had the opportunity of discussing the matter in detail with my client, and he is prepared to cooperate fully with your investigation on the strict understanding that, in doing so, he is allowing you to process his highly sensitive personal data. I am instructed that should any of that personal data find its way into the public domain, I am to commence High Court proceedings against the Avon and Somerset Constabulary and to pursue those proceedings vigorously and to the full extent of the law.'

Dixon thought he could hear Charlesworth throwing up his lunch next door.

'But, let's be clear,' continued Crosby. 'We're talking about leaks. If any of what my client reveals in this interview finds its way into the newspapers, you – by which I mean the police – will be held responsible.'

'Let's cut to the chase, then,' Dixon said, turning to Ratcliffe. 'Malcolm, are you the artist commonly known as Van Gard.'

'Yes.'

Time for Dixon to act the poker player and wipe that self-satisfied smirk off Crosby's face. He'd known it was coming anyway; that much was clear from Crosby's little opening speech. 'Good, well, that saves us a lot of time, doesn't it?' He dropped the single key on the table in front of Ratcliffe. 'Tell me about this key.'

'I've got one of the railway arches at Bedminster, third one along. I use it for storage and it's my studio.'

'And what will we find there?'

'A van with a moped in the back. Spray paints, stencils.' Ratcliffe folded his arms. 'The sort of stuff you'd expect to find in an artist's studio, I suppose.'

'How long have you been operating under the name Van Gard?'

'Twenty years.'

'How many people know your identity?'

'A handful, no more than that. Trusted friends.'

Dixon waited.

'My wife. Trudy Lister, of course. A couple of street artists who help me out from time to time.'

'What with?'

Ratcliffe raised himself up in his chair. 'Logistics, mainly. I needed a diversion at the model village, so they kicked off on the other side. That sort of thing.'

'Names?'

'I have advised my client not to reveal the names of the street artists who know his identity,' said Crosby. 'It cannot possibly be relevant to your investigation.'

'Where were you on the night of—'

'My client has previously given details of his whereabouts at the relevant times, and it is my understanding that those details have been checked and verified by the police in the course of your investigation.'

'"Trudy Lister, of course",' said Dixon with a hint of sarcasm.

'My wife knows, if that's what you're asking.'

Dixon slid a photograph across the table. 'Do you recognise this?' he asked.

'It's not one of mine,' said Ratcliffe. 'Yes, it's a stencil, but the shading is very clumsy.'

'What do you think it's a picture of? I'll give you a clue – it appeared on the side of the toilet block at Brean in the days after Emma Carpenter's death.'

'I guess it's supposed to be Emma Carpenter then, isn't it?'

'Perhaps I can clarify one thing,' said Crosby, sitting up. 'Malcolm, how many street artists are out there now using stencils?'

'It's very common. When I started there were a few others, a handful maybe, but I was the only one doing it commercially; loads of people have jumped on the bandwagon now.'

'Explain this to me then, Malcolm.' Dixon leaned forward over the table. 'Emma is actively looking to reveal your identity as part of her thesis, a thesis that you've seen and are aware of, and then the next thing is she's dead. You can imagine what I'm thinking, can't you?'

'There have been loads of attempts to unmask me over the years and none of them got close. There was even a TV documentary done by an old student and she never worked it out. Journalists too. What are you suggesting, that I killed them all? I think you'll find they're still alive, if you'd care to check. And I thought Emma's death was an accident anyway.'

'What about Seb Cook's then? He was thrown from the bridge over the M32.' Dixon slid another image across the table. 'This is a still taken from CCTV at the scene. It shows an individual we'd very much like to speak to in connection with Seb's murder, walking away in the direction of Lower Easton.'

'Not me. I was with Trudy. I've already told you.'

'Do you own a hoodie?'

'I own a coat with a hood.'

'And this.' Another photograph. 'This is a painting that appeared on the bridge later that same night.'

'My client has already said there are any number of artists out there using stencils. There is nothing unique in that style.'

'When was the last time you visited the Cotswolds?' asked Dixon, changing tack.

'I went to a hotel with Trudy last year. Well, I say hotel, it was more of a pub, really. The Mermaid at Burford.'

'Which just happens to be the pub where Evie worked during her holidays.'

'It's a small world, and Trudy and I went last November, during the term time.'

'When you went to Emma's funeral, do you remember a van parked in the lay-by on the main road?'

'Not really. Trudy and I went in my car to the crem. After that we went back to Emma's house for the funeral tea and then came home. We weren't there long.'

'There was a private detective in that van, keeping a neighbour under surveillance. Then next thing is he disappears, and six months later we're fishing his remains out of the Tone.'

'I'm sorry, I really don't see what this has got to do with me.' Ratcliffe's eyes darted to his solicitor, seeking reassurance.

'His name was Barry Mercer, and his right foot is still missing,' said Dixon, sliding a photograph of the painting on the side of the pumping station across the table. 'What d'you make of that?'

Ratcliffe studied the picture in front of him. 'It's a foot stamping on a camera, but I did *not* paint it, and I did *not* kill him, whoever he was. I was with Trudy the whole time at the funeral. There'll be CCTV, I expect, and you can check the traffic cameras too. We went on the M5 and came back that way as well.'

'Do you have anything else to put to my client?' asked Crosby.

'You use an offshore company, I think,' replied Dixon. 'In the Cayman Islands?'

'I have advised my client not to discuss his financial arrangements. They cannot possibly be relevant to your investigation, and they are both perfectly legal and above board, as well as being private. If needs be, we can supply details in due course.'

'In that case, I am suspending this interview at three-twenty-four, pending further enquiries.'

'What further enquiries?' demanded Crosby.

'We need to check the movements of your client's van and moped for a start, and search his studio.'

'And in the meantime, he is free to leave?'

'If your client tries to leave, Mr Crosby, he will be arrested and detained, but he's cooperating fully, isn't he, so that won't be necessary, will it?'

◆ ◆ ◆

'Well, that was bloody marvellous,' said Charlesworth, cornering Dixon and Louise in the corridor outside the interview room. 'You've proved he's Van Gard, but what good's that? If it gets in the papers, he's going to sue us.'

'He'd need to prove the leak came from us.'

'They usually do, don't they? Police stations leak like sieves.'

'But he'd need to prove it, Sir, which is a very different thing from thinking it probably did.'

'It's not as if it's taken us much further, is it? You can't prove he's done anything wrong at all.' Charlesworth was getting hotter under the collar. 'If you're not careful, we'll find ourselves on the wrong end of a wrongful arrest claim as well.'

'He's not under arrest, Sir,' replied Dixon, opening the swing door and heading for the lift.

He waited until the lift doors closed behind Louise. 'If you've got anything to say, now's your chance.'

'Do you want to be there when we search his railway arch?'

'No.'

'I'll get them checking the cameras for his van and moped then.'

'And I want a forensic gait analysis done. There'll be footage of him walking in here, and we can compare it to the CCTV footage we've got from the night Seb Cook was killed.'

'That sounds a bit like clutching at straws.'

'More like a last throw of the dice, but we need to know if he's lying, don't we.'

◆ ◆ ◆

Dixon was sitting in the corner of the canteen, enjoying a late lunch – although 'enjoying' was probably the wrong word; a grated Red Leicester cheese baguette was all they had left. Actually, 'hiding' was probably a better word too: *hiding* in the corner of the canteen.

He hadn't been ready to jump, but the disappearance of Evie Clarke had changed everything. It had left him with two choices. Keep digging, however long it took, and hope he made the breakthrough in time to save her, or jump in with both feet and hope for the best. Even if some people did think he was barking up the wrong tree.

Actually, that was wrong too. 'Some people' was more like 'everyone except Jane'.

He makes things happen was a phrase he'd heard more than once. His old boss Peter Lewis had used it, and it had come up again at the promotion board, an interviewer quoting from his personnel file. Only it didn't seem to be working this time.

Things were happening. People were dying and pictures were being painted on walls, but Dixon felt like a rabbit caught in headlights – one that panics and runs in the wrong direction.

'There you are,' said Jane, sitting down next to him. 'Lou got hold of someone at Oxford and emailed over the footage. A detailed analysis will take several days but they said they'd have a look at it and ring you. Where's your phone?'

Dixon slid it out of his jacket pocket and placed it on the table in front of Jane.

'Were you watching the interview?' he asked.

'You're close, and it'll turn out you're closer than you know.'

'How's Monty?'

'Fine,' replied Jane, sliding his phone towards him when it started buzzing on the table. 'You'd better get that.'

'Dixon.'

'Professor Anne Tideswell speaking. I was asked to review some footage and ring you.'

'Yes, thank you.'

'Have you used forensic gait analysis before?'

'Yes.' A long time ago in London and Dixon hadn't been the SIO, but she didn't need to know that.

'It's about comparison, one person's walk compared to another, which is presumably why you sent me the two clips?'

'It is.'

'Well, look, I'm not sure if this is good or bad news, but they're not the same person.'

Jane was leaning over, listening to both sides of the conversation.

'How sure are you?' he asked.

'Quite sure. The gaits are very different – to the trained eye that is, mind you. The man walking along the corridor has good movement in both lower legs and his feet spring equally into the forward step. Not so the character on the CCTV footage. There's no spring from his right lower leg at all. He masks it well with a kick of the knee, and you'd be hard pressed to notice it at a casual glance.'

'And what does that tell you?'

'Ideally I'd need to see him walking towards the camera, or left to right rather than right to left, especially as it's his right leg, but I'd say it's prosthetic.'

Chapter Twenty-Six

'A prosthetic leg?' Charlesworth seemed to be hopping from one foot to the other in sympathy. 'You've got him then. That lad from the car breaker's?'

'Jane's gone to pick him up,' replied Dixon, trying to edge past him and get to the canteen before it closed.

'You don't sound terribly optimistic, if I may say so.'

'He may have had motive to kill Barry Mercer, but what about the others?' Dixon was looking over Charlesworth's shoulder at the double doors of the Professional Standards Department, opening slowly. 'I'm getting him in because it would be negligent not to. Check his alibis, tick the boxes, move on.'

Carlisle had picked his moment with care, clearly not prepared to tackle Dixon without a referee on hand. Charlesworth was probably in on it too, given that he didn't even bother to turn around at the sound of Carlisle's approaching footsteps. Orchestrated then; a pincer movement.

Gits.

'Dixon, I was after the files you've had down from Fishponds, the ones Barry Mercer and Dave Harding worked on together.' Carlisle was hovering behind Charlesworth, using him as a human shield, possibly.

Jane would've told Dixon to take a deep breath and count to ten right about now.

Fuck that.

'They're material evidence in a multiple murder investigation and you can't have them.' A suitable pause, followed by a 'Sir' loaded with sarcasm.

An audience had gathered on the landing below, outside the canteen, all of them looking up, expecting to see fists flying, probably.

'Now then, chaps,' said Charlesworth. 'There was something else you wanted to say to Nick, I think, Marcus.'

'Yes, well, I . . .'

Carlisle was shifting from one foot to the other now.

'I just wanted to say it was nothing personal.'

'Bollocks.' Definitely no count of ten before that one. But Dixon remembered only too well the glee on Carlisle's face, and that of his sidekick, Larkin, when they had arrested him for murder. The smirks. 'You had a DCI in your sights; it was like watching Traffic when they pull over a Ferrari, all their Christmases come at once.'

'Now, steady on.'

'Well, all's well that ends well, Nick.' Charlesworth was doing his best.

'Look, I need those files,' said Carlisle.

'You can have copies,' said Dixon, turning for the stairs at the far end of the landing. 'I'll get them sent over in the morning.'

Jane and Sarah were sitting opposite Ben Clifford in interview room 1 by the time Dixon sat down in the video suite to watch the feed and eat the rest of his baguette in peace. He was the only one there. Louise had wanted to watch it, but had been tasked with isolating footage of Clifford walking along the corridor, then emailing it to Anne Tideswell for gait comparison. Dixon wasn't optimistic. By the time the comparison had been completed, they'd have checked Clifford's alibis and excluded him from the investigation.

Mercifully, there was no one sitting next to Dixon to take a bet on it.

No lawyer, nothing to hide, apparently; Clifford's alibi was the same each time. He spent a lot of time with his girlfriend by all accounts, but then Dixon spent a lot of time with Jane, so he could hardly criticise a fellow for that. Cinema, pub; it wouldn't take long to check and then let him go.

Dixon had been doing a lot of that today. Ratcliffe had been let go a couple of hours earlier, his solicitor huffing and puffing about harassment on the way out. Dixon had politely reminded him that all three of the victims thus far were either current or former students of his client. No doubt Dixon would need to speak to him again, and if that was harassment, then so be it.

Or words to that effect.

He tapped out a text message and watched on the monitor as Jane picked up her phone off the table and read it. She understood. She always understood.

Picking up Monty. Will be on the beach. Gore Road.

◆　◆　◆

It was a section of old brick wall, just along from the lighthouse. Sometimes it was sticking out of the sand quite a bit, so you had to climb up on top of it. Other times it was deeper in the sand and you could just sit down. It depended on the tides.

Tonight it was almost covered. Dixon sat with his legs stretched out in front of him, heels digging into the soft sand.

He was watching Monty's white coat in the moonlight as the dog pottered along the lines of seaweed that had been washed up. He'd never been one of those dogs for whom life was one long buffet, but occasionally he ate something he shouldn't. Rarely sick though, which was a bonus in a rented cottage.

They'd parked at the end of Gore Road and walked along as far as the wreck on Berrow Beach before turning back.

Three dead, one missing, and all he'd achieved so far was unmasking an anonymous street artist.

The Gloucestershire force were doing all they could their end, according to Mark Pearce who was still up there; a missing person investigation by the numbers, and getting nowhere. High risk, threat to life, it made no difference.

Dixon was missing something. He knew that. Actually, it was bloody obvious for all to see. Yes, he'd made something happen, but it was the wrong thing, and it had got him precisely nowhere. It hadn't helped that the press had got hold of it. 'A forty-two-year-old man is helping police with their enquiries.'

That hadn't done much to calm Charlesworth's nerves either.

Several anguished phone calls with Evie Clarke's parents had followed, not that Dixon could tell them much; just that whoever it was had been released.

He slid his phone out of his pocket and scrolled through the images that he'd taken of the death messages. Emma Carpenter's, an unidentified pair of hands administering an injection, then Seb Cook falling on to the southbound M32 carriageway, and lastly Barry Mercer's missing right foot stamping on a camera.

Lastly, so far. And that was a good sign. It felt reasonable to assume that no death message for Evie Clarke meant she was still alive.

Painted by the same person – not very well, by all accounts – using stencils.

Deborah Potter had suggested getting a psychologist to look at them, but Dixon knew all he needed to know. Whoever it was thought that he or she couldn't be caught; or realised it was inevitable they would be and didn't care.

Taunting the police, possibly.

What more could a psychologist tell him?

A light emerged behind him from the dunes, Monty running towards it. Jane then, taking more care with where she placed her feet in the dark. Dixon must've trodden in God knows what.

'We let him go,' she said, sitting down on the wall next to Dixon. 'It's not Clifford.'

'Never thought it was.'

'How far did you walk?' she asked.

'The wreck and back.'

'Deborah Potter asked me to remind you about the press conference in the morning.' A hint of anxiety in Jane's voice. 'So, what happens now?'

'I've got another job interview on Monday afternoon,' replied Dixon. 'That firm in Yeovil.'

'You're not still going to that, surely?'

'Wills and probate.'

'You'll love that. Making wills for little old biddies, and winding up their estates when they've gone. For heaven's sake, ring and cancel it first thing Monday morning.'

'How far did you get with Barry Mercer?'

Jane's eyes were following Monty in the darkness. 'I thought you were pursuing the Van Gard angle?'

'I'm not exactly getting anywhere, am I?'

'It connects all the victims.'

'Mercer wasn't trying to expose Van Gard, was he?'

'Well, we're working our way through his surveillance files and have eliminated everybody we've spoken to so far.'

Dixon stood up, rummaging in his pocket for a dog poo bag. 'I got it wrong.'

'About Ratcliffe maybe, although we know he's Van Gard.'

'Not about Ratcliffe. He's in this thing up to his bloody neck, I just don't know how or why. Yet.'

'Really?'

'Yes, really.' Dixon was picking up shards of glass that were half buried in the sand and glinting in the moonlight. 'Plays havoc with dogs' paws, this bloody stuff. I do wish people would be more careful,' he said, dropping them in the bag.

'What were you wrong about?'

'Barry Mercer,' replied Dixon, shining the light on his phone at the sand in front of him. 'He wasn't killed because of someone he *saw* at Emma's funeral. It's more subtle than that. He was killed because of someone he *recognised* at Emma's funeral. The question is, how did he recognise them?'

'Welcome back.'

'Thank you.'

Chapter Twenty-Seven

Dixon arrived at Express Park just after six. A couple of hours' sleep on the sofa – at Jane's insistence – had been enough, and it meant he could get out of the cottage without waking her up; but not before he'd sneaked into their bedroom and switched her alarm off.

He was walking along the landing, watching for movement at the far end, lights on in the Professional Standards Department. At this time in the morning?

Maybe Mercer would be the key to unlocking this, he thought. He glanced down at Monty trotting along beside him, then up at the CCTV camera, and wondered how long it would be before the building manager was after him.

He'd not made much progress tackling it from the Bristol end – the street art end – so maybe a change of tack was called for.

Barry Mercer had recognised someone at Emma Carpenter's funeral. And that had got him killed.

The light on in the incident room turned out to be Sarah.

'Superintendent Carlisle was after those files again,' she said, filling the kettle. 'I've had a look at them and—'

'What did you tell him?'

'That they'd be going down to admin to be copied as soon as the office was open.'

'What are you doing in this early anyway?' Dixon asked.

'Couldn't sleep.'

There was a lot of it about.

'Leave that. It's not your job to make the tea.'

'Oh, right.' Sarah was watching Monty sniffing along the base of the units, looking for crumbs. 'So this is the famous Monty?'

'Famous?'

'He kept a search team at bay for hours, didn't he?'

That was another indignity Dixon had been trying to forget; languishing in a cell, officers executing a search warrant at his cottage. At least Jane had got Monty out before Armed Response had turned up.

'And he's supposed to have been the one who woke you up when the Albanians came calling,' continued Sarah. 'He's a legend.'

'That he is.' Dixon was filling two mugs. 'Sugar?'

'Er, no, thank you.'

'Talk to me about Barry Mercer,' said Dixon, placing a mug of tea on the desk in front of Sarah.

'Jane's probably the one to—'

'She's asleep.'

'Oh, right. Well, we've been working our way through his surveillance cases. Seriously boring. You'd think it would be interesting, wouldn't you? Fun, even, but it's not. Hours and hours watching someone, and the highlight of the day is catching them carrying a bag of shopping. I'm sure as hell not doing that when I leave the police.' She reached down and opened the bottom drawer of her workstation. 'I was having a look at these,' she said, dropping a small pile of thin files on the desk. 'They're the ones PSD are after, Dave Harding and Barry Mercer the investigating officers on all of them.'

'Anything interesting?'

'This one,' Sarah replied, picking up one of the thicker files – still no more than an inch – from the top of the pile. 'Causing death by dangerous driving.' She placed the file in Dixon's outstretched hand. 'The accident was in 2002 at junction 3 on the M32, and we've had a murder at junction 3 and a death message has appeared there. It may be a coincidence, I suppose.'

'We don't believe in those.'

'Then you've got one of the witnesses.' A slight pause for dramatic effect. 'Malcolm Ratcliffe.'

Dramatic effect or comic timing, perhaps? Dixon wasn't sure which. He sat down at a workstation and opened the file.

Date of accident: 28 February 2002.

The Crown against Christopher Green.

Date of trial: 14 October 2002.

Plea: not guilty.

Verdict: guilty.

Sentence: three years' imprisonment.

Dixon recognised Dave Harding's handwriting. It was a bit more of a scribble these days perhaps, but this was Dave's all right.

The file had originally been opened as a major investigation, the coding changed from murder to causing death by dangerous driving. The investigating officers were both uniformed too, so no doubt CID had not been convinced by the murder charge. Dixon flicked through the correspondence pin, quickly finding a memo from CID. 'No evidence to support Green's version of events . . . warrants no further investigation by CID.'

Start with the interview then, and find out what Green's version of events was.

The interviewing officers were hardly a surprise: Police Sergeant Barry Mercer and Police Constable David Harding. The interview took place at Fishponds police station on the afternoon of 28 February 2002. Dixon skipped the formalities, quickly finding the exchange that mattered:

'What happened then?'

'I was northbound on the M32. There were three figures behind the Armco barrier on the nearside. I could see them in my headlights, which were on full beam. I slowed as I approached, then one of them pushed the other over the barrier and into the path of my lorry. There was nothing I could do. I braked as hard as I could, and tried to swerve, but it was too late. There was a thud from the front nearside, then the rear wheels went over something. I stopped and ran back.'

'You said there were three people behind the Armco barrier. Where were the other two?'

'Gone.'

'Was anybody else there by this time?'

'Another car had pulled up and the driver was on the phone to you lot, according to his passenger.'

'Can you describe the two people you saw behind the barrier?'

'Not really. They were both wearing hoods, either hoodies or hooded coats; dark clothing. I thought they were spraying graffiti on the wall, to be honest. I'm sure I saw a white spray can in the hand of one of them, and it looked like there was something on the wall.'

'Did one of them push Jackson, or both?'

'One of them. I saw a kick, then this figure fall back over the barrier.'

'The pathologist found no evidence of a kick.'

'Hardly surprising after the poor bloke had been hit by my lorry.'

That explained the original murder coding: an allegation that the victim had been pushed into the path of a lorry taken seriously, at least until it had been dismissed as fantasy on the part of the driver, perhaps.

Green had been arrested at the scene and the tachograph seized. Odd that there was no statement from the arresting officer. Dixon flicked through the statements. There should have been one, with the tachograph introduced in evidence by it and exhibited to it.

The statement from the victim's mother made grim reading – Mary Ogunwe. Jackson had been an only child and a talented street artist; his tag – JAKZ – becoming well known across the city, not that anyone had known his real name. Popular too, by all accounts. Worked in the Subway Gallery by day, a DJ and rapper on the club scene by night. Killed instantly, the post mortem report document-ing multiple catastrophic injuries.

Dixon would no doubt be crossing swords with Trevor Crosby again soon, a word with Ratcliffe about his witness statement dated 1 March 2002 likely to happen sooner rather than later. Yes, Ratcliffe had fled the scene, but that was because he had been spray painting the underpass and was worried about a criminal damage charge. A third year student at the University of Avon then, head of the art department now and a successful contem-porary artist too.

Ratcliffe's statement was clear about the accident: Jackson was standing outside the Armco barrier when a speeding lorry veered to the left and hit him. Ratcliffe had seen the lorry approaching and shouted, but it was too late. And he remembered the driver, who appeared distracted – rolling a cigarette, possibly.

Dixon flicked back to the interview.

'Do you smoke?'

'I roll my own.'

Add that to a tachograph that documented excessive speed and driving for seven hours without a break, and it was easy to see why CID had dropped it.

Easy to see why a jury had convicted Green of causing death by dangerous driving.

'Morning, Sir,' said Louise, making a beeline for the kettle.

'No time for that, Lou.' Dixon closed the file and dropped it on the workstation. 'Sarah, we need Roger Poland to review Jackson Ogunwe's post mortem. Make sure he sees the notes and photographs as well.'

'Yes, Sir.'

'Set up another interview with Ratcliffe for this afternoon, and we need to see Mary Ogunwe as well. Sooner rather than later.'

'You haven't forgotten the press conference, have you?' Louise asked.

'We'll be back in plenty of time.'

'Where are we going?'

'To get Dave out of bed.'

'Looks like you were barking up the right tree after all then, Sir,' said Louise, her sentence punctuated by Dixon banging on the door of Dave Harding's terraced house in Devonshire Street, so hard that the door knocker was joining in. 'Sorry.'

'Don't be. I was right, but for all the wrong reasons.'

Dixon had parked next to a van that had been reversed up to the metal fence at the far end of the road, the railway tracks beyond, the sound of a speeding train flying past deafening to those not used to it.

'Do you want me to see if I can get round the back?' asked Louise. 'There's an alley just there.'

'Don't bother,' replied Dixon, his hand to the glass of the front window while he looked through the gap in the curtains. 'I can see the dozy bugger fast asleep on the sofa.' Dixon squatted down and shouted through the letterbox. 'I'm counting to ten, Dave, then I'm getting a battering ram.'

'I'll try ringing him again.'

'He's moving.' Dixon was looking through the letterbox. 'Dave, it's Nick Dixon and I've got Lou with me. Let us in, will you?'

Jogging bottoms and a filthy T-shirt; unshaven. Crumpled, even by Dave's standards.

'He doesn't look good,' whispered Dixon. 'Drinking even more heavily than usual.'

'Hardly surprising. I'll put the kettle on when we get in there; make him a coffee.'

The door opened slowly, Dave's eyes scanning the houses on the opposite side of the road. 'Curtain twitching brigade,' he mumbled, before turning away, seeking refuge in the darkness of his front room.

Dixon followed, watching him pick up each of the empty lager cans lined up on the coffee table and shake them, looking for the dregs. 'Lou's doing you a coffee,' he said, flicking on the light, the sound of a kettle being filled from a tap in the kitchen.

'Thanks.'

'New Inn, was it?'

Dave was blinking furiously. 'It's a bit of a dive, but he has a relaxed attitude to opening hours.'

'You eat there too?'

'Crisps and a pasty in the microwave, if you're lucky. He doesn't do food.' Dave had sat down on the arm of the sofa and was shielding his eyes from the ceiling light. 'I really need to get a shade for that bulb.'

Louise appeared in the doorway, holding up a silver carton containing the remains of something hidden under several layers of mould. 'Where are your bin bags, Dave?' she demanded.

'There should be some under the sink.'

'Junction 3 on the M32,' said Dixon, watching for a reaction.

Dave looked up, slowly. 'Christopher Green,' he said. 'Killed a graffiti artist with his lorry one night. He tried to say the lad had been pushed, but we all knew that was bollocks. We reckoned he was rolling a fag and took his eye off the road.'

'Does the name Malcolm Ratcliffe mean anything to you?'

'Was he the witness who came forward a couple of days later?'

'Yes.'

'Seemed like a decent enough lad. At Bristol University, I think, or it might have been UAB. One of them anyway. Ran off because he didn't want to get done for criminal damage. He'd have got thrown off his course. There was some half-finished daub on the underpass. The council cleaned it off a week or so later.'

Louise appeared, a mug of hot black coffee in one hand and a half-filled bin liner in the other. 'Your back door's locked,' she said, handing the mug to Dave. 'And you've got no milk.'

'Key's on top of the door frame.'

'I can't reach that.'

'Just leave it on the back door mat,' replied Dave. 'I'll put it out later.'

'You won't though, will you?'

Dave frowned. 'Is this why Barry was killed?'

'I don't know, Dave,' replied Dixon. 'All I do know is that Barry was keeping an eye on Emma Carpenter's neighbour the day of her funeral, and Ratcliffe was there.'

'Look, we all knew Green was lying,' said Dave. 'All that crap about Jackson being pushed in front of his lorry. Barry was determined to get him, so he switched the tachograph.'

229

'He falsified evidence?'

'It was one of the cases I reported. The original tachograph confirmed Green was travelling within the speed limit – I can't remember what that was, maybe fifty miles an hour – and he'd taken his break too. So Barry switched it for one that said he was speeding and hadn't taken a break. That's where the causing death by dangerous driving charge came from.'

'Without that it would've been driving without due care and attention,' said Dixon. 'A few points on his licence and a fine.'

'There was no causing death by careless driving back then and all we had was Ratcliffe's statement that Green was distracted and swerved.' Dave took a swig of coffee.

'Why did Barry do it?'

'To make sure Green got what he deserved.'

'There was no other reason.'

'Like what?'

Louise had sat down on the arm at the other end of the sofa and was making notes.

'Money,' said Dixon.

Dave sighed. 'I suspected he'd taken a bribe, but it was never proven. Actually, nothing was ever proven; Barry left the force before it got that far. I don't think he was given a choice, mind you.'

'And where do you suspect this money came from?'

'Ratcliffe's father. He was some big noise in the Bristol office of an insurance company, until it closed. Like I say, PSD never proved any of this and they were crawling all over Barry for months after I reported him. It was still harsh on Green, I thought. It was the early hours, pitch dark, and they were wearing dark clothing because they were up to no good. And then the victim was on the wrong side of the crash barrier as well.'

'Unless you believe Green's version of events?'

'That Jackson was pushed?' Dave drained his coffee and put his mug on the coffee table, pushing it in amongst the empty beer cans. 'Who by?'

'Green said in interview there were two people there, in addition to Jackson.'

'That was never proven, and the occupants of the car that came up behind the lorry said they saw no one at all.'

'You remember this case pretty well, don't you,' said Dixon.

'It was the straw that broke the camel's back,' said Dave, with a heavy sigh. 'When he switched the tachograph it didn't sit well with me.'

'When did you report him?'

'About a year later, which is not something I'm proud of either. I should've done it straightaway. And you think Barry's dead because of this?'

Dixon took a deep breath. 'Barry, Emma Carpenter, Sebastian Cook, and now a girl called Evie Clarke has gone missing.'

'Four people?' Dave had his head in his hands. 'Because of this case?'

'Possibly. Seb Cook was thrown from the bridge at junction 3 on to the carriageway below, and we've got a death message on the parapet. Scroll right,' said Dixon, handing Dave his phone.

'That's supposed to be Barry's foot, stamping on the camera?' asked Dave.

'Barry's right foot is still missing,' replied Louise, placing her hand on Dave's shoulder.

'Who are the others?' he asked.

'They're all either current or former students of UAB. All known to each other and known to be trying to unmask Van Gard.'

'The artist?'

'We know who he is,' said Louise. 'But he's got an alibi for each killing.'

'Do you know what became of Christopher Green, Dave?' asked Dixon.

'Not really. I seem to remember he had a bit of trouble inside and ended up doing more than his three years, but how much extra time and what for, I couldn't tell you.'

'Is there somewhere you can go and stay?' asked Louise. 'How about your ex-wife?'

'Go and stay? You think I'm at risk?'

'If it is Green,' replied Dixon, 'and he's killed Barry Mercer because of this, then we can't guarantee he won't come after you as well. As far as he's concerned you were both the investigating officers in the case. You interviewed him.'

'I'll be fine, Sir. Thanks for your concern and all that, but he'd never find me here. I'm not even on the electoral roll yet. I only moved in a few months ago.'

Dixon unlocked the back door and carried the black bag to the bin at the end of the garden path. Paved, it was somehow still overgrown with weeds, even in the depths of winter. The pungent smell of last night's booze followed him down the garden path from the open kitchen door. A trip to the bottle bank wouldn't go amiss either, thought Dixon, glancing along the empty bottles lined up against the wall of the terraced house.

Dave was leaning against the kitchen sink when Dixon walked back inside, his arms folded tightly across his chest, watching Louise stacking his dishwasher.

'Where are your dishwasher tablets?' she asked.

'Not got any.'

'Typical.' She picked up the Fairy Liquid from the worktop, the bottle sticking in the congealed washing up liquid around the base, squirted some into the dishwasher and slammed the door. 'That'll have to do,' she said, over the noise of the machine coming to life.

'Thanks.'

'The half-finished painting on the wall,' said Dixon. 'You said it was cleaned off by the council?'

'Yeah,' replied Dave. 'There were pictures of it in the *Bristol Post*, then a couple of weeks later it was gone. It just left a clean patch where the jet washers had done their bit.'

'What was it a painting of?'

'Does it matter?'

Dixon decided to let that one go as he turned for the front door.

Louise waited until it slammed behind them. 'He'll let us get clear before he heads for the off-licence, I expect,' she said, glancing over her shoulder. 'I'm guessing you'll want Green's prison record and the photos from the *Bristol Post*?'

'We'll have a bit of fun with Professional Standards too,' said Dixon. 'I want their file on Barry Mercer.' He spun around and banged on the front door, reaching up to bang on it again just as it opened. 'There's no statement on the file from the arresting officer exhibiting the tachograph, Dave. Who was it? D'you remember?'

Chapter Twenty-Eight

'You git.'

'Thank you, Sergeant.'

Jane was standing in the kitchen when Dixon opened the back door of the cottage, a long baggy T-shirt hiding her bump, both hands wrapped around a mug of decaffeinated coffee; the jar with the green lid was still out by the kettle.

Dixon slipped off Monty's lead and allowed the dog to run in; bowl first – empty – then jump up at Jane.

'You have fed him?'

'Six o'clock this morning,' replied Dixon.

'You shouldn't have let me sleep in.'

'Yes, he should,' replied Louise, appearing around the corner of the cottage. 'You're carrying a passenger, as my husband used to say.'

'Lucy's arriving this afternoon, don't forget. It's supposed to be my hen do tonight.'

Dixon raised his eyebrows.

'I know, I know. I'll cancel it. It's not as if I can have a drink anyway.'

'Sorry.'

'You've got that look,' said Jane, her eyes fixed on Dixon's face. 'Like you're on to something.'

'He is,' said Louise.

'We are,' he replied. 'Green – it's one of the files Dave and Mercer worked on together; a death by dangerous driving. Get the others copied and they can go to PSD. Keep that one.'

'Where are you going?'

'Bristol.'

'What about the press conference?'

'Get Vicky Thomas to cancel it. We're close and there's a missing girl to find. I haven't got time to muck about in front of TV cameras.'

'Yes, Sir,' said Jane, snapping her heels together for effect; bare foot, though, so there was no click.

'And jump to it. It's no use lying around in bed all day.'

Dixon and Louise disappeared around the side of the cottage before Jane could find something to throw. She'd been looking, but wasn't quick enough.

'You're brave,' mumbled Louise, climbing into the passenger seat of Dixon's Land Rover.

'I'll pay for it later.'

'Where to first?'

'Jackson's mother.'

Freshly painted in salmon pink, new doors and windows; a terrace of flat-roofed houses in Campbell Street, St Paul's, each three storeys including the basement steps down to a separate front door.

'Mrs Ogunwe is number 9,' said Louise. '9a must be the basement flat.'

Even the railings had been painted, a Hunters 'For sale' board attached to them with cable ties. The meter cupboard on the outside wall needed a new door on it, but it was a small point, and Dixon had had enough of estate agents lately anyway.

Louise knocked on the frosted glass pane in the front door, a figure looming up quickly on the inside.

'Mary Ogunwe?' asked Dixon.

'Are you here for the viewing?'

'I'm afraid not.'

'Police then. Someone rang me and told me you were coming.' She stepped back, allowing Dixon and Louise into the hall. 'I've got a viewing at ten, but the agent is coming, so I just keep out of the way and let them get on with it.'

'Where are you moving to?' asked Louise.

'My son is dead, and now my husband is dead, so I'm going to live with my sister in Jamaica. Going home, I suppose, but I've been here so long it doesn't feel like it. Through here,' she said, opening the sitting room door. 'Now, what was it you wanted to talk to me about? The girl I spoke to on the phone didn't say.'

'Can I call you Mary?' asked Dixon.

'Please do.'

'I'm really sorry to do this to you, Mary, but I need to ask you some questions about Jackson.'

Mary was holding on to the back of the sofa to steady herself, her eyes welling up. 'I thought it was about the burglary two doors down.'

'I'm afraid not. Look, there's no way of dressing this up, so I'm going to come straight out with it. We're looking again at the accident and exploring the possibility that Jackson was actually pushed into the path of the lorry.'

'Murdered, you mean?' She flicked a newspaper off the arm of the sofa and sat down, one hand still holding on to the back. 'Just like the lorry driver said?'

'Yes.'

'After all these years.' She looked up at the picture hanging on the wall above the mantelpiece: Jesus Christ on the cross. 'God moves in mysterious ways.' Her fingers closing around a crucifix that had been in her cardigan pocket. 'My husband died only three months ago; oh, he would have dearly loved to have been here for this.'

The estate agent obviously hadn't had the decluttering conversation with Mary, or if he had, she'd ignored it. Either that or she didn't think of family photos as 'clutter'. Dixon could understand that. Father and son, separately and together, all in silver frames and lined up along the mantelpiece.

'What do you think happened?' he asked, taking his cue from Mary, who clearly had something to say.

'He was a good boy, my Jackson. God fearing, well behaved. Yes, he was a graffiti artist, but a good one with a style all of his own.'

'Do you have any photographs of his work?'

'Some,' replied Mary, standing up. She walked over to a built-in cupboard beside the fireplace, opened the bottom door and took out a large scrapbook. 'These are newspaper cuttings and photos I found in his room after he'd . . .' She couldn't bring herself to say it, instead handing the scrapbook to Dixon. Then she sat down on the sofa next to Louise, forcing a smile as she did so. 'He was like all the rest, to begin with. Spray painting their tags on the walls everywhere. JAKZ, with a "z" on the end. I saw it several times on the embankments and bridges on the way into Temple Meads. My husband would scold him whenever he saw it. In the end we got him to study art at college and he wanted to go to university. Then he was gone.'

'He was studying art?'

'Yes, at City of Bristol. He'd dropped out, as kids do, but we persuaded him to go back and study Art and Design. He loved it, was good at it too. Then they killed him and stole his style.'

'Who did?'

'Van Gard.' Mary's teeth were gritted now. 'It should've been Jackson, not him. Look at the scrapbook!'

Dixon opened it, several newspaper cuttings Sellotaped to the first page. The *Bristol Post* from September 2001: 'Stencils take Upfest by storm', accompanied by a photograph of JAKZ on a scaffolding platform, back to the camera, spray can in hand, putting the finishing touches to a stencilled image – an old man sitting on a low stool, holding a red balloon, real sand and a bucket and spade at his feet.

'I've still got some of his stencils upstairs,' volunteered Mary. 'Would you like to see them?'

'Can I keep the scrapbook?' asked Dixon, conscious that he was asking a lot.

Mary hesitated. 'Will I get it back?'

'I guarantee it.'

'Then you may. I trust you.'

Dixon and Louise followed Mary up the stairs and into the back bedroom, watching her slide a large portfolio case out from under the bed. 'He was just getting going really, but he liked the stencils because it meant he could do more complex paintings in double-quick time; less chance of getting caught,' she said, running the zip around the case and opening it out on the bed.

'Who was he friendly with at the time?'

'I don't know, really. He'd met some new people at college and was starting to make friends on the street art scene too, but I don't know who. He was working in the gallery too.'

'Was he in a relationship?'

'Not that I know of,' replied Mary. She held a stencil up to the light. 'You can't really see what it is, but the skill is in the shading, then it comes to life.'

There were some partially cut stencils in the portfolio case, and sketches of stencils to come.

'Such plans, such promise,' said Mary, with a heavy sigh. 'There are lots of people doing it now, copying Van Gard, with their stencils and bright colours, but Jackson was doing it first and Van Gard took it from him.'

'Did you tell the police at the time?' asked Dixon. 'That you suspected Jackson had been murdered?'

'Yes. We went to the police station and spoke to a sergeant, but he said it had been looked at and there was no evidence.'

'Police Sergeant Mercer?'

'That was him.' Mary nodded. 'We made a nuisance of ourselves, I'm afraid. Went in nearly every day for weeks, asking for news, but got none. We even went to see the lorry driver, Christopher. I looked into his eyes and we prayed together and cried together. He was telling the truth. I know it.' Mary sat down on the end of the bed. 'Poor man. Where is he now?'

'We don't know.'

'Three years in prison for something he didn't do.' Mary was wringing her hands, her fingers interlocked. 'But he had faith, so God willing, that saw him through his ordeal.'

They were standing on the doorstep before Mary spoke again. She'd been lost in her own thoughts and memories as she trudged down the stairs. 'I'm going to take the property off the market and stay to see this through,' she said. 'For Jackson's sake and for my husband, Wilfrid's.' She was staring at the scrapbook tucked under Dixon's arm. 'I want justice, not revenge. God help me, but I cannot forgive.'

Chapter Twenty-Nine

Jane's text arrived just as Dixon turned into Birdman Grange on the edge of Whitchurch.

'A nice touch that,' he muttered.

'What is?'

'Sells off Birdman Haulage for housing, and the development is named Birdman Grange. Then he buys a house here. Dennis Birdman, 6 Birdman Grange.'

'Must be a knob,' said Louise.

Dixon wrenched on the handbrake, then reached for his phone. It was Jane after all:

> *Roger wants to know how urgently you need him to look at Ogunwe's PM*

Dixon tapped out a reply, chuckling to himself as he did so. A little mischief to lighten the darkest of days:

> *He's not still in bed as well, is he? :-)*

Piss off. Jx

Tell him it's DROP EVERYTHING URGENT!

Will do.

'Right then,' said Dixon, dropping his phone back into his jacket pocket. 'Let's go and see what this knob has got to say for himself, shall we?'

'There it is, the big one in the corner,' said Louise. 'Surprise, surprise.'

Double garage, sideways on to the house; bay windows either side of the front door, a Christmas tree in both; a large wreath hanging from the reproduction door knocker; mistletoe hanging from the hall light visible through the small leaded window to the side of the front door.

It was supposed to be a joyous time of year – more so getting married on Christmas Eve – but Jane's hen do had gone and no doubt his stag do would as well. Not that cancelling that would be such a hardship, but it was all part of the tradition of these things.

'Why do people insist on killing each other at Christmas?' he said, immediately kicking himself that he'd said it out loud.

'It's bloody inconsiderate, if you ask me,' said Louise, with an emphatic nod.

Dixon hadn't, but decided not to tell her that. Best just to knock on the door instead.

'What d'you want?' demanded the man, snatching open the door. He was untangling a set of Christmas lights, or trying to.

'Dennis Birdman?'

'Yes.'

'Police, Sir,' said Dixon, warrant card at the ready.

'Yes, someone did call. You'll need to be quick, we're getting ready for a party this evening.'

'May we come in?'

'Must you?'

Louise coughed behind him; stifling a chuckle, possibly.

'Four people are dead and one is missing, so yes, we must. And I should warn you, it'll take as long as it takes.'

'Oh, right.' Birdman dropped the tangle of lights in a box on the hall table and turned, shouting along the corridor in the direction of the kitchen at the back of the house. 'Police are here, Chloe. We'll be in the living room.' He closed the front door behind Dixon and Louise. 'Does my wife need to . . .'

'No, Sir.'

White leather sofa, white marble fireplace; even the artificial Christmas tree was white.

Birdman took a small cigar from a silver box on the glass coffee table and lit it, before sitting down in a white leather armchair. 'How can I help?' he asked.

Red trousers and a white shirt. The scene reminded Dixon of one of Van Gard's stencilled paintings; or one of Jackson's perhaps.

'We need to ask you about a road traffic accident that took place in 2002.'

'2002? How the bloody hell am I supposed to remember that far back?'

'You'll remember this one,' replied Dixon, calmly. 'One of your drivers was prosecuted for causing death by dangerous driving.'

Birdman took a drag on his cigar and blew the smoke out through his nose. 'Yeah, I remember that one, of course I do. Chris Green, the poor bastard. It was out on the M32, junction 3.'

'Can you remember where he was going?'

'He was in an empty tipper, heading up to the Midlands for a load of aggregate. He said the lad was pushed out in front of him,

242

but there was no evidence, so they got him on failing to observe driving time and speeding. But let's be frank about it, the reality was that someone had died and it was always going to be the driver's fault. Chris didn't stand a chance.'

'Was he a good driver?'

'Yes. Always reliable, and it was the first time he'd overrun the tacho time limit. He wasn't known for speeding either, so it came as a surprise, but you can't argue with a tachograph, can you?'

'Unless it's been switched,' said Dixon.

'Not by me it bloody well wasn't.'

'I'm not suggesting that at all.'

'Who switched it then?'

'I really can't say.'

'There was a witness who said he was rolling a fag as well, but Chris used to roll them in the canteen, ready for the road. We had a prefab we used as a staffroom and there was tea and coffee and sandwiches. You'd see him in the corner rolling all these fags before he hit the road.' Birdman shrugged. 'This was back when it was legal to smoke behind the wheel. Now they'll do you for not being in proper control.'

'And it's a workplace,' said Louise.

'Yeah, they'll do you for that too,' said Birdman. 'Smoking in the workplace. I keep saying "they", but it's *you*, isn't it?'

'Not really *us*.'

'Sheesh. He was stitched up good and bloody proper, wasn't he?'

'Have you seen him since he got out?' asked Dixon.

'No.' Birdman was screwing the remains of his cigar into an ashtray he had balanced on the arm of his chair. 'He got in a lot of trouble inside. Ended up doing about eighteen years all told, I think; we'd closed down by the time he got out. Diesel prices. I tried selling the business as a going concern, but no one wanted it. In the end I got planning permission on the land and sold to a developer; made more money that way anyway.'

'Eighteen years?' Dixon frowned. 'He was sentenced to three.'

'Someone attacked him in the nick. I'm sure I heard about it at the time. Self defence, he claimed, but they did him for manslaughter and added to his sentence for the privilege.' Birdman stood up and headed for the cigar box on the coffee table. 'He went a bit loopy, by all accounts. What's your interest in it, anyway?'

'We're looking at it again as part of a wider investigation into three murders.'

'Looking at it again?'

'Yes.'

'All right then, ask the accident investigator this: junction 3 is no more than two hundred yards from the end of the A4032 with its thirty limit, right. So, you tell me how he's going faster than fifty when he reaches junction 3? There's no way a tipper would accelerate that fast, even empty.'

'The witness said he swerved—'

'Bollocks. These things are heavy, even when they're empty, and they don't swerve like a car. If he'd been able to wrench the wheel over then he'd probably have hit the bridge. There'd have been no time to correct it. And, don't forget, you're raised up in the driver's cab, so the chances are he wouldn't have seen anyone by the crash barrier anyway. What were they wearing?'

'Dark clothes.'

'There you are then. A swerve implies that Chris saw the bloke late and yanked the wheel over, but if that's right, they'd have already been out of view down on the nearside. You see what I'm saying?'

'Did you give evidence at Green's trial?'

'I wasn't asked. His lawyer just wanted a character reference from his employer, so I wrote a letter and that was it. But I don't believe he swerved, and I don't believe he could have been speeding by the time he reached junction 3, even with the hammer down.'

'Assuming he stuck to the speed limit on the A4032,' said Dixon.

'Yeah, but like I said, Chris wasn't known for speeding. Some drivers were, but not him.'

'Can you confirm what hours he worked that day?'

'All the records have gone, I'm afraid.' Birdman was lighting another cigar. 'When we sold up I got a commercial shredding firm in and they did the lot. No point in keeping it.'

'Was there an insurance claim as a result of the accident?'

'No. I notified my insurers, and they were expecting one from the dead lad's family; but he was over eighteen and had no dependants, so it never came. The insurers did pay for Chris's defence though, so my premium went through the roof anyway.'

'And you believed him when he said someone pushed the victim in front of his lorry?'

'I did.'

Chapter Thirty

Press conference put back to 2pm. Charlesworth says you're to be there. You've already missed one, he says. Jx

What about Ratcliffe?

3. It's the earliest his solicitor can get here.

'Where to now then, Sir?' asked Louise. She was sitting in the driver's seat of Dixon's Land Rover, the signal being the usual lobbing of the keys in her direction.

'Musgrove Park,' replied Dixon. 'Let's go and see what Roger's got to say for himself.'

He opened the scrapbook and spent the drive south reading it from cover to cover; all of the newspaper cuttings and articles, letters too. There were even several pages torn out of a book – JAKZ mentioned as a rising star of the Bristol Street Art Movement. A chapter on Upfest with a photograph of his stencilled painting, and another chapter entitled 'How Street Art Went Boom'; with artists such as Van Gard 'expected to break down art market boundaries', some of the pieces were already selling for eye-watering sums of money.

Money. There must be more to this than that, surely?

'I was just about to ring you.' Poland was leaning out of a window at the back of the pathology lab at Musgrove Park Hospital. His office, hopefully, thought Dixon, although he was wearing a shirt open at the neck rather than his scrubs. Not in the middle of a post mortem, then. 'Come round the side and I'll open the fire escape.'

'Won't the alarm go off?'

'It's broken.'

A loud metallic clunk echoed around the courtyard at the back, two smokers sitting in the garden startled by the noise, more faces appearing at the windows opposite the fire door as it swung open.

'Who are they?' asked Dixon.

'Physiotherapy department on the ground floor,' replied Poland. 'Orthopaedics above.'

'I suppose you're nice and close for when something goes wrong.'

'Tee hee.'

'We need to have a chat about the stag do,' said Dixon, squeezing past Poland's large frame in the doorway.

'Yes, I know. Cancel it.' Poland slammed the door behind Louise, jerking the bar into place with another clank.

'Better had. Sorry.'

'Jane's cancelled her hen do, if it's any consolation,' offered Louise.

'Through there,' said Poland, gesturing to his office.

Dixon glanced into the lab, two bodies lying on slabs next to each other, covered in green sheets, mercifully. 'Anything interesting?' he asked, with a nod in that direction.

'A house fire over at Langport. Smoke inhalation.' Poland sat down on the swivel chair behind his desk and produced a bottle of scotch from the bottom drawer of his desk.

'Too early, Roger.'

'Not for me, thanks,' said Louise.

'Oh, right. Fine,' he said, slipping one plastic cup off the stack. 'Which d'you want to talk about first?'

'Eh?'

'Emma Carpenter or Jackson Ogunwe?'

'You've looked at Emma Carpenter's post mortem as well?'

'A senior police officer turns up at an inquest and calls into question a colleague's PM findings. I was required to review it as a matter of routine. Internal protocol, you might say.'

'And?'

'He's right and you're wrong.'

Dixon sat back on the edge of the windowsill. 'Go on.'

'There's no evidence of foul play,' said Poland, pouring himself a whisky. 'Insulin levels are consistent with the suggested dosing – two lots of double the usual amount – and she'd taken a sleeping pill. There are two injection sites, but no other marks on the body at all – none consistent with restraint anyway – apart from old injection sites and finger prick blood tests. I've looked at the notes and the photographs.'

'I never questioned any of that, Roger,' replied Dixon. 'It doesn't mean there wasn't foul play, though. Just that there's no evidence of it. I'll have to get a confession in that case, won't I?'

'Who from?' Louise should've known better and seemed relieved when Poland came to her rescue.

'Between you and me, Davidson took it a bit personally.' Poland took a swig of scotch. 'Sensitive to criticism, but he'll need to get used to it in this line of work. I'll be having a word with him about it at some point, over a beer.'

'He'll get over it. What about Jackson?'

'Have you seen the photographs?' asked Poland. 'I can just see you turning up at that post mortem.'

'I can imagine.'

'Poor lad was hit by a tipper lorry going at fifty-plus miles an hour. Looks like he went under the back wheels too.' Poland turned his computer screen to face Dixon. 'You need to look at them, I'm afraid, so brace yourself.'

'How on earth did they do the identification?' asked Louise, closing her eyes.

'Teeth and DNA,' replied Poland. 'Okay, so let's take it in order. The first point of impact is the upper body, left side. There's a catastrophic injury to the left side of his head, multiple skull fractures, so it looks like his head hit the front wing, possibly somewhere above the bumper. He'd have felt nothing after that.'

'That's something, I suppose,' said Dixon.

'There are tyre marks on the lower legs and crushing injuries to the leg bones, as you'd expect, so somehow he must've got turned on impact and dragged under the back wheels. Those were the conclusions of the original PM, and I must say, I agree with them.'

'Is that it?'

'Well, actually, no it isn't *it*.'

'Thank God for that.'

'It's an easy trap to fall into. Determining the cause of a particular injury or bruise in this situation is more of an art than a science sometimes, and things can often be missed. Add to that the fact the Bristol pathologist back then wasn't known for being entirely sober all the time, and it was an evening PM.'

'Was he asked to look for evidence of a push?'

'There's no record of it in his notes.'

'And you've found evidence of a push?'

Poland scrolled through more photographs, then pointed at the screen. 'That's the boy's torso.'

'What are we looking at?' asked Louise.

'Bear in mind it was February and he was wearing several layers of clothing,' replied Poland. 'Good job, really, otherwise the body really would have been in a mess.'

Dixon leaned forward, tipping his head at the screen. 'That curved bruise in the middle of his chest,' he said, following the line with his index finger.

'The best I can say is it's consistent with a shoe.' Poland was sucking his teeth. 'Or a stamp. I think someone might have stamped on him.'

'Or kicked him backwards over the crash barrier?'

'It's possible.' Poland was mulling it over. 'It might explain why there are no injuries to the pelvic area too. If he'd been standing up when he'd been hit, then the whole of his left side would've taken the impact, rather than just his upper body.'

'Unless he was trying to get out of the way,' said Dixon. 'Maybe he saw the lorry late and—'

'Yes, but if he threw himself forward . . .' Louise's voice ran out of steam, unsure where it was taking her.

'Look, there are no shoe imprint marks,' said Poland, 'but then you wouldn't get those through clothing anyway. Just a curved bruise. I can say it's possibly consistent with a shoe, but that's as good as it gets.'

'Hardly "beyond reasonable doubt", is it?' Dixon was still staring at the computer screen. 'Was there a second PM, for the defence?' he asked.

'No record of it,' replied Poland. 'Probably didn't think there was a lot of point, given that it really is impossible to say with any degree of certainty what caused a particular injury in an impact like that.'

'Probably legally aided,' said Louise.

Dixon was watching the smokers in the garden behind the pathology lab – different ones this time, both of them dragging oxygen bottles on wheels, thin tubes behind their ears and up their noses.

'Who?' he asked.

'Green.'

'The insurers paid for his defence.'

'I wonder why there was no second PM, in that case?'

'And I'm wondering why there was no mention of that bruise in the PM report,' replied Dixon. 'Although it probably wouldn't have made much difference in the face of that tachograph. Did we request the original out of store? It's just a copy on the file.'

'Not yet,' replied Louise, shaking her head.

'Get it, will you?'

'Yes, Sir.' She put on her seatbelt and then started the engine. 'Where to now?'

'Express Park.' Dixon grimaced. 'I suppose I'd better show up for that bloody press conference.'

Louise parked in the visitors' car park twenty minutes later, Dixon having spent the short drive going through the scrapbook. Again.

'Ah, there you are.' Reg's voice from behind the reception desk as Dixon and Louise tried to sneak in the front doors. Dixon knew that Charlesworth would be watching the staff entrance, waiting for him to swipe in. 'There's a retired sergeant waiting to see you, Sir. Down the far end.'

Sitting on the bench seat at the far end of the reception area, well away from everyone else: an older man reading a newspaper – greying hair, wool coat, hat and scarf.

'Are you looking for me?' asked Dixon, standing over him.

'Con Dugdale,' said the man, standing up, almost to attention. 'Ex-traffic, Sir.'

Old habits die hard, obviously.

'I was phoned this morning about an old fate-acc of mine on the M32. I couldn't remember the case, I'm afraid, so I thought I'd pop in and have a look at my report, see if it rang any bells. I've retired down here now. Live in Burnham. Fatal accidents were my thing, back in the day.'

'I'll get the file,' said Louise, turning for the security door.

Dixon sat down next to Dugdale on the bench, watching several TV vans arrive in the visitors' car park and block in his Land Rover. 'It was February 2002. A tipper lorry and a graffiti artist at junction 3. The driver alleged the victim had been pushed into the path of his lorry.'

'I do remember it in that case.' Dugdale sat up. 'There was an independent witness who put the victim outside the crash barrier, from memory. Stepping back to admire his work, probably; there was graffiti on the wall. The witness said he thought the lorry swerved, but that was unlikely in my opinion because the braking didn't start until well after the collision point. A swerve implies the driver reacted – you'd brake and turn the wheel at the same time – but he clearly didn't brake for at least a good second after the impact. The skid started well beyond the collision point; big skid too, from a twelve-wheeler. The tacho was damaging for the driver more than anything else; his undoing, really.'

'It's been alleged the tachograph was switched.'

'Switched by who?'

'Not you, don't worry,' replied Dixon. 'The truth of it seems to be that he wasn't speeding and hadn't overrun his time.'

'Bloody hell.'

'Would it have made a difference?'

'Yes, it would. He'd still have been charged with driving without due care and attention – he should've seen him and he didn't. He'd have pleaded guilty to that, most likely, and walked away with a few points and a fine. Causing death by careless driving didn't exist back then, so it was only the tacho that got it up to a dangerous.'

'When I spoke to the owner of the haulage firm, he said Green was not known for speeding, so assuming he was going at thirty miles an hour when he reached the end of the A-whatever-it-is, could he have been exceeding the speed limit by the time he reached junction 3? The owner of the firm says not, even accelerating hard.'

'That's probably right, even with an empty tipper. It's not that far.'

'That's what the original tachograph said, apparently. Did you give evidence at the trial?'

'Yes, I think so. I didn't tend to have much involvement with cases after the accident investigation finished, though. I'd submit my report and that would be that. On to the next one, I'm afraid.'

◆ ◆ ◆

'Close to making an arrest?' Charlesworth had the decency to wait until the door of the media suite had closed behind them. 'That wasn't in the briefing I was given.'

'Nor mine,' said Potter. 'There's nothing in the Policy Log either. I checked.'

'I haven't updated it yet,' replied Dixon.

'Well, are you close to making an arrest?' demanded Charlesworth.

'No.'

Vicky Thomas had been lurking behind Charlesworth, but couldn't help sticking her sharp nose in. She'd been irritating enough as the humble press officer, but now she had been elevated to head of corporate communications she was going to be unstoppable. 'That's misleading the press. Does our reputation no end of damage if it comes out.' She shook her head, her hair stuck rigid by hairspray. 'It'll take me ages to restore confidence in our press briefings.'

'They're only here for the gory details anyway,' said Dixon. 'We might as well make use of them.'

'That's not how it's supposed to—'

'And what was all that about the M32 in February 2002?' interrupted Charlesworth.

'You still haven't been on that training course, have you?' asked Vicky Thomas, glaring at Dixon. 'Handling the media is an integral part of being a DCI – building relationships, networking. It's my own fault. I'll organise it for the new year.'

'Thank you, Vicky,' said Charlesworth.

The idea of 'networking' turned Dixon's stomach. It brought back memories of the legal profession, representing the firm at this breakfast or that lunch, purely because no one else could be bothered to go. Still, it meant that he hadn't had to answer Charlesworth's question about the M32. Every cloud, and all that.

'You've requested a tachograph out of evidence too.'

Bollocks.

'Is it relevant?'

'In my opinion, it is, Sir,' replied Dixon.

'Explain.'

'Barry Mercer was the senior investigating officer and now he's dead.'

'We know.'

'Malcolm Ratcliffe was a witness to the collision and now makes vast sums of money – which he sends to an offshore company – from selling artwork in the style of the victim of that collision, a victim that the driver says was pushed in front of his lorry. If that's right, and it could be because the tachograph was switched, then it's possible Ratcliffe killed Jackson Ogunwe and stole his artistic identity.'

'It sounds plausible,' said Potter.

'Mercer saw Ratcliffe at Emma Carpenter's funeral and, who knows, maybe he tried to blackmail him? My guess is we'll never know, but Mercer had to die as a consequence,' continued Dixon.

'What about the students and the other bloke, Slime Zee or whatever his name was?' asked Charlesworth.

'They were trying to unmask Van Gard and Ratcliffe wasn't having any of that. Not only would Van Gard lose his anonymity and his appeal, but it might well have raised the same questions I'm about to ask him about that accident on the M32.'

'He's here?'

'Interview room one,' replied Dixon, looking at his watch. 'In ten minutes.'

'Just be careful.' Charlesworth pursed his lips. 'There's an awful lot of assumptions in there. You've still got no real evidence Emma Carpenter was murdered at all. Or that Jackson Ogunwe was pushed. We'll watch from the video suite, I think, Deborah.'

Chapter Thirty-One

'It's called "using your initiative".' Jane glanced across at Sarah sitting nervously in the passenger seat. 'It was good work, and if you're right, we may just blow this whole thing wide open.'

'I thought you were supposed to be running the incident room?'

'It'll be fine. Initiative is encouraged, and besides, I'm nurturing young talent, just like the ACC said.'

Jane turned into the car breaker's yard and parked in the empty staff car park. The crusher was silent, no screech of twisting metal to drown out the train lumbering by on the tracks on the far side, accelerating out of Bridgwater railway station.

She banged on the door of the Portakabin, then opened it without waiting for an invitation. As Dixon always said, best to take them by surprise.

Colin Higgs sat up sharply. 'What d'you want on a Sunday?' He folded up his newspaper and dropped it on the floor beside his chair. 'Oh, it's you. Sorry, I didn't recognise you in civvies, lamb,' he said.

'This is Detective Sergeant Jane Winter,' said Sarah. 'And I wouldn't call her *lamb*, if I were you.'

'Right, sorry.' Higgs's face reddened.

Jane looked at Sarah and nodded.

'Mr Higgs, am I right in thinking that you sell items on eBay from an account with the username "Higgsy1971"?'

'Yeah, I do. Occasionally,' he replied, defensively. 'It's just crap people leave behind in the cars. Once they scrap it and sign the vehicle over to me, it's mine, so I can do what I want with it.'

Jane was peering behind the closed blinds at the windowsills, piled high with old CDs, binoculars, dashcams and other 'crap'.

'You'd be amazed what people leave behind. Stuff that's gone right under the seat, y'know.' A toothy grin, nervously watching Jane working her way along the windows at the back of the Portakabin.

'When I looked at your auction history,' continued Sarah, 'I saw that you sold several higher value items about six months ago. Do you remember them?'

'Like what?'

'Two zoom lenses.' Reading from her notebook. 'One was a Canon KJ13x6B KRSD BCTV, whatever all that means. It started at ninety-nine pence and went for three thousand, three hundred pounds.'

'Er, yeah, I remember that. It was left in a van.'

'A white Vauxhall Combo, registration number BL08 ZVN.'

'May have been, yeah.' Arms folded tightly across his chest now.

'But when I asked, you said you hadn't had a Combo through here for ages.'

'I may have been mistaken, I suppose.'

'Only, that zoom lens has been identified as having belonged to a Mr Barry Mercer, whose dismembered body was found in the Tone last week.'

Sarah was getting the hang of this already, thought Jane, stifling a smile.

'Now, wait a minute, I didn't kill him. I didn't kill anyone.'

'But you do admit that a Vauxhall Combo van went through your Authorised Treatment Facility six months ago?'

'This bloke brought it in, but he didn't say nothing about no murder. Just that it had to be got rid of.'

Jane looked at Sarah and coughed.

'Colin Higgs, I am arresting you on suspicion of handling stolen goods,' said Sarah.

Jane was unplugging the computer on the desk, ready to take it to High Tech.

'You can't take that!'

'I think you'll find we can, Mr Higgs,' replied Jane.

'You do not have to say anything when questioned,' continued Sarah, 'but it may harm your defence if you do not mention when questioned something you later rely on in court. Anything you do say may be given in evidence.'

Word perfect; shame Sarah was a probationer, really.

'I don't know anything about a murder. All right?' Higgs was watching Jane take a pair of handcuffs out of her pocket. 'Look, this bloke wanted this van crushed. It's long gone now, probably on a container ship to China to be turned into baked bean cans. He never mentioned any cameras or anything, but there they were, so I thought, why not? Might as well make a few quid on the deal.'

Arms dragged behind his back, handcuffs snapping closed around his wrists.

'It was Ben's father, all right. He brought the van in; said I owed his family a favour – after what happened to Ben, with his leg, like.'

Louise dealt with the formalities, Dixon trying not to look up at the camera in the corner of the interview room. It reminded him of some all-knowing, all-seeing eye, like the one from *The Lord of the Rings*. A brooding, evil presence. Actually, it was only Charlesworth and Potter watching the feed in the video suite.

Still, there was something bugging Dixon about it. Charlesworth always took a passing interest in his cases, mainly because they had been high profile ones of late and media interest always made him nervous. But Dixon couldn't get rid of the feeling there was more to it than that this time.

Maybe it was because it was his first case back, and he should be flattered the ACC was taking such a keen interest in his welfare?

Dixon felt a nudge from Louise, sitting to his left.

'Detective Chief Inspector Nicholas Dixon,' he said, identifying himself for the tape. Then it was back to trying not to look up at the camera. And stewing on Trevor Crosby's whispered sentence that Dixon had caught the tail end of when he walked into the interview room. 'Remember, Malcolm, they can't prove a thing after all this time.'

'You are still under caution,' said Louise. 'Do you understand?'

'I do.'

Dixon was supposed to be saying that himself in a couple of days.

'Right then, Malcolm,' he said. 'Here's what I think. I think Christopher Green was telling the truth all along. I think Jackson was pushed in front of his lorry.'

'That is pure speculation,' said Crosby, spelling it out for the tape.

'Actually, it's not. We know the tachograph was falsified. Switched, to make it appear that Green had been speeding and exceeding his driving time when he hadn't and wasn't.'

'Switched by whom?' asked Crosby, emphasising the 'm'.

'Police Sergeant Barry Mercer,' replied Dixon. 'You will recall that it was the discovery of his dismembered body that started this investigation.'

'My client has an alibi for the murder of Barry Mercer, that you've checked, I believe?'

'Twice. But we're here to talk about the road traffic accident on the M32.' Dixon opened a file on the desk in front of him and slid a copy of a newspaper cutting across the table. 'That was taken from the *Bristol Post* on the first of March 2002. It's a report of the accident, without much detail really, but what's interesting about it is the photograph of the half-finished painting Jackson had been working on. Do you remember that, Malcolm?'

Ratcliffe leaned forward and looked at the newspaper cutting. 'Not really.'

'Either you do or you don't.'

'There was a painting, but I can't remember the subject or anything like that. It was dark.'

'Of course it was.' Dixon gave a reassuring smile, but his eyes probably gave the sarcasm away. 'You see, what's interesting about it is not the subject, it's the style. The painting is stencilled, a style we would now normally associate with you – or should I say Van Gard.'

'Stencilling is mainstream now.'

'But it wasn't back then, was it?'

Silence.

'Jackson was breaking new ground,' continued Dixon. 'A rising star of the Bristol Street Art Movement, according to the book I read. There's even a photograph of him working on a piece at the 2001 Upfest. Back to the camera, hoodie up. All you anonymous artists are the same, aren't you?'

'What are you saying?' asked Crosby.

'I'm saying that your client killed Jackson Ogunwe by pushing him in front of Christopher Green's tipper lorry, and then stole his artistic style. The first stencilled Van Gard, verified anyway, appeared in September 2002 on a wall in Highbridge. Your trademark black stencilling on a white wall, with a burst of red,' said Dixon, turning back to Ratcliffe.

'I didn't push Jackson in front of the lorry,' said Ratcliffe. 'He was standing outside the crash barrier and the lorry driver was distracted. He tried to swerve at the last minute, but it was too late and he hit him.'

'There are several things wrong with that version of events, Malcolm, but we'll come to that in a minute,' said Dixon. 'What I'd like to know is this. Jackson was working on a stencilled image. You can see that in the photograph. So, where was the stencil?'

'What d'you mean?'

'It's a simple question, surely? There was no stencil found at the scene, not on his body or anywhere else for that matter, otherwise it would have been admitted in evidence. So, where did it go?'

'I don't know.'

'You didn't have it on you when you attended the police station a couple of days later, did you?'

'No.'

'Must've been a shock that, the driver alleging Jackson was pushed and you being arrested when you arrived.'

'My client gave a statement at the time and was quickly eliminated from enquiries,' said Crosby. 'We need to be clear about that, for the interview record.'

'But where was the stencil?'

'My client has answered that question, Inspector. He said he doesn't know.'

'Odd that it mysteriously disappeared, don't you think?'

'I really have no idea where it went,' said Ratcliffe, his face flushed.

'Sticking with the photograph in the *Bristol Post* then,' said Dixon. 'There's a second painting in the background, in a very different style. Can you see it?'

'There's something there, yes.'

'Was that what you were working on?'

'I don't remember.'

'Oh, come on, Malcolm. What else were you doing down there? You were down behind the crash barrier painting on the wall of the underpass, weren't you?'

Crosby leaned across and began whispering in Ratcliffe's ear.

'Look, I'm investigating four murders and a girl is still missing. I'm really not interested in a historic case of criminal damage. All right?'

'Yes,' replied Ratcliffe. 'I was down there with Jackson and we were both painting. I must've been ten yards away, maybe. It's difficult to see from that photo. I can't remember what it was I was painting. It wasn't much; you didn't have time down there.'

'How well did you know him?'

'Not that well. We'd met through the street art scene. We always tried to work in pairs in case something happened.'

'Like what?'

'You lot coming along was the main thing. Two people running in different directions have a better chance of both getting away.' Ratcliffe shrugged. 'We were just kids back then.'

'Did your father pay Police Sergeant Mercer to switch the tachograph?'

The sudden change of tack took Ratcliffe and Crosby by surprise. Both sat up.

'My father is dead.'

'That wasn't the question, Malcolm.'

'No, he didn't.'

'You said the tipper lorry swerved in your statement at the time. Did you give that evidence in court?'

'Yes.'

'Was it challenged by the defence?'

'Not specifically. They tried to say my whole statement was a lie.'

'Was it?'

'No.'

Dixon slid a photograph across the table. 'What does that image tell you?'

Silence.

'That the lorry skidded in a straight line, perhaps?' Dixon folded his arms. 'It's hardly going to have done that if it swerved, is it.'

'My client is not a trained road traffic accident investigator.'

'All right, this is your last chance to tell us what happened, Malcolm,' said Dixon, sliding another photograph out of the folder on the table in front of him. 'This is a photograph of Jackson Ogunwe's torso taken at the post mortem examination on twenty-eighth February 2002. It shows what is possibly a shoe mark in the middle of his chest. What have you got to say about that?'

Crosby reached forward and snatched the photograph before Ratcliffe could look at it. 'That could be anything,' he said. 'The victim was hit by a tipper lorry travelling at nearly sixty miles an hour in a fifty limit. He'd have suffered catastrophic injuries.' Crosby pushed the photograph back to Dixon. 'I'm advising you not to look at it, Malcolm. It's pure speculation.'

Ratcliffe arched his back. 'If that's what my solicitor says, then who am I to argue.'

'What shoes would you have been wearing that night?' asked Dixon.

'Trainers, probably. In case we had to run for it.'

'Do you still have them?'

'God, no.' Ratcliffe chuckled. 'Have you still got your trainers from twenty years ago?'

'Look, I think this has gone on long enough,' said Crosby. 'Either you terminate this interview now, or I shall advise my client not to answer any further questions.'

'Fine.' Dixon stood up. 'This interview is terminated at fifteen-forty-six.'

'And I trust this is the last my client will hear of this nonsense.'

'I doubt that very much, Mr Crosby,' said Dixon. 'I doubt that very much.'

Chapter Thirty-Two

'You'll never guess what she's gone and done,' said Jane, grinning at Dixon when he and Louise appeared at the top of the stairs.

They'd managed to get out of the interview room and into the comparative safety of the lift before Charlesworth and Potter had been able to catch up with them. 'Who?'

'You tell him, Sarah.'

'You remember the Portakabin at the car breaker's yard?' Sarah's face reddened when she looked up from behind her computer. 'There were all these padded envelopes and a set of scales. It reminded me of my brother; he used to do a bit of selling on eBay and had a set of scales to calculate the postage. So, I had a trawl through completed listings of photographic equipment, starting six months ago. On my phone, at night. I was checking for a business seller because you can see the registered address. Anyway, there was a zoom lens and the seller's address was the car breaker's.'

'Where is he?'

'Downstairs,' replied Jane. 'She nicked him for handling stolen goods.'

'We checked with Barry Mercer's secretary, Carol, and she confirmed the zoom lens belonged to him,' continued Sarah. 'So we're contacting the other buyers of photographic equipment and trying to get the stuff back. There's another zoom lens and a camera.'

'What happened to the van?' asked Dixon.

'Long gone,' replied Jane.

'Have you interviewed him?'

'Jane did. She let me sit in, though.'

'The van was brought in by Warren Clifford, Ben's father,' said Jane. 'He said Higgs owed the family a favour because of what happened to Ben.'

'Have we had Green's prison record yet?' asked Dixon.

'Not yet.'

'Chase that up, will you, Jane?'

'I was going to go with Sarah and pick up—'

'I'd like a senior officer dealing with the Prison Service,' interrupted Dixon. 'We'll pick up Ben's father, don't worry.'

Dixon drove down to the end of the lane and turned at the bottom, parking on the nearside verge, the wheels of his Land Rover sinking in the soft mud.

'How long?' he asked.

'About five minutes, they said; just coming through Curry Rivel now,' replied Sarah, sitting in the passenger seat. 'We'd better wait. Jane's just emailed over his previous.'

'Go on.'

'Do you want the dishonesty or the violence?'

'Both.'

'Goes right back to 1982. Feltham Young Offenders Institute; eighteen months for affray and actual bodily harm. Then there's theft, criminal damage, obtaining a pecuniary advantage by deception, drink driving, another assault, and the most recent is three years for grievous bodily harm. Nothing for the last six months though, so maybe he's calmed down a bit?'

'I wonder if his path crossed with Green's when he was inside?'

'Shall I ask Jane to check?'

'Better had. You wearing a stab vest?'

'Under my coat,' replied Sarah. 'You think Green's behind this?' she asked, tapping out a text message.

'He's got a motive for killing Mercer, if he was stitched up over the accident. Causing death by dangerous driving; three years and it cost him eighteen. It doesn't tie in with the others somehow, does it?'

'Not really.'

'Or maybe it does, we just don't know how or why yet.' Dixon was watching a dog walker in his rear view mirror. 'Who asked you to have a look at Mercer's missing person file in the first place?' he asked, idly.

'The ACC.'

'And you're enjoying CID?'

'Very much, Sir, thank you,' replied Sarah. 'I always wanted to be a dog handler, but now I think I'll be a detective.'

'A dog handler sounds fun, but you spend most of your time lying under hedges, waiting for something to happen. Then, when it does, it's over in seconds. Have a dog as a pet, then you get the best of both worlds.'

'We've got a retriever.'

'There you are then.'

A patrol car appeared out on the main road, slowing by the entrance to the lane. The driver flashed his headlights, then turned into a lay-by. Seconds later, Dixon's phone was buzzing in his pocket.

'You got somebody with you, Nige?'

'Yes, Sir.'

'It's the first house in the lane. Park across the drive and we'd better have the battering ram, just in case. He's got form, so I hope you're wearing stab vests.'

'We were warned, Sir, don't worry.'

'All right, let's go.' Dixon accelerated up the lane and parked in front of Cole's patrol car, which had beaten him to it and was already blocking the drive. 'Good lad, is Nigel,' he said.

'This is Sandra MacIntyre,' said Cole, gesturing to the uniformed officer standing next to him. 'She may look small, but she doesn't take any shit.'

'Round the back with Sarah, please, Sandra,' said Dixon. 'We'll go in the front, Nige.'

Cole snatched the battering ram from MacIntyre.

A count of ten once the others had disappeared around the side of the dormer bungalow. 'They'll be in position by now,' Dixon said, ringing the doorbell.

Footsteps, two people, then a shrill voice from behind the door, 'Who is it?'

'Police.'

'He's not here.'

'Who isn't?'

'Ben. He's gone into Taunton.'

'We're here to speak to your husband, Mrs Clifford,' replied Dixon. He recognised the voice, and the attitude.

Silence.

'Let's have that battering ram, please, Constable.'

'All right, all right, there's no need for that.' The door opened. 'What's he gone and done now?'

The large figure of Warren Clifford standing behind his wife – cowering almost.

'Do you want to tell her, or shall I, Warren?' asked Dixon.

A glance over his shoulder, the unmistakable outline of a police uniform standing outside the frosted glass of the back door, Sarah watching through the kitchen window.

'C'mon then, what's he supposed to have done?'

Clifford was standing at the bottom of the stairs, both hands gripping the wooden balusters, rocking backwards and forwards, hitting his head on the handrail. 'I did it for Ben,' he said, his voice tremulous. 'I can't go back to prison.'

'Warren Clifford, I am arresting you on suspicion of the murder of Barry Mercer.' Dixon gestured to Cole, who stepped forward, handcuffs at the ready.

'Murder? I never murdered no one. You've got this all wrong.' Shaking now, pulling hard on the balusters – good weapons if they came loose.

'You do not have to say anything, but it may harm your defence if you do not mention when questioned something you later rely on in court.'

Sarah and MacIntyre had opened the back door silently and were creeping into the kitchen.

'Anything you do say may be given in evidence.'

MacIntyre reached up slowly and took hold of Clifford's right wrist. 'Hands, Warren,' she said. 'Behind your back, please.'

'Who's Barry Mercer?' demanded Mrs Clifford. 'Is he that bloke they fished out the Tone?'

'He is,' replied Dixon, breathing a silent sigh of relief as Clifford put his hands behind his back.

'I never killed him,' said Clifford. 'You want to know what happened, I'll tell you because I sure as bloody hell ain't going back to prison for something I haven't done.'

Dixon waited. Clifford had been cautioned, so if he had something to get off his chest, let him.

'This bloke rang me; said there was a van outside the house with a private detective in it, keeping an eye on Ben, spying on him, trying to catch him taking the piss so they could get his injury claim thrown out. So, I went out to give him a piece of my mind. I got him out of the van and gave him a slap, but that was it. I didn't kill him.'

'When was this?' asked Dixon.

'The day of the Carpenter girl's funeral. Later on, after everyone had gone.'

'There must be more to it than that, you dozy bugger.'

A nice line of questioning from his wife, thought Dixon. He wouldn't have put it quite like that himself, but she'd got the gist of it.

'I knocked him down, all right. He was out for the count on the grass verge out there, when this bloke stuck his bloody nose in, a right do-gooder, bundled him into his car and said he'd take him to hospital. I put the van in the garage and left it for a couple of days. When no one came back for it, I got Higgs to put it through his crusher. I never heard no more about it, and to be honest, I didn't bloody well care.'

'You told me it was your brother's van,' said Mrs Clifford. 'It was there for bloody days . . . Who the hell are they?' she asked, watching two Scientific Services vans parking in the lane outside.

'The search team,' replied Dixon.

'Where's your warrant?'

'We don't need one, as it happens. Your husband has been arrested for murder, and a search is necessary to preserve evidence.'

'Look, all I kept from the van was the USB sticks,' said Clifford. 'The rest went to the crusher.'

'Where are they?' asked Dixon.

'In my toolbox in the garage. They've got film of Ben on them.'

'That's why he settled the case, innit? You told our son he was being watched?'

'No, I didn't,' insisted Clifford, talking to his wife over his shoulder as he was being manoeuvred towards the front door by Cole and MacIntyre. 'Ben never knew anything about this. I just persuaded him to take the offer that was on the table. Who knows what other footage they'd got of him, and it was a good deal, for fuck's sake. The lawyer said so.'

Dixon watched as the search team squeezed into the bungalow past Clifford on his way out. There was then the narrow gap to negotiate between the hedge and the line of cars in the drive; not easy without getting saturated.

'You take the Land Rover back, will you, Sarah,' said Dixon, dropping his car keys into her hand. 'I'll go with Nigel in the patrol car.'

'D'you want me to hang on here, Guv?' asked MacIntyre.

'Thank you.' Dixon managed to mask his wince; he hated being called 'guv'. 'Nige will come back for you when we've booked Clifford in.'

A hand on top of Clifford's head and he was unceremoniously pushed into the back of the patrol car. Then Cole leaned in to do up the seatbelt.

'Easily fooled, is she, your missus?' asked Dixon, when Cole was turning out on to the main road.

'Eh?'

Cole was watching Clifford in the rear view mirror, Dixon having turned in the passenger seat to look over his shoulder. 'All that crap about a good Samaritan rescuing Mercer from your beating. You know, I think she actually believed it.'

'It's bloody true, that's why.'

'Three years for GBH. What was it, a knife?'

'A pool cue.'

'Nice.'

'I don't lie,' said Clifford.

'Except when you're obtaining a pecuniary advantage by deception.'

'That was different. I'm telling you, I didn't kill Mercer.'

'This good Samaritan, who just happened to chance upon the scene, what did he look like?' Dixon was trying his best, but his sarcasm was in danger of slipping through.

'Just like a normal bloke. Dark hair.' Clifford was fidgeting in the back of the patrol car, his hands still behind his back.

'What was he wearing?'

'Jeans and a coat. Brown, I think. Trainers, possibly. I can have a go at a Photofit, if you like.'

'Had you seen him before?'

'No.'

Dixon slid his phone out of his jacket pocket and looked again at Jane's text message. 'And you're sure you'd never seen him before?'

'Yes.'

Cole was driving slowly out across the Levels when another patrol car flashed past them, blue light flashing and siren wailing.

'Do you know what that was, Warren? That was your phone, computer, iPad and the USB sticks on the way to our High Tech department. You know, it's amazing what you can get off a phone these days, isn't it, Constable?'

'Yes, Sir,' replied Cole, his eyes fixed on the road ahead.

'Call logs for a start. Then there's email.'

'I don't know what you're getting at.'

'You're going to need a solicitor, Warren,' said Dixon, feigning concern. 'At the moment, you're looking at conspiracy to murder, at the very least, and that's a life sentence. More likely a straight murder charge; joint enterprise. We'll leave that to the Crown Prosecution Service, though.'

'I didn't know he was going to kill him.'

'Christopher Green?'

'Yes.'

'So, let me make sure I understand this correctly, the man you said you'd never seen before is actually Christopher Green?'

'Yes.'

'The same Christopher Green you shared a cell with at Wakefield for three months, according to the Prison Service.'

Clifford was sitting back, banging his head against the headrest behind him. 'Look, Green rang me and told me Mercer was outside, spying on Ben. So, I went out. That bit was true. I gave him a bit of a slap and then Green turned up and laid into him as well. Then he took him away in his car. I don't know where he took him, I didn't ask and he didn't tell me. He just told me to get rid of the van, which I thought I'd done.'

'You got rid of the van, all right, but not the cameras. We found them on eBay.'

'For fuck's sake.' Through gritted teeth.

'The sad thing is, Warren, I bet there was nothing on the footage that suggested Ben was exaggerating his claim. Far from his claim being thrown out, the insurers might well have increased their offer when they'd seen it. Happens all the time.'

'What would you know about it?'

Chapter Thirty-Three

'Drawing a blank on Green, Sir,' said Louise, her head popping up from behind her computer. 'No trace of him anywhere.'

'Did Clifford cause any trouble?' asked Jane.

'Quiet as a mouse,' replied Sarah. 'He's downstairs now, waiting for his solicitor.'

Dixon was scrutinising the whiteboards, not that there was much new information on them, except photographs of Higgs and Clifford side by side, looking remarkably like Stan and Ollie. 'What about Green's prison record?'

'They emailed it over, so I printed it off for you.' Louise was holding up a bundle of paper. 'We're still waiting for his medical records.'

'Anything interesting?'

'Very. You'll never guess who else he shared a cell with.'

'Who?'

'The open prison at Plymouth, for the last month before they were both released.'

'Who?' demanded Dixon, doing his best not to stamp his foot.

'Denton Miller.'

'What was he in for?'

'VAT fraud.' Louise had switched off her computer and stood up, slinging her handbag over her shoulder. 'From company director to caretaker in one easy step. Do you want me to drive while you read that?'

'Sarah's got the keys.'

'Oh yeah,' she said, rummaging in her pockets.

'Jane, you and Sarah interview Clifford and Higgs when they're ready, please.'

'You're off to Bristol, I suppose?'

Charlesworth's car was still in the visitors' car park at the front of the police centre, so forty miles away in Bristol seemed a good place to be. 'We need to speak to Miller.'

'I'll tell Charlesworth when he comes looking for you then, shall I?'

'Thanks.'

'He was waving a press release about, announcing two arrests.'

'Tell him not yet. Not till we've got Green.'

'If you say so,' said Jane, clearly not relishing the prospect.

'It's on the top floor,' offered Sarah, when Dixon and Louise headed for the door to the staff car park, Louise waving the keys in her direction in reply.

'Turn right out of Express Park,' said Dixon, when they were waiting on the electric ramp for the gates to open.

'Right?'

'Dave's place in Devonshire Street. It's down near the railway station.'

Louise knew better than to ask.

Dixon was still flicking through Green's prison record when Louise spoke again. 'What number is it again?' she asked, the Land Rover creeping along the narrow street, cars parked on both sides.

'Twenty-nine,' said Dixon.

'This one then.' Louise stopped and looked up at the terraced property on the driver's side. 'Lights are on. Where shall I park?'

'Just wait here a minute.'

Dixon slid out of the Land Rover and looked through the letterbox. Someone was moving in the kitchen at the back of the house, so he let the flap drop back with a clang and then banged on the door.

'Yes, Sir,' said Dave, answering the door quickly. Clean shaven, sober too, but then it was just before five.

'Going somewhere?' asked Dixon.

'I had a go at one of those dating apps,' replied Dave, looking sheepish. 'The one where the women make the first move. And someone did.'

'You haven't got time for that,' said Dixon. 'Get in.'

Dave leaned over and waved to Louise, still sitting in Dixon's Land Rover, the engine ticking over.

'Where are we going?' he asked.

'You're staying at my place.'

'What for?'

Dixon pushed past Dave into the hall and closed the front door behind them. 'Christopher Green killed Barry Mercer. We've got everybody out looking for him now, but there's no sign.'

'Green?' Dave let out a sharp sigh. 'That little shit.'

'He served eighteen years in the end – killed someone inside – and it's not beyond the realms of possibility he might come looking for you.'

'He's welcome to.'

'Grow up, Dave. You were investigating officer with Mercer. You interviewed Green and you were there when he was charged. I bet you were in court too, when he was sent down.'

'I've got a date. We're meeting at the Bristol and Exeter at six, and I'm not missing that.'

'Who with?'

'Her name's Ange, that's all I know. She's local, got a kid and a dog; that's all it says on her profile. Looks a bit of all right though, if the photo's not too old.' Dave squeezed past Dixon and reached down behind the front door curtain. 'Look, Sir, I only moved here six weeks ago. I'm not even on the electoral roll yet. How could he possibly find me here?'

'Is your ex-wife still at home?'

'It's empty and there's a sale going through. She's at her mother's in Chester,' replied Dave, producing a telescopic hiking pole that had been hidden in the corner behind the folds of the open curtain. The rubber bung on the end was gone, revealing a sharpened metal spike. 'Besides, I always keep this handy, just in case.' He grinned. 'You can never be too careful in our line of work.'

'I'll get uniform to swing by from time to time.' Dixon opened the front door. 'Make sure you've got your phone on you. And don't get too pissed.'

◆ ◆ ◆

'I was just closing up,' said Miller, through the glass doors of the art department at UAB an hour later, right about the time Dave would be meeting Ange. Dixon had arranged for a patrol car to be on hand, and two officers in civvies in the bar.

'I let the cleaners in and lock up at six,' continued Miller. 'Who are you looking for? They've all gone home by now.'

'You, Mr Miller,' replied Dixon.

'Oh, right.' Fumbling for the keys, dangling from a chain tied to his belt. 'You'd better come in.'

Dixon was distracted by someone wheeling a trolley down at the far end of the corridor, the squeak of the wheel soon drowned out by the rattle of keys and a snap of the lock behind him.

'What was it you wanted to see me about?' asked Miller.

'VAT fraud,' replied Dixon.

Eyes darting from side to side. 'We'll go in my office, if that's all right. Some people know my past, but most don't,' said Miller. 'And it's not something you want to broadcast.'

The click of their heels on the tiled floor; the trolley wheel echoing along the corridor.

'I was quite open about it at my interview,' said Miller, closing the door of his office behind Dixon and Louise. 'You have to be, don't you. I mean, in a place like this they do a database check anyway. Then how would it look if I'd lied about it?'

'You were sentenced to twelve months?'

'Served six.' Miller shrugged. 'Silly, really. How I ever expected to get away with it, I don't know, but I was desperate. Cash flow got tight, you know how it is. The old fictional invoices came to the rescue; invoices for purchases you've never made, but you can reclaim the VAT. Seemed like free money at the time. Till HM Customs and Excise are knocking on your door.'

Open blue UAB fleece over a white T-shirt, jeans flecked with paint that had been through the washing machine umpteen times.

'What line of business were you in?'

'Importing terracotta flower pots from Portugal. And what a bloody nightmare that became after Brexit.' Miller gritted his teeth. 'I bloody well voted for it too, didn't I?'

'How long have you been here?'

'Pretty much since I got out. They've been very good, to be honest. The taxman bankrupted me, disqualified me from acting as a director, dissolved my company, sent me to prison, took my house while I was in there. Then my wife divorced me, but UAB stepped in and gave me a job. God knows where I'd be now if they hadn't done that.'

'I wanted to ask you about your last few weeks at the open prison in Plymouth.'

'Counting down the days by then,' muttered Miller.

'You shared a cell with Christopher Green.'

'Not a nice bloke.'

Dixon had perched on the windowsill, his back to the bike sheds in the courtyard behind the art department. He glanced at Louise, who was leaning on a filing cabinet, making notes. 'Did you get to know him well?'

'Not really. It was only four weeks or so, and we were allowed out during the day anyway.'

'Where did you go?'

'I got a job at a car wash.'

'And what did Green do with his days?'

'No idea, I'm afraid.'

'Did he tell you what he was in for?'

Miller gave up trying to see what Louise was writing and sat down behind his desk. 'Causing death by dangerous driving, originally. He said he was innocent, but then everyone does, so you take it with a pinch of salt. That was a three-year stretch and he served a sod of a lot longer than that. There was a fight and he stabbed someone with a sharpened toothbrush; self defence, he said, but they added to his sentence for that – manslaughter, I think. There was a fight with a screw as well, took him hostage. That was more time. He served the lot, so in the end they couldn't keep him in any longer and out he walked a couple of days before me.'

'What was he like?' asked Dixon.

'Angry. If I had to sum him up in one word, it would be angry.'

'He had a lot to be angry about.'

'Stitched up by the police, he said, but worse than that, they mucked up his diabetes treatment when he was in prison; the wrong insulin, no insulin. Then he got circulation trouble, gangrene, and lost a couple of toes on his right foot. I think he was more angry about that than anything else. He tried suing the Prison Service, but you know what it's like if you're on the inside.'

'When was that?'

'Maybe halfway through his stretch.' Miller paused, then tutted. 'I'm not sure why I say that, really. He must've said something that gave me that impression, I suppose. Truth is, I don't really know.'

Dixon slid his phone out of his jacket pocket and opened up the photo album, clicking on a video. 'Have a look at this short bit of film and tell me if you know who that is,' he said, handing his phone to Miller. He watched Miller watching the footage – a flicker of recognition, perhaps.

'Is this him?' asked Miller.

'You tell me.'

'Could be, I suppose. Right sort of build and he had a slight limp. Can't see his face, though.'

'Have you been in touch with him since you both got out?'

'No way.' Miller cringed. 'He's not the sort of bloke you'd want to keep in touch with, to be honest; out for what he can get.'

'Feels like he's owed by society, I imagine.'

'Funny you should say that. He used that exact phrase once. "Society owes me," he said, "and I'm going to collect."'

'Did he ever talk of friends or family?'

'He had a sister in Clacton, I think. Somewhere like that.'

'What about transport?'

'An old car he gave to her when he was sent down, I think. It was some sort of classic, but nothing special. A Sunbeam or something like that. He used to take it round the classic car shows, he said, back when he was a very different person.'

'Do you know where he might have gone?' asked Dixon. 'Did he talk about his plans for when he got out?'

'You mean apart from collecting on what society owed him?'

Dixon remained impassive.

'He was looking forward to going racing, I remember that. The dogs. His nearest track was Swindon.'

'Have you got a phone number for him?'

'No bloody fear.' Miller laughed at the very idea. 'If I had I'd have thrown it in the bin. I'm on to a good thing here and I sure as hell wouldn't want him turning up and buggering it up for me. It's bad enough with you lot sniffing around all the time. I'm sure some of the lecturers think I've been up to something.'

Chapter Thirty-Four

'Let's chase up Green's medical records, Lou,' said Dixon. He'd watched Miller lock the glass doors from the inside and then walk back to his office.

'I know what you're thinking,' said Louise, 'but they checked Miller's ID when they took a formal statement from him; all checks out.'

It had been Miller's name on the door of the office too.

'Let's check with the gait specialist if the footage we've got could be a man missing the toes on his right foot. I know she said it was a prosthetic leg, but one limp looks much the same as any other to me.'

'And me.'

They ran from the shelter of the canopy at the front of the building across to Dixon's Land Rover, Louise pulling her jacket up over her head. Dixon opened the passenger door first, then ran round to the driver's side, reaching into the back for the dog towel as he climbed in.

'Here,' he said, offering the towel to Louise.

'No thanks.'

'It's clean.'

'I'm fine.'

'You know, for someone he couldn't stand and spent very little time talking to, Miller knew an awful lot about Green.' Dixon was drying his hands and face on the towel. Then he lobbed it into the back of the Land Rover. 'I don't think we asked one question he didn't know the answer to.'

'We checked him out.'

'ID can be forged,' said Dixon, turning the key. And there it was, the missing piece of the jigsaw puzzle, staring him in the face the whole time he had been speaking to Miller.

Dixon reached under the driver's seat and pulled out Green's prison record. Inside fly leaf, under health conditions: diabetes; type 1.

'Have we got a contact at the Prison Service?' he asked

'Jane has.'

'Get her to ring them now, I need to know if Denton Miller is diabetic and I need to know now.'

Dixon watched the rain running down the windscreen while Louise rang Jane; a short conversation, followed by a short wait before Jane rang back.

'No.'

Short it may have been, but it had felt like a lifetime.

Chapter Thirty-Five

'Stab vests,' said Dixon. 'There are some in the box under the bench seat.'

'Are you going to tell me what's going on?' asked Louise, standing by the open back door of the Land Rover, the rain trickling down her face.

Dixon handed her a stab vest. 'Miller is Green.'

'How d'you know?'

'A single drop of blood on his T-shirt. I get it when I inject myself through my shirt.'

'It could've been paint.'

'The paint on his trousers was old, and the brushes in his office haven't been used for days. It was blood.'

'So, where's the real Denton Miller?' asked Louise, zipping up her vest.

'Dead, probably,' replied Dixon. 'We'll worry about him later.'

Banging on the glass doors now, much harder and they'd shatter. Louise calling for backup on her phone.

'Police. Open up,' shouted Dixon, when a cleaner appeared along the corridor, nervously edging towards the doors. He slammed his warrant card against the glass. 'Open this door now!'

'I don't have a key.'

First door on the right was the canteen. Dixon had glanced in on his way past. 'The fire exit in the far corner of the canteen. Open it.'

'I can't do that.'

'Open it now.'

Dixon and Louise ran along the front of the building, watching the cleaner through the window as she weaved her way between the tables towards the fire door.

'Kick the bar. Do it now.'

Sirens in the distance.

A solid metallic clunk and the fire door swung open.

'Leave it open,' said Dixon, shouting over the fire alarm that had gone off as he ran past the bewildered cleaner. 'There'll be uniformed officers behind us.'

Sliding on the polished floor, Dixon and Louise stopped outside the door to Miller's office. Locked from the inside.

'Shit!' Dixon took a step back; then brought his foot up, kicking at the lock.

Louise had her cheek pressed to the glass of the window adjacent to Miller's office door, trying to look along the back of the building. 'His window's open, Sir,' she said. 'Looks like he's long gone.'

Another kick and the door swung open.

'Fuck it.' Louise had been right. The office was empty, the window opened wide enough to climb out of, rain collecting on the windowsill where Dixon had been sitting only twenty minutes ago.

'He can't have gone far, Sir. He stopped to do this before he left,' said Louise, gesturing to the wall opposite the window.

Stencilled, the paint still shiny and wet, running down the wall in places.

A windmill, bright red blood dripping from one of the sails.

'Left in a hurry, though,' she continued. 'His coat's still hanging on the back of the door.'

Dixon jumped out of the window, landing heavily in the sodden flower bed beneath. There had been three bicycles in the bike racks when he had been talking to Miller; now there were two and a set of wheel tracks in the wet grass. He followed them across the lawn, stopping on the far side, the tracks disappearing on the wet road surface, the last of the grass on the wheels deposited on the tarmac when the bicycle bounced down off the pavement. After that he could've gone anywhere.

Two uniformed police officers arrived on foot behind him, puffing hard.

'Which way'd he go, Sir?'

'No idea.' Dixon shook his head. 'Paint-spattered blue jeans, white T-shirt, blue fleece; on a bicycle. Get the description circulated and the helicopter up if it's available.'

'Yes, Sir.'

Dixon trudged back towards the open window, uniformed officers streaming out of another fire door further along and fanning out across the grass.

Blue lights were reflecting off the windows, the sirens almost drowning out the fire alarm.

The flash on the camera on Louise's phone was going off when Dixon walked into the office, Louise taking pictures of the stencilled painting on the wall.

'He's long gone,' said Dixon.

'See the leading edge of this sail,' said Louise, pointing at the one from which blood was dripping, the drips running down the wall and collecting in a puddle of red paint on a table that had been pushed against the wall. 'It's a blade, if you look closely, Sir.'

'I had noticed.'

'What the bloody hell is going on here?'

Dixon spun round. 'Mr Ratcliffe, fancy seeing you here.'

'I'm a key holder, so I got a call when the fire alarm went off.'

'I take it you knew the man calling himself Denton Miller was actually Christopher Green?'

'Of course I knew. It's why I gave him the job.'

'You never said.'

'You never asked.'

'Guilt, was it?'

'I think I'd better have my solicitor present before I answer any more of your questions.'

'I think you better had,' replied Dixon.

Chapter Thirty-Six

'Do you know how many windmills there are in Gloucestershire?'

Dixon was sitting in the passenger seat of his Land Rover, Louise speeding north on the M32 as fast as the diesel engine would allow. He leaned forward in his seat, his phone to his ear, and looked up at the bridge when they went under the roundabout at junction 3. The stencilled image of Sebastian Cook falling was still there, on the parapet, right above the inside lane. That was Slime Zee's death message.

This one was Evie Clarke's.

'Check them all,' Dixon said, into his phone. 'You've seen the picture?'

'Louise Willmott sent it to me.' Detective Inspector Coates sighed on the other end of the line. 'There must be at least twenty-five in the Cotswolds alone.'

'Evie Clarke is in one of them and she *may* still be alive.'

'We haven't got enough boots on the ground.'

'Then you'll need to work out how you're going to explain that to her parents, won't you, Inspector.'

Dixon rang off.

'Are they going to check them?' asked Louise.

'They don't have a lot of choice.' The screen of Dixon's phone lit up, then it started buzzing in his hand. 'An unidentified number,' he mumbled.

'The gait specialist was going to ring you. What's the dialling code?'

'01865.'

'That's Oxford.'

'Dixon.'

'It's Anne Tideswell, Inspector. I had a message to ring you.'

'We've got a suspect. There's no prosthetic leg, but he's lost some or all of the toes on his right foot.'

'That would do it.'

'Hardly limps at all though. Not when I've seen him.'

'Walking normally, it's far easier to disguise a limp. I might see it, but to the untrained eye it can become almost invisible, specially if they've practised. In the CCTV footage he's walking at speed and it's far more difficult to hide a limp in that situation. Do we know which toes?'

'We're still waiting for his medical records.'

'If it's his big toe then it becomes more difficult to hide the limp, but if he's still got that one then that might explain it. We spring forward off that toe more than any of the others. What caused it?'

'Diabetic complications.'

'Might well be the other toes then. I'd like to have a look at his medical records when you get them.'

'Thank you.' Dixon rang off and plugged his phone into the charger dangling from the cigarette lighter. 'Hardly an exact science, is it, gait analysis?'

'What is?' asked Louise.

'DNA.'

'Yeah, we've been unlucky there. There should've been something on Seb Cook if there'd been a struggle on the bridge, but we found nothing. And we were never going to find any on Barry Mercer.'

'I don't believe there was a struggle with Cook. Get him to look over the railings, grab his ankles and over he goes. Emma Carpenter was cremated, and there'd been people going in and out of her bedroom for six months.'

'Do you think Evie Clarke's still alive?'

'Her mother seems to think so.'

'What d'you think?'

'I think she was killed within a few hours of disappearing.'

'Me too.'

The rest of the drive to Cirencester was thinking time, Dixon watching the headlights flashing by on the other side of the road; brooding. Green had been right under his nose the whole time. Killing with precision and care, until he'd known the police were on to him. Then it had got bloody.

His one mistake had been trusting those idiots to get rid of Mercer's van, but then it probably hadn't occurred to him that the dismembered body would ever be found.

Who the hell had heard of magnet fishing, let alone tried it?

Dixon wondered whether the investigation had triggered the murders of Seb Cook and Evie Clarke. It was a question that had come up before in previous cases, but the answer was always the same. They'd have died anyway. Maybe Green would've taken more time and care over it, but the end result would've been the same. More funerals.

Now Green was on the run, Dixon kicking himself that he hadn't made the connection quicker.

It had been a drop-everything-and-find-him moment, and he was grateful to be on the road north, well out of the way of Charlesworth and his moaning about overtime and the cost of it all. Helicopter up, doors being kicked in all over Somerset.

And now Gloucestershire too.

Louise parked on the double yellow lines outside Cirencester police station.

The front doors were locked, the reception area closed; lights off.

'Shuts at five, would you believe it?'

Dixon spun round to find a man walking past on the pavement, a sheepdog perfectly to heel.

'Useless buggers, they are,' continued the man, with a dismissive wave.

Lights were on in the offices upstairs.

'Ring Coates and tell him we're here, will you, Lou,' said Dixon, rattling the huge steel gates at the side; they were locked too.

He just caught the movement in the upstairs window, then the lights came on in reception.

'Come in, Sir,' said Coates, locking the doors behind them. 'We're working our way through the windmills. There's a list on Wikipedia that gives the grid references, and we've got cars out all over the county. We're even checking those that have been converted, and the sites of others that it says have been demolished. Flat out, we are.'

'Nothing yet?'

'Nothing.' Coates opened the security door at the bottom of a flight of stairs.

'Have you told Mr and Mrs Clarke?'

'Thought it best not to, at least until we have some news one way or the other.'

The CID room on the second floor was all but deserted, two officers on phones, but the rest were out searching windmills, hopefully.

The whiteboard on the wall looked much like the one at Express Park, the same photographs of the same people and places. The same arrows and annotations.

A colour photograph of the windmill Green had painted on the wall of his office was front and centre, printed on thicker paper than was provided at Express Park. The ink hadn't curled the edges, although the blood dripping from the sail and puddling up on the table underneath looked more orange than red. The printer running out of ink, probably.

'Have you circulated this?'

'No point,' replied Coates. 'We're checking every windmill anyway, so what difference would it make?'

The look on Dixon's face must've been enough.

'I'll do it now.'

The list of Gloucestershire windmills had been printed off Wikipedia and stuck to the glass partition next to the whiteboard, one of the officers on the phones occasionally getting up, walking over to it and ticking off one that had been checked. It reminded Dixon of a scene from an old war film – ground staff ticking off aircraft that had returned safely, or gone missing perhaps.

Angels One Five, or something like that.

A young community support officer was hovering in the doorway, clearly nervous at the prospect of entering the hallowed ground of the CID room.

'What d'you want?' asked Coates.

'You uploaded a picture of a windmill, Sir,' he replied. 'And asked if anyone recognised it. Only I do.'

'Really?'

'It's Tysoe Windmill. Same shape and everything.'

'That one's not in our area,' said one of the CID officers, his hand over the speaker on his phone. 'It hasn't got any sails either. I checked.'

'Yes it has. It was restored earlier this year. New door, finial, sails and everything.'

'Are you sure?' asked Dixon.

'My nan lives in Tysoe and I take her dog up to the windmill for a walk when we go over there. It's in Warwickshire though.'

'Make the call,' said Dixon to Coates. Then he turned to the young PCSO. 'Can you take us there?'

'Yes, Sir.'

'How long?'

'It's about an hour from here, less if we blue light it.'

Chapter Thirty-Seven

The lay-by at the bottom of the hill was occupied by two police cars, a dog van and an ambulance by the time Dixon arrived on the edge of Tysoe.

Rural Warwickshire looked much the same as rural Somerset: rolling fields, lights from small villages visible in the distance, high hedges. The roads were wider though, that was one advantage. No deep rhynes either side waiting to trap the unwary – that was another.

An officer stepped out into the road in front of Dixon's Land Rover, his arm raised.

'Keep moving, please, Sir,' he said. 'There's nothing to see here.'

Dixon knew there was. He'd had the call from Coates.

'Oh right. Sorry, Sir,' said the officer, when Dixon pointed to the blue light on the roof. He gestured to the grass verge on the opposite side of the road. 'Would you mind parking over there, Sir? You'll be fine in a Land Rover, only I'm keeping that space for Scientific and there's a pathologist on the way too. Torches and wellington boots, if you've got them.'

Dixon kept a torch in the glovebox and a pair of wellies in the back.

'It's not too bad underfoot,' said the young PCSO. Luke somebody; they'd been halfway to Tysoe before Dixon had remembered the introductions. A bright lad, all the same. 'You'll be fine in those,' he said, shining his torch at Louise's leather boots.

'Thanks.'

'Is this as close as we can get?' asked Dixon.

'There's a farm track the other side of the hill,' replied the uniformed officer, who was still standing in the middle of the road. 'It's steeper, but you wouldn't get through the ford at the bottom. Well, you would in your Defender, but we wouldn't get Scientific's van up there, that's for sure.'

'All right, we'll walk.'

A new steel gate in a gap in the hedge, then the path turned left along the hedge. Dixon shone his torch up the hill, the direct line to the top gate taking him right across the open field; the open *ploughed* field.

'You'd lose your wellies in that mud, Sir,' said Luke. 'They leave a bit round the edge for walkers.'

The sound of a sliding van door down on the road behind them echoed in the trees as they turned in the corner of the field and followed the hedge up the hill, and a line of footprints in the wet grass.

Torches flickering up by the windmill, shafts of light climbing skyward and illuminating low cloud. No light coming from inside the windmill, though – the officers sensible enough to keep out until Scientific arrived. No doubt Warwickshire would have a crime scene manager on the way too. Best to get in and out before they arrived.

An owl hooted in the distance, just as the drizzle began to fall again. Dixon pulled up the collar of his coat while he waited his turn to squeeze through the kissing gate at the top of the field, his torch catching the sodden fleece of a sheep sheltering under the hedge on the far side.

The inevitable dog bag hooked on a branch, like some sort of warped Christmas decoration.

The last bit was the steepest, but then it always seemed to be; it was the same with any climb up any hill.

Five officers and a paramedic, standing in a circle, their torches all shining in the same direction.

'D'you mind?' said Dixon, shielding his eyes from the light.

'DCI Dixon, Sir?' asked a police sergeant.

'Yes.'

'PC Danvers got here first and made the call. No one's been in since then, apart from the paramedic. Nobody comes up here much, this time of year, except the occasional dog walker.'

'She's been dead for a while,' said the paramedic. 'Days, I'd say. Well past CPR, I'm afraid.'

Dixon shone his torch up at the windmill, the sails stationary. It was small, no more than two storeys high, of old red brick with a shiny new finial on the top that reflected the torchlight. The door was standing open, small, arched and solid oak; a padlock bracket snapped open.

'How did you get through this?' asked Dixon.

'I got the key from a Mr Baxter, Sir,' replied an officer with a German shepherd on a short lead. 'He's the chair of the Friends of Tysoe Windmill, lives down the hill. The key didn't fit, though – the padlock had been changed – so I had to break it anyway.'

Dixon had expected an empty shell, but the windmill was cramped inside. Full of timber cogs and wheels, vertical and horizontal, the milling stone underneath. It looked like it was in perfect working order.

He ducked and stepped in through the small door; the wall behind him sloped inwards and made standing up difficult.

'Are you sure you should be . . . ?' Louise gave up when she realised Dixon was going in, whatever she said.

He squeezed around the side of the millstone, ducking under the grinding wheel.

And there she was.

Curled up in the foetal position under a small flight of wooden steps on the far side of the windmill, a pool of blood congealed on the stone floor. Some had soaked into the cracks in the flagstones, some had been soaked up by the dregs of flour lying under the millstone.

Throat cut.

'It's Evie,' said Dixon, stepping back out into the darkness.

Chapter Thirty-Eight

Dixon passed four Scientific Services officers trudging up the hill on his way down. Two were carrying metal cases that looked more like glitter balls in the torchlight. The other two were carrying arc lamps. Behind them came a man in white overalls carrying a clipboard.

'DCI Dixon, is it?' he asked.

Dixon nodded.

'Designated crime scene manager. I'm told you went in the windmill without authorisation and without PPE. I'm going to be making a report . . .'

Tempting, but Dixon kept walking, the voice tailing off as he disappeared into the darkness.

Cars and vans were blocking the road by the time he let the metal gate slam behind him at the top of the lay-by. Two Scientific Services vans, a Volvo estate – the pathologist probably, they all seemed to drive Volvos – more marked cars, some Gloucestershire in amongst the Warwickshire now, blue lights flashing.

Coates was striding towards them, weaving his way between the vehicles. 'Is it her?' he asked.

'It is.'

'I'd better get someone to go and tell the family.'

'I'll go,' said Dixon. 'It needs to be somebody they know, and somebody senior. Is the pathologist here?'

'I'm just on my way up there now,' replied a woman who was just setting off up the hill; green overalls and white wellington boots. She stopped and turned by the gate, a metal briefcase in her hand. 'What can I do for you?'

'I need a best estimate of when she died before I go in to see her parents. They're an hour away by car.'

'I can do that.'

'Thanks.'

'Shall I ring the liaison officer and let her know you're coming?' asked Coates. 'Her name's Sally Coker.'

'Text her. She's to say nothing to the family.'

'I'll stay here if you don't mind, Sir,' said Luke. 'There are some of my lot here now, so I can get a lift back with them.'

'Thank you for your help,' Dixon said.

The drive south was conducted in silence and darkness, the only voice penetrating the monotonous growl of the diesel engine the satnav on Louise's phone.

'In one hundred yards turn left.'

'Turn left.'

They were waiting at a set of traffic lights on the edge of Burford when the phone rang, Dixon listening to her end of the conversation, Louise repeating much of what the pathologist was saying for his benefit.

'Throat cut from left to right. Clean. Severed the carotid artery left side. Less than a minute. No immediate sign of other injuries, except restraint, so probable cause of death. No sign of sexual

299

assault. Somewhere between seventy-two and ninety-six hours, so soon after she disappeared. Thank you.'

The mother's instinct had been wrong; clouded by wishful thinking.

'She's been dead the whole time,' said Louise, staring straight ahead. 'You'd like to think you'd know, but the truth is you don't – you can't.'

A light was on in the house opposite the Clarkes' when Dixon parked across the drive, the door opening as he took the blue light off the roof of his Land Rover and dropped it in a box on the floor behind the driver's seat.

He watched a man approaching, silhouetted against the lights behind him. Dark clothes, only a dog collar catching the light.

The Clarkes lived opposite the vicarage then.

'Do you have news for them?' asked the vicar.

'Are they religious, Reverend?' asked Dixon.

'They are members of my church.'

'You'd better come with us.'

The lights were on upstairs and down, curtains open, light streaming out and illuminating three cars squeezed on to the drive.

'I've not long left them,' said the vicar, in a hushed voice. 'We prayed together.'

Dixon reached up for the bell, the door opening before he had a chance to press it; the family liaison officer, mercifully.

'I was expecting you, Sir,' Sally said. 'Evie's parents are in the kitchen. Their son has gone to his grandparents', so he's out of the way.'

Then the kitchen door opened. Mr Clarke was standing in the doorway, his wife sitting at the pine table behind him.

Mr Clarke looked first at Dixon, then the vicar, then back to Dixon. 'You've found her.'

The family liaison officer hastily closed the front door behind them.

'There'll need to be a formal identification, but yes, we have, Mr Clarke,' replied Dixon. 'I'm sorry.' He didn't feel the need to spell it out; the presence of the vicar and the looks on their faces had been enough.

Mr Clarke looked up at the ceiling and let out a long sigh, the pain of not knowing being slowly replaced by acceptance of the inevitable, perhaps. Behind him, his wife tried to stand up, but slumped back into her chair, sobbing, acceptance of the inevitable manifesting itself in a gut-wrenching scream.

'You'd better come through,' said Mr Clarke.

The vicar stepped forward, kneeling next to Mrs Clarke, holding her hands tight.

'It's late,' said Mr Clarke. 'Have you eaten?'

'We're fine, thank you,' replied Dixon

'Tea, then.'

'I'll make it.' Sally was grateful for something to do, probably.

Mrs Clarke was rocking backwards and forwards in her chair, the vicar still holding her hands. Then she stopped abruptly and looked up. 'Have you seen Evie?' she asked, her eyes burning into Dixon's.

'I have.'

'Was she . . .' The words wouldn't come, lost in a long, slow gasp. She was twisting a handkerchief tightly, fighting to compose herself, to ask the question. 'Was she raped?'

'Not as far as we can tell. I saw no sign of sexual assault and the pathologist has confirmed—'

'Where is she?' asked Clarke.

'We found her in a windmill at a place called Tysoe,' replied Dixon. 'According to the pathologist, Evie's been dead for between seventy-two and ninety-six hours, so she was killed very soon after she disappeared on Thursday night.'

'I really thought she was alive,' mumbled Mrs Clarke.

'How did she die?'

Dixon had known that one was coming. It always did. 'There's a lot to confirm in the coming days,' he said. 'There'll need to be a post mortem, which will confirm the cause of her death.'

'You saw her,' said Clarke. 'You must know. How did my daughter die?'

Dixon looked at Mrs Clarke, her eyes wide, pleading. She nodded, in response to Dixon's unspoken question. 'If you're sure,' he said.

'We are.'

'Her throat had been cut, severing the carotid artery in the left side of her neck.'

'Death would have come very quickly,' said the vicar, with a comforting smile. 'She's at peace now, with the Lord.'

'Sally will be able to give you more news as soon as it becomes available,' said Dixon.

'I want to see her,' said Mrs Clarke. 'Is she still at the windmill?'

'It's a crime scene,' replied Sally, stepping forward and putting her arm around Mrs Clarke, the sound of a kettle boiling on the worktop behind her. 'It's very tightly controlled. When the Forensics team have done their bit, Evie will be moved to the mortuary and we can go and see her there.'

'When?'

'It's likely to be tomorrow now.'

'At peace with the Lord,' muttered Mr Clarke. 'Well, I'm bloody well not.' He turned to Dixon. 'They said you'd made arrests?'

'Two, but not the man who killed Evie. We know who he is and there are hundreds of officers looking for him, across Gloucestershire and Somerset.'

'You do something for me. You find him and you kill him.' Mr Clarke's composure was cracking, his breathing deepening. 'You do that for me. For us. You kill him.'

The vicar stood up. 'He can't do that, and you can't ask that of him.'

'Yes, we can.' Mrs Clarke started to sob again.

'There's no way I'm sitting in court watching that man grinning at me from the dock, then getting life with a minimum of twenty years. What's that all about? Life should mean life, and if it doesn't I want him dead.' Mr Clarke sat down at the table, his head in his hands, sobbing uncontrollably.

Sally Coker looked at Dixon and then nodded in the direction of the door. 'I'll make your excuses,' she mouthed.

Dixon and Louise stepped back into the corridor, Mr Clarke's shouts following them to the front door.

'You do that for us. You find him and you kill him!'

Chapter Thirty-Nine

It was just after two in the morning when Dixon finally dropped Louise back to her car at Express Park.

'Get some sleep, Lou,' he said, before watching her running up the ramp to the staff car park. Dixon knew what would happen when she got home; Louise had spent most of the drive south telling him. Her four-year-old daughter was about to be woken up and hugged for all she was worth, then they'd both fall asleep in each other's arms.

Delivering death messages was never easy at the best of times, but telling a parent their child was dead – murdered – was the worst. Worse still for a police officer who was a parent.

Dixon was dreading that.

Movement in the floor to ceiling windows on the second floor caught his attention, Jane waving at him and pointing at the ground; the universal signal to stay where you are. Dixon got the message. He switched off the engine and slid out of the driver's seat, watching Jane turn and run towards the stairs.

Then the side entrance burst open, Jane running with her phone to her ear.

'It's Lucy,' she said, breathing heavily. 'Billy's just dropped her home—'

'At this time of night?'

Jane waved Dixon's question away. 'And there's a death message on the wall of the cottage.'

'Our cottage?'

'Our cottage.'

Dixon snatched the phone from Jane. 'Where are you now?'

'In Billy's car,' whispered Lucy. 'We're parked over the road in the pub car park, lights off so no one can see us.'

'Get Billy to take you back to Westonzoyland.'

'What about Monty?'

'He's at Jane's parents in Worle. Tell me about the picture.'

'It's a stencil,' replied Lucy, the sound of an engine starting in the background. 'There's a coffin with a police helmet on the top and then there's blood dripping from one corner. That goes down the wall to a puddle of paint on the ground. I've got a photo of it. I'll send it over when I ring off.'

'Where are you now?'

'Going out towards the A38. There's no one around.'

'Tell Billy to take the M5, and stay on the line till you get out there.'

Dixon handed the phone to Jane and snatched open the door of the Land Rover.

'The police centre's the safest place, if he's coming after you,' said Jane, putting the phone back to her ear.

'It's not me,' replied Dixon, climbing into the driver's seat. 'It's Dave.'

'I'm coming with you.'

Jane opened the passenger door before Dixon could stop her, switching her phone to loudspeaker and dropping it in her lap while she put on her seatbelt.

'We're out on the A38,' said Lucy. 'There's no one behind us.'

Dixon handed his phone to Jane as he accelerated out of Express Park. 'Try Dave,' he said.

He got up to seventy miles an hour along Bristol Road, the deafening roar of the diesel engine all but drowning out conversation.

'It's ringing out,' shouted Jane.

'Call it in then. 29 Devonshire Street. We'll need Armed Response.'

'We're out on the M5 now,' said Lucy, still on the line on Jane's phone. 'No one followed us down the slip road and it's deserted.'

'Go back to Billy's, Lucy, and stay there,' shouted Dixon.

Jane disconnected the call with one hand and dropped her phone into her jacket pocket, still talking to Control on Dixon's phone.

He accelerated hard off the roundabout and into Polden Street, then left again into Devonshire Street.

The streetlights had gone off at half past midnight, plunging the terraced houses either side into pitch darkness – all except a single shaft of light coming from an open door, halfway down on the right. It lit up a car, parked in the road outside, lights off, driver's door standing open.

Whoever it was had turned at the bottom and parked ready to make a quick getaway, but Dixon's Land Rover now blocked the escape route.

He switched off his headlights and allowed the Land Rover to creep forwards, undoing his seatbelt at the same time.

Movement in the light streaming from the open doorway, then a figure running to the parked car, the driver's door slamming shut.

The headlights came on, lighting up the Land Rover.

'Is it him?' asked Jane.

'Let's find out,' replied Dixon. He accelerated hard, switching his lights back on; full beam, blue light on the roof. 'Yes, it is,' he said, watching Green climb out of the car and run towards the far end of the street.

Dixon stamped on his brakes and jumped out of the Land Rover, running across to Dave's open front door, Jane right behind him.

Dave was leaning against the door pillar, his right hand pressed to the right side of his neck, blood seeping out from between his fingers. 'I got him with this,' he said, grinning blood-streaked teeth and holding up the hiking pole in his other hand, blood dripping from the sharpened spike on the end.

Jane squeezed in behind Dave and tried to hold him up as the first sirens in the distance broke the silence.

'I'm going after Green,' said Dixon. He flicked on the light on his phone, then he turned and ran along the pavement towards the far end of the road.

Two cars and a white Transit van had reversed up to the high railings, blood smeared on the bonnet of the van indicating which way Green had gone. That and a blood-smeared knife lying on the tarmac beneath the front wheel.

Dixon followed: bonnet, roof, then a jump over the fence into the railway siding beyond.

He hesitated on the roof of the van, looking for movement in the darkness, a figure picking his way across the railway lines just visible in the headlights of a vehicle turning on the far side. Then Green was gone, stumbling into the darkness once more.

Dixon shone the light on his phone at the ground beneath the fence, the glow just enough to make out the gravel embankment below and, beyond that, the rusting tracks of the disused siding. Precious little vegetation to break his fall either, except for a few stinging nettles. Still, Green had done it and was banking on Dixon not following, no doubt.

He launched himself over the fence, his feet sliding on the gravel as he landed heavily, the drop further than he had been expecting. He'd hit the ground from this height often enough when rock climbing and knew to roll on landing – left to avoid the nettles – but instead he pitched backwards into the fence, hitting his head on a steel post. Then he was up and picking his way across the deserted siding towards the main line.

Shining the light ahead of him, he followed a gravel path of sorts across the tracks; rusting, rarely used, the air thick with the smell of diesel, the gravel beneath his feet coated with God knows what.

A signal box marked the edge of the main line, a figure on all fours across the tracks beyond.

Cackling.

The sirens were getting closer, louder, blue lights now reflecting off the rooftops of Devonshire Street.

'You have to help me,' sneered Green, lurching to his feet, stumbling backwards. 'It's your job.' His hand was pressed to his neck just like Dave's had been. 'He stuck me with a bloody walking stick.' Blood was bubbling up when he spoke, Dixon could see it in the lights.

Then the brakes on the freight train came on.

Late, but you wouldn't expect someone to be standing in the middle of the track at this time of night.

The squeal of the brakes almost drowned out Green's shout, but not the sickening thud that followed, Dixon watching the freight cars sliding past one by one, towering over him, wheels locked, sparks flying.

'Whatever,' he said, turning away.

Chapter Forty

Jane was sitting in the doorway, leaning against the open front door, cradling Dave in her arms, his legs stretched out in front of him across the pavement. She looked up at Dixon, tears leaving streaks in the blood spattered all over her face.

'He's gone,' she said. 'Just died in my arms.'

Dave's shirt had been ripped open, revealing more stab wounds in his stomach and chest.

'They tried CPR but it was no good; he'd lost too much blood.'

Bloodstained bandages were lying on the pavement, in amongst ripped-open packets and syringes, rubber gloves and an oxygen mask smeared with blood. A defibrillator too, the green cover spattered with blood.

'I had to put him down so they could try that, but I wasn't leaving him.'

Further along the pavement, two paramedics were sitting on a doorstep, one of them pulling hard on a cigarette.

Dixon leaned over and closed Dave's eyes with the flat of his hand.

'Where's Green?' asked Jane.

'Under a freight train.'

'Good.'

'Did Dave say anything?' asked Dixon.

'Wife, pension,' Jane sighed. 'And that's it, he was gone.'

Dixon sat down on the doorstep next to her and watched several uniformed officers ushering nosy neighbours back indoors, not that he could hear what was being said, the helicopter now hovering over the railway line. The freight train would've taken a mile or so to stop, and some people's parcels would be late the following day, but that was just tough.

'You've got blood on the back of your head,' said Jane.

'I'm fine.' Dixon ran his fingers through his hair and inspected the result; hardly enough to worry about – not compared to Dave anyway. 'I wonder how his date went?'

Jane frowned. 'Dave had a date?'

'I called here on the way up to Burford; tried to get him to go and stay at the cottage, but he had a date with someone he met online. Ange, her name was.'

'We'd better find her.'

'We will.'

'You dozy bloody . . .' The voice tailed off, Dixon and Jane looking up to find Mark Pearce standing over them. He was staring at Dave's body, tears welling up. 'Where's Green?' he asked.

'Dead, out on the railway lines,' replied Dixon. 'Dave got him.'

'He always gave a good account of himself.' Mark closed his eyes for a second. 'You two go and get yourselves cleaned up. I'll stay with him.'

'It's fine, Mark,' said Jane.

'No, really. I'd like to. I've worked with him for six years, the least I can do is be with him now. I wasn't when it mattered.'

Chapter Forty-One

A Scientific Services van was parked outside the cottage when Dixon and Jane arrived home just after dawn, after several hours spent at Express Park dealing with the formalities; a long shower for Jane, her clothes bagged up for evidence, then witness statements, wearing jogging bottoms and an ASP fleece.

An arc lamp had been set up on the pavement, the light shining at the wall of the cottage next to the front door, which was actually in the lane at the side; photographs, samples of the paint, dusting for fingerprints, the usual stuff.

Not that there was any doubt who'd painted it. The stencils and spray cans had been found in the back of Green's car that Dixon had blocked in outside Dave's house.

'When can we get rid of it?' asked Jane, staring at the stencilled image on the wall.

'As soon as you like,' replied the Scientific Services officer. 'We've finished with it.'

'I'll get Billy to do it. There's a tin of masonry paint in the shed that's the right colour. He'll be over in a bit with Lucy.'

'You need to get some sleep,' said Dixon, opening the door.

'Where are you going?'

'Pick up Monty, then back to Express Park.'

'It's over, surely?'

'Bar the shouting.'

Jane fell backwards on to the sofa and closed her eyes.

'Oh no you don't. Bed.' Dixon took her by the wrists and gently pulled her to her feet, wrapping his arms around her waist.

'I can't believe he's dead,' she said. 'If only we'd got there a bit—'

'ACC's here.' The call came from outside, the front door of the cottage still standing open, light from the arc lamp streaming in.

'I'll put the kettle on,' said Jane, heading for the sanctuary of the kitchen.

'Can I come in?'

'Yes, Sir.'

'Very sad about Dave Harding,' said Charlesworth, tucking his hat under his arm. 'And Evie Clarke, of course.' He was looking nervously around the cottage, behind the sofa and up the stairs.

'Monty's at Jane's parents.'

'Oh, right. Thank you.'

'Coffee, Sir?' asked Jane, from the kitchen.

'No, thank you. Look, Nick, we've got a statement from the train driver. He says he saw Green late, blames his dark clothing. You can imagine it, I expect.' Charlesworth cleared his throat. 'But he says he also saw a second figure by the tracks. I'm guessing that was you?'

'Yes, Sir.'

'There was no time to get him out of the way, I suppose?'

'I followed Green across the siding, made an assessment of the risk and decided it was unsafe to follow him on to the main line, so I retreated to a safe distance whilst keeping the suspect under observation at all times. It's all in my witness statement.'

'Unlike you to follow procedure.'

'I'm about to become a husband and father.'

'Quite.'

'Has someone spoken to Dave Harding's widow?' asked Dixon.

'I thought he was getting a divorce?'

'Getting, not got. They're still married, and Dave's last wishes were that she should get his pension.'

Jane was standing in the kitchen doorway, a milk carton in her hand. 'I was there when he died, Sir,' she said. 'If it wasn't for Dave, Green would've got away. He deserves a posthumous commendation, at the very least.'

'It's just a shame he was facing that file tampering allegation.' Charlesworth's sentence was punctuated by another catch of the throat; deliberate this time, to hide his embarrassment. 'Professional Standards have to complete their investigation, and if they find evidence he was responsible then his pension will be forfeited.'

Dixon wasn't letting that pass; not now, not ever. 'I wonder if we might have a word in private, Sir? Outside, perhaps.'

'Er, yes, fine.'

Charlesworth followed Dixon round the back of the cottage and into the yard. The Scientific Service officers had packed up the last of their equipment and were leaving.

'What is it, Nick?'

Dixon was standing behind Jane's car and turned his back on the cottage, conscious that she was watching from the bedroom window and was a passable lipreader.

'I am satisfied that Dave Harding did not tamper with Barry Mercer's missing person file, Sir.'

'The PSD are not, and they'll need to complete their investigation,' replied a clearly exasperated Charlesworth. And not just because it was drizzling again.

'I was surprised to find there was no copy of the arresting officer's witness statement on Green's causing death by dangerous driving file. The same officer would've been responsible for seizing the tachograph and introducing it in evidence. There's a photocopy of the tachograph on the file, but no statement.'

'Don't tell me he tampered with that file as well.'

Dixon took a deep breath. 'No, Sir, he did not.'

'Who did then?' Charlesworth was becoming agitated now, although the beads of sweat on his forehead could've been raindrops, possibly. 'D'you know?'

'The photocopy of the tachograph is only one-sided,' continued Dixon. 'Whoever copied it failed to do the back with the exhibit label on it, so I got the original out of store.' Dixon slid a piece of paper out of his jacket pocket and unfolded it. 'Exhibit DC1,' he said, reading from the label on the reverse. 'Dated twenty-eighth February 2002, exhibited to the witness statement of Police Constable 2176 David Charlesworth.'

The blood drained from Charlesworth's face.

'Keep it,' said Dixon, holding the photocopy in his outstretched hand, the paper sagging in the rain. 'I've made several copies. Double-sided this time.'

Charlesworth snatched the document, screwed it into a ball and stuffed it in his trouser pocket.

'I looked at the transcript of the trial and your evidence was agreed by the defence, so when did you find out Mercer had switched the tachograph exhibited to your witness statement? I'm guessing it was later.'

'Much later.' Charlesworth was breathing heavily through his nose. 'It was when Harding made his complaint about Mercer's conduct, although I'd been promoted and transferred to Portishead by then.'

'I'm assuming you stepped forward and supported him in that complaint then?' asked Dixon. Another question he knew the answer to, but he asked it all the same, just to watch Charlesworth squirm.

'To my lasting shame and embarrassment, I did not.'

'Career first.'

'Yes.'

'Dave Harding died in the line of duty, Sir. It was thanks to him that a multiple murderer was caught and he's going to be recognised for that. His widow's going to get his pension too, and if I hear any suggestion that the file tampering allegation is being pinned on him, I will make it my life's work to prove who really did tamper with that file. Do we understand each other?'

'You'd never be able to prove it.'

'Care to bet on that?' Dixon remained impassive. 'And besides, I wouldn't need to. The "no smoke without fire" merchants would have a field day at your expense.'

Silence.

'Do we understand each other? Sir.'

'We do.'

'Asking a probationer to review Mercer's missing person file was a good idea, but you picked on the wrong one. Sarah's got brains.'

'So it seems.' Charlesworth was deliberately averting his gaze from the upstairs window, where Jane was standing, her frown growing ever deeper. 'Does anyone else know about this?'

'No.'

'I'd be grateful if you kept it that way.'

'I will, Sir,' replied Dixon. 'But for her sake, not yours.'

315

Chapter Forty-Two

'Is it true?' Louise had been crying, her eyes red, traces of mascara on her cheeks. She was standing on the edge of a small gaggle of officers – some in uniform, others in civvies – on the landing outside the canteen, waiting for it to open. The news had clearly reached the catering staff too. 'They're all wearing black armbands in there,' she said.

The animated conversation petered out, the faces turning towards Dixon one by one.

'Yes, it's true,' he said. He raised his voice slightly, his tone sombre. 'Detective Constable Dave Harding died in the early hours of this morning. He was attacked by Christopher Green on his doorstep, and in the course of the struggle was able to inflict an injury on Green that later proved fatal.'

'He got the bastard.'

Dixon didn't recognise the officer, but he did the sentiment. 'Yes, he did. Green collapsed on the main line while trying to make his escape and was hit by a freight train.'

The word 'good' stood out from the otherwise indistinguishable murmur.

And 'good old Dave'; that would become a common refrain, no doubt.

'Where's Jane?' asked Louise, when the other officers turned back to the canteen, the doors being unlocked from the inside.

'Getting some sleep,' replied Dixon. 'Dave died in her arms, so she's a bit . . . she just needs a bit of time.'

'She's a copper.' Louise was looking along the corridor, over Dixon's shoulder. 'And she's got a job to do.'

He spun round to find Jane striding along the landing towards them.

'Couldn't sleep,' she said, walking straight past, towards the stairs up to the second floor.

The incident room was crowded, Louise sitting down at a workstation at the front, next to Sarah. The computer was on, Louise's coat slung over the back of the chair, the customary signs that it was taken. Otherwise it was standing room only, Deborah Potter hovering at the front, pretending to look at the whiteboard.

'Would you like to say a few words, Ma'am?' asked Dixon.

'You can handle it,' she said.

'Thank you.'

The chatter stopped abruptly when Dixon stepped to the front of the incident room.

'Detective Constable David Harding was a hard-working, loyal and honest police officer, and I was privileged to work with him. Many of you knew him, and it is a testament to him that there are so many of you here this morning. He died in the early hours of this morning in the line of duty. It is entirely thanks to Dave that Christopher Green is no longer a threat to the public, but there is still work to be done in this investigation and we owe it to Dave to do it to the best of our ability.'

'He should never have been suspended.' The voice was taut, the face hidden behind one of the many computers.

Dixon glanced at Potter, her face reddening.

'The decision taken to suspend him for the purposes of this investigation was the right one,' continued Dixon, cutting the word 'technically' off the end of his sentence. 'But let me be absolutely clear: Dave was eliminated from our enquiries very early and there is no suggestion whatsoever that he played any part in the murder of Barry Mercer. They were former colleagues, and both were investigating officers in the prosecution of Christopher Green in 2002 for an offence of causing death by dangerous driving. Dave was a victim in this case, not a suspect.'

'Dave would never tamper with a file either.' The same voice again. Dixon thought he recognised it this time.

'I am satisfied that Dave did not tamper with the file,' he said. 'And I fully expect him to be exonerated formally in due course.'

'He'd better be.'

Dixon let that one go. 'Does anyone have any questions?'

'Did anyone actually see Green die, Sir?' A uniformed sergeant at the back.

'I did,' replied Dixon. 'It was the Parcelforce train going at seventy miles an hour and I was a few feet away when it hit him.'

'Thank you, Sir,' replied the sergeant, nodding his understanding.

'How did Dave die, Sir?' asked another.

'He was attacked with a knife and defended himself with a hiking pole.'

'Was he alone when he died, Sir?'

'Detective Sergeant Jane Winter and I got there just after the attack, and Jane was with him when he passed away.'

She was perched on the edge of a table at the side of the incident room, several hands reaching across to pat her on the back.

'Dave leaves a widow,' continued Dixon. 'And there'll be a collection in due course. No doubt you'll all give generously. Funeral arrangements to be confirmed.'

'Good old Dave.'

'Those of you not directly involved in the investigation, I'm sure you have places you need to be.'

Potter used the crowd dispersing as cover. 'Who was that, half-way back, on about the file tampering?'

'I don't know, Ma'am,' replied Dixon, lying. 'I couldn't quite see where the voice came from, I'm afraid.'

'Presumably you'll be wrapping things up now?'

'There are questions, and I've still got Ratcliffe in custody downstairs.'

'The clock's ticking, remember,' said Potter, heading for the stairs. 'Twenty-four hours, and you brought him in late yesterday afternoon.'

'I'm sure I can find a superintendent who will grant me an extension.'

'Don't bank on it.'

The crowd had gone, leaving empty workstations covered in plastic coffee cups behind them.

'One killer,' said Dixon. 'Two different motives. Barry Mercer and Dave were murdered because Green blamed them for his 2002 causing death by dangerous driving conviction, and everything that flowed from that. Emma Carpenter, Sebastian Cook and Evie Clarke were killed because they were trying to unmask Van Gard and we've got him downstairs, in custody. What we need to be able to do is prove Malcolm Ratcliffe was instrumental in their murders; that he gave the orders. I want him for murder, not just conspiracy.'

'I've got the funeral footage that Mercer filmed,' said Sarah. 'It was on the flash drives we found in Warren Clifford's garage. There's not much, mind you.'

'Ratcliffe must've told Green that Mercer had seen him at the funeral. Maybe there was a confrontation?'

'The footage just shows people arriving for the funeral tea,' said Sarah. 'No argument; nothing like that.'

'Let's check Green's and Ratcliffe's mobile phone records. We need to go over Ratcliffe's alibis too; check them, and then check them again. Track Green's car on traffic cameras.'

'I'll do that,' said Mark, his head popping up from behind the computer Dixon had been keeping his eye on.

'What are you doing here?' asked Dixon.

'I came in when they took Dave.' Mark shrugged. 'Nowhere else to go, except home to an empty flat.'

'You haven't slept.'

'Neither have you.'

Another one to let go. 'The file tampering allegation is in hand. Just leave it, Mark.'

'Yes, Sir.'

'Let's make some enquiries about the real Denton Miller. Green took his identity, and probably his life, so I'm not holding my breath.'

'I'll do that,' volunteered Sarah.

'Ratcliffe's solicitor is hopping up and down, Sir,' said Louise. 'Demanding to know when you're intending to interview his client. He's in reception, apparently.'

'Where's this footage from the funeral?' Dixon asked.

'I've got it here,' Sarah replied, opening a file on the computer in front of her. 'It's only a few seconds, but I've got several stills from it and enlarged them.' She clicked Play.

The camera was focused on the front of the Cliffords' bungalow, an out-of-focus car passing in front of the lens and the murmur of voices in the background somewhere.

'I think that's the side window,' said Sarah. 'Now it moves to the back window to look along the lane.'

All went dark as the camera swept across the inside of the van, the lens not having time to refocus. Then it was looking out of the back, along the lane towards the Carpenters' bungalow, cars parked on both sides of the road, another backed up to the stile at the far end.

People were walking with umbrellas above their heads, all in the direction of the open front door. All in black too, apart from a group of younger mourners in bright colours. It was a scene played out at umpteen funerals every day.

'Watch the SUV there,' said Sarah, pointing at the screen, a large dark vehicle parked facing away from the camera.

'That's Malcolm Ratcliffe getting out the driver's side,' said Louise. 'And that's Trudy Lister in the front passenger seat, but who's that getting out of the back?'

'Dominic Meek,' replied Sarah. 'Teaches Developing Practice and Professional Practice at UAB.'

'The family did say there were some people they didn't know,' offered Jane.

'Neither Malcolm Ratcliffe nor Trudy Lister mentioned him being there,' muttered Dixon.

'We've got a statement from him.' Sarah was holding a piece of paper up in front of her, waiting for someone to snatch it. 'Makes no mention of being at Emma Carpenter's funeral either.'

Chapter Forty-Three

'I was never asked!'

Dominic Meek was standing in front of a canvas in the studio at UAB, a paintbrush in one hand and a palette in the other. An oil painting, not that Dixon could make out what it was supposed to be. A dismal failure at Creative Analysis, but then he could live with that.

The art department was a hive of activity, although that was mainly Scientific Services officers tearing the head of department's and the caretaker's offices apart.

Meek was watching the search of Ratcliffe's office through the glass partition. 'You can't seriously think Malcolm's involved in this?'

Dixon treated it as a rhetorical question.

Black jeans and a blue T-shirt, both smeared with paint. There were even flecks of paint in Meek's beard and on the lenses of his spectacles.

'Were you aware that the man claiming to be Denton Miller was not actually who he said he was?'

'No. I'm just a junior lecturer here. I'm not involved in recruitment decisions or anything like that. I'd seen this bloke around, and I knew the caretaker's name was Denton, and we'd spoken a couple of times, maybe.' Meek was waving his paintbrush in the air, giving the impression he was conducting an orchestra.

'What about?'

'His hatred of modern art, mainly, and how it's just pretentious crap. He said Creative Analysis was just teaching students how to justify the fact they had no talent, which is a fair point in some cases.'

'Have you seen the picture on the wall of his office?'

'I poked my head around the door, yes.'

'He painted it.'

'He said using stencils was painting by numbers. Anybody could do it. Some artists go for satire; he offered sarcasm.'

'Evie Clarke was found dead in a windmill last night, with her throat cut.' It was as close as Dixon could get to wiping the smirk off Meek's face.

'Evie's dead?'

'His real name was Christopher Green,' Dixon said. 'And he'd just been released from prison.'

'Prison?'

'What was the relationship like between Malcolm Ratcliffe and Green?' asked Dixon.

'As you would expect. Malcolm was head of department and Dent . . . Green, or whatever his name was, was the caretaker. We had issues come up at staff meetings that Malcolm said he'd raise with him. Boring stuff – litter, lavatory paper running out in the loos, that sort of crap. They weren't best mates, if that's what you're asking?'

'Were you aware there was a history between them?'

'No.' Hands on his hips now; more paint on his T-shirt. 'What history?'

'You say you weren't asked whether you were at Emma Carpenter's funeral when your original statement was taken?'

'No, I wasn't.'

'And you didn't think to mention it?'

'No, I'm sorry, I didn't,' he replied, dropping his paintbrush – bristles first – into a jar of white spirit. 'I've never had dealings with the police before and I just answered the questions I was asked, as best I could. That's what we're supposed to do, isn't it?'

'You'll have to forgive me if I'm a little brusque this morning,' said Dixon. 'Christopher Green stabbed a colleague of mine to death in the early hours of this morning.'

Meek froze. 'I'm sorry. Nobody said anything to me, just that it was part of the ongoing enquiry into Emma Carpenter's death.'

'And Evie Clarke's.' Dixon had spotted the flecks of blood on the sleeve of his jacket on the drive up to Bristol, but couldn't be sure whether it was Dave's or Green's. Or both, perhaps. It made a stark contrast with the flecks of paint. 'How well did you know Emma and Evie?' he asked.

'They were both on my Developing Practice course last year, and Evie was doing Professional Practice this year.'

'Were you here when Sebastian Cook was a student?'

'Name doesn't ring a bell, so he must've been here before my time. I've only been here two years.'

'Went by the name of Slime Zee,' replied Dixon. 'Green threw him off a bridge at junction 3 of the M32.'

Meek sat down on a tall stool; his face was much the same colour as his shirt now, behind the beard and the paint.

Dixon had his attention, so now was the time to ask the important questions. 'Tell me what happened at Emma's funeral,' he said.

'Nothing, really,' replied Meek, clearly thinking it an odd question. 'It was just a funeral. I was in the car with Malcolm and Trudy and we met the family at Taunton Crematorium. Then afterwards we went back to their house for the funeral tea. Curry Rivel, I think it was. We weren't there long.'

'Do you remember a white van parked in a lay-by on the main road?'

'Yes. The driver was talking to Malcolm when I came out, but I thought it was just about parking or something. Malcolm looked at the back bumper of his car, so I thought maybe someone had reversed into it?'

'Where was Trudy?'

'Already in the car, I think. In the front passenger seat.'

'Had Mr Ratcliffe seen you when he looked at the bumper?'

'Yes.'

'And could you hear what was being said?'

'Not close enough, I'm afraid, and when I approached, the man scrambled up the bank, got back in his van and drove off. They never mentioned it and I just got in the car and we came home.'

'Are you familiar with Van Gard's work?'

'Everybody is, surely? Even the non-arty types.'

'Do you rate it?'

'I'm not a huge fan of the street art scene to be honest, and leave teaching that to Trudy. There's this big mystery about Van Gard's identity; a few people know who they are, but—'

'They?' interrupted Dixon.

'Sorry.' Meek's face reddened. 'Force of habit. I don't know how Van Gard identifies, so university guidelines tell us to use gender neutral pronouns.'

'Would it surprise you to learn that Mr Ratcliffe has admitted to being Van Gard?'

'Malcolm? I never thought he was talented enough, to be honest. But, for God's sake, don't tell him I said so.'

◆ ◆ ◆

The arc lamps were still blazing in Green's office, Dixon staring at Evie Clarke's death message. The table had gone, taking with it the puddle of red paint.

He'd never have the chance to ask Green why he had painted them now, although he had a fairly good idea. This was a man who hated the establishment, the police, the prison service; who blamed them for the systematic destruction of his life. First his job, then his wife, house and health; an eighteen-year transformation into a man with a burning grievance.

He had been taunting the police.

That explained the deaths of Dave and Barry Mercer, but why would he be killing students who threatened to expose Van Gard? If Dixon was a betting man, he'd place his money *on* money.

Plastic crates were lined up along the wall in the corridor outside, each containing several evidence bags and labelled on top. Nothing terribly exciting, but then you'd hardly keep anything incriminating in such a public setting.

Or would you?

A piece of paper had been found Sellotaped to the underside of a filing cabinet drawer, the evidence bag marked 'Login details, unidentified'. Dixon slid a pen out of his jacket pocket and crossed out 'unidentified', writing 'BITCOIN WALLET' above it.

Killing to protect his blackmail victim, his source of money. And a rich source it was too, provided Van Gard remained anonymous.

It would make for an interesting conversation with Ratcliffe when he got back to Express Park.

'Shall we have a look in Ratcliffe's office, while we've got the chance?' asked Louise. 'Scientific have almost finished in there.'

'Why not?' Dixon gave a tired smile. 'You never know what we might find.'

Ratcliffe's computer had gone to High Tech, a very nice top-of-the-range Mac, but that was about it, the wireless keyboard and mouse still sitting on the glass desk.

'Bugger all in here,' said the Scientific Services officer, his mask pulled down below his chin. Even the plastic crate on the floor just inside the door was empty.

It didn't bode well.

'The filing cabinet's just confidential student personnel files and stuff like that. I did get someone to open it and had a look.'

Dixon was working his way along the bookshelves. One caught his eye: *What Happened to Art?: A Guide for the Puzzled*. It could have been written for him. Then he stopped.

'Did you get a copy of the book those pictures of Jackson Ogunwe had been torn out of – the ones in his mother's scrapbook.'

'No, sorry, Sir. It's out of print. I rang round the libraries, but no one's got a copy.'

'Yes, they have.'

And there it was. In between a biography of Andy Warhol and a copy of *Modern Art: A History from Impressionism to Today*.

Vanguard, Bristol Street Art: The Evolution of a Global Movement. Dixon held the spine in his right hand and flicked through the pages. None missing, which was a bonus. He turned to the chapter on Upfest, finding the pictures of Jackson. There were even pictures of the underpass at junction 3 on the M32.

A little light reading for the journey home, thought Dixon, lobbing Louise his car keys.

Chapter Forty-Four

A gin and tonic at lunchtime wasn't entirely unusual during the Christmas holidays. The drink was in her left hand, a cigarette clenched between her teeth, when Trudy Lister opened the front door of her flat.

'You again,' she said, without moving her lips.

Louise had spent much of the drive over to Clifton reminding Dixon that time was running out to charge or release Ratcliffe, although much of it had gone in one ear and out the other, Dixon absorbed in the Bristol Street Art Movement.

He brushed past her into the flat, Trudy making a token effort to block his path before stepping back.

'What d'you want?'

'I want to know about your relationship with Malcolm Ratcliffe,' replied Dixon, following the light at the end of the corridor into her studio. Something was on a plinth in the bay window – something half-finished, hopefully – and an apron draped over a stool.

'God, who told you about that?'

Dixon waited.

'It started a long time ago. Wendy knows about it, but we've got past it and we all get on, all right?' Flicking her ash into an empty can of gin and tonic on the mantelpiece.

'How did it start?'

'A drunken fumble when we were away at some conference or other. It must've been ten years ago and it lasted, maybe, eighteen months. Then we sat down and had a perfectly adult conversation about what the bloody hell we were doing and where it was going.' Trudy took a drag on her cigarette, holding the smoke in while she continued. 'We both said nowhere, basically, so that was it. An entirely mutual decision. We parted friends and have remained so ever since.'

'He's admitted to being Van Gard.'

'That's because he is Van Gard,' she replied, exhaling at the same time.

'Which means you lied.'

'Of course I lied, about *that*.'

'Dominic Meek expressed surprise.' Dixon was looking at the pictures on the wall, pretty much every available space taken – a mixture of framed artworks and photographs.

'That's mainly work by my students,' said Trudy, following Dixon, but at least having the courtesy to turn away when she exhaled. 'Some of them have been very talented. Others not so.'

'What about Meek?'

'Mediocrity, and jealous with it,' she replied, with a dismissive wave that deposited ash on the dustsheet.

'I recognise that one,' said Dixon, leaning in to look closely at a black and white photograph on the wall.

'That was taken by Emma Carpenter. It's Van Gard's *Ebbing Tide*. A very famous piece.' Three people in a rowing boat, the image stencilled on a tiled wall in a flooded subway, waves added just above the water level. The bow was real, cut off a real boat and

329

bolted to the wall, giving it a three-dimensional quality. 'It was one of Van Gard's first installations. In a subway at Bedminster; there's one that's always flooded.'

'Where is it now?'

'It was moved to a gallery in London. They had to, the boat was blocking the path.'

'What's the significance of that?' asked Dixon, pointing at the name stencilled on the bow.

'God, you'd fail Creative Analysis, wouldn't you?' Trudy shook her head. 'It's a lifeboat from a fictional ship called the *Corporate Creed*. It's satire.'

'I'll take your word for that.'

'And a play on words.' Trudy could scarcely hide the incredulity in her voice. 'You don't approve?'

'It's not my place to approve or disapprove. I'm just a humble police officer.'

'There's nothing humble about you.'

'Are you still involved in the street scene?' asked Dixon, deciding a change of subject was called for.

'I have to stay up to date because I lecture on it, but I only paint on canvas these days. I dabble with sculpture too,' Trudy said, gesturing to the bay window.

'You were at UAB yourself, I gather?'

'Late nineties. I left in 2000, had a few years in London and then came back.'

'With a conviction for criminal damage?'

'It's a badge of honour for a street artist – at least it was back then. Nowadays finding legal venues is far easier, so there's no need to risk it.'

'And that didn't stop you getting a job at the university?'

'I think it helped, actually.' She dropped her cigarette end into the empty can of gin and tonic, a wisp of smoke rising.

'Did you know Jackson Ogunwe?' asked Dixon. 'He was active in the street art movement until 2002.'

'JAKZ,' said Trudy. 'Yes, I knew him. We did a painting together at Upfest the year before he died. There's a picture of us on some scaffolding on the side of an end terrace in Cheltenham Road. It's long gone now, but there's a book with it in.'

'I've got Mr Ratcliffe's copy in my car.'

'There's another, bigger one we did on the side of a block of flats. That's still there, that one. TRDZ was my tag back then, but we move on, don't we?' She lit another cigarette. 'I did a guerrilla piece that year too, but the less said about that the better. It was just a daub in a subway. I'd had a few too many.'

'Did you know what happened to Jackson?'

'He was hit by a lorry down in the underpass on the M32. It was very sad. We lost another that year too. A lad by the name of DVD; David somebody. He'd abseiled over the top of Avon Gorge to paint the cliff and fell to his death. It was the bit under the suspension bridge there.'

'Tell me about the piece you and Jackson did on the side of the flats.'

'You've seen it, surely?' replied Trudy, sitting down on the stool. 'It's something of a Bristol landmark and you can hardly miss it.'

'As we've established, I think, I'm hopeless at Creative Analysis.'

'It took us the whole week; over six floors. It's a man in a suit and a bowler hat pouring blood from a paint pot. I think it might have been the See No Evil festival, that came before Upfest. Anyway, he's pouring the blood down a drain, and we had a puddle on the ground at the bottom of the block around a real drain, so it was part painting and part installation.'

'A bit like *Ebbing Tide*, with the bow of the boat?'

'Yes, I suppose.'

'Same satirical message?'

'Corporate greed was the theme of the day. It's moved on to climate activism now. A lot of the street art you see is focused on that. Priorities change, things move on.'

'Have you seen the painting on the wall of Green's office?'

'I popped in earlier and Dominic showed it to me.'

'He seems to be mimicking your puddles of blood,' said Dixon. 'There's been one underneath each of his paintings.'

'I really don't know what to say to that, I'm afraid.'

'How well did you know Green, although you'd have known him as Denton Miller, of course?'

'Hardly at all. He was just the caretaker.'

'Did you know he was the driver of the lorry that killed Jackson Ogunwe?'

'Was he?' Trudy puffed out her cheeks. 'No, I never knew that.'

'You knew that unmasking Van Gard was a central theme of Emma Carpenter's project, though?' Dixon was examining the sculpture on the plinth in the bay window; half-finished had been optimistic, more like just started. He resisted the temptation to ask what it was supposed to be. 'Did that ever cause you to question her death? Ask yourself whether it was deliberate?'

'Whether she was murdered?'

'Seb Cook and Evie Clarke both were.'

'It didn't, but I suppose when you stop and think about it.'

'How well did Malcolm Ratcliffe and Green get on?'

'I don't know. As far as I'm aware, it was just a professional relationship. There were issues from time to time that he had to take up with the caretaker, but that was it. There are other departments in the building and I'd imagine their heads had the same relationship with Denton, or Green, or whatever you want to call him.'

'Was Green blackmailing Malcolm?'

'If he was, Malcolm certainly never said anything to me!'

'Why didn't you mention that Dominic Meek had been at Emma Carpenter's funeral when you were first asked about it?'

'I must've forgotten. I didn't really want to be there at all and was on autopilot for most of the day if you must know. I had a couple of them in the car on the way down,' she said, gesturing to the can of gin and tonic. 'To help me get through the day.'

'Do you remember a white van parked outside the Carpenters' house?'

'Malcolm said some bloke had backed into his car, but it hadn't done any damage so they went their separate ways without exchanging details.'

'What are you doing for Christmas?' asked Dixon, turning for the door. 'Not going anywhere, I hope.'

'Just to my parents' in Bath,' replied Trudy. 'Mum's not well and Dad's struggling a bit with it all. I do what I can, when I can.'

◆ ◆ ◆

'I've got the chief super on the phone,' said Louise, her phone pressed to her ear. 'Wants to know if you want the extension for Ratcliffe or not.'

'Tell her yes.'

'You heard that, Ma'am,' said Louise. 'I really don't know.' Louise rang off.

'What was it you really don't know?' asked Dixon.

'She asked me if we were making any progress.'

A Scientific Services van was waiting for them at the railway arches, Donald Watson having said he'd meet them there. It was the one place Dixon hadn't been; the one place he hadn't got the feel of.

'There wasn't a lot here,' said Watson, unlocking the main door. 'Well, there is, just not a lot that's terribly useful. I didn't think so, anyway. Lots of Ratcliffe's fingerprints, but then he doesn't deny being Van Gard, does he?'

'Anyone else's?'

'There's a partial in the paint on a half-finished Airfix tank. We're checking, but there's no match on the system at first pass.'

'Chase it up, will you, Lou?' asked Dixon.

'What is it?' Watson grinned. 'Don't trust yourself to speak to fingerprinting, is it?'

Dixon ignored the jibe.

'The bloke who planted your dabs is long gone,' continued Watson. 'He's been charged with perverting the course of justice too.'

'I know.'

'What's your problem, then?' Watson switched on the lights; large strip lighting overhead and several lamps along a worktop.

Dixon wasn't entirely sure whether Watson was waiting for a reply, but he wasn't getting one.

'This lot must be worth a pretty packet,' said Louise.

'It won't be when he goes to prison,' muttered Dixon.

'We've got a full inventory,' replied Watson. 'So, don't get tempted.'

Sketches, half-finished models; stencils that had been used and others that hadn't. Photographs stuck on the walls with masking tape. Dixon had been through the report from Scientific, and all the appendices, scrolling through the photographs at length.

'We think the half-finished tank was a first go at the one he used at the model village,' said Watson. 'It's a big Airfix Challenger battle tank. It's got the words "new model army" on the side, but the final version had "peace? keeping-force" on it.'

'Four hundred thousand that one went for.' Louise's voice was loaded with disbelief.

'I do like these installations,' continued Watson. 'Three-dimensional works that transform the perception of a space.'

'Bollocks.'

'I googled it.'

'What's in here?' asked Dixon, gesturing to an old chest freezer.

'Rolls of paper. We looked at some of them, but they're just dummy runs with the stencils. He tapes a big sheet of paper to the wall and has a practice. Time is of the essence when he gets out there for real, I suppose.'

'Let's have a look at them,' said Dixon.

'All of them?'

'All of them.'

Chapter Forty-Five

Standing room only in the video suite, everyone watching the feed from interview room 1. The audience included Charlesworth and Potter, according to Jane's text; she was standing behind them.

'I really must protest, Inspector,' said Crosby. 'My client has been here for over twenty-four hours—'

'A custody extension was granted by a chief superintendent.'

'That's not the point.'

'I think you'll find it is.'

'Is my wife here?' asked Ratcliffe.

'She is,' replied Dixon.

'Can I see her?'

Louise stepped in to go through the formalities, which was a relief. It was always a shame to start off an interview on a glum note.

'Let's start from the beginning again, shall we?' Dixon hesitated, allowing time for Crosby to step in, surprised that he didn't. 'The road traffic accident on the twenty-eighth of February 2002.'

'I lied,' said Ratcliffe. 'Jackson was pushed into the path of the lorry. My father paid Barry Mercer to switch the tachograph and pin it on Christopher Green. I'm only sorry I haven't had the courage to come clean before now, and so many people have lost their lives as a result.'

'Your father paid Mercer?'

'Father's dead now, so you can't touch him. He was looking after his son. I put him in an impossible position, and I only hope your child doesn't do the same to you one day.'

'Who pushed Jackson?'

'I did. We were fighting and it was self defence.'

'How?'

'I kicked him. I was just trying to get him away from me.'

'Show me.'

Ratcliffe stood up, visibly shaking, one hand on the back of the chair for support. 'I kicked out, so,' he said, kicking his left leg out in front of him. 'And Jackson went back over the crash barrier.'

'Leading with your toe?'

'I suppose so.'

'Did you know the lorry was there?'

'I don't remember seeing the lights or hearing the engine even, not until after Jackson fell back over the barrier. I suppose I must've pushed him into the path of the lorry, but I wasn't trying to kill him.'

Dixon could imagine the high-fives and fist-pumping going on in the video suite, and that was just Charlesworth; a guilty plea to manslaughter and there'd be no scrutiny of what happened to the tachograph.

'Did the lorry brake?'

'After the impact. He had no time before, the poor sod.'

'Okay, so while we're on a roll, let's take it forward to when Green got out of prison.'

'He'd been following me for days; cornered me at the railway arches one night, held a knife to my throat, said my lies had cost him eighteen years of his life. He was going to kill me, so I offered him money. What else could I do? He said there was no amount of money, so I told him I was Van Gard and it turned out there was – half of everything.' Ratcliffe took a deep breath. 'He wanted a job at the uni so he could be close by – keep an eye on me – and I got him the caretaker's job.'

'When was this?'

'A couple of years ago, when he got out of prison.'

'How was the money transferred?'

'Directly from the offshore account. I'd transfer it to him in Bitcoin.'

'What about Emma Carpenter?'

'She came to see me one day and set out her plans for her project; said she'd found Van Gard's studio in a railway arch and it was just a matter of time before she caught him red-handed. She was going to make the big reveal in her thesis. I didn't know what to do. If my identity came out that would be the end of it, so I told Green and he said he'd deal with it. The next thing I know Emma's dead. I want to make it clear that I did not know he was going to kill her.'

'What did you think he was going to do? Take her out to lunch and have a quiet word?'

'I don't know.'

'Why didn't you report it?'

'How could I? It would have all come out. The lies, my identity, everything.'

'And Barry Mercer?'

'What were the chances of that? I turn up to Emma's funeral and there he is. I don't know what he was doing there, but he comes marching over, reminds me he switched the tachograph to keep me out of trouble, and demands money. His business was going down the drain, or something. Green had always suspected Mercer was the one who switched the tachograph, so that was an easy one. I told him where to find Mercer and that was that. Problem solved. Trudy and Dominic saw me talking to Mercer at the funeral, so I just said a car had clipped my bumper.'

'Sebastian Cook?'

'It was getting out of hand by then. Green was getting carried away, enjoying himself, if you ask me.'

'I *am* asking you, Malcolm.'

'He killed Seb and Evie because he thought Emma might have told them who Van Gard was. I pleaded with him not to, but he did it anyway. I had no idea he was going to go after your colleague, either – I swear. That was Green acting entirely alone. I had no reason to want Detective Constable Harding out of the way. He was no threat to me.'

'So, let me clarify this for the tape,' said Dixon. 'You're admitting to the manslaughter of Jackson Ogunwe. Is that correct?'

'No,' replied Crosby, stepping in. 'My client says that he kicked Ogunwe in self defence, who then fell back over the Armco barrier into the path of the lorry. My client made it clear he did not know the lorry was there.'

'The murder of Emma Carpenter?'

'My client says he asked Green for help, who said, and I quote, "that he would deal with it". At that point Mr Ratcliffe had no idea that it was Green's intention to kill Emma.'

'Barry Mercer.'

Crosby looked at Ratcliffe and raised his eyebrows.

Ratcliffe was sucking his teeth, breathing heavily through his nose. 'I knew that Green was likely to kill Mercer when I told him where to find him, yes.'

'For the avoidance of doubt, my client makes no such admission in relation to the murders of Sebastian Cook, Evie Clarke and

David Harding. Those murders were committed by Christopher Green acting entirely alone.'

◆　◆　◆

Dixon stepped out into the corridor to find himself caught in yet another pincer movement – a new tactic he'd need to be on the lookout for – Potter to his right, Charlesworth on his left. There was no chance of escape.

'Well done, Nick,' said Potter.

'That's it then,' said Charlesworth. 'A charging decision from the CPS will be simple enough, and then you can get some well-earned rest. And get married.'

That was a conversation he needed to have with Jane – the idea of their wedding taking place while she was still washing Dave's blood out of her hair hardly filling him with joy.

'We may postpone that until after Dave's funeral, Sir,' replied Dixon. 'I haven't had the chance to speak to Jane about it yet.'

'Quite understand.' Charlesworth smiled. 'Nice to get a confession that wraps everything up neatly, all the same.'

'Yes, it is, Sir,' replied Dixon. 'Shame it's a load of bollocks.'

Chapter Forty-Six

'Wraps everything up neatly,' Charlesworth had said.

Too neatly.

Every 'i' dotted, every 't' crossed, while admitting to the barest minimum he could get away with.

'Ratcliffe is seriously asking us to believe he killed Jackson Ogunwe in self defence, didn't know Emma was going to be killed, and pleaded with Green not to kill Seb Cook and Evie Clarke. And you lot think that's an excuse to crack open the Prosecco?'

Jane knew better, and Louise; Mark too. Even the probationer, Sarah, was still sitting at her workstation.

The team from Portishead was gathered around a table at the back of the incident room, several plastic cups scattered around two empty bottles of sparkling wine.

'That's it, Guv, surely,' said one, with a shrug. 'He's admitted it. We thought . . .' His voice tailed off.

'Go home,' said Dixon.

'Really?'

'Eight o'clock, sharp. There's going to be a lot to do to get this ready for trial.'

'Yes, Sir.'

Dixon turned away, trying not to listen to the murmuring as the officers drifted off in the direction of the door to the staff car park. He felt sure there was an 'arrogant git' in there somewhere; he'd been called worse.

'Is his wife still down in reception?'

'She's gone, Sir,' replied Sarah. 'She looked distraught when I told her he was confessing; said she'd see him in hell, and left. I did tell her she might be able to see him tomorrow at court, but I don't know whether she'll come or not. She didn't say.'

'What are we all doing then?'

'I'm still on the traffic cameras,' replied Mark.

'I was just going through the mobile phone records, Sir,' said Sarah. 'Nothing to report, sadly, but then Ratcliffe and Green worked in the same building, so they probably did everything face to face.'

Dixon sat down on the edge of Jane's workstation, looked at her and smiled. 'We need to have a conversation about Christmas Eve.'

'I know.'

'What exactly is it you don't like about his confession, Sir?' asked Sarah. It was the question nobody else dared ask; usually left unspoken until Dixon was ready to tell them.

'Everything Green said about the accident on the M32 was true. We know that now. He was in the wrong place at the wrong time and ended up with his life in tatters. He took his revenge for that, and Dave paid the price for Barry Mercer's dishonesty, but the starting point is that Green's version of events is true.'

'What I don't get is why he didn't appeal his conviction when it came out that the tachograph had been switched?' Sarah again.

'It's in the dates,' replied Dixon. 'He'd already had twelve years added to his sentence for manslaughter by then, so there'd have been no point. He wasn't getting out, was he?'

'Green said there were two people down on the carriageway, in addition to Jackson,' said Jane. 'It's in his police interview.'

'Which means Ratcliffe is protecting someone,' continued Dixon. 'And that's what I don't like about his confession.'

'So, what happens now?'

'We go through everything again with that line of enquiry front and centre.'

Jane stood up. 'I'll put the kettle on.'

Dixon pushed the two tables at the back of the incident room together and unrolled one of the large pieces of paper he had found in the old chest freezer at the railway arch, an empty bottle of Prosecco in each top corner to keep it flat.

'Here,' said Sarah, offering him a hole punch and a stapler for the bottom corners. 'What is it?' she asked.

Jane and Mark were standing behind him too, exchanging puzzled looks.

'It's an early version of Van Gard's *Ebbing Tide* – a practice run. He'd stick big pieces of paper like this one on the wall in the railway arch, to see what the stencil looked like for real.'

'Can't be much light in a railway arch,' said Sarah.

'He works at night.'

'Yeah.'

'What's so special about it?' asked Mark.

'It's probably worth a bob or two,' said Louise.

'Apart from that.'

'We're seeing it without the bow, which would've been *installed* when the painting was finished.'

'It looks remarkably like the unfinished painting Jackson Ogunwe was working on the night he was killed.' Louise was leaning over, her hands outstretched, mimicking the position of the bow.

'Everybody thought it was unfinished,' said Dixon. 'The council painted over it a few weeks later, but I've enlarged the photo from the *Bristol Post*.' He unfolded a piece of A3 paper and dropped it on the table. 'They're almost identical, except the faces of the people. They're a bit blurred, perhaps.'

Louise was studying the faces of the figures in the rowing boat. She had brushed aside the copy of the *Bristol Post* and was looking at the full-sized practice stencil. 'Is it me, or is that Trudy Lister's face?' she asked, tipping her head. Then she used the palm of her hand to block out the nose and mouth. 'It's her eyes, surely?'

'Have we got the original image from the *Bristol Post*?' asked Dixon.

'I chased them up this morning,' replied Jane. 'It's in my email; arrived this afternoon.'

'Can I see it?' asked Dixon.

Jane handed him her phone, the image on the screen.

Dixon zoomed in on the faces in the boat. 'Trudy said that Emma had a photograph of Van Gard at work on her laptop.'

'Well, I couldn't see one. There are several of Ratcliffe, but none of him *at work*,' said Sarah. 'They're on my computer, if you want to have another look yourself.'

Dixon didn't notice the mug of coffee at his elbow until it was stone cold. The photographs of street artists had been taken at night, often out of range for the camera flash to be of use, streetlights offering the only illumination. The hoodies didn't help, either.

Underpasses, subways, backstreets at night, main streets in broad daylight. Then the photographs switched to a gallery.

And there it was.

Two people smiling at the camera, arm in arm; one wearing a dinner jacket and tie, the other a ball gown. At a party of some sort, their glasses filled with champagne.

Dixon leaned back in his chair and closed his eyes, letting out a long slow sigh through his nose, becoming aware of footsteps closing in behind him, a small crowd gathering.

'Who's that with him?' asked Mark.

'Van Gard,' he replied, opening his eyes.

'Yeah, we know Ratcliffe is.'

'They both are.'

Chapter Forty-Seven

'Can I come?' Sarah had asked.

'You need to finish what you started,' Dixon had replied.

Now they were standing in the departure lounge at Bristol Airport. Dixon, Louise and Sarah, all watching Jane talking to officers from the British Transport Police.

Lights were moving out on the runway, Dixon more used to seeing aircraft in the night sky above when he was out on the beach with Monty; flashing red and white lights, the moon lighting up the vapour trails. Seeing them at close quarters was most disconcerting, and a painful reminder of why he hated flying at the best of times. The idea that those things could get off the ground at all defied logic – for a humble police officer, anyway.

'She's in the AspirePlus Lounge,' said Jane, walking over. 'And they've grounded the flight, so she's not going anywhere.'

They followed the BTP officers across the concourse, all but deserted at this time of night; a few people stretched out on the seats, others curled up on the floor, their heads resting on their suitcases.

Dixon glanced up at the flight board, the departure for Grand Cayman still showing as 'On time'.

'How did you know she'd be on this flight?' asked one of the BTP officers.

'It's the only one going to the Cayman Islands,' replied Dixon. 'It's where all her money is.' He was peering through the glass door, careful not to show his face.

It looked more like a wine bar than an airport lounge, stools arranged around a bar in the middle of the room, two men in suits propping it up, not that it needed it.

Further along, the bar area gave way to comfortable seating arranged in snugs with colour-matched partitioning and rugs on the floor, fresh flowers on the tables. Some were occupied, but not all.

The view through the internal floor to ceiling windows was blocked by screens; the view outside much the same as from the rest of the departure lounge: the runway, aircraft taxiing, the roar of the engines.

'Go in, Jane, have a wander round and see if you can see her. She's already checked in, so she'll only have hand luggage.' Dixon had already made sure of that, baggage handlers busily unloading the plane, much to their annoyance. 'You're shitting me!' had been the exact phrase, but he had ignored it.

'That was close,' said Jane, puffing out her cheeks as the door closed behind her a minute or so later. 'The bloke behind the bar asked me for my lounge pass, so I showed him my warrant card.'

'Is she in there?'

'Down the far end, last section in the window, sitting in the corner with her back to the bar. She's wearing a wool coat with a fur collar. It's almost up to her ears. A fur lined hat too.'

'Empty seats?'

'One next to her and both opposite.'

'You'll have to sit this one out,' said Dixon, turning to Louise and Sarah. 'She knows your faces.'

'We'll watch the door with these lads,' replied Louise, gesturing to the BTP officers.

'Is there another exit?' Dixon asked.

'No, Sir. Just loos down the far end.'

'Right then. Jane, go in, act casual and sit down opposite her. Read a magazine or something. Look bored.'

'I can manage that,' said Jane.

Sarah looked as if she was about to throw up.

'You all right?' asked Dixon.

'Fine, Sir.'

'Anyone would think you were the one about to be arrested for murder.'

Jane pushed open the door of the lounge, Dixon watching her as she walked along the aisle between the tables and the lounge seating. A couple of people glanced up at her as she went past, but most were asleep or had earphones on.

'Where's your office?' asked Dixon.

'Far side of the concourse, Sir,' replied one of the BTP officers.

'We'll go there when we've arrested her.'

'Yes, Sir.'

Dixon let the door slam behind him, Louise and Sarah on the inside now, sitting at the bar, the steward placing two glasses of sparkling water in front of them. Then Dixon walked along the aisle. Jane looked up and saw him coming, quickly turning back to her magazine: *Going Places*.

He sat down in the vacant seat opposite Jane.

'Going somewhere, Wendy? Grand Cayman, changing at Amsterdam and Atlanta? I should imagine you'll be relieved you're not going to have to endure that.'

She recognised the voice, her eyes closing; staying shut as her breathing deepened.

'Wendy Ratcliffe, I am arresting you on suspicion of the murders of Barry Mercer, Emma Carpenter, Sebastian Cook and Evie Clarke.'

Wendy opened her eyes and turned to face him, the blood draining from her cheeks, visible even under the rouge.

'You do not have to say anything, but it may harm your defence if you do not mention when questioned something you later rely on in court.'

'How did you know?' she asked.

'Anything you do say may be given in evidence.'

Jane was gesturing to someone behind the partition – a nosy bystander, probably.

'It's fine,' she mouthed.

'It's Trudy Lister sitting in the boat in *Ebbing Tide*, but in the original version, painted by Jackson Ogunwe, it was you.'

'The council scrubbed that off years ago.'

'There was a photo in the *Bristol Post*. His mother kept a scrapbook with it in.'

Wendy was pretending to admire her painted fingernails. 'Jackson had no vision,' she said. 'Didn't my husband confess to killing him?'

'He lied.'

'I thought you proved he was Van Gard?'

'You both are.'

Silence.

'Dominic Meek said he was surprised. He didn't think your husband had the talent.'

'He hasn't.'

'But you do?'

'Yes, I do.'

'We had a pathologist – a very good one – look again at Jackson's post mortem, the notes and photographs, and he spotted an injury on Jackson's chest that he thought was a stamp, where someone had stamped on Jackson, but it was a kick, wasn't it?'

'Yes.'

'The foot sideways on. Your husband got that wrong.'

Wendy sneered. 'Useless.'

'When did you give up Karate?'

'Not the trophy in the display cabinet?'

Dixon nodded.

'Jackson couldn't see the commercial possibilities. There was money to be made, lots of it, but he was happy scurrying about in the gutter, painting walls and subways. We had something new and it was only going to last so long. We were arguing down on the M32, he was standing by the crash barrier and I kicked out. The next thing I know he's under the lorry. Malcolm said to run, so I ran.'

'Carrying the bow of the rowing boat.'

'It was only papier mâché. We were going to glue it on the wall. It was later we decided to use the real thing and bolt it on.' Wendy folded her arms. 'It makes a bolder statement.' She was watching Jane making notes, pausing to allow her to catch up. 'Malcolm said it was him and got his father to get him out of trouble, and that was that. We became Van Gard, as well as husband and wife; a match made in hell.' A heavy sigh. 'Malcolm did the stencilling and I did everything else, and I mean *everything*. I was the artistic director and the business brains.'

'Until Emma Carpenter came along?'

'Trudy mentioned Emma's project to me at a Christmas drinks last year. Trudy knew Malcolm was Van Gard, but not that I was involved too. I suppose you know she and Malcolm had an affair?'

'We do.'

Wendy curled her lip. 'He assured me it was just sex.'

'That's all right then.'

'Not really, but I got over it. Then Malcolm said the girl had found the studio. I didn't know what to do.'

Dixon slid the colour photograph out of his pocket and handed it to Wendy. 'Van Gard at a launch party of some sort?' he asked.

'An exhibition at a gallery in the Kings Road.' Wendy handed the photograph back. 'She knew we were both Van Gard, I suppose?'

'Looks like it.'

'I was right to have her killed then.' Oddly calm.

Jane looked up.

'Oh, don't be so precious,' snapped Wendy. 'The child was going to expose us. What bloody right had she to do that?'

'So, she had to die,' said Dixon.

'Yes, she did. We had Green hanging around our necks by then, the grubby little man. He'd caught up with Malcolm and was threatening to kill him, so Malcolm offered him money.'

'He was blackmailing you?'

'Green was blackmailing Malcolm, not me. I was using *him* – "do what I say or the money stops". *I* told him to kill Emma, told him she was diabetic and suggested an insulin overdose; switching the pens was his idea, and he managed to get in and out of her house without being spotted. I thought we'd got away with it, until you stuck your nose in.'

'And Barry Mercer?'

'*I* told him to deal with Barry Mercer. It was messy, but time was short.'

'Your husband says that he told Green where to find Mercer.'

'He's lying to protect me. Again.'

'We'll be able to check your mobile phone records easily enough.'

'I don't have one of those ghastly little things.'

'You were the business brains?' A little bit of flattery to keep her talking.

'I was. And we made millions. Used a solicitor who's bound by client confidentiality and had the auction proceeds sent offshore to the Cayman Islands, but then you know that.'

'I do. The taxman will do shortly as well.'

'That's hardly going to worry me where I'm going, is it?'

'What about your children?'

'They're adults now and can look after themselves.'

'If I were you, I'd work on showing a bit of remorse,' said Dixon, standing up. 'Always goes down well with a judge.'

'Remorse?' Wendy gave a wry smile. 'I have some for the Cook boy and Evie Clarke, I suppose. They didn't deserve to die. Their only crime was knowing what Emma was up to, but I wasn't taking any chances. Once Emma's inquest was adjourned, and her death was being treated as suspicious, there was a chance they'd tell people she was about to unmask Van Gard. That would've put me in the frame for two murders, so what's two more?' She shook her head. 'Your colleague too; that was nothing to do with me. That was Green all on his own, for reasons of his own. He knew you were on to us by then – you'd found Mercer in the river – and he said he had a score to settle before you caught up with him.'

'Why did he paint the death messages?'

'He was having a bit of fun – taunting the police, he said. I think he knew it was just a matter of time by then, anyway.' She stood up, holding her hands out, wrists together, fists clenched. 'I think I've said enough. In front or behind?'

'Behind,' replied Jane.

Dixon waited until the handcuffs snapped shut. He looked down at the magazine on the glass table top.

Going Places.

'Wasn't quite what I had in mind,' muttered Wendy.

Chapter Forty-Eight

Dixon was glad it was raining. It seemed appropriate, somehow.

The figure in the distance could've been anybody, but he knew it was Jane, if only because of the large white dog walking beside her. They were down by the waterline, on the other side of a muddy channel between the sandbanks, the tide coming in over the flats. Downwind of him, so Dixon tried a whistle; the first few notes of the theme to *The Vikings*.

Monty looked more like a Dalmatian by the time he arrived at Dixon's feet, spattered with grey mud. Still, it was better than blood.

'Bath for you when we get home,' he said, the dog jumping up at him, showering him with muddy water.

Jane was wading across the narrow channel towards them, the murky water almost up to the top of her wellington boots.

'How'd you get on?' she asked.

'There was a lot of crying, but she was grateful to have the scrapbook back, and to know what really happened to her son. Said she'll stay for the trial and then go back to Jamaica.'

'Here.' Jane was holding a sodden tennis ball between the tips of her thumb and index finger. 'You can have this.'

'Thanks.'

'Did we get a charging decision out of the CPS?'

'Perverting the course of justice for him; she's having the book thrown at her. Manslaughter for Jackson Ogunwe, then the murders of Emma Carpenter, Barry Mercer, Seb Cook and Evie Clarke.' Dixon dropped the ball at his feet and kicked it towards the soft sand of the dunes. 'I wanted to charge him with the lot, but she's adamant he knew nothing and there's no other evidence.'

'Shame. And no one pays for Dave's death.'

'Green did, the old fashioned way.'

'Yeah.'

'Keep walking or pub?' asked Dixon. 'We've got twenty minutes before it gets dark.'

'Let's keep going,' replied Jane. 'Have you been home?'

'Not yet.'

'You won't have seen the letter then.' Walking side by side now, holding hands as the last of the daylight gave way to darkness. 'Landlord's selling up. Wants to know if we want to buy it, before he puts it on the market.'

'What d'you think?'

'It'll do for a couple of years. We'll need a garden eventually, for the children, but it's convenient for the time being.'

Dixon pretended not to notice her use of the plural; children it is then. 'Right opposite the Red Cow.'

'I was thinking of the motorway.'

'That as well.'

Jane flicked back the hood of her coat when the rain eased off, the lights of Hinkley Point twinkling on the far side of the estuary. 'I rang the vicar. Explained.'

Dixon was watching Monty sniffing along the lines of fetid black seaweed, the tennis ball abandoned and just visible rolling towards the muddy channel. 'What about everyone else?'

'Nobody was surprised, given what's happened.' Jane shrugged. 'I think they were expecting it, to be honest. It's hardly the time.'

'When's the funeral?' he asked, picking up the ball before it reached the water.

'Not until the new year, after we get back from the Lakes. We might as well go,' said Jane. 'I cancelled the hotel, but the cottage is still booked. I thought Lucy and Billy could come.'

'Why not?'

'There's plenty of time to get married,' she said, squeezing his hand. 'We've got the rest of our lives.'

'I'm sure I'll get to say "I do" one day.'

'You will. And you'll say it to me.'

Dixon stopped, pulling his hand from Jane's. He was staring at the sand at his feet. 'There's something you need to know.'

'What?'

'About the man you're planning to marry. I'm not the man you think I am.'

'You're worrying me now.' Jane's eyes narrowed. 'Just tell me. Whatever it is.'

'Green,' said Dixon, blowing a heavy sigh out through his nose. 'There was time. I saw the train coming and there was time to get him off the tracks, out of the way. I looked into his eyes, and then I watched him die.'

'Is that it?'

'That's it.'

'Fuck him.' Jane took his hand and carried on walking, pulling him with her. 'Green killed five people – six, if you include the real Denton Miller; there's still no sign of him – and you're worried you didn't risk your life to save his.' She smiled. 'That's why I love you. Deep down, you're a daft sod.'

'Remind me never to go magnet fishing on the Levels.'

'You reckon that's where Miller is?'

'He could be anywhere – dismembered and in the Tone, buried in a shallow grave. Who knows? A dog walker or a magnet fisherman will find him one day.'

'That kid, Sarah, did well, I thought,' Jane said, changing the subject.

'She's going to work with Nige in the Rural Crimes team for the rest of her probation,' replied Dixon. 'Said she wants to join CID after that. As soon as she can, anyway.'

'So, have we heard the last of this legal profession crap, or what?'

'I rang the recruitment agent and told them to forget it.'

'Thank God for that.' Jane took the tennis ball from Dixon's hand and threw it along the sand, appearing mildly irritated when Monty ignored it. 'Charlesworth was sniffing around earlier, being as nice as pie. He even made a coffee and sat drinking it with us. It was quite unnerving.'

'Where was I?'

'Down in the interview room. He kept going on about what a great officer Dave was and how he's arranging for a funeral with full honours, even though he was technically on suspension at the time of his death.'

'I should bloody well think so.'

'Asked me to tell you that Professional Standards are going to drop their investigation into the file tampering too.'

'Really.' Matter of fact.

'You don't sound surprised.'

'I'm not.'

'Do you know who did it?'

Dixon stopped, took a deep breath, and said, 'I do.'

Author's Note

I very much hope you enjoyed reading *Death Message*.

I'm embarrassed to admit that I was not a huge fan of street art, but the research for the novel has given me the opportunity to learn more about it, and even come to appreciate it. The Bristol scene is one of the most established and highly regarded in the world, with some of the most talented artists working anywhere – a real jewel in the city's crown. It's been a real treat to delve into it, rather than just speeding past the paintings and installations, as we all tend to do as we go about our busy daily lives.

Next time you're out and about, I'd highly recommend taking a moment to stop and admire the talent freely on display.

I had a lot of fun with the death messages themselves too, although I am nothing like talented enough to be able to recreate them. I wasn't even allowed to take art 'O' level at school and I can still remember the conversation with my art teacher; being told politely but firmly that it would have been a waste of everybody's time, including my own.

There are several people to thank as always, first and foremost among them my wife, Shelley, who dutifully reads the manuscript on a daily basis (whether she wants to or not!). My dear friend Rod Glanville, who is my harshest critic and worth his weight in gold for it.

David Hall and Clare Paul have once again been extraordinarily generous with their help and advice. Their local knowledge of the Levels is invaluable to say the least. And David's encyclopaedic knowledge of all things Land Rover.

A huge 'thank you' must also go to the team at Thomas & Mercer, in particular, Victoria Haslam, Rebecca Hills and Ian Pindar.

And lastly a shout out to the narrator of the audiobooks, Simon Mattacks, who does such a cracking job. Thank you, Simon!

Damien Boyd
Devon, UK
January 2023

About the Author

Damien Boyd is a solicitor by training and draws on his extensive experience of criminal law, along with a spell in the Crown Prosecution Service, to write fast-paced crime thrillers featuring Detective Inspector Nick Dixon.

Follow the Author on Amazon

If you enjoyed this book, follow Damien Boyd on Amazon to be notified when the author releases a new book!

To do this, please follow these instructions:

Desktop:

1) Search for the author's name on Amazon or in the Amazon App.
2) Click on the author's name to arrive on their Amazon page.
3) Click the 'Follow' button.

Mobile and Tablet:

1) Search for the author's name on Amazon or in the Amazon App.
2) Click on one of the author's books.
3) Click on the author's name to arrive on their Amazon page.
4) Click the 'Follow' button.

Kindle eReader and Kindle App:

If you enjoyed this book on a Kindle eReader or in the Kindle App, you will find the author 'Follow' button after the last page.